STILLWATER

A JACK MCBRIDE MYSTERY

MELISSA LENHARDT

Skyhorse Publishing

Skyhorse Publishing books may be purchased in bulk at special discounts for sales promotion, corporate gifts, fund-raising, or educational purposes. Special editions can also be created to specifications. For details, contact the Special Sales Department, Skyhorse Publishing, 307 West 36th Street, 11th Floor, New York, NY 10018 or info@skyhorsepublishing.com.

Skyhorse® and Skyhorse Publishing® are registered trademarks of Skyhorse Publishing, Inc.®, a Delaware corporation.

Visit our website at www.skyhorsepublishing.com.

10 9 8 7 6 5 4 3 2 1

Library of Congress Cataloging-in-Publication Data is available on file.

Cover design by Brian Peterson
Cover photo: Shutterstock

Print ISBN: 978-1-63450-226-9
Ebook ISBN: 978-1-5107-0071-0

Printed in the United States of America

For Jay

CHAPTER ONE

Thursday

I

A line of flashing blue and red lights led the way to a pale green single-wide trailer. Firemen, sheriff deputies, and EMTs huddled in front of the house, talking, looking around, and laughing. All eyes turned to Jack McBride's car as it pulled into the dirt-packed front yard, which doubled as the driveway.

Jack set the alarm on his phone. "Stay in the car," he told his thirteen-year-old son, Ethan. He opened the door, got out, and leaned back in. "I mean it."

"I *know*, Dad."

Neighbors grouped behind yellow crime-scene tape. Some wore pajamas, others wore work clothes. Women held babies, children craned their necks to see better, eager for information to share at school. A young officer guarded them—Officer Nathan Starling.

It was his file that had fallen from Jack's lap when he was startled awake by the early morning call. If Jack hadn't read Starling was the youngest and newest member of the force, he would have guessed it from his role as crowd control. Starling shifted on his feet and looked over his shoulder at the crowd, as if debating whether he should leave his post to introduce himself or stay put. Jack waved an acknowledgment to him and moved toward the trailer.

Jack nodded at the group of first responders as he walked by and received a couple of muttered hellos in return. Some looked from Jack to Ethan and then back. Jack climbed the uneven concrete steps, stopped at the door, and put on paper booties and gloves. Behind him, he heard a low conversation start back up, the words *alone, wife,* and *no one knows* carrying across the yard as if announced through a bullhorn. The screen door slapped shut behind him, cutting off the rest of the conversation.

The smell of chili, paprika, and cumin hung in the air of the trailer. Flimsy wooden cabinets topped with a chipped orange Formica counter were wedged against the back wall of the main room by a strip of ugly, peeling linoleum. Brown shag carpet, flattened by years of traffic, marked off the living area of the room. Left of the door, under a loud window unit dripping condensation, sat a couch of indeterminate color too large for the room. A black-haired man with bloodshot eyes and a green tinge underneath his dark skin sat on the couch, chewing his nails. He looked up at Jack and stopped chewing—a signal for his leg to start bouncing. A bull-necked police officer, his thumbs crooked underneath his gun belt, stood guard over the man.

"Officer Freeman," Jack said.

If Michael Freeman was surprised Jack knew who he was, he didn't show it. His face remained expressionless.

"Chief McBride."

A third officer stood at the mouth of the hallway to the right with a portly, elderly man. Relief washed over the officer's face. He moved forward, hand outstretched. "Chief McBride," he said. "Miner Jesson. This here is Doc Poole."

Jack shook their hands. "Sorry to meet you under these circumstances, Dr. Poole."

"Helluva case to get on your first day, eh?" the doctor said.

Jack nodded and gave a brief smile. He pulled gloves and more paper booties from his coat pocket and handed them to Jesson and the doctor. Jack walked down the hall and entered the room. Jesson stopped at the door.

"Gilberto and Rosa Ramos," Jesson said. "Found dead this morning by Diego Vasquez." He jerked his thumb in the direction of the man sitting on the couch. "Says he's Rosa's brother. He don't speak much English, but from what I gathered, he came to pick Gilberto up for work and heard the baby screaming. When no one answered, he let himself in. Door was open. Found them just like that."

They were both nude. The woman lay face down, covering half of the man's body. The right side of the man's head was blown across the pillow. Blood and brain matter were sprayed across the bed, under the woman and onto the floor. A clump of long dark hair was stuck to the window with blood. Her right arm extended across the man's chest, a gun held lightly in her grip.

Jack walked around the bed.

Doc Poole stood next to Officer Jesson. "It takes a special kind of anger to kill someone you are in the middle of fucking, doncha think?" Doc Poole said. "Ever see that in the F-B-I?" Derision dripped from every letter.

Jack ignored him. "Where's the baby?"

Jack hoped the revulsion on Jesson's face meant scenes like this were rare in Stillwater. If he had wanted to deal with shit like this on a regular basis, he would have taken a better-paying job in a larger town.

"Officer Jesson?" Jack said. "Where's the baby?"

"Oh. It's with a neighbor."

"Has anyone called CPS?"

"Why?"

"To take care of the baby."

"The neighbor offered."

"And what do we know about this neighbor?"

He shrugged. "She didn't speak much English."

"So, she could be in the next county by now?"

"Oh, I doubt that," Jesson said. "She seemed like a nice sort. Very motherly."

Jack cocked his head and puzzled over whether his most senior officer was ignorant, naive, or an amazing judge of character.

He turned his attention to Doc Poole. "What's the time of death?"

"Sometime last night."

"Can you be more specific?"

"Didn't see the need. Seems pretty obvious what happened."

"Oh, are you a detective?"

"No. I'm a general practitioner."

"You're the JP, aren't you?"

"No. I used to be." He chuckled. "Too old for this now."

"Yet, here you are."

"JP is on the way, Chief," Jesson said.

Jack kept his focus on Doctor Poole. "So you heard this over the radio and decided to come? Or did someone call you?"

"Well, I—"

"Do you have the instruments necessary to establish a time of death?"

"Not with me, but—"

"Then get off my crime scene."

The little man straightened his shoulders and lifted his chin. "I can see why Jane Maxwell liked you." He started to leave but turned back. "We do things different here in Stillwater."

"Not anymore we don't," Jack said.

Jesson watched in slack-jawed astonishment as Doc Poole walked away. Jack waited for him to explain what the man had been doing there or to contradict Jack kicking him off the scene. Instead, Jesson snapped on his left glove and stepped into the room.

"Ever seen anything like this, Officer Jesson?"

"Call me Miner." He shook his head. "Don't get many murders here."

Thank God. "Assuming this is a murder-suicide, like it looks," Jack said. "What else do you see?"

Miner stepped toward the bed, turned green, swallowed. Stepped back. "Nice gun. Beretta M92. Preferred by military wannabes and veterans. Would've thought the gun'd fallen out of her hand, what with the recoil."

"Me too. Do you know the victims? Ever been in any trouble with the police?"

"I ran their names on the way over. No record of them."

"Which means they're illegal."

"Probably."

"Diego?"

"Says he's new in town. Haven't run him yet, but illegal as well, I imagine."

"But he stayed until you got here anyway?"

Miner nodded.

"Huh." Jack removed his gloves. "Who's responsible for processing the crime scene?"

"For something like this? The county crime-scene tech. Yourke County got a nice mobile unit last year. He's on his way."

"ETA?"

Miner shrugged. "Probably pretty quick. It's only ten miles to Yourkeville. I'm surprised he ain't here."

Jack walked back to the living room. He could feel the vibrations of Diego's bouncing leg through the floor. He motioned for Freeman to come into the hall.

Michael Freeman stared down the witness, freezing the man in place. He was Jack's height but at least fifty pounds heavier; seven pounds of Kevlar and forty-three of muscle. The short sleeves of his perfectly pressed uniform shirt bunched above his bulging biceps. Miner, by contrast, was so slight of build, his rumpled uniform might have been handed down from a taller, fatter brother. One was prepared for an invasion, one looked like he'd rather be fishing. Their dissimilarities didn't stop there. Freeman's eyes were vacant, neither hostile nor compassionate. Jack knew he would perform any task given him without comment or question. Miner's eyes were large, brown, and in constant motion.

"Freeman, get your crime-scene kit and take pictures. Start in the bedroom. After the tech has processed the scene, search all of the drawers and photograph what's inside. In the closet, under the bed. Everything. While the tech is working, unless he needs your help, photograph the rest of the house and outside."

"Yes, sir." He left.

"Miner, you talk to the neighbors. See if anyone heard anything, what Rosa and Gilberto's relationship was like, if they've seen anyone around lately that shouldn't be around."

"All right," he drawled.

"First, find the baby and call CPS. Shouldn't there be another cop here?"

"He quit."

Jack nodded. One fewer person to have to win over and one more thing to add to his to-do list: hire. "Get one of those sheriff's deputies out there to guard the front door. Tell him not to let anyone in this house that isn't properly booted and gloved. I'll talk to Diego."

The man on the couch stood as Jack approached.

Jack motioned for him to sit down. "*Hola, Diego. Me llamo es Jack McBride.*"

"*Bueno. Habla espanol?*"

"*Sí.*"

The man relaxed, as Jack knew he would. Jack continued in Spanish. "Tell me what happened."

"I came to pick Gilberto up for work. I got to the door, heard the baby screaming, and came in.

"I found the baby in her crib, red-faced, like she'd been crying a long time." Diego leaned over, elbows on his knees, and stared at his clasped hands.

"I knew it was bad. If they were in the house, they would not have let Carmen cry like that. I walked to their bedroom. Before I got to the door, I could smell the blood. The shit. I didn't want to look, I wish I didn't, but I thought one of them might be okay." He wiped his eyes roughly. The palms of his hands were wet. "I called 911 and waited."

"You did the right thing." Diego nodded his head and stared at the floor. "But," Jack continued, "I have to wonder: why?"

Diego's head jerked up, his expression a mixture of anger and defensiveness. "Because you can't trust us wetbacks to follow the law?"

"No. Because by doing so, you risk being deported if you are here illegally. Officer Jesson seems to think you are. Is he right?"

Diego's leg jiggled.

"Diego, I'm not immigration. I don't care. I'm not about to deport someone who cared so much about his friends, he stayed around to help even when it wasn't in his best interests."

Diego's leg stilled, but his hand found its way to his mouth. He chewed on the outside of this thumb.

"So, why did you stay?"

He removed his thumb, then spit whatever was in his mouth to the floor. Jack tried not to cringe. "That ain't right," Diego said. He returned his finger to his mouth.

"What?"

"Rosa would never kill Gilberto."

"Diego, come on. This happens all the time."

"No, man. My little sister wouldn't do that." He motioned toward the bedroom. "I'm telling you."

"It looks like she did it. People go crazy sometimes, do things that are very out of character."

"You aren't listening to me, *vato*."

"You aren't saying anything, Diego. Of course you don't think your sister would blow Gilberto's brains out while fucking him and then shoot herself. But you aren't giving me any other reason why this might have happened. Or who might have done it."

Diego glared at him. "I don't know."

"Were Gilberto and Rosa acting normal?"

"Yeah."

"No fights?"

"I didn't see any."

"They have any enemies?"

"How would I know? I've just been here a few days."

"Drugs."

"They take them? No."

"Deal?"

Diego laughed. "No."

"Where are you staying, Diego?"

Diego shifted on the couch and didn't answer.

"You're staying here, aren't you?"

"Yes."

"Where were you last night?"

"I was down the street."

"With who?"

"A girl named Esperanza."

"All night?"

"From about midnight."

Jack sighed. "You know this doesn't look good, Diego."

"When I left, they were still alive."

"When did you get back?"

"About 6:30. I called the police right away."

And he didn't leave, nor did he try to solidify the murder-suicide theory by saying they were having problems. He went out of his way to say it wasn't possible. He was either incredibly stupid or not guilty.

Jack stood. "All right, Diego."

"Can I go?"

"Where would you go?"

Diego didn't answer.

"Stay here until I get back. Then I'll take you to the station to get your statement."

"I didn't do nothing."

"Then you have nothing to worry about."

Diego looked away. His nervous tics returned in force. Jack didn't think he killed his sister and brother-in-law, but no one with a clear conscience would be so fidgety. He was hiding something.

A sheriff's deputy entered the trailer.

"I'll be back soon. Sit tight," Jack said.

Jack told the deputy to guard Diego as well as the crime scene until he returned. He opened the screen door and stepped outside.

A shaft of sunlight pierced through the clouds and shone across the hood of Jack's car. Ethan sat in the center of the beam, glaring at his father through the windshield.

II

"Are you serious?"

"Come on, Ethan. It isn't that bad."

"You're right. It's horrible."

Jack leaned across Ethan and looked out the window. "It does look like something out of *The Walking Dead*."

Ethan rolled his eyes and tried not to smile. His dad was not allowed to be funny while Ethan was mad at him. Ethan scowled. "So, what am I supposed to do after school?"

"I'll pick you up this afternoon and we'll talk about it."

"Have you even *thought* about it?"

Jack's face tightened, his knuckles turned white on the steering wheel. "Yes, Ethan. We'll talk about it after school. I have to go. Have a good day."

There. That was the dad it was easy to be mad at. Ethan jerked open the car door. "Whatever." He slammed it, hoping that his dad could feel his anger. But no. Ethan stood on the empty school sidewalk and watched his dad drive off without a wave.

School or home? A day of trying to make friends with a bunch of country bumpkins or a house full of unopened moving boxes and an empty refrigerator? Two crappy choices. Just like Mom used to give him.

"You can have green beans or broccoli. Which do you choose?"

"I want potatoes."

"You can have green beans or broccoli. Which do you choose?"

"Jesus, Jules. Just let him have potatoes."

Okay, so his dad wasn't *all* bad. Lately, though, it was his dad giving him the crappy choices, if he even gave him a choice at all.

Ethan looked at the school. It was long, low, and brown, with bushes pruned down to sticks and very little grass. It might look like something from a zombie apocalypse, but it *would* make a pretty cool picture. Add a couple of filters, get the light just right, and it might even look good. From what Ethan had seen of the town, it was full of run-down buildings like this. That was something. How pathetic that the most exciting thing in his life now was taking pictures of crappy buildings.

Choice number three: grab his camera and explore the town. He put his backpack over both shoulders and started walking in the direction he thought his house was.

Screw Stillwater and Eisenhower Junior High.

He didn't want to be here. This school or this town. His dad never asked Ethan what he wanted. He just came home one day and said he had a new job. Ethan's first reaction was relief. He could get away from all the stupid people who knew the stupid thing he did. Then he'd thought of his mom. Did this mean she wasn't coming back? Did she know where they were? Had something awful happened to her and his dad just hadn't told him?

Then his dad said they were moving, not with the FBI to another city somewhere cool like Colorado or California, but to a tiny town in nowhere Texas. As freaking police chief. Sure, Ethan knew his dad was technically in law enforcement, being an FBI agent, but a police chief? Was he going to start wearing some ugly uniform and a cowboy hat? Arresting stinky rednecks in overalls and dirty caps for drugs and disorderly conduct? Ethan couldn't see it. His dad was a well-dressed desk jockey. He sat in a generic black car, drinking coffee, casing out terrorist safe houses and saving the world. He drank expensive beer, got his hair cut every three weeks, polished his dress shoes while watching ESPN, and had five dark suits that all looked so much alike you had to look real close to tell them apart. He flossed twice a day, was clean-shaven, and had eyelashes so long they looked fake. (For the record, Ethan only knew that because his mom used to tease his dad about his supermodel eyelashes.) Jack McBride was a city boy, through and through. Everyone here was going to hate him on sight. There was no way he would last in this town.

Ethan stopped at the end of the crumbling sidewalk. He could hate his dad for a lot of reasons, but people who didn't know him couldn't. They hadn't earned the right. Ethan figured they would soon enough, but he didn't want to be the cause of problems for his dad. At least not on the first day. Skipping school would cause a bunch of problems. He hadn't told anyone, especially his dad, but Ethan had resolved to try to get along here in Podunk, Texas. Not to make life easy on his dad, but maybe if he acted real good, somehow his mom would find out and come back. Ethan sighed, turned, and stumbled over the crack in the sidewalk. He kicked a chunk of loose concrete and trudged back to the school.

The inside of the school was just as bad as the outside. Worse, actually, since it smelled like oranges. In front of him was the office. To the left and right were long halls lined with lockers and classroom doors. The hall to the left ended at a door with a sign labeling it as the library. Sunshine streamed through the glass doors at the end of the hall to the right. Ethan turned and looked back at the front door.

"You've got to be fucking kidding me."

"You lost?"

A young woman stared at him from the office door. Ethan took a step back and gripped the shoulder strap of his backpack. Great. Caught cussing in the first minute.

There goes my resolution to turn over a new leaf.

What would happen next? A talk with the principal? Detention? Corporal punishment? Surely not. No one did that anymore. Though, *this* school might. These rednecks probably believed in that crap. This looked like the type of school that would have a big wooden paddle with holes drilled into the face. His Uncle Eddie said those were the worst. Dad didn't know firsthand. Of course.

The woman standing in the doorway of the office was young, pretty, and, Ethan realized, trying very hard not to laugh.

His grip loosened and his shoulders relaxed. "It'd be pretty tough to get lost in a one-hall school," Ethan replied.

"Good point. You must be Ethan. Come on in. I'll get you squared away." She opened the door wider and stood aside. "I'm Paige Grant," she said. She smelled like flowers and her lips were shiny with red lip gloss. Ethan wanted to smile but his lips had turned to cement. He looked at the floor instead.

Ms. Grant leaned over the counter and picked up Ethan's schedule. "Here you go," she said. "Have a seat and look it over. Principal Courcey wants to say hi to you."

"Why?" Ethan asked. A principal had never personally greeted him before.

"She does it with all the new students."

"You get a lot of those here?"

Ms. Grant laughed. "Not many, no." She tilted her head to the side and appraised him. "The girls are going to love you."

Ethan's neck burned.

"The boys are going to hate you."

"Great," Ethan said.

He dropped his backpack to the floor and fell into an uncomfortable chair. A dusty orange Cheeto lay forgotten in the corner. A ring of grease had seeped out of it and onto the Army green linoleum tile. Gross. Ethan vowed to never eat a Cheeto again.

He tore his eyes away and read his schedule: English, Science, Math, Lunch, Social Studies, Gym, Art.

A small woman emerged from one of the offices behind the counter. "Ethan McBride! Welcome to Eisenhower Junior High!"

He had never seen a principal with so much enthusiasm and energy. In his varied experience, they were usually frazzled and beaten down and happy not to know your name. If they knew your name, that usually meant you were a troublemaker. Of course those were schools with seven hundred-plus students. A small school in a small town was different, he guessed.

"Hello, Principal Courcey." He held out his hand and smiled. Adults loved that crap.

"Well, look at those manners!" Big voice for a little woman, but her grip was weak. Dad said never to trust a weak handshake. "What a little gentleman. I like it."

Ethan caught Paige Grant's eye. She winked at him and picked up the phone.

"I've seen your transcript. You're a good student. Maybe a little challenged with math but that's okay. We'll get you up to speed in no time. Even so, you've had really good test scores, which is great. STAAR testing is coming up, you know. I see you have your schedule." She turned to Ms. Grant. "Let's get someone—" she started.

Paige Grant replaced the phone. "I've already called Mrs. Wright's room for Olivia. Their schedules are almost the same." She smiled so sweetly and innocently at him, Ethan immediately became suspicious.

"Excellent!" Principal Courcey clapped her hands. "Well! I hope this is the last time I see you in the office!"

She gripped his shoulder, leaned forward, and said in an undertone, "I'm sure we won't have any of the same issues you had at your previous school, will we?" Her large smile could not mask the threat in her brittle, green eyes. Ethan tried to not cringe as her thin fingers dug into his shoulders.

So, my principal is Dolores Umbridge. Good to know.

"No, ma'am."

She released him and patted his shoulder. "Good. Have a nice day."

"Yes, ma'am. It was a pleasure meeting you."

Courcey turned, her hard eyes searching Ethan for any sign of sarcasm. Ethan, a master at faking out adults when he wanted, showed her every one of his teeth.

"I like your necklace. My mom has one just like it," he lied.

Courcey's eyes narrowed. "How nice."

"Bye," Ethan said, waving and smiling. When Courcey closed the door of her office, he dropped the smile and sat down to wait for Olivia, whoever she was.

He sighed. *Why can't it ever be easy?*

The door opened and a girl stormed in. "What is so important that you had to get me out of English?"

"Olivia, meet our newest eighth grader, Ethan McBride," Paige Grant said with a mischievous smile.

The girl turned and stared. He half expected her to be as hostile to him as she was to Ms. Grant. Instead, her eyes widened, her face turned red, and she looked away. "Hi," she said. She rounded on the young woman, making Ethan say hi to her back. She whispered to Ms. Grant, who laughed.

"You two have basically the same schedule so I thought you could show him around today."

"Troy has the same schedule as I do," Olivia said.

"Does he? I didn't know."

Olivia said something else in a low voice. Ethan was pretty sure he heard the word *dead*.

"Come on." Olivia walked out the door.

He picked up his backpack and followed.

"Let's find your locker." She held her hand out for his schedule. She turned it over. "Locker 526. It's around the corner at the end of the hall."

"Gosh, I hope I make it to class on time."

She ignored him. "This is the fifth- and sixth-grade hall. That," she jerked her thumb over her shoulder, "is the seventh-grade hall. The eighth-grade hall is around the corner from the library."

"So there are *two* halls. Very impressive."

"Just what we need. Another sarcastic eighth grader."

They rounded the corner into the eighth-grade hall and stopped at his locker. "You'll spend most of your time in this hall. The school doesn't allow backpacks in the classroom. Or cell phones, iPods. Any electronics." She handed his schedule back.

Ethan tried to open the combination lock three times, his face getting hotter with each attempt.

"Want me to try?" Olivia asked.

"No. I can get it."

"Whatever. I'd like to get back to class before the bell rings."

"Is English that interesting?"

"It's better than watching you try to open a lock. Good grief." She pushed Ethan aside. She twisted the lock around and back and pulled the handle. "Grab a spiral and a pen." She walked off down the hall before he could respond.

She was waiting outside a door halfway down the hall. When he was almost there, she entered the room, leaving him to walk into a room full of strangers by himself.

Olivia sat in the front row, of course. A middle-aged teacher with flyaway hair was looking at him over her reading glasses. "Class, we have a new student. Come in, come in! Ethan, isn't it?"

"Yes, ma'am."

"I'm Mrs. Wright. There's a seat in the back corner."

Ethan settled into his desk and stared at the backs of his new classmates. From this angle, they looked like every other classmate he'd ever had. A few girls were sneaking glances back at him. The boys, who were in the back of the room with him, were mostly ignoring him, though a boy sitting behind Olivia turned and waved.

"Troy," Mrs. Wright said, "eyes on me, please. Ethan, just grab a textbook from that shelf next to you. Page 145."

The class ended with a pop quiz over a book he read in seventh grade. Students filed out of the room, placing the quiz on the teacher's desk. Mrs. Wright gave him a warm smile. "Welcome to Stillwater, Ethan."

"Thank you, Mrs. Wright."

Olivia and the friendly boy were waiting for him outside the classroom. "This is my brother, Troy," Olivia said, without preamble. "His locker is close to yours so he's going to show you around the rest of the day."

"Hey," Ethan said.

"Hey," Troy said.

They weaved through the throng of curious eighth graders. Ethan kept his eyes down. "That's got to be a record," Ethan said.

"What?"

"I've never made an enemy in the first hour of school. Usually it's around lunch time."

"Have you moved around a lot?"

"A little."

"Weird." Troy unlocked his locker. "I've lived here all my life. I can't imagine going to a different school."

"You get used to it," Ethan said. Groups of girls were walking past, staring at him and giggling. The boys puffed out their chests and continued to pointedly ignore him. "Some of it, anyway."

Troy closed his locker. "Olivia doesn't hate you."

Ethan opened his locker on the first try. Of course. "Well, she doesn't like me."

"Olivia likes everybody."

"Could've fooled me."

"She gets like that when she's mad."

"I didn't do anything to piss her off."

"Oh, she's not mad at you. She's mad at Paige."

"The woman from the office? Why?"

"Sisters are always mad at each other, it seems like."

"They're sisters?"

"Yep." Troy was nodding at people as they walked down the hall. "So, your dad is the new police chief."

"Yeah."

"What does your mom do?"

"She's a consultant."

"No idea what that is."

"Me either." As lies went, though, it was pretty good. Generic and uninteresting enough to not encourage more questions.

"She not move here with y'all?"

Usually.

"How did you know that?"

"Everybody knows that."

Ethan rummaged in his locker and let that sink in for a moment. He didn't know a thing about this kid, or the town, the school, or anyone in the town, and it seemed that they knew everything about him. His stomach dropped at the thought.

"So, your parents separated? Divorced?"

"She's on a business trip."

"Oh. Cool."

Ethan slammed his locker door and started walking. He didn't want to think of his mom right now. Starting a new school was bad enough; the last thing he needed to do was start crying.

III

Desperate for coffee and running on fumes, Jack pulled into the Chevron, started the gas pump, and walked inside.

A bell jingled. All conversation stopped, all eyes turned to him. Next to the front windows to his right were three booths, one occupied with four old men. Steaming cups of coffee sat in front of each. Behind the counter stood a man wearing oversized overalls and an International Harvester hat that had seen its fair share of harvests. Jack nodded and said, "Morning," and made for the coffee pot at the back of the store.

He poured four cups, snapped on the lids, and wedged the cups into a cardboard traveler. He shoved a handful of creamers, sweeteners, sugars, and stir straws in his coat pocket. Balancing the traveler in one hand, he walked to the counter to pay, pulling two honey buns off a shelf on the way.

The man behind the counter rang him. "Two dollars and sixteen cents."

Jack held his wallet open. "Two dollars for all of this?"

"Cops get coffee free."

Jack smiled. "Thanks, but I'd rather pay for all of it."

The clerk glanced over Jack's shoulder before adjusting the price. "Six fifty-five."

Jack handed him a ten, received his change, and put his honey buns in his empty coat pocket. He was almost out the door when one of the men from the booth spoke up. "Hear you got a pretty grisly scene out there at the trailer park."

Jack paused, his hand on the door handle. "Where did you hear that?"

The man shrugged. "Small town. News travels fast."

The other men stared into their coffee cups. The clerk leaned against the back counter, arms crossed over his ample chest, and watched. An avalanche of new ice fell in the icemaker. The coffee pot clicked off. Strains of country music, tinny and flat, floated from a radio on the counter behind the clerk. Breakfast taquitos and hot dogs rolled in their warmer. The man who spoke drank his coffee, placed the cup on the table, and said, "Careful you don't get your nice shoes dirty."

Jack smirked. "Always my top priority," he said and pushed through the door.

∼

Jack parked behind the crime-scene van. In the twenty minutes he was gone, the crowd around the trailer had grown, as had the line of rubber-neckers on the road.

Nathan Starling stood in the same spot, his back to the crowd. He didn't seem to mind being on the periphery of the action, but looked happy to just be involved in something bigger than him. The cup of coffee Jack gave him brought out all of the nervous gratitude typical in a young man overwhelmed by his superiors. Jack talked to him for a minute, thanked him for taking care of the edge of the scene, and told him they would all meet later today to discuss the case. Starling yes-sir'd Jack to death and Jack walked away, smiling at his eagerness.

Diego sat on the couch and watched Mike Freeman take pictures of everything. With no expression, Freeman thanked Jack for the coffee but said he didn't drink it. Jack gave it to Diego, took his own cup from the carrier, placed Miner's coffee on the kitchen table, and walked down the hall.

Sheriff Ann Newberry stood outside the bedroom door, watching the tech process the scene. In her early fifties and a law-enforcement lifer, Ann Newberry started her career as a prison guard at the women's penitentiary in Gatesville, Texas. She attended night classes at Central Texas College, worked twelve-hour shifts, and raised her daughter by herself. She was tough, fair, intelligent, and incorruptible. Her razor-sharp wit was all the more deadly—very few people realized she was making fun of them. Jack had known her for almost twenty years, since he had worked with her on a nationwide prison gang case his first year with the Agency. He had liked her immediately. The fact she was the sheriff of Yourke County had been one of the items in the "pro" column when he was deciding whether to take this job.

"Jack McBride." Her voice was deeper than the last time he'd talked to her.

They shook hands. "Still smoking a pack a day, I hear."

"Well, everyone dies of something."

"Good to see you, Ann."

She moved aside. They stood together in the doorway and watched the tech take pictures. "Nasty business," she said.

"Not the first case I wanted to catch."

"I suppose not." She crossed her arms over her chest. "You just missed the coroner. She put the time of death between midnight and two. Had Josh over there—" the crime-scene tech looked up and nodded "—do a quick GSR check on ol' Diego out there. He's clean, so *he* wasn't the shooter. Looked these two up before I came. No records, never been questioned about anything. Clean except for the fact they're illegal, that is."

"Yeah, that's what Miner said. I've got him out questioning the neighbors."

Ann snorted. "He won't get very far, even if he could speak Spanish. They aren't going to talk to the police, especially Miner."

"Why especially Miner?"

"He was with Buck Pollard longer than anyone."

Buck Pollard. The name hung over Stillwater like a pall. The former police chief had abruptly retired in June, with no explanation other than age and a desire to do a little more fishin'. During Jack's interview process, which had happened mostly over the phone, Pollard's retirement was glossed over so quickly and smoothly Jack knew something was sketchy. Jack's research had turned up very little except an excellent crime rate and whispers of corruption, though no formal investigation had ever been instigated.

"Are you saying Miner's corrupt?"

Ann shrugged. "He hasn't been implicated." She turned to face Jack. She hadn't changed much from when Jack had first met her. Petite, with a pixie hair cut and blue eyes, she still reminded him of Peter Pan, though unlike Peter, age was starting to show in the generous amount of gray sprinkled through her hair and the fine lines around her eyes.

"I can't believe you took this job."

"Why?" Jack sipped his coffee.

"Captain Ambition patrolling a dying town?"

Jack winced at the nickname bestowed on him by older, slower, and less intelligent agents during the prison gang case. He hadn't heard it in a while. Ann had enough contacts that Jack was sure she knew the story, or at least part of the story, of why he left the Agency. The Ann he remembered was always direct; he wondered why she was fishing instead of asking straight out. If she asked, he would answer. But he hated passive-aggressive bullshit. He kept his eyes on the two bodies and changed the subject. "What's your gut instinct on this?"

"She was either one vindictive bitch or someone did a crappy job trying to make this look like a murder-suicide."

He nodded.

Ann patted him on the shoulder. "Come down to Yourkeville first chance you get. I'll give you the lowdown on Yourke County."

"Oh, no need. I Googled it," Jack said.

"Really?" Ann said. "What did Google say?"

"It was Wikipedia, actually. You have a booming meth business, lots of child abuse, spousal abuse, and hot checks."

"Don't forget endemic corruption."

"Does that include the sheriff's department?"

She laughed. "I don't care why you're here, I'm just glad you are. It's going to be a helluva lot more fun around here with you stirring the pot." She walked down the hall and waved over her shoulder. "Try to stay out of trouble, McBride."

The second interrogation of Diego Vasquez yielded nothing new. He was steadfast in his belief that Rosa and Gilberto were happily married and neither of them had enemies; the couple basked in the glow of perfection of the recently deceased. Their faults and imperfections would be glossed over for weeks and eventually only talked about in apologetic tones or with an indulgent laugh.

Jack parked Diego in one of the three damp holding cells in the City Hall basement and heard an earful of Spanish insults for his trouble. When Diego finished, Jack said, "This is for your own protection."

"How's that?"

"If you're right and Rosa didn't do this, then maybe the killer was there for *you*. Ever thought of that?"

Diego paused, and then said, "No one wants to kill me."

"Maybe, maybe not. But just to be safe." Jack jingled the keys in his pocket. "I'll bring you some lunch. Burger okay?"

"I'm not hungry."

"I'll bring it anyway. Get some rest," Jack said.

Jack walked up the back stairs of City Hall to the second-floor offices that served as the city police station. Space was at a premium, which meant every room was cramped and pulled double duty. The break room was also the interrogation room. The radio operator was crammed in the storage closet. Four deputies shared two offices. The only office on the second floor that wasn't doubled up was Jack's.

A large wooden desk with a well-worn brown leather office chair sat in the center of the large rectangular office. To the left, five mismatched chairs surrounded a round wooden table on which sat an empty, dirty ashtray on loan from the 1970s. Metal filing cabinets of various ages, colors, and heights took up every available inch of space on the east and west walls. Behind the desk, the northern wall was a bank of leaded glass windows overlooking the Cypress River, the natural boundary of Stillwater's square. Through the willows lining the river bank, Jack could just make out the back of his house across the water.

Jack pulled the chair out from under the desk, draped his jacket on the back, and sat down. The town had only five policemen including the chief, and the simplicity of the single hall with five offices was initially appealing to Jack, but now he was here, committed and in charge, it seemed second rate and dingy.

Jack opened the middle desk drawer while he waited for the bulky desktop computer to boot up. Bent paper clips, stubby pencils with broken leads and nubby erasers, Bic pens, their clear barrels smeared inside with exploded blue ink, dried-out Liquid Paper, a torn portion of carbon paper—did anyone even use this stuff anymore?—thumb tacks, an empty can of Skol, a dried-out stamp pad, and a date stamp last used on April 26, 1993. He closed the drawer, noting that it neither opened all the way nor closed all the way. On the edge of the left side of the desk, a portion of the wooden top was discolored and worn down in the perfect shape of a boot heel. He imagined a bald fat man reclining in the chair, a pair of pointy-toed cowboy boots propped up on the desk, a paper cup of dip spit balanced on his round stomach.

Susan Grant, the receptionist, knocked on the door jamb, the lid of an envelope box overflowing with office supplies balanced on her arm. "Did Buck clean you out?"

"Yes, he did."

She placed the box on his desk. "I have the key to the supply closet. I also order the supplies, so if there's something we don't have that you need, just let me know."

"Can I get a new desk and a new computer?"

She smiled. "The big stuff goes through Earl, the city manager."

Jack pulled the box forward, opened a side drawer, and dumped the contents inside. Susan leaned forward, a stricken expression on her face, before recalling herself and straightening. She bit her lip and said, "My daughter says Ethan is all settled in at school."

"Your daughter?"

"My oldest, Paige. She graduated last year. Now she works in the office at Eisenhower. She made sure my youngest two, Troy and Olivia, met Ethan this morning."

"That was nice of her."

"What will Ethan do after school?"

Jack ran his hands over the top of the desk. Despite what he had told Ethan, he hadn't given it nearly enough thought. He didn't have the neighborhood friends to help out now—the parents who had been so willing to help him out after Julie left, but whose good nature and helpfulness ran its course when weeks passed and suspicions mounted. Though Jack hadn't thought of specifics, his ability to cope on his own was part of the reason he took a job in a small town. Not the only reason, or even the biggest reason, but it played a part.

Susan waited for an answer. "Not sure, yet," Jack said. The computer on his desk lit up, saving him elaborating. "Looks like I need a password."

Susan came around the desk, opened the drawer, grimaced again, pulled out a pink pad of sticky notes and a pen, and closed the drawer with a snap. She wrote CHIEF and PSSWRD in tiny, block letters. "Here. Be sure to change it." She pulled the note off and stuck it on the desk and laid the pen next to it. "I need to get back up front." She pointed at the phone. "I'm zero on the intercom. Page me if you need me."

Jack was relieved she didn't offer to help with Ethan. He would have taken her up on it and, if past was predictor of future behavior, which he knew it was, he would have taken advantage of Susan's good nature in the end.

She turned at the door. "Don't forget about your ten o'clock at the bank."

Jack was taken aback. He *had* forgotten. "How did you know about that?"

"Ellie called. Thought you might forget with everything going on."

Jack looked at his watch. "I guess I better get over there since technically Ethan and I are trespassing until I sign the papers." He still couldn't believe Ellie let him move into the house before finalizing the paperwork. He supposed she thought it was a safe bet since he was the chief of police. Jack walked around the desk, putting on his jacket as he went. He stood in the doorway, facing Susan, and adjusted his collar. "My desk drawer is driving you crazy, isn't it?"

She blushed. "How did you know that?"

"If it makes you feel better to organize it, be my guest. Feel free to fix my middle drawer while you're at it."

Susan walked around the desk and opened the side drawer. "Can't you fix it?"

"Probably not."

Susan's mouth curled into a smirk. "If you can't fix a desk drawer, then you probably bought the wrong house."

IV

Jack's footsteps echoed around Stillwater National Bank's expansive and surprisingly quiet lobby. Behind the nearest teller window, a woman in an outdated uniform glanced up, first with curiosity, then recognition. She patted her gray, tightly permed hair (which Jack guessed hadn't moved an inch in thirty years), and with homespun professionalism asked him, "How can I help you, sir?" She had a thick, Southern drawl and a wide smile.

"Jack McBride. I have an appointment."

"Yes, sir. If you'd like to have a seat," she said. She motioned across the lobby to a group of chairs huddled around a coffee table. Jack took in the stiff, old-fashioned chairs and decided to stand.

Though not large, the bank was impressive in the way old banks were. The entire building, from the facade to the inside with its gleaming white marble floors, tall ceilings, chandeliers, and heavy oak desks centered on oriental rugs, spoke of permanence, a safe place to put your money and store your valuables. The bank customers, most older than fifty years old, were straight out of central casting for a small-town, old-fashioned drama. A couple of farmers, a house painter, a lawyer, and a retired schoolteacher, if Jack wasn't mistaken, stood at the two counters in the middle of the lobby, filling out deposit slips, counting their money, signing checks, and trying to hide their interest in the tall stranger standing in the middle of the bank.

Sure don't look like no cop I've ever seen. City boy for sure. Jesus H. Christ.

Moved here to get his son away from the city. He's a troublemaker, no doubt.

He won't last a week.

A woman, dressed identically to the teller who greeted Jack but thirty years younger, rose from behind one of the desks and approached him.

"Welcome to Stillwater, Chief McBride." She held out her hand and smiled. "I'm Ellie Martin. It's nice to finally meet you in person."

Jack smiled. Her smooth alto twang was as intriguing as he remembered. "Call me Jack, please. And, we've met before. At Valerie Patterson's funeral."

Ellie brushed a piece of wispy hair not tied back in her loose bun away from her face. "Of course. I wasn't sure if you remembered. Right this way."

As he followed Ellie Martin, years of FBI training kicked in. Jack had assessed, catalogued, and profiled her by the time she sat down and looked up from the single stack of papers on her desk.

She was attractive but unremarkable, taller than average, around five-feet-eight. Jack could tell little about her figure; the uniform she wore was twenty years out of style and unflattering. Jack remembered his grandmother wearing a similar outfit back in the 1970s. Her skirt was loose at the hips and the waist bunched beneath a thin leather belt, telltale signs of significant weight loss. She walked with her head held high, but without even a bit of sway to her hips. He guessed that no one had ever given her an appreciative whistle as she walked down the street. Ellie Martin would be good conversationalist but not the woman men went out of their way to buy a beer for. All of her best friends would be beautiful, nice, and loyal—a rare combination that Ellie had a knack for attracting—and would sincerely argue with her when she laughed at her bad luck with men. Jack guessed she was around his age, though she could have been as young as thirty-five or as old as forty-five.

She motioned for him to have a seat. "I hear you've had an eventful morning."

Jack sat back and crossed his legs. "Yes. Not exactly what I was hoping for on my first day."

"I imagine not. What a tragedy."

"I don't suppose you knew them?"

"Actually, I did. Slightly. Gilberto was a day laborer, as you probably know. He helped me move few weeks ago. Back in July."

"Do you know the names of the other day laborers?"

She scrunched her nose. "Only one. Raul. They wait for work at the Chevron. You might be able to find him there. Sorry I can't be more help."

"It is a help. Thank you."

She tucked the errant strand of hair behind her ear and said, "Did your son make it to school all right?"

"How did you know I had a son?"

"I believe Jane mentioned it." She waved her hand. "I don't mean to pry. I'm sorry."

"No, not at all. It's just—"

"Weird that a stranger knows. That's a small town for you."

"To answer your question, yes. Ethan made it to school okay. Susan—Grant, the receptionist—"

Ellie smiled. "I've known Susan since sophomore year in high school."

Jack paused, felt his face redden for the first time in years. "Of course you do. I bet you know everyone in town."

"Pretty much."

"Susan said Ethan is squared away."

"Good."

Jack thought back to the morning and a dozen ways he could have made it go easier. In the moment, it had been difficult to stop and think of what would be the best way to react to his emotional, hormonal, angry teenager, especially in the morning when Jack's moods were not conducive to coddling, coaxing, and commiserating. For almost a year, their time together had been an extended version of the quiet game. So far, Ethan was winning.

If Ellie Martin saw Jack's discomfort at thoughts of his son, she didn't let on. "I believe we have everything in order for you. Your bank account is open, and checks are on order. Though who uses checks these days? Still." She pushed a thin checkbook across the desk. "These are temporary. Your ATM card will come in the mail. Direct deposit with the city has been set up. Your mortgage is set up for auto payment also. I take it all of your utilities were connected when you arrived?"

"Yes."

"Good." She folded her hands on the desk and leaned forward slightly. Jack noticed a chicken pox scar just under her left eyebrow. Her eyes looked more green than hazel now and had a combination of intelligence and humor he rarely saw, but was always attracted to.

"You have beautiful eyes."

Ellie Martin straightened, her mouth gaping in astonishment. Jack couldn't believe he had said it either. The click of her teeth as she clamped her mouth shut was audible. She dropped her eyes to the stack of papers on her desk.

"I'm so sorry," Jack said. "That was, uh." He cleared his throat. "Completely inappropriate. I don't know why I said that. I mean, I do. You do have beautiful eyes. But—" But what? Jesus Christ. What was he doing?

She regained her composure sooner than Jack. "Thank you," she said. Her voice cracked as she said it. She looked at her folded hands and cleared her throat. When she looked back at Jack she had regained some, though not all, of her professionalism. Her voice was slightly higher than normal when she asked, "How are you settling in?"

He grasped the conversational life raft. "We haven't, really. Lots of boxes."

"I find the best thing to do is to focus on one room a day. Makes it more manageable," Ellie said.

"Have you moved often?"

"No. I've lived in Stillwater all my life."

"Oh." He couldn't fathom it. Why would someone choose to stay in a small town like this for their entire life? What life events kept her in a town where there were limited possibilities for success instead of moving to a city where opportunities were endless? Early marriage? Children? Parents? Lack of ambition? Or maybe she wanted to be an important person in a small town instead of one of millions in a city.

"Are you profiling me?"

He shifted in his chair, caught out. Thank God she seemed amused instead of offended. Still, he feigned ignorance. "Sorry?"

"Either I've sprouted a second head or you were trying very hard to figure out why I've lived in Stillwater my entire life."

"I'm usually much more subtle about it."

"I would hope so."

"Or maybe you're more perceptive than most."

"Maybe I am. Though I wish I'd been half as perceptive when I was younger."

"Don't we all? Would have saved a lot of needless drama."

"You, too?"

Jack nodded. He wondered how long her hair was. It had been shoulder length a year ago. Were the light streaks in her hair natural or out of a bottle? Regardless, he imagined her hair was soft, silky even. He looked away.

*Jesus, McBride. What are you thinking about? You have two dead peo-
ple in a trailer not a mile from here and instead of finishing your business as
quickly as possible, you're pondering the texture and color of a woman's hair
whom you've seen twice and talked to on the phone a couple of times?*

"Jack?"

Her voice jerked him back into the present. She had called him Jack.
Huh.

"How did you become so perceptive?" he asked, just remembering the
thread of their conversation. Poor Gilberto and Rosa would have to wait.
"Hard-earned experience?"

"Maybe," she replied. "Or maybe I've just read a lot of mysteries."

"You mean the ones where there's a new chief of police in town and
he needs the help of the local preacher, hair dresser, or bank executive to
solve crimes?"

"A bank executive?"

"Sure, why not?"

"I can't imagine ten-key skills would come in handy in solving crimes."

"You would be a forensic accountant on the side."

"Would I? What is that?" she asked.

"They follow the money. There's always a money trail."

Her eyes narrowed and her smile dropped a fraction. "My guess is it
wouldn't be very interesting to read about," she said.

"Maybe you're right. Not like the ones with the cats and the recipes.
They're surprisingly good, you know."

"You expect me to believe you read cozy mysteries?"

He shrugged. "It takes the edge off of a long day."

She shook her head and chuckled. "Well, our book wouldn't have
recipes. I can't cook. Can you?"

"No. I bet you have a cat, though. Named Sherlock. Or Watson. Or
maybe Mr. Darcy. No, wait." He put his hand to his chin. "You named
your cat after Poe's detective. Can't remember his name. French-sounding,
though."

"Maupin."

Jack grinned. "Am I right?"

She inhaled and paused, as if she was about to confess his brilliance. "No." She sighed. "I don't have a cat. You aren't a very good profiler, are you?" Her whiskey-soaked chuckle stirred an emotion inside Jack he had thought was long dead.

"I guess not."

"That's okay. Your secret is safe with me."

Jack studied her. They'd met so briefly at the funeral, and he'd been distracted with his own personal problems, so he hadn't paid much attention to her. He remembered her voice, her eyes, her protectiveness of Valerie's parents, and her spunk. He couldn't help but smile; he suspected she would hate being called *spunky*. Now, she wore little makeup, apparently not concerned with masking the small lines around her eyes or the faint freckles dusting her nose. When she smiled, which was often, the left side of her mouth crooked up higher than her right, making her look mischievous, ready to pull an epic prank. Her fingers were long and thin; her nails were manicured but without polish. She wore no ring, nor was there a shiny strip of skin on an accidentally naked ring finger. Jack felt a pang of pity for all the men who hadn't bothered to buy Ellie Martin a beer.

A blush crept up her neck to her cheeks. She looked down at her desk. Could she read his mind? He looked around the bank to find something boring and innocuous to talk about. They spoke at the same time.

"This is an int—"

She held out a file. "The signed—"

They stopped, like two embarrassed teenagers struggling to make conversation on a first date. Blushing suited her. "You go," Jack said.

"No, you."

"I was just saying this is an interesting building."

And she was off, rattling information about the building. "This is one of the oldest buildings in Stillwater. One of the first built of stone, which is why it survived the 1889 fire. It was designed and built in 1882 by Jean Robichaux. He was from France via Louisiana, as you might expect with a name like Robichaux. But he was forgiven for the sin of being a

Frenchman when he married a local girl. He lived in Stillwater for sixty years, until his death in—" She took a breath. "And I'm rambling. I'm sorry. I didn't mean to bore you. I forget sometimes that other people aren't as interested in history as I am."

"I'm not bored," Jack said, though he had no idea what she had just told him. Her voice soothed him, pushed out of his mind all the shit that led to him sitting in this chair, across a desk from a woman he was finding he wanted to get in a quiet corner of a dark bar and talk to for hours.

"I guess I know who I need to see if I have questions about Stillwater," Jack said with a smile, hoping to put her at ease as well as mask what he was feeling.

"Of course. I'd be happy to help."

She picked up the forgotten file and laid it on the desk in front of him. "Are you ready to close on your new house?"

Jack sat forward. "And your old one."

She opened the file. "If you will just sign where it is marked." She removed a pen from the stand on her desk and handed it to him. "You might want to flex your hand. There's a lot to sign."

Jack flipped open the file and signed below the seller's signature, Elliot Yourke. Jack looked up. "Yourke? As in Yourkeville? Yourke County?"

Ellie stared at the paperwork. "Yes. I'm a descendent of the founders."

"You really *are* the person to go to for information."

She nodded. "My mind is full of useless information, and I love to bore people with it."

"I doubt that." Jack scrawled his signature. "Elliot?"

"Dad wanted a son."

"I like it."

"Well, it could be worse, Juan Miguel."

Jack chuckled and kept signing. "Are you making fun of my legal name, Elliot?"

"I would never make fun of a man carrying a gun."

Jack glanced up at Ellie and found her smirking. He laughed. "My mother's ancestors are the founders of San Antonio," he said.

"Wow. Way to scoreboard me."

"I only trot that fact out when I'm trying to impress people." His pen hovered over the contract. He glanced up at Ellie, who was blushing and focusing on her hands. Jack smiled and kept signing. "My mom was the first Ibáñez to marry an Anglo, which they never forgave her for. My older brother got the Anglo name, I got Juan Miguel."

He continued to sign and initial, sign and initial, trusting everything was in order but not really caring one way or the other. Contracts had been his least favorite subject in law school. "Done." Jack put the pen down.

She pulled the folder to her and checked the signatures. "I've made a list of local repairmen and a designer you can call when you are ready to start renovations."

"Thank you," Jack said. "I'm going to do most of the renovations myself."

Her eyebrows arched. Her lopsided grin deepened the dimple on her left cheek. "Really? Are you a handyman?"

"Not particularly, but how hard can it be?"

She didn't laugh, but he could tell she wanted to. "Well, keep the list anyway. Just in case."

The phone on her desk beeped. "Excuse me," she said. After she replaced the receiver she stood. "Mrs. Maxwell is ready to see you."

Every person they walked past, customer and coworker alike, lifted their head and greeted her with either a silent nod or a smiling hello. It was obvious Ellie Martin was well liked and respected.

They stopped in front of a desk protecting a glass door with the name, JANE MAXWELL, PRESIDENT, painted in black, block letters. An older woman with a phone held to her ear held up a finger. She was dressed identically to Ellie but somehow didn't look ridiculous. She replaced the receiver, came around the desk, and had pulled Jack into a hug before Ellie could make the introduction. Stunned, Jack patted Shirley Underwood lightly on the back.

"Thank you for catching my daughter's killer," Shirley said, with an emphatic squeeze. Ellie pursed her lips and tried not to look amused at

Jack's discomfort. Shirley held Jack at arm's length. Her eyes were shiny with unshed tears. Jack reached for his handkerchief, an old-fashioned affectation that had proved valuable over the course of his career. Shirley took the crisp white cloth and dabbed at her eyes.

"You're welcome," Jack said.

Shirley nodded quickly and sniffed. "She was a wonderful daughter."

"I'm glad I was able to help."

"Help? From what I was told, you solved the case."

Jack put his hands in his pockets and jingled his keys, wondering how she knew his role in solving the case at all. He supposed the lead detective in Emerson had told the family. "No, I was part of a larger team." He looked toward the closed door, then at his watch.

"The mayor's on the phone," Shirley explained. "Shouldn't be but a minute."

Ellie handed the woman the file full of Jack's paperwork.

"Then I'll leave him in your capable hands." She looked Jack in the eye and extended her hand. "Good luck, Jack."

Her grip was firm, her palm dry. Her hand hummed with energy beneath his. He held her hand a fraction longer than he should have. Her smile stayed in place but her brows furrowed so slightly Jack thought he imagined it.

"I hope to see you again soon, Ellie."

She removed her hand from his. "In a town the size of Stillwater, it will be tough to avoid."

She turned to the woman at the desk. "Bye, Shirley. I'll talk to you later."

"Bye, darlin'."

Ellie walked through the lobby, greeting people as she went. She stopped and hugged an old man in overalls and spoke to him for a few minutes. While the man talked, Ellie focused on him completely, mischievous smile in place. She threw her head back and laughed. The old man basked in her attention.

"I'm sure gonna miss that girl," Shirley said.

Jack turned back to Mrs. Underwood. "Where's she going?"

"Across the street. She's opening her own business. Living in the remodeled second floor. Friday was her last day but she insisted on coming in today to get you all squared away."

Jack glanced back at Ellie, who was walking out the door, waving at someone.

"Why don't you have a seat, Chief?"

Jack looked at his watch. He suddenly wanted to leave as soon as possible. "I really should get back. Could we reschedule this?"

"She'll be done in a minute. Your crime scene isn't going anywhere." Shirley settled herself behind her desk. "Have you ever lived in a small town?"

"No. Army bases. San Antonio."

"Are you married?"

"I'd rather not talk about my personal life."

"Oh, I understand. Trust me. I only ask because if you aren't there are going to be lots of women setting their sights on you." She pointedly looked at his bare left ring finger. "There aren't many single men like you in Stillwater."

"Like me?"

"Young, handsome, and powerful."

"Powerful?" Jack laughed.

"Too bad Ellie's not one to go chasing after men. Not that she don't like men, mind you. She just had a pretty bad marriage. I think she views men and marriage as more trouble than they're worth."

"She could be right," Jack said. He checked his watch again, trying to hide the stab of disappointment from Shirley's comments and wondering what Ellie would think about Shirley Underwood talking so freely about her to a virtual stranger.

"No, she isn't. Take it from someone who's been married for forty-seven years. She just hasn't found the right man yet."

"You believe in true love, Mrs. Underwood?"

"Of course I do. I think everyone does, deep down. Don't you?"

Did he? Not really. "It's a nice idea."

"Apparently, you haven't found the right woman, either. Well, you'll have ample chance. The women in this county are going to be all over you like white on rice, whether you're married or not. There's a couple of women you should steer clear of, truth be told. If you need any advice in that area, you just let me know. Not that I would ever say a bad word about anyone. No, sir. I don't like to gossip. But, living here all my life . . ." She leaned forward again. "I know where all the bodies are buried."

"Thank you, Mrs. Underwood, but I'm not interested in dating." As soon as he said it, he knew it was a lie.

"Sometimes, what you are or aren't interested in don't matter in the least." Her phone beeped. "She's ready for you." Mrs. Underwood rose and, after a cursory knock on the opaque glass, opened the door and announced him.

Jane Maxwell, bank president and mayor of Stillwater, rose as Jack entered her office. She looked the part of a kindly grandmother in her conservative suit (apparently the bank uniform rule did not extend to her), choker of large pearls, and head of softly permed silver hair. Upon closer inspection, Jack saw the care that had been taken to conceal the dark circles beneath her shrewd blue eyes.

"Chief McBride, how good to see you again."

"And you, Mayor Maxwell," Jack said, shaking her small hand.

"Sit. Sit." She settled back into her chair, closed her eyes briefly before composing herself and saying, "Shirley, some coffee, please." The door closed with a soft click. "I take it you're settling in?"

"Yes." He thought with dread of all the boxes left to unpack.

Shirley returned, carrying a tray loaded with a pot of coffee, cups, and saucers. "Cream or sugar?" she asked Jack.

"Both, thank you," he replied.

Shirley poured, doctored, and handed him the cup. "I meant to tell you, Chief McBride, since Ellie is gone, if you have any questions or need anything else done, don't hesitate to give me a call." She served her boss and retreated from the room.

"You look amused, Mr. McBride," Jane Maxwell said over the rim of her cup, her slight European accent more pronounced on the word *amused*.

"Not amused, exactly. Just bewildered."

"The Bank of Stillwater prides itself on being the best bank in Yourke County. I could bore you with how we've held onto the traditions that our customers cling to while embracing the technology that they demand, but when it comes right down to it, what is bewildering you is the small-town friendliness. Get used to it, Mr. McBride."

"It'll be torture, I'm sure," he replied.

"Have you ever lived in a small town?"

"Army bases, which are similar, I suppose."

"Then you understand how it works. Everyone will know everything you do, or at least think they know. Because of your situation, you will be watched. Closely."

Jack sipped his coffee. "My situation?"

"An outsider replacing a native son."

"He retired, didn't he?"

She paused. "Yes."

"Voluntarily?"

"Buck Pollard was part of the police department for over forty-five years. He wielded an enormous amount of power. That is not easy to give up."

He noticed she didn't answer the question. "You think he will try to undermine my position?"

"Of course he will. But he will not do it directly. He is related to half of the county."

"Wonderful."

"You will be inundated with well-meaning citizens wanting to do things for you. Be careful what favors you take. There is always a price."

"And I won't know who they are really coming from."

She shook her head.

"What price will Shirley exact? Or Ellie?"

"None. Neither is related to Pollard." Jane gave a wry smile. "After what you did to solve Valerie's murder, Shirley would give you an organ if necessary. And Ellie? I'm not sure Ellie has ever asked for a favor from anyone. It's probably why she is the one person in town who is universally liked. That and the fact that she is level-headed and fair."

"I'm surprised you let her leave."

"I didn't do it willingly, I assure you. I'm not sure where or when she got her powers of persuasion. She was always a very tractable young woman."

Jack sipped his coffee, imagining there were very few times someone had bested Jane Maxwell. His admiration for Ellie Martin grew.

Jane set her cup down. "As chief of police, it would probably be best to avoid freebies altogether. If you're here long enough, there will be a scandal. There always is. Everything you've done until that point will be scrutinized. Don't give your enemies ammunition."

"I've been here barely forty-eight hours and I already have enemies and a scandal?"

"The man in charge always has enemies. Better that you learn now. One more thing."

"What?"

"I'm a direct person. I don't sugarcoat or pussyfoot around. I don't want you to do it with me and I will never do it with you. If I ask you a question, I expect complete honesty."

Jack set his cup and saucer on the desk. "As do I."

Her smile was enigmatic. He saw the lie coming before she said it. "Of course."

V

With a name like Miner Jesson, Jack expected his most senior officer to have a pot belly from too much fried food, a receding hairline, and blunt, square fingers with cuticles perpetually stained with engine grease.

Instead, a middle-aged man of slight build with sallow skin, dark hair, and crooked teeth stood next to him in the Ramoses' front yard waiting for Mike Freeman to return. Nathan Starling was taping the front door of the trailer. Jack stared at Miner, trying to place who exactly he reminded him of, while Miner tried to ignore Jack's gaze. At least Jack was right about the fingers.

Miner stared at the darkening sky. "Looks like rain."

Jack followed his gaze. "It does."

"Sure do need it." He hesitated and then said, "I just want you to know, I hold no ill will toward you." The words tumbled out of Miner's mouth.

"Why would you?"

"I was up for the chief's job."

"Were you?"

"I didn't want it. I only applied because . . ." He stopped and looked at Jack. "It seemed like I should, being the senior officer."

"Why didn't you want the job?"

He sighed. "Paperwork ain't my strong suit. Neither is dealing with the politics. Don't want the hassle."

"Now you're making me second-guess my decision."

"Don't go saying that. You're just what this town needs."

"What's that?"

"An outsider. I'm glad you're here. I'm looking forward to working with you. Hope to learn a little something. Prove the old saying about old dogs wrong."

Jack smiled. "We'll see what we can do."

Nathan Starling walked over just as Mike Freeman drove into the yard. Starling's eyes were rimmed with dark circles. "Thank you for the coffee this morning, Chief. I don't think I would have made it without it."

"You're welcome. You work the night shift?"

"Yes, sir." Starling looked at his watch. "Go on in six hours."

"Why don't you go home and get some rest. I can fill you in later."

"Oh, I'd like to stay and hear everything, if that's all right."

Jack shrugged in reply but liked the kid's enthusiasm.

Freeman walked over and handed a thick manila envelope to Jack. "Sorry I'm late. Been in Yourkeville, printing these out."

"We don't have a printer?" Jack opened the envelope and pulled out the top picture. It was a close up of Gilberto's blown-apart head.

"Not one that can print that quality of pictures," Miner said. "Haven't had much need for one."

"As she was leaving today, Sheriff Newberry said I could use theirs," Freeman said. "Pretty unlike her to offer help like that."

Jack looked up from the pictures. "Why do you say that?"

"She and Buck didn't exactly get along," Miner said.

"I guess she likes you," Starling piped up.

"I worked with Sheriff Newberry on a case, years ago," Jack explained, though he felt he shouldn't have had to. "Miner, what did you find out?"

"Not much. The Mexicans that probably knew them best couldn't speak very good English. I got a lot of no's, which I took to mean after some trial and error that none of them believed Rosa would kill Gilberto then herself. A few trailers down lives Edna Stamps, retired secretary. Lived in the trailer park for going on thirty years, way before it transitioned to mainly Mexicans. She had generally good things to say about the Ramoses. Didn't know them very well, but said she never heard them arguing and screaming at each other like some of the other families. Said they walked around the neighborhood every night, pushing their baby in a stroller. Also said Rosa brought her a meal one day last year when she was sick. When I asked her if she was surprised by what happened she said she stopped being surprised by anything after 9/11."

"What does that mean?" Freeman asked.

"I think she just stopped being surprised at the evil in the world."

"I hope I never stop being surprised at the evil in the world," Jack mumbled. "All right. Miner, give me the list of people you talked to and I'll go out tomorrow and talk to them in Spanish."

Miner took a small notebook and pencil from his pocket and started writing names.

"I've got Diego locked up at City Hall," Jack said. "I'm running a check on him, but it might be a while. Depends on how helpful Mexican law enforcement wants to be." Jack watched as Miner wrote in his book. "Did you not write the information down as you talked to them?"

Miner kept his eyes on his notes. "No . . . Nathan, if you want to get a couple extra hours sleep, I'll cover your patrol until ten," Miner said.

Starling glanced at Jack. "Oh, that's okay. I'll be fine."

"No, I think it's an excellent idea," Jack said. "Go on home, get some sleep." Reluctantly, Starling left.

"If there's nothing else," Freeman said, "I better get out to the school. Teenagers in a school zone, the tickets just write themselves."

Jack watched Miner write out the names, first and last, and addresses of his interviewees in large, slanting letters. "I've got to pick Ethan up from school," Jack said.

"All right. What are we doing with Vasquez?"

"Take him down to County."

"Thought you weren't going to deport him."

"I don't want to, but the only way to keep him from bolting is to keep him in custody. We don't have the facilities."

Miner nodded in agreement. "I can take him for you."

"I'll call for transport. I suppose that's available."

"Sure."

"I need you to find a day laborer named Raul. Ellie Martin says he worked with Gilberto when they helped her move."

"All right. Anything else?" He tore the paper from his notebook and handed it to Jack.

"Yeah, where's a good place to eat?"

VI

"How was your day?"

Jack and Ethan sat in a red Formica booth at the Dairy Queen, waiting on their burgers. Since Jack picked up Ethan, his son hadn't said a word.

"And don't shrug your answer to me," Jack said, cutting off Ethan's shrug as it started. "It takes two people, talking, to have a conversation." Ethan glared at him. "In case you didn't know," Jack finished.

"You've never cared how my day was before."

Jack sighed. The camaraderie they found on their summer road trip had vanished as soon as Jack told Ethan they were moving. Check that— it vanished when Jack told Ethan *where* they were moving. Jack wasn't surprised; he even understood where Ethan was coming from. To a point. But Jack needed a job. His pride wouldn't let him go back to the Agency, even if they wanted him to. So far, nothing indicated they did.

He and Ethan had been four weeks into their road trip, somewhere in Montana, when Jack got the call. He thought it was the call he'd been waiting for, the one where someone from the Agency reached out to ask him to come back. Instead, his former partner told him about a chief of police position she heard about. Small town. Small force. Low crime. Less stress.

"Low pay?" he added. His six months' savings cushion was dwindling at an alarming rate.

"Low cost of living, too. Let me give them your number. At least talk to them."

Ethan had been asleep in the back seat, music pulsing from the head-phones on his ears.

"Where is it?"

"East Texas. Stillwater."

Now, here they were. New place, same difficult relationship.

"Don't act like I never asked about your day or what was going on when I got home, Ethan. I'm not an absentee father because I worked late sometimes."

"Sometimes," Ethan scoffed. "Try four out of five nights a week."

Ethan said it, but Jack heard his wife's accusing voice. From the comments Ethan had been making for the last year, it was plain Julie had spent lots of time complaining to Ethan about Jack, his job, and all of the horrible things he did to her and the family. It would be so easy to do the same, to tell Ethan about his mother, her abandonment, where she was, what she was doing and with whom, but Jack refrained. Okay, he lied, but the truth would destroy Ethan's opinion of his mother. As much as Jack hated Julie and what she did, he wouldn't do that. If Julie ever came back, Jack had no doubt Ethan would eventually see through her. He was a smart kid. He didn't ever want Julie to be able to accuse him of poisoning her son against her. Sometimes taking the high road was damn hard.

"Well, here I am now. Picking you up from school, trying to have a conversation with you, and all you can do is shrug your shoulders and give me attitude."

Ethan sat up and plastered on a smile. "My day was great, Dad! Half the school hated me because I'm your son. The other half tried to be my best friend because I'm new and apparently have hair like some vampire dude. Those were mostly girls. The ugly ones."

"A vampire dude?"

Ethan slumped back down in his seat, played with the white plastic saltshaker. "It's not funny, Dad."

Jack cleared his throat. "Absolutely not."

Seeing Jack's fake seriousness made Ethan give a small, embarrassed smile. "It's *really* not funny."

"Come on. It's pretty funny. . . . If it makes you feel any better, some old man at the gas station made fun of my shoes."

Ethan leaned back and looked under the table. "They *are* a little gay for the country."

Jack looked at his favorite square-toed loafers. "Since most of the gay men I know have pretty good taste, I'll take that as a compliment."

Two cowboys with heavily starched long-sleeved shirts, jeans with a heavy crease down the front of their legs, and straw cowboy hats stood at the counter ordering Hunger-Busters and steak fingers. "Not much competition for style around here," Ethan said. He dumped salt and pepper together into a pile.

A perky high school girl who grinned at Ethan for longer than appropriate delivered their food. Ethan scarfed down his burger and was halfway done with his fries before Jack had taken five bites.

"What happened with your case?" Ethan asked. Jack noted for future reference that food softened Ethan's attitude. He wanted to fill Ethan in on everything, happy to have a safe, common ground, but he knew better. He didn't need his son accidentally lobbing information grenades into the middle of Stillwater's rumor mill.

"Not much," Jack said. "Most of the people that live around the victims are Hispanic and the officer that interviewed them doesn't speak the language. I'm going back tomorrow afternoon to do interviews. I'd like to go in the morning, but my day is full of meetings."

"Why don't we go now?" Ethan asked.

"No."

"I'll just hang back. Talk to the kids."

"You don't know Spanish."

"A little. Anyway, they probably speak English."

"I can't take my son to question witnesses."

"You're the chief. You can do whatever you want."

"It's because I'm the chief that I can't do whatever I want. The guy before me did too much of that. I have to set a new tone—and fast."

"He took his kids to crime scenes?"

Jack sighed. "I don't know. He was corrupt, is what I meant. I have to be extra careful what I do. Taking my teenage son to interview witnesses is a bad way to start."

"You took me to the crime scene this morning."

"I didn't have any choice. And you stayed in the car."

Ethan finished his fries and slumped back into his seat. "Was the old chief's name Jackson?"

"No. Why?"

"Some kid cornered me in the locker room, talking about you taking his uncle's job or something."

"Did he hit you?"

Ethan laughed. "No. Just flexed his muscles, scowled and tried to string together three-letter words into a sentence. He's big and stupid."

Jack wiped his hands on a flimsy paper napkin and considered his son while he finished chewing his burger. "Have you ever gotten into a fight?"

Ethan looked at his dad from under his eyebrows. "Shouldn't you know that?"

"Do you tell me everything that happens to you?"

"No."

"Did you tell Mom everything?"

Ethan shook his head.

Jack held his hands out in surrender. Ethan poured more salt and pepper onto the table. "Stop that," Jack said.

Ethan swept the grains onto the floor.

Jack gritted his teeth. "How old are you? Seven? Now that girl will have to clean up your mess."

"She gets paid, doesn't she?"

Jack felt the conversation getting away from him, which Jack suspected was Ethan's goal. He steered it back on track.

"Do you know what to do if you're in a fight?"

"Run?"

"Only if you want to continue to be picked on."

Ethan stared at him. "Are you telling me to fight?"

"I would never tell you to pick a fight. But, if someone takes a swipe at you, you won't get in trouble from me for fighting back."

Ethan's eyes widened. "Mom said never—"

"She's not here, is she?"

Jack regretted it immediately. He braced himself for the lie he would have to tell when Ethan asked where she was. But Ethan didn't ask. Instead, he slumped in his chair—Jack feared he was going to slide right under the table soon—and stared out the window at the parking lot.

"Things are different here," Jack said. "I'm chief of police, which means that I'm going to make enemies. If I throw some kid's mom or dad in jail, they may try to retaliate by picking a fight with you."

"Awesome. I'm so glad you decided to move us to this crappy town."

"The first, and best, thing to do is walk away. Always. But, sometimes, you just have to stand up for yourself. And your friends."

"Well, I don't have any of those right now."

"You will." Jack piled his empty wrappers on the tray. "Now. We need to talk about what you're going to do after school. I'm not always going to be able to pick you up."

"I know."

"Think you're old enough to stay at the house by yourself until I get home?"

Ethan looked at his father, his eyes wary. "Really? You'd let me do that?"

"Sure. I did it when I was your age."

"Sweet."

"But there are conditions."

"What kind of conditions did Grandmother put on you and Uncle Eddie?"

"Don't fight and don't burn the house down."

"Burn the house down? Seriously?"

"Uncle Eddie."

Ethan beamed and Jack tamped down the flame of jealousy Ethan's bottomless well of admiration for Eddie always ignited. Ethan didn't know about all of the shit Eddie had created for their mother and Jack over the years. One or the other of them was always cleaning up Eddie's messes, even now. Jack and his mother had joked that having an FBI agent brother and politician mother who could get Eddie out of almost any jam was probably not the best thing in the world for a troublemaker like Sean Edward McBride. But, for all his faults, Eddie was one hell of a fun uncle.

"Have you talked to Uncle Eddie lately?" Ethan asked.

"A few weeks ago."

"Is he going to come visit?"

Jack shrugged. "Maybe," he lied. His conversation with his brother hadn't gone well. Eddie had never liked Julie—a disdain that was mutual—and had not been shy about telling Jack, each time they talked, how he had been right about her all along. There was nothing more infuriating than hearing "I told you so," in every conceivable way, from your older brother.

"Anyway," Jack said. "That's not all."

"Of course it's not."

"You have to have your homework done by the time I get home."

Ethan crossed his arms over his chest.

"Your room has to be clean, your bed made every day."

"Dad."

"You can't have friends over unless I know about it well beforehand."

"Like I said, I have no friends."

"Absolutely no girls at the house when I'm not there."

Ethan rolled his eyes. "Like any girls would want to hang out with me."

"If you want to go somewhere, you have to call me."

"Where the fu—" Ethan stopped. "Where would I possibly want to go?"

"On days it's raining, I'll try to pick you up, but again, I might not always be able to. You'll have to walk."

"Sure. Whatever."

"If I have to work the night shift, I'm going to get a sitter, though."

"Absolutely not. I'm going to be fourteen in a week."

"*Fourteen-year-old boy dies in a fiery blaze while dad at work.* Still a shitty headline."

"*D-a-ad,*" Ethan said, rolling his eyes, "stop with the headline thing. Nothing's going to happen."

"Because when I work at night, I'm getting a sitter. I'll make sure she's pretty."

"Oh my God, just stop talking." Ethan got up and headed for the door.

"Hey. Help me clean this up."

Ethan sighed with his entire upper body, as only a teenager could, heaped the trash onto the red tray and threw it away.

When they were in the car, Jack said, "Tomorrow morning I have a breakfast meeting. You'll have to ride your bike."

"Okay."

Jack turned the ignition. "Come on. Let's drive the route."

VII

Diego Vasquez sat in a wobbly chair in the police station break room. He stared out the window, his leg jiggling, and his eyes in constant motion. He sniffed, wiped his nose with the back of his hand, stared at the slick residue, and wiped it on his jeans. Freeman stood over him in much the same attitude as earlier—arms crossed, feet wide, expressionless. Diego avoided looking at him.

Jack observed through the two-way mirror in his office. He didn't know what was weirder—being able to see everything that went on in the break room from his office or the fact that the break room doubled as the interrogation room. He rubbed his forehead and sighed.

It just gets better and better.

He slapped the manila folder he was holding on his leg and walked into the break room.

"*Hola*, Diego," Jack said. He nodded for Freeman to leave, which he did without a word.

Diego didn't answer. He stared out the window so intently Jack was compelled to follow his gaze. Through the sheets of rain and the gaps between the vacant downtown buildings, Jack could just see the river in the distance. A boom of thunder shook the leaded glass windows. A crack of lightning lit the sky, turning the depressing downtown scene an eerie silver, before reverting to the gray shroud of rain. It was 4:30 in the afternoon but looked like midnight.

Jack opened the manila folder and read the information he had just received from the Mexican authorities. "Rosa Ruiz Iban Ramos. Born on November 28, 1990, to Jesus Iban and Carmen Ruiz." Jack looked up at the baby-faced man sitting in front of him. Diego stared at the folder, chewing his thumb. Diego's chair wobbled with every jerk of his leg, tapping a steady rhythm on the floor. Jack tried to ignore it. "We have no record of when she arrived in the US, nor when she was married to Gilberto, if they were even married."

Diego shot him a dirty look. "They were married."

Jack shrugged. He couldn't care less. "Thing is, Diego, Rosa has lots of sisters. Eight, in fact. But no brothers. Weird, huh? With you, her brother, sitting right in front of me." Jack leaned forward and said, in exaggerated astonishment, "You don't exist, Diego."

Jack replaced the sheet of paper, closed the folder, and sat back, hands on the table. He tapped his fingers like a drummer. He slammed his hands on the table and lurched forward. Diego didn't flinch.

"God, you don't know how I envy you. To be able to just—" Jack snapped his fingers, "disappear. Not a care in the world. No one to look after, answer to. Just go where the road takes me. I mean who *hasn't* dreamed of doing that? Bitchy wife. Ungrateful kids. Overbearing parents. Horrible bosses. Maybe we do something we'd like to forget. See something we shouldn't." Diego's eyes hardened. Jack noted it, pretended to ignore it, and continued. "Oh, there's hundreds—thousands—of reasons to disappear. But . . ." He sat back in his chair and threw up his hands. They settled on his thighs. "It's all just a fantasy. No one ever does it, or not many, anyway. Those who do are the ones who believe that what they want—that saving their skin, scratching whatever itch they have at the moment—is more important than any responsibility they may have, any commitment they made."

Jack stopped. He could hear the bitterness in his voice himself. He took a deep breath and smiled and waved his hand in dismissal. "I'm sure none of that pertains to you. A man like that, a man who's running from something, wouldn't have stuck around, would he? This is just a mix-up with the records down in Mexico, I bet. They've got bigger fish to fry than keeping accurate records, what with all the cartel murders and such. It's a war zone down there." Jack waited, let the silence expand into the crevices of the room. He tapped the table with the folder and stood. "I'll do a little more digging." He stopped at the door and turned.

"Of course . . . Rosa has cousins."

Jack returned to his chair. All of the nervous tics Diego had worked so hard to exhibit evaporated. "Probably hundreds of them. Twenty-two brothers and sisters between Rosa's parents." Jack leaned forward, whispered. "Is that it, Diego? Are you her cousin?"

"I ain't nobody, man."

Still whispering, Jack replied, "Come on, Diego. Everybody's somebody. And I think you're somebody special."

"No man. I ain't."

"Are you really going to make me go to all that effort to find out who you are, to talk to the Mexican authorities, dig around in their files, talk to the DEA, Border Patrol, INS, ATF, FBI, when you can just tell me, right now, who you are?"

Diego looked at the two-way mirror over Jack's shoulder. "Who's back there?"

"I have no idea. Probably no one."

"That big dude back there?"

"Freeman? Maybe."

Diego's eyes blazed, and Jack saw how dangerous this man could be. The transformation was breathtaking. "I ain't saying a word unless you can promise me no one but you will know."

"I can't promise that."

He sat back, the fidgety illegal again. "I guess Rosa killed Gilberto then killed herself."

Jack looked at the mirror, then back at Diego. "All right. Let's hear it."

"They'd been fighting. Gilberto'd been out drinking with me since I got here, having a good time. She didn't like that, with the new baby and all. We'd been drinking that night, before he went home and I went down to Esperanza's. I guess Rosa'd had too much."

"Where'd she get the gun?"

Diego shrugged. "I never seen it before. Honest to God. Maybe she had it hid in one of those bins under her bed. She liked to hide stuff."

"Their deaths had nothing to do with you."

Diego leaned forward and whispered. "You want to know more, get me out of this room." He raised his eyebrows, sat back, and stared out the window.

Jack stood, took out his phone, and pointed it at Diego. "Hey." When Diego looked at him, Jack took the picture and smiled. "Sit tight."

Jack found Freeman at his desk, filling out a report.

"Hey. I'm taking Vasquez to County."

"I can do that for you."

"I got it. Want to stop in and see Sheriff Newberry while I'm there." It was a weak reason for the chief to be transporting a prisoner, especially on his first day on the job, but Freeman seemed to buy it easily enough.

Jack called Ethan, told him he would be a little late, and promised to bring him dinner. The kid was going to eat him into the poorhouse.

Jack hung up and watched Freeman. Freeman seemed straightforward; unmarried, former military police, two tours in Iraq, a health nut, and bit of a meathead. Freeman would follow orders. If the orders happened to line up with the rules? So much the better. If not, so what?

Why didn't Diego want to talk in front of him?

"What's your take on him?"

"Vasquez?" Freeman asked.

"Yeah. You've been around him some."

The chair creaked as Freeman leaned back. His hair was cut high and tight, military style, and was so blond he almost looked bald. "Fidgety bastard. My guess is he's some low-level drug mule from Mexico who came up here to get away from all the crazy shit going on down there."

A much more nuanced answer than Jack expected. "Think he brought trouble with him?"

"Maybe."

Jack leaned against the desk. "A cartel wouldn't try to make it look like murder-suicide. They'd just kill them and walk away. Maybe pin a note to their chest with an ice pick. And why not wait around and kill Diego?"

Freeman shrugged. "Expected him to be home when he wasn't? No chance since. He's been in custody. Get anything from Mexico yet?"

"No. Nothing through the state either. Would you run him through the Feds? I was going to do it when I got back, but if you could do it, it would save some time." Jack pulled his phone out. "I'll forward his picture to you. I may be gone for a while, getting him processed. I'll be late in the morning. Have the Rotary breakfast."

"Sounds like fun."

"Maybe in some alternate universe."

Freeman grinned. "Susan's been fielding calls from every women's group in town. They all can't wait to meet you," he said in a sing-song voice.

Jack pocketed his phone and pointed at his deputy. "Watch it, or I'll make you go in my place."

"I take it all back. Be careful on the road," Freeman said. "Weather's terrible."

"Will do."

VIII

Visibility was five feet. Maybe.

The wipers worked frantically to clear the windshield. Gusts of wind buffeted the car, knocking it onto the shoulder before Jack could compensate. Knuckles white on the steering wheel, he jerked the car to the left, crossing over the centerline and back into his lane.

Jack glanced in the rearview mirror at Diego Vasquez. He stared out the window, expressionless.

"All right, we're alone. Talk."

Diego remained silent. Jack drove a mile before speaking again. "I have a theory. Want to hear it?"

Silence.

"You're a cousin—it will be easy to figure out which one with your picture and fingerprints." Jack glanced back. Diego stared at him in the mirror. "Dairy Queen cups are surprisingly good for fingerprints.

"When we send your picture and prints to the DEA, my guess is you'll come up quick. Hell, there might even be a reward for you, though Freeman thinks you're a low-level drug mule. Not smart enough to be in charge.

"You ran up here because you saw something you shouldn't have. Turned you off the drug trade. Maybe you were a snitch and they sent someone up here to kill you."

The wind suddenly changed direction, jerking the car to the left as a boom of thunder shook the earth and lightning ripped across the sky. Jack jerked the car to the right, thankful there were no other cars on the road. He slowed the car and looked back at Diego.

He was gone.

Jack turned. Through the protective screen, he saw Diego slumped down in the seat, hands cuffed behind him, eyes rolled back in his head in the throes of a seizure. Blood dribbled down his right cheek from where his head hit the window. Jack slammed on the brakes and skidded to a stop on the shoulder.

Jack was soaked through as soon as he stepped out of the car. He ran around, pulling the handcuff key out of his pocket as he went. He jerked open the back door, unbuckled Diego, and turned him on his side. Jack was leaning across his prisoner and had unlocked the first cuff when Diego sat up and smashed his forehead twice against Jack's in quick succession. He followed it with a weak punch to the face, but Jack was too dazed to respond. Diego kicked at Jack, who flew out of the car and landed on his back in the waterlogged ditch.

Jack felt the thunder in the earth and saw lightning crawl across the sky but heard nothing. Sound was muffled. Rain pelted his face, blurring his vision. There was a pulling on his clothes, his suit coat pockets, and his pants pocket. He felt the snap release on his hip holster, his sidearm jerked out. Diego, hair plastered to his head, eyes glittering with amusement, leaned over Jack. Jack's gun was in his right hand, his phone in his left.

"I probably shouldn't have stayed this morning," Diego said in English. "But Rosa is family. Nothing is more important than family." He shook his head. "I like you, *vato*, but going to jail isn't part of my plan. No hard feelings, huh?"

Diego lifted his arm. The last thing Jack saw was the butt of his gun rushing toward him.

IX

The leg of the chair pounded on the floor—*boom, boom, boom*—with every jerk of Diego's leg.

Jack leaned across the table, grabbed the front of Diego's shirt. "Stop shaking your fucking leg."

Diego's eyes turned black. He smiled. "No hard feelings, *vato*." Diego put the gun to Jack's head and pulled the trigger.

Jack jerked awake. The room was dark, save a faint glow of greenish light. Jack moved his head and groaned. An ice pick pierced his temple.

"Chief?"

A woman's voice, calm and soothing.

"Julie?"

"No. I'm Nurse Lowe. You're in the hospital." She was in her fifties, slightly overweight, with gentle hands and a kind, compassionate face. She smiled at Jack, grasped his hand and squeezed.

"Where?"

"The hospital. You've been in an accident. You're going to be just fine, though." She squeezed his hand again. "I'm going to get the doctor."

She left, her footsteps soft on the floor. Jack lifted his hand to shield his eyes from the slash of light through the opened door. The door closed with a small click, throwing him into semidarkness again.

He closed his eyes and swallowed, fighting nausea. Through the pounding in his head and the sharp pain in his temple, he tried to remember what had happened. The last thing he remembered was calling Ethan. Then, Nurse Lowe.

Ethan. Where was Ethan?

He covered his eyes with his hand and tentatively opened them, peeking through his fingers. Outside it was dark, and rain pelted against the window.

What time was it?

The door to his room opened and Nurse Lowe entered, followed by Miner Jesson and middle-aged man wearing a white coat.

"Chief McBride," the doctor said. "I'm Doctor Poole."

"Where's Ethan?"

"He's in the hall. We'll bring him in in a minute."

Jack's heart slowed. Ethan was okay. He stared at the man in the coat. "Poole? You look different."

The doctor smiled. "You met my father yesterday."

Jack blinked. Licked his rough lips. Miner's face was creased with worry. "Hey, Miner," Jack said, though to Jack's ears it sounded like, "hiner." He couldn't put his lips together. Why was that?

"Chief."

"Wha' happe . . . ?" He didn't have the energy to say it all. Miner was a smart man. Smarter than he let on. He'd figure it out. Or not. Whatever. Jack didn't care.

Doctor Poole stepped forward, blocking Jack's view of Miner. It was a fuzzy view at best. Miner stepped back into the shadows. Doctor Poole pulled out a penlight and shined it in Jack's eyes. Jack closed his eyes and raised his hand. "Ow." Poole the Younger clicked the penlight off and put it in his breast pocket.

"Are you nauseated, Chief?"

"Yeah."

"Head hurt?"

"Yeah."

Poole smiled. "I'd be surprised if it didn't. You took a pretty big beating."

Jack forced himself to enunciate. "Wha' happened." That was good. He bet he could drive right now if he had to.

Miner stepped forward. "We were hoping you could tell us."

Jack lifted his hands off the bed. They felt light, like feathers, until they plopped back down. Weird.

"Do you remember interrogating Vasquez this afternoon?"

"Vasquez?" A wobbly chair came to mind, but nothing else. "No."

"Freeman said you interrogated him about 4:00, for about ten minutes, then took him to County. About an hour later, a local plumber found you in the ditch off of Yourkeville Highway, soaked through and apparently pistol whipped."

"Where's Ethan?"

"He's outside," Miner said.

Jack tried to sit up. The room started spinning. Poole put a gentle hand on his shoulder. "We're going to keep you here overnight," he said. "For observation."

Jack felt like he should protest, but he was too busy swallowing the bile that rose in his throat. He slumped back on the pillow. Nurse Lowe was next to him, fussing over him, looking so very sweet and comforting. Jack smiled at her. He would bet she gave great hugs. Grandmotherly. He shouldn't ask her for a hug. *Don't ask her for a hug.* "Than' you."

She winked at him. "I'll go get that handsome son of yours."

Poole patted him on the shoulder. "I'll be back later. Rest."

Miner stepped forward, staring at Jack's face. "I look that bad?"

Miner grimaced. "Pretty bad. You have six stitches in your left eyebrow and your right eye is swollen shut."

"No wonder you're a blur."

"You're going to have an impressive shiner."

"Ladies love that shit." It hurt when Jack laughed.

"They found your patrol car near the county line."

Jack nodded.

"Vasquez torched it."

"'Course he did."

The door opened. Ethan peeked around. "Dad?"

"Hey, buddy."

Ethan rushed forward. When he saw his dad's face, fully, his mouth gaped and his eyes reddened. "Jesus, Dad. Are you okay?"

Jack lifted his hand. Ethan took it. "Yeah. I'm fine. I'm going to be fine."

"What happened?"

"I don't remember." He squeezed Ethan's hand. "Sorry I didn't bring dinner."

Ethan shook his head rapidly. "Whatever, Dad. Should I call Mom? Tell her to come?"

Jack felt a stab of guilt stronger than the pounding in his head. "No. Miner will take care of it." He saw Susan Grant in the background, clutching a huge purse in front of her. Why did women carry such big purses? Were they really necessary? What was she doing here? "Hey, Susan."

She stepped forward. "Sam—Doctor Poole—said you need to stay overnight. Ethan will stay with us."

Jack smiled faintly. "Thanks."

Ethan held Jack's hand, but his gaze was riveted to Jack's bruised and swollen face. "You need anything, Dad?"

Jack opened his mouth, closed it, then smiled. "I have no idea."

Nurse Lowe stepped forward. "He needs rest. Off with you."

"I'll be back in the morning," Ethan said.

"No, go to school. I'll be fine."

"But, Dad . . ."

"No, really. Go to school. I'll see you when you get home tomorrow." Ethan leaned over and hugged Jack.

"Love you," Ethan whispered.

Jack hugged him with one arm. "I love you, too." His throat thickened; he couldn't remember the last time he said those words to his son. He lifted his arm full of tubes and pulled Ethan closer. "We're going to be fine." Ethan nodded into Jack's shoulder, and sniffed.

Jack patted Ethan on the back, and his son straightened. "See ya," he said, face red and splotchy, and walked quickly out the door. Susan followed.

Miner stood at the foot of the bed. "Is there someone you want me to call, Chief?"

Jack thought of Julie and, for the first time in months, wished she were with him. "No," he said.

Miner nodded and didn't press. "I'll bring you some clothes in the morning. I'll take care of things at the station. Don't you worry."

"Where's my phone, Miner?"

"Wasn't on you." Miner looked at the hat he held in his hand, then back up at Jack. "Neither was your gun. I've already reported it stolen."

"Shit. I liked that gun."

"Come on, Miner," Nurse Lowe said. "Let the man rest. You can do this in the morning." She hustled Miner out the door.

Jack watched the rain and thought of his wife, wondered where she was. He hadn't had the heart to tell Ethan that the emails Jack had sent her over the last year were sometimes opened, but always unanswered. Julie had walked out of their lives so cleanly and completely that there were times Jack wondered if she ever existed, if she was nothing more than a figment of his imagination. Then the proof they had once been in love and happy would walk in the room, ear buds in, the musty, sour smell of puberty following him like the contrail of a jet.

He swallowed, with difficulty, the hatred and resentment he felt toward his wife. Apparently those emotions could pierce through his foggy mind. She should be here, if for no other reason than for Ethan, to comfort him when he was so obviously upset at seeing Jack like this. Instead, a stranger was taking care of him, mothering him, reassuring Ethan that everything would be okay.

As soon as the idea of calling his own mother occurred to Jack, he dismissed it. The last thing he needed was the former lieutenant governor of Texas swooping in and taking over their lives. His brother, Eddie, was an option, but he hadn't talked to Eddie in weeks and hadn't left things well with him the last time they spoke. That Eddie had been completely right was even more reason to not call him.

Jack drifted in and out of consciousness, vaguely aware of Nurse Lowe coming and going, low voices, the rain lashing against the window. Eddie and the Lieutenant Governor stood at the foot of his bed, shaking their heads.

"I told you so, bro."

"Don't you worry," his mother said. She held her speaker's gavel in her right hand. "I'll take care of everything."

A large man appeared next to her, holding a cup of coffee. "Told you you'd ruin your shoes."

"I liked those shoes," Jack mumbled.

Diego leaned against the window, wearing Jack's suit—hell, he even had Jack's haircut. Julie stood next to him. Diego held Jack's gun to her head. "You weren't part of the deal, *vato*. No hard feelings." Lightning flashed behind them, throwing them into shadow, the gunshot rang out. When the lightning faded, they were gone.

Jack stood at the top of a bluff, looking down over Stillwater. A golden glow suffused the town, softening the ugliness, making Stillwater seem quaint instead of shabby. A soft breeze ruffled his loose linen shirt, shook the blood orange leaves on the trees. Vibrant green grass threaded between his toes, cooled his feet. He breathed in. The faint smell of wood smoke tickled his nose.

A woman pulled at his hand. "Are you coming?" she asked. Her voice was as smooth as poured chocolate. He wanted to wrap himself in her voice and take a long nap.

She tugged on his hand again. He followed. She glanced back, but did not turn. He saw the line of her jaw, the slope of her nose, the corner of her eye crinkle, and she laughed. His heart leapt at the sound, the shared private joke, and he laughed with her. The sun flared over her shoulder, blinding him. He lifted his hand to shield his eyes, and when he put it down, she was gone.

CHAPTER TWO

Friday

I

Ellie Martin had been part of Stillwater football in some form or fashion for most of her forty-two years. She liked football—had been the star of the powderpuff football game in 1984 when her freshman class beat the seniors, a contentious bit of Stillwater Snipes history even to this day—but for Ellie, the game was secondary, the background music to what she enjoyed most of all: watching the pageant of a small-town community. The best vantage point for that was the concession stand.

Everyone, at one point or another throughout the game or season, came to the home-side concession stand. Most were regulars—coming at the same time during the game, ordering the same thing, making the same bit of small talk. Others came infrequently, their visits memorable for their rarity. Many conversations were ended midsentence, the press of the line demanding attention, with promises to call, catch lunch, or talk more at church made with a wave or nod, depending on how overloaded arms were with burgers, hot dogs, Cokes, candy, and popcorn.

The Stillwater Snipes Booster Club had been running the home-side concession stand for as long as anyone could remember. Game prep went on with little explanation or direction. Everyone knew their job and did it, decked out in various types of Snipes spirit wear: logoed golf shirts, bedazzled denim shirts and trucker hats, homemade Snipes earrings and necklaces made by a past president of the booster club, oversized hoodies and fleeces when the weather turned cooler. Conversation leaned toward gossip—school, church, and town. The concession stand was right behind the Cut-n-Curl and bank in Stillwater grapevine importance. Ellie'd been at the center of Stillwater chatter too many times in her life to want to participate. Only a fool wouldn't listen. The topic of conversation at this meaningless, pre-district game, however, was more interesting than usual: Jack McBride.

"Hardly a great way to start his job. Losin' a criminal and getting pistol-whipped on his first day."

"Don't forget that illegal stole his cruiser and set it on fire."

"Buck Pollard never had anything like that happen."

"I'm sure Buck Pollard had plenty happen you never knew about."

"You think it's a coincidence Stillwater has its first murders in years on McBride's first day?"

"What's that supposed to mean?"

"I'm just sayin'."

"How on Earth could Buck Pollard have stopped a Mexican from killing her husband and herself? That's the stupidest thing I've ever heard."

"Weren't no murder-suicide. Double murder. Drug-related from what I hear."

"Well, if it's drug-related, then maybe Buck would have stopped it."

Everyone went silent and exchanged furtive glances, waiting for lightning to strike them all down for the audacity of talking against Pollard. It was an open secret that crime was so low in Stillwater because of Pollard's machinations—illegal and legal—instead of his crime-fighting abilities. A good portion of the town was incensed when he left, not willing to trade their false sense of security for a rule-following Fed. Too many people were willing to sweep the town's problems under the rug and pretend they didn't exist.

Though the world didn't end with the vague implication about Pollard, the women changed the subject anyway.

"I heard Earl told the Chief yesterday morning he had a hiring freeze. Of course, had to change his mind this morning."

"Well, it was stupid of Earl to do that anyway. Can't run the town on four policemen, let alone three."

"If he don't got the money, he don't got the money."

"Oh, I'm sure he can find it somewhere."

"I heard the chief's already interviewin' outsiders for the open officer position."

"I doubt he's interviewed anyone yet. Have you seen him? He don't look like he knows where he is."

Ellie looked up through the concession window. Jack McBride leaned against the fence circling the field, listening to Miner but looking in the direction of the concession stand. Surely he couldn't hear their conversation.

"Rachel Lowe told me it was a bad one. He left the hospital this morning against Young Poole's orders."

"He don't look like the type who would take orders from anyone."

"Don't let Jane Maxwell hear you say that."

Everyone laughed. Ellie kept her head down and stocked the drink cooler. It was the first sensible thing they'd said.

"Rachel Lowe doesn't need to be telling anyone anything."

"My point was why ain't he interviewing local men? There's plenty that want the job. Lord knows there's just as many that need it."

"Maybe he will. My guess is none are qualified."

"Are you kidding me? Plenty of men in this town are good with a gun. My cousin, Curtis, is the best marksman in the county."

"He was also thrown in jail for growing weed."

"That was a long time ago. He's reformed. Plus, that experience would only make him a better officer. He has insight into the criminal mind."

"Well, I think it's awfully early to be telling the chief how to do his job. Give him a chance to get adjusted, make a difference."

"Clear the cobwebs out from getting the tar beat out of him."

"We all need to wait a while to pass judgment. Then you can tell him how to do his job if it ain't up to your standards."

A new voice entered the discussion. "If you ask me, a little outside blood is just what this town needs." Everyone stopped and stared at the woman standing in the doorway of the concession stand.

Stillwater Snipes Football Booster President Kelly Dudley Jackson Kendrick had a way of stopping conversation, either by lobbing verbal bombs into the middle of innocuous discussions or just by entering a room. That was to be expected by the only Stillwater girl to place in the Miss Texas pageant, an achievement she continued to get mileage off of twenty-five years after the fact.

"Just in time, Miss America—all the work's done," Ellie said.

"I know, and I'm sorry, y'all," Kelly said, voice full of contrition. "My client in Yourkeville is from Maine, of all places, and doesn't understand about Friday nights. It took her three hours to decide between two shades of gray."

"You just said we need outside blood and you're making fun of a woman from Maine?"

"I didn't mean Yankee blood. McBride's mother was Lieutenant Governor, for heaven's sake."

"Are y'all talkin' about the new chief?" Michelle Ryan, a woman Ellie had known her entire life and disliked for almost as long, stood at the window of the concession stand. Ellie rolled her eyes and focused on stocking Dr Peppers in the drinks cooler. Michelle was like a heat-seeking missile; locking in on wherever Ellie and Kelly were and making a point to rub salt into old wounds with either a veiled barb about past events or by merely existing in the same space. Michelle angled herself so she could talk to them while staring at Jack McBride.

Kelly's smile was sweet and sarcastic. "Have you met him?"

"Not yet."

"That's right. You only go in for married men."

Michelle glanced at Ellie, and raised her eyebrow with a smirk. *And there it is.* Activity in the concession stand increased, as if none of the gossipy women were in the least bit interested in the newest installment of a long-standing feud.

Ellie could feel the grapevine reaching out and entwining itself around her. "Come on, Kelly, help me bring some Diet Cokes in." Ellie grabbed Kelly's arm, and dragged her out of the small building.

"I can't stand that cow," Kelly said when they were out of earshot.

"I know," Ellie said. "Everybody knows."

"I can't believe you can be in the same room with her."

"Technically, we weren't in the same room."

Kelly crossed her arms, cocked her hip, and tapped her foot.

Ellie stood in front of her petite friend and placed her hands on her shoulders. "It was ten years ago. Time to let it go."

"I don't like people messing with my Ellie Bellie," Kelly said. "And how can you be so easy to forgive? She basically ruined your life."

"I want to move on. It would help if you'd stop alluding to it in every conversation with her."

Kelly's shoulders slumped. "Shit, you're right." She scrunched up her face. "I'm sorry."

"It's fine. Just don't do it again."

"Okay, but if she mentions it or alludes to it, I'm going to kick her ass for you."

Ellie clutched her hands in front of her chest and batted her eyes. "My champion."

"Shut up." She pushed Ellie's shoulder. With a grin, Ellie pushed back.

"Now, help me." Ellie released the tailgate of a truck filled with concession supplies.

"*Is* McBride married?" Kelly asked.

"How would I know?" She shoved a case of drinks in Kelly's arms.

"You met him. Sold your house to him."

"We didn't talk about his personal life."

"Was there a woman's name on the paperwork?"

"No. Take that in and stock the cooler. If Michelle is still around, don't say a word to her." Kelly opened her mouth to speak, but Ellie lifted her finger and pointed it at her friend. "Don't even look at her."

"Fine," Kelly said. She walked off, calling over her shoulder, "You better hurry back in. I can't be held responsible for what I say if she looks at me the wrong way."

"Just need to find the Skittles," Ellie replied.

She climbed into the back of the truck and shifted everything around until she found the right box. Ellie lifted the box of candy and wrinkled her nose against the faint, fruity aroma of tropical Skittles. She liked the original flavor better, but these sold like gangbusters, along with Sour Patch Kids. Her mouth puckered at the thought of the tangy candy. She stacked a box of Snickers on top to block the smell and picked her way back through the supplies to the tailgate. She put the boxes down and was about to jump out of the truck when she spied Jack McBride walking toward her.

"Hi," she said. She tried not to flinch at the sight of the stitches over his eyebrow or the dark purple bruise around his right eye. His gaze was unfocused, as if trying to place her. Ellie placed her hand across her chest. "Ellie. Ellie Martin."

He grinned. "I knew who you were. Do I look that out of it?"

"A little."

"Need some help?" he asked. He held out his hand.

She didn't, but she took his hand anyway. "Thanks." She jumped down. "Good to see you."

"You, too." He stared at her, rather stupidly, and held her hand a little too long. She pulled her hand away and picked up the candy.

"Let me get that," he said.

"That's okay. I've got it."

"You look different," he said.

She motioned vaguely to her jeans and T-shirt and almost dropped the candy. "No uniform."

Jack reached out and took the boxes from her. His eyes lost focus again and then cleared. "Oh, right," he said. He gave a self-deprecating laugh. "Sorry. I guess I am still a little foggy. I meant your hair." He waved his hand near his neck. "You've cut it, right?"

"Yes, she did." Kelly was back, a huge smile on her face. "You must be the new chief of police. I'm Kelly Kendrick."

"Jack McBride," he said, offering his hand. "Nice to meet you." Ellie thought she saw Jack's gaze travel up and down her friend quickly, taking her in.

"No offense, but you look awful, Chief," Kelly said.

"None taken. Ethan can barely look at me."

"Ethan?" Kelly asked.

"My son."

Kelly caught sight of Jack's gun. "I heard you lost that."

"It's my backup."

"Is that a Beretta?"

"Yeah. You know guns?"

"A little. What did you have before?"

He answered but Ellie tuned out their gun talk. Not many men could resist Kelly's charms and good looks. With her recent obsession with guns, she was the walking wet dream of every redneck east of Dallas. And why not? She was one of those women who looked good all the time, no matter what she wore. Worse yet, it was effortless. Ellie, though four inches taller than her best friend, felt the familiar sensation of receding into the background under the glare of Kelly's personality.

"Kelly Kendrick. Where have I heard that name?" Jack addressed Ellie, jolting her out of uncharitable thoughts of her friend.

"It's on the list I gave you. The interior designer."

"Did you really?" Kelly threw her arms around Ellie's neck, pulling her down into a hug. "That's why I love you. Always looking out for me." Still hugging Ellie, she addressed Jack. "We look out for each other."

"I can see that."

He wore an expression that made Ellie assume he was checking off every bullet point in his profile of the two of them. The urge to flee his knowing smirk overwhelmed her.

"I've been wanting to get my hands on that house for years. Ellie never would let me at it."

"Why not?" Jack said.

"I hated that house," Ellie said, more vehemently than she intended. Jack raised his eyebrows, but didn't comment.

"Oh, she took good care of it," Kelly said, quickly. "It just needs updating. You call me when you're ready to get started. Come on, Ellie. Get back to work." She said to Jack, "She holds everything together in there."

"No I don't," Ellie said, but she was happy to use the excuse to leave. She relieved Jack of the boxes he held. "Thanks. Enjoy the game."

Kelly waited for her, arms crossed, foot tapping, just as Ellie knew she would be. Ignoring her was Ellie's role in the drama. She opened the freezer door and stacked chocolate candy bars inside. Kelly moved close enough to her so the rest of the women couldn't hear, which of course made them all curious.

"You're holding out on me," Kelly whispered.

"How?"

"Doesn't he remind you of someone?"

He did, but Ellie hadn't wanted to admit it. Once she did, she would never be able to deny the resemblance, just as she could never look at a map of the United States without thinking Florida looked like a penis. She had Joe Dan Weeks to thank for that one.

Luckily, Kelly knew Ellie well enough to skirt the subject, if only slightly. "He's a little older than his picture in the paper and much better looking. Even with the bruises and stitches." She leaned forward and whispered, "Those make him a little sexy. Gives that conservative, buttoned-up exterior a bit of danger."

"If you say so."

"What do you say?"

"I say the game started. I need to get to work, and you need to go cheer for Seth."

Kelly craned her neck to see the field. Her son, Seth, was the senior quarterback and was being recruited by smaller Texas colleges. His goal was to play at the University of Texas, which, considering his size and armstrength, was a pipe dream. For the past six months, Seth had been working out regularly with Mike Freeman and had vastly improved his strength, agility, and quickness. He might be able to walk on at Texas as a slot receiver, but he wasn't quite ready to give up on his quarterback dream.

"Defense is on the field," Kelly said. "I'll help a bit."

They used the first quarter, which was always slow, to catch up. Kelly described a project she was working on in Yourkeville. Ellie stocked the hotdog condiments, half-listening to Kelly and half-watching Jack McBride. Jack rested his left arm on the top of the fence, his right hand rested on his holster. The long sleeves of his blue dress shirt were rolled halfway up his forearms. The soles of his expensive loafers were caked in mud.

Ellie had known whom Jack McBride looked like from the moment she set eyes on him a year earlier at Valerie Patterson's funeral. The resemblance was so striking, she had excused herself from the receiving line and called the prison to make sure her ex-husband hadn't been paroled or let out for good behavior. She knew better than anyone that if Jinx Martin wanted something bad enough, he could behave well enough to get it.

But, no. Jinx was safely in Huntsville and Jack McBride was nothing like him. Not that it mattered. Despite what Kelly told Michelle Ryan, and Ellie's evasion of the question, she knew Jack McBride was married.

"And then she told me she had fallen in love with me at first sight and we consummated our mutual attraction on her new Pottery Barn couch."

Ellie's head shot up. "What?"

"So you *are* listening," Kelly said.

"Of course I am," Ellie lied. "I'm just distracted by the fifty boxes of books I have to shelve tomorrow with more being delivered on Monday."

"What are you doing here?"

"Helping a friend."

Kelly tilted her head to the side. "Have you been working at the concession stand all these years just to help me?" Kelly turned Ellie toward the exit. "Go. Your business is more important than selling a few hotdogs for unappreciative, pimply football players."

Ellie turned back around. "But what if Michelle comes back? Who will stand between you? Maybe I should warn Miner."

"Miner, bless his heart. I can hear him now, 'Now, ladies, what's goin' on here? What are two purty ladies like you fightin' fur?'"

Ellie laughed. Kelly was an excellent mimic. "If things get dicey with Michelle, I'm sure the Chief will come to your rescue."

Jesus. Why did she say that? She knew. Of course she knew. Apparently, it didn't matter how old you were, or how hard you tried, some childhood insecurities lasted a lifetime.

"You think?" Kelly said, either oblivious to Ellie's anxieties or pointedly ignoring them. Ellie had never known which. "Because he kept looking at you the whole time I was talking."

"No, he didn't."

"How would you know? You were studying your shoes the whole time. They're ugly, by the way."

"All rain boots are ugly."

"Mine aren't." Kelly wiggled her foot. Her paisley-printed cowboy rain boots *were* pretty cute. "You need a pop of color down there."

"That sounds wrong on every level."

"Only because your mind is in the gutter." She leaned close and whispered, "Which means you need to get laid. Bet Jack McBride would oblige."

"If you don't let me go, people are going to start rumors about us."

Kelly released her. "Oh, they already talk. You know that. I mean, why else would two devastatingly attractive women not be married unless they were lesbians? And lesbians *together*? God, think of all the barflies out at The Gristmill who get mileage out of that rumor."

"I'd rather not."

"Come on, it's funny."

Ellie's mouth twitched. "Okay, it's funny."

Kelly shooed her away. "Go on. Get out of here before the rush starts. I'll come by after and tell you about all the mistakes I made, just to make you feel better."

"Perfect."

"Chill a bottle. Love your hair. Throw those hideous boots in the trash. Now go," Kelly said with a playful push.

Ellie walked away, grinning. She would chill two bottles of wine and rope Kelly into helping her shelve some books. She walked behind the bleachers, skirting running children and trying to ignore the teenagers making out in the shadows. The parking lot was empty, save a few late-comers. Ellie was opening her car when someone called her name, startling her.

"I didn't mean to scare you," Jack McBride said as he approached.

Ellie dropped her hand from her chest and forced a smile. "That's okay."

"You leaving?"

"Kelly relieved me of duty. Obviously she forgot I hold it all together."

"She thinks very highly of you."

"She does. Undeservedly so."

"I doubt that. Seems like everyone thinks highly of you."

"Maybe this week they do. It can change like that." She snapped her fingers.

He studied her, a tiny smile tugging the corner of his lips. The PA announcer's voice echoed off the high school. Jack looked over his shoulder at the field and back at Ellie. "Don't you like football?"

"What self-respecting Texan doesn't like Friday night football?"

"You didn't answer the question."

"Do *you* like football?"

He leaned forward and whispered. "I'm more of a basketball fan."

She mimicked him. "So am I."

His small smile turned into a mischievous grin. His hand was in his pocket, jingling his keys. The crowd erupted in a loud cheer. The announcer's voice boomed around them. Jack winced.

"Are you all right?"

"Just a headache."

"Should you be here? All this noise can't be good for you."

"It's why I'm checking the parking lot. To get away from the noise."

"Find anything interesting out here?"

"No, though a little kid waylaid me behind the stands, told me he found a skeleton."

"Really?"

He nodded and shrugged.

"You know it's probably a cow," Ellie said.

"Oh. I should have thought of that. . . . Well, I'll check it out anyway." He stared at her with the same spacey expression from earlier.

"What is it? Are you feeling okay?"

"No. I'll be fine. Mind if I lean against your car?"

"Of course not."

He leaned his back against her rear driver's side door and took a deep breath. His face was pale. "Are you sure you're okay?" She reached out to touch his forehead to check his temperature, but caught herself. She jerked her hand back. "Sorry."

"Why are you apologizing? Do I have a fever?" He leaned his head toward her. Reluctantly, she placed the back of her hand against his forehead, careful to avoid his fresh stitches. He was a little warm.

"You might. Is that common with concussions?"

"I don't know."

"Do you want me to take you home?"

"No, Ethan's here. I drove."

"Right."

They leaned against her car, staring at the football field. Ellie shoved her hands in her pockets to keep herself from touching him. He needed someone to take care of him and she, uncharacteristically, wanted to do it. She had zero experience taking care of others or being taken care of. When she was sick, she took care of herself. People who craved attention when they were sick irritated her—cancer patients and people with terminal illnesses notwithstanding. She wasn't coldhearted, just ignorant of the desire to nurture and be nurtured in return.

Until now.

She felt his eyes on her. What was he thinking? Was he comparing her to Kelly? Was he—

Enough of this. If she traveled too far down this road, she would hate herself for being petty and immature. She'd battled her private insecurities and prejudices enough to know they were easily vanquished with determined focus on things at which she excelled. At the moment, that distraction would be her new business, which she needed to get back to. She was formulating just what to say to get rid of Jack McBride when he spoke.

"Have you ever met someone and felt a connection almost immediately?"

She studied him. The memory of their conversation at the bank rushed forward. The jolt she felt when he shook her hand. His smile.

"Yes." She looked down and dug the toe of her ugly boot into the gravel. "Kelly has that effect on people."

"Kelly?" He paused. "I'm not talking about Kelly." His voice was gentle, as though coaxing a terrified kitten from a ledge.

Ellie cleared her throat. She wasn't ready for this, didn't want it. "I really should go." She turned to open her car door, but he stepped closer to her.

She could smell the faint scent of his aftershave and see the tiny broken blood vessels in his eyes, which lingered on her lips. She edged away from him. His eyes moved to hers, his good eyebrow arched, and the corner of his mouth quirked up.

"Are you scared of me?"

Terrified, but she would never admit it. It was bad enough her insecurities were so plain to him. Her spine stiffened. . . . He sure wasn't acting like a married man, she realized.

"Can I ask you something?" she said.

"Sure."

"Why Stillwater?"

The shift from good humor to wariness was barely perceptible. "Why not?"

"FBI agent to small-town police chief?"

She waited until he had to answer either with the truth or a creative lie.

"My son and I needed a change. Stillwater seemed like a good choice."

She noticed he didn't mention his wife. "Why don't I believe you?"

Jack shrugged. "It's the truth."

"But not the full truth."

He narrowed his eyes and jingled the change in his pocket, as though debating how much he could trust her. She held his gaze and his face softened. What did he read in her?

"The last year has been difficult, personally and professionally. When I heard of this job," he shrugged, "I thought small-town living might be a nice change." He leaned his shoulder against her car. "Despite my shitty first day—" He let his eyes travel over her. It should have been offensive, but his expression was so appreciative and full of something Ellie didn't want to name, she flushed with chagrin. "—I think it was a good decision," he finished.

A car pulled through the parking lot and beeped its horn. Ellie jumped and instinctively waved at the driver.

Jack chuckled. "You do know everyone in town."

She had no idea who she just waved at, but didn't want to admit it. "Almost. I have to go." She got in the car and turned it on.

Jack stepped into the gap of the open door, his hand on the top of the window, and leaned down. The stadium lights behind him cast his face in shadow, but his eyes were bright. For the first time he looked ill at ease, embarrassed, vulnerable, in a way that had nothing to do with his head injury. Her stomach felt like it had jumped on an out-of-control merry-go-round and was holding on for dear life.

He opened his mouth to speak, but she got out her words first. "Take care of yourself, Jack. Good luck with the skeleton."

His disappointment was clear. He straightened, nodded. "Drive carefully, Ellie."

She closed the door, relieved to have a solid barrier between her and a world of trouble.

CHAPTER THREE

Saturday

I

She was close. Too close. He could see the flecks of brown in her eyes, the way her lips parted before curling into a smile. She leaned into him, her breasts brushed his chest and he—

"Get up. We're going to see a skeleton."

His body trembled, but not from excitement—someone was shaking him. Ethan slapped the offending hand away. "What?"

"Your room smells like gym socks."

"Go away, Dad." Ethan pulled the covers over his head. Maybe if he could get back to sleep, the dream could pick up where it left off.

"How can your room smell this bad? We've been here less than a week."

"Go *away*, Dad."

"Get up. It's nine-thirty. We have to be somewhere at ten."

"I don't have to be anywhere at ten."

Jack ripped the covers from Ethan. Cold air hit his body like a pail of ice water. Ethan pulled his knees to his chest, hoping to cover up his boner. Not that his father would (a) notice, (b) care, or (c) say anything if he did notice or care. There were moments he hated his dad beyond all reason, and this was one of them.

"You can be a real asshole, Dad."

"I thought my mom was an asshole when I was thirteen, too. You'll get over it."

Ethan looked at him. Couldn't he do *anything* to piss his dad off?

"Plus," Jack continued, "I could be a whole lot worse if I wanted. Now, get up. We're going to see a skeleton."

Ethan rubbed his eyes. "A skeleton?"

Jack walked to the door. "I made breakfast. Hurry up." He left.

"I don't think the skeleton will care if we're late."

Ethan dropped his hand to the bed and sighed. The dream wasn't coming back, that was for sure. Did he even want it to? How would he be able to look at Olivia the next time he saw her with that dream in his mind? Maybe it would fade away like most of his dreams did. He rubbed his chest where he had felt her breasts. That had been awfully realistic. And hard to forget.

He picked up the clothes on the floor nearest the bed, dressed, and walked down the stairs. His pace quickened as the smell of bacon hit him.

Ethan stopped at the doorway of the kitchen. His dad was at the stove scrambling eggs in a skillet. Tortillas, cheese, bacon, and tater tots were on the table along with two plates. More shocking than his dad cooking breakfast, which used to be a Saturday morning staple, was the lack of boxes in the kitchen. When Ethan and his dad had returned from the football game the night before, there had been a small path from the back door through the kitchen and every inch of the counter surface had been covered in boxes. Now it was spotless.

"How long have you been up?" Ethan asked. He sat down at the table.

Jack turned the gas off on the stove, grabbed a trivet from a drawer, and brought the skillet full of eggs to the table. "A while."

The bruise on his dad's face looked even worse today.

"How do you feel?"

"Better."

"I looked up concussions online. Insomnia is a side effect."

"You looked it up?" His dad seemed really happy he'd taken the time.

"Yeah." Ethan wasn't really hungry; he rarely was when he first got up. But his dad went to the trouble to make breakfast and he had saved Ethan from unpacking the kitchen. He piled everything on a tortilla, folded it in half, and took a bite. Okay, maybe he was hungry. "We're going to see a skeleton?" A bit of egg fell out of his mouth. He expected his dad to mention it but he didn't.

"A kid came up to me last night and said he found a skeleton. Thought we'd check it out. Most likely it's animal bones."

"Most likely it's a waste of time." He shoved the rest of his burrito in his mouth and made another.

Jack shrugged. "Maybe. But, if it's a cow skull, we'll take it and hang it on the wall."

"Gross. . . . Do you feel good enough to go out?" Ethan asked. "You probably should rest today."

"I'm fine," Jack said.

They ate in silence, his dad staring off into space. Ethan shifted in his chair and spoke the question he'd been working up the courage to ask since his dad got home from the hospital. "Have you talked to Mom?"

His dad stopped chewing. "No. Have you?"

Ethan's shoulders dropped. "You told me not to call her. I've emailed her a couple of times."

Jack nodded. "So have I."

"She knows where we are?"

"Yes, Ethan. She knows where we are."

"Does she know what happened to you?"

"Yes."

"When is she coming home?"

Jack sighed. "I wish I knew." He stood and dumped three quarters of his taco in the trash.

Ethan felt a glimmer of hope. It was the longest conversation they had about his mother in months. His dad wanted his mother to come home. Happiness welled within him, giving him the confidence to ask the next question.

"Who was the lady you were talking to last night?"

"What lady?"

"In the parking lot."

"Oh, she sold us the house."

"She's a realtor?"

"No, it was her house. She owns the bookstore downtown. We need to get going. Help me clean up."

Within five minutes, the kitchen was clean and they were on the road. Within ten, they parked in front of a run-down, white wooden house just across the river and outside the city limits. The metal mailbox was dented and without a flag or door. Two canvas lawn chairs, one green and one blue, both faded, sat on the porch. Empty beer bottles sat forgotten in the cup holders. Cigarette butts were strewn around the chairs like confetti. Through the open screen door, Ethan heard SpongeBob and Patrick try to explain imagination to Squidward. Ethan stood at the bottom of the concrete steps, his hands shoved deep in the pockets of his cargo shorts, while his dad knocked on the door. He wanted to take out his phone and snap pictures of this house, but he didn't want the people who lived there to catch him.

The woman who came to the door was younger than Ethan expected. She had black circles under her eyes, her hair was a tangled mess, and her soft rolls of fat strained against her too-small clothes. She didn't seem to recognize Jack until her gaze traveled to the badge that hung on a chain around his neck.

The fog slowly cleared from her eyes. "You came." She turned her head slightly to the side, trying not to look over her shoulder. "I didn't think you would."

"Obviously," Ethan said under his breath.

"I didn't get your name last night," Jack said.

"Edie. Edie Wood."

A young boy pushed through the space between Edie and the door. "Want me to show you the skeleton?"

Jack nodded. "I sure do."

"Come on." He bounded down the stairs and stopped at the sight of Ethan. "Who are you?"

"Ethan."

"I'm Billy. Come on."

The boy took off around the house. Ethan looked at his father, who shrugged. They followed.

"Do I need to come?" Edie Wood asked.

"I don't think it's necessary," Jack said.

Visibly relieved, she went inside.

Billy crawled through the barbed wire fence behind the house and waited patiently for Jack and Ethan. As soon as Jack was through, Billy took off. The three followed a cow path through the pasture. Billy turned left at the tree line and walked on. Ethan pulled out his phone and took pictures.

"Is this your land?" Jack said.

"No," Billy replied.

"You're allowed to play back here?" Ethan asked. He snapped a picture of the boy leading them down the cow path, the sky and land enormous, dwarfing him. *Cool*.

"As long as I don't bother the cows."

"What cows?"

Billy pointed downriver. A herd of cows stood on the bank, chewing their cud and watching them. A large gray bull with a hump on his back and long ears snorted and walked in their direction. "Watch out for that one. He'll charge you." Billy ducked into a small opening in the brush on the bank of the river, leaving Ethan and Jack staring at the bull, which had become too interested in them.

Ethan snapped a picture just before Jack pushed him into the gap. Billy was waiting on the bank of the swollen river by a downed tree. "Cross here." He hopped up on the tree and walked his way across.

The other side of the river was densely wooded. Underbrush, briars, and felled trees made progress difficult. Billy kept pushing through, winding in and around the undergrowth, finding small trails Ethan would have never noticed and flipping tree branches and briars back into Ethan's face on a regular basis. Ethan's legs were going to be a map of scratches and punctures. His dad had been smart enough to wear jeans and hiking boots. Ethan thought traipsing through the woods was kinda fun—he was getting some good pictures and it would be a good story to tell Troy—but knew his dad was getting angrier and angrier by the minute. Jack was not the outdoorsy type. The boots were more for show than actual hiking.

Finally, they burst through the underbrush to an open area. A large tree, much like the one that spanned the river, had fallen and had taken much of the surrounding vegetation with it. The trunk was at least five feet tall and the root system sticking out of the ground at the far end of the clearing was easily twice as high. Billy stood by the roots of the tree, reminding Ethan of the picture of a man dwarfed by a redwood tree he had seen in one of his textbooks. He snapped a picture.

Billy pointed. "I told you so."

Ethan and Jack walked down the length of the tree trunk. Ethan ran his free hand along the long burnt gash on the side of the tree as his dad outpaced him to the end. When Jack reached the proud boy, his jaw, which had been set in a hard, angry line, slackened into an astonished gape. Ethan walked around the two of them and stopped. Partially buried in the loamy soil, the vacant eye of a human skull stared up at them.

II

Ethan stared at the water stain on his ceiling. He didn't think it was possible to be more bored than he was. Stillwater sucked. There was nothing to do and no one to do it with. His dad would be at the skeleton crime scene all day today and probably tomorrow. Troy wasn't answering his texts, and he wasn't about to text Olivia. The dream from the morning was too fresh.

He thought of texting Mitra, the only other friend he'd made since Thursday, but she was a girl and a Muslim. Her father probably kept a close eye on her texts. Was that being racist? Maybe Mitra's family wasn't religious or strict. How devout could they be living among all these rednecks? She was, as far as Ethan could tell, the only Muslim in the whole school. That had to suck. So, he texted her. They could be outsiders together.

Bored 2 death. Wuts thar 2 do in this town?

He tossed his phone on the bed and went to his computer. No reply from his mom. Why did he even expect one?

His phone beeped.

Nothing. That's why I'm in Tyler with my mom. Need anything from Dillards? Makeup? Perfume?

Ethan smiled. Mitra was the only person he knew who used almost perfect grammar in texts. It was dorky. And . . . cute.

Perfume samples wud be nice.

Okay. :) Where is your dad?

Crime scene. Thinking of taking pics of town. Where shld I go?

Downtown, German church, the Bottom.

The bottom?

It's the poor part of town.

Would I get mugged?

Doubt it.

Pass. wuts the german church?

Down the street from you. Overgrown road on the left. On a bluff. Great view. Gotta go. Be careful, E.

Sure, Mom.

She sent an emoji with the tongue sticking out. She was much chattier while texting than in person. Whenever he talked to her, she always seemed on the verge of blushing. Ethan knew it had nothing to do with him and everything to do with Troy. Of course, Troy was too clueless to see Mitra liked him. Ethan wasn't about to clue him in.

Ethan replaced his camera battery with the fully charged spare, got his longboard, and headed downtown, figuring he would end at the German church. If he had his directions right, he would get a sunset picture from up there. He texted his dad about what he was doing and received a return text thanking him for the update and the same warning to be careful.

At the end of River Road, he turned left. There was no sidewalk, so he picked his board up and walked on the beaten path next to the road. He crossed the rusty iron bridge that spanned the river and took the first street on the left.

An alley ran next to the river behind what looked like a warehouse. Ethan took several pictures, adjusted his settings until he got the exposure he wanted, and started shooting. Even though downtown was empty and depressing, Stillwater made a great subject. He skated around the dead-end square, taking as many pictures of empty lots as buildings. What had his dad been thinking, taking this job? He took a few shots of City Hall and wondered where his dad's office was.

At the end of the main street, on the edge of the square, were the only two buildings that could be called cool. One was all white columns and marble. Ethan would have known it was a bank even without STILLWATER NATIONAL BANK chiseled over the door. Less cool than impressive. Ethan took pictures of it because he felt the building expected him to.

The building across the street was the really cool one. It was a two-story red stone building with tall windows along the front and sides. The front door was set in the corner facing the square. Tiny white octagonal tiles were set before the door, with ROBICHAUX written in bright blue tiles in the middle. A small balcony with a shiny wrought-iron railing ran along the second floor. Sheer curtains fluttered from the open French doors on the upper tier, whipping around two bright orange iron chairs and a small table. Planter boxes overflowing with flowers and vines hung from the railing. It was serene; the most welcoming subject he'd found so far. Ethan lifted his camera and started shooting.

He was surprised when a woman wandered out, sipping something out of a mug and reading a book. She sat without taking her eyes off her book, placing her cup on the table and kicking her feet on the railing in front of her. Ethan took ten or twenty shots before he realized who she was.

He looked up from his viewfinder. It was the woman his dad talked to at the game. Twice. Ethan hadn't told his dad that he saw him both times. His dad acted like she was barely an acquaintance. And how could she be anything else? This was their fourth day in town.

Ethan's eye went back to the viewfinder and zoomed in. She was reading *The Lord of the Rings*. Dork. She wasn't very far into it. Ethan wondered how she could read it at all. He moved his camera to her face. She wore black-rimmed reading glasses, like a hipster. God, adults looked so stupid when they tried to act young. Ethan guessed she was pretty, for a mom. She couldn't hold a candle to his mom, though.

The woman wrinkled her nose, closed the book, and tossed it on the table. Maybe she wasn't a dork. She picked up her coffee, took her glasses off, and placed them on the book. She stared off into space and sipped her drink. One side of her mouth curled into a wicked smile. Suddenly, Ethan liked her. He snapped a few pictures.

He almost dropped his camera when she turned her head and looked right at him. She looked as alarmed as he felt. She squinted at him, then her face cleared into relief and . . . nervousness? She stood, leaned on the railing, and waved. He turned to see if she was waving at someone else. When he realized she wasn't, he almost bolted. He was caught, though. Better face the music and apologize. Dad would be pissed Ethan was taking pictures of people without asking. He said it was like eavesdropping or being a peeping tom. But some of Ethan's best shots were of people when they didn't know he was shooting. When people posed, he didn't feel like he saw the real person.

"Hi," she called.

"Hi."

Ethan looked around, searching for a means of escape. Nothing.

"You must be Ethan."

"Yes, ma'am." Strangers knowing who he was would never *not* be weird. He crossed the street and stood almost directly under her balcony.

"You look like your dad."

Ethan shrugged. People always said that and he never knew how to respond. Thanks? Yuck? Dude, he's like, old?

"I'm Ellie Martin."

"Nice to meet you, Mrs. Martin."

"Call me Ellie. I'm nobody's mom." She nodded to his camera. "Taking pictures?"

"Yeah. Do you mind?"

"No. As long as you delete the ugly ones. You didn't catch me picking my nose, did you?"

"No."

"Have you ever caught someone doing that?"

"Not yet."

There was a long, awkward silence. Ethan didn't know what to say to his dad most of the time—how could he be expected to talk to a stranger, and a woman?

"You caught me taking a break. I better get back." She pointed over her shoulder with her thumb. "Be careful."

"Okay." Did everyone think he was some kind of daredevil?

"Happy shooting."

She grimaced when she said it, but thankfully didn't apologize for it. Instead, she bolted inside, stumbling over one of the chairs.

Adults are so weird, Ethan thought as he waited for the light to turn at the corner of Main and Broadway. The salty, greasy aroma of french fries and hamburgers coming from the Dairy Queen across the street made Ethan's stomach growl. He had only three dollars in his string bag, maybe enough for some fries, but a drink would be stretching it. He crossed the street and went into the gas station on the other corner instead. A fat man in overalls stood behind the counter. A couple of old men sat in the booths in the front window. Ethan stared at the ground and walked to the candy aisle. He put his longboard down, fished his money out of his string bag, and put his camera inside. He would need both hands to hold his drink and eat his candy bar. He brought a cookies and cream Hershey bar and the biggest fountain drink he could afford to the counter. The clerk eyed him suspiciously. Ethan gave him a brief smile and kept his eyes on his purchases.

"Three oh six."

Ethan put the three dollars on the counter.

"Got six cents?" the clerk asked.

"No, sir."

Surely the guy would spot him six cents. The 7-Eleven in Emerson used to do it all the time for him and his friends. They always put money in the community thing when they could because they always ended up needing it.

Without a word, the man scraped six cents out of a small bowl next to the register and dropped it into the cash drawer.

"Thank you," Ethan mumbled.

He put the candy bar in his pocket and left with the drink and long-board in his hands. He sat at the far end of the gas station, ate his candy bar in three bites, drank half of his Dr Pepper, and pulled his camera back out. Within minutes, he was back on the streets, taking pictures.

He saw the entire town in less than an hour, including the Bottom. It was by far the most interesting area, more run-down than the rest of town for sure, but that's why it was interesting. He never felt unsafe, either, though he did generate some interest from the residents. Ethan wondered why the roads in that area were so full of potholes, some of them almost dirt tracks, when in the other areas the roads were smooth and well cared for. But, besides the Bottom, the rest of the town was kind of boring. The yards were all brown from the hot summer. Flowers had long since died. Leaves on the trees were a dark, exhausted green. The streets were mostly deserted, though he got a sick shot of a car up on blocks. Ethan was riding down a narrow street near the high school when a cop car pulled up behind him and beeped its siren. Ethan moved over into a yard and waited for the car to go by. He was surprised when it stopped next to him.

A large cop got out of the car. He looked up and down the street and adjusted his holster before swaggering over to Ethan. Ethan's palms started to sweat, though he knew he hadn't done anything wrong.

"Son, what's your name?"

"Ethan."

"What you are doing?"

"Riding my longboard."

"Where."

"On the street."

"You need to keep it to the sidewalks."

Ethan looked up and down the streets. "Where are they?"

"Where are what?"

"The sidewalks? I haven't seen one."

"Are you being smart?"

"No, sir. I believe technically I'm being ignorant. I really don't know where the sidewalks are."

The cop scowled. Ethan smiled then laughed. This was a prank—this dude had to know who he was. Probably his dad sent him to scare Ethan. Anyway, like Ellie said, he looked just like his dad. Could this guy really not see it?

"What's so funny?"

"You're pranking me, aren't you?"

"No. We've had complaints from residents about a strange boy taking pictures all over town. Others have called in about a skateboarder. Say you've been prowling. Making trouble."

Ethan felt his face burn. He wasn't strange and he hadn't done anything wrong or hurt anybody. He had been minding his own business and didn't deserve this cop harassing him or strangers telling stories about him. "I'm not making trouble; I'm just taking pictures of vacant lots and junky cars. I didn't know I needed permission. Who would I contact for that? The mayor of Shitwater?"

"Son, you better watch your mouth."

"I'm not your son. My name is Ethan *McBride*." Ethan put his board on the ground and skated off.

"Where do you think you're going?"

"Away from you."

The cop grabbed his arm and jerked him off the board. Ethan dropped his drink. Ice exploded all over the pavement and started melting immediately. Ethan looked around, hoping there was someone near to help him. The street, like all the others, was deserted. Anyway, he assumed no one would help the strange skateboarder. The man's eyes were a cold blue. His name badge said FREEMAN. Ethan wasn't about to give this oaf the satisfaction of knowing his arm was going numb.

"Where did you get that drink?"

"The gas station."

"Where's the candy bar?"

"I ate . . . how did you know I got a candy bar?"

"Abe called, said you stole it. Where is it?"

"I didn't steal it."

"That's what he says."

"He's lying."

"Why would he do that?"

"How would I know?"

Freeman released his arm. "I'll let you go this time, but if I hear you stealing again—"

"I didn't steal that candy bar. I paid for it."

"With your history, who's going to believe you?"

Ethan froze. How would this guy know his history? Did his dad tell him? No way. No freaking way his dad would tell this guy. If not his dad, though, who? Principal Courcey? The shoplifting incident was in his school file since it happened on a field trip. On the "permanent record" parents always threatened kids with. Maybe the principal was spreading it around town. Ethan knew he had been right to hate that woman.

"Now, pick your skateboard up and walk home. I won't tell your dad about this, but if I hear about you causing trouble again, I won't be as nice."

The edges of Ethan's vision were turning red. He struggled to hold his tongue. Through gritted teeth, he managed to say, "Yes, sir."

Ethan walked away as quickly as possible without running.

Ten minutes later, he was back on River Road. He made sure there wasn't a cop around, put his longboard on the ground, and skated the short distance home. The walk calmed him. He couldn't decide whether he should tell his dad and, if so, what he should say. His dad probably wouldn't believe him. That necklace was going to follow Ethan the rest of his life.

Ethan got a Dr Pepper from the fridge and went to the front porch. He sat on the swing and scanned through the pictures he'd taken that day. Mrs. Martin—Ellie—was kind of pretty, in an average, sporty sort of way. She had nice eyes. Friendly. He wondered about the big secret that had made her smile. Ethan raced through the shots, making it look like a movie. He'd had his camera set to continuous and didn't realize he had taken so many. He laughed at her grimace. Apparently, she didn't like *The Lord of the Rings*. If he had to choose which one captured her real self, he would say the photo of the wicked smile, for sure.

A police cruiser drove down the street. Ethan thought it might be his dad, but the car drove on by. Freeman was at the wheel.

"Jackwagon," Ethan muttered.

The car turned left a little ways down the road. Ethan assumed it was turning around since River Road was a dead end. What was it with Stillwater and dead end roads? Summed up the whole town as far as Ethan was concerned. Instead, the car disappeared.

Five minutes went by and Freeman didn't return. A red Jeep rolled down the street and turned at the same spot. Ethan draped his camera over his shoulder, descended the porch stairs, and followed.

Ethan stayed close to the trees and listened intently as he climbed the steep grass track, which barely passed for a road. He wanted to be able to jump into the trees in case Freeman drove back down. When Ethan saw the steeple, he knew this was the German church Mitra had mentioned. He cut into the trees and crept closer. Freeman's cruiser and the Jeep were parked next to each other in front of the church. Ethan made sure his camera's time stamp was on and started taking pictures; he wanted to get proof of that asshole goofing off on the job.

Neither Freeman nor the other guy were in their cars. Maybe they were in the church. Ethan didn't want to risk leaving his hiding spot to find out. He sat down behind a tree, started the timer on his phone, and waited. Fifteen minutes later, Freeman and the guy came back to their cars, got in each, and drove off. Ethan turned off his timer, waited for the sound of their cars to fade away, and walked to the church.

Might as well get some shots while I'm here.

He'd worry about Freeman later.

CHAPTER FOUR

Sunday

I

Sunday morning dawned hot and clear. In the deepest part of the woods, the bright, unrelenting sun burned through the gaping hole in the canopy of mature oaks, cottonwoods, mimosas, and pines and onto the working men and women. Squirrels, birds, and raccoons silently watched the activity from the hollows and branches of the nearby trees.

A thin, weather-beaten man in khaki dungarees and a sweat-stained straw fedora stood on the inside of the crime-scene tape. He held the skull gently, reverently, and moved his hands over the yellowed surface. Jack stood outside of the tape. He held a stainless-steel coffee traveler in his right hand and watched the amateur archaeologists work.

"Sorry, Jack. This isn't an ancient Indian or settler."

Jack let out a quick sigh.

"That's the bad news. The good news is it isn't recent either. That should be less trouble for you."

"How old, Hugh?"

Hugh Barnes shrugged. "Won't know that until I get it all back to my lab. No upper dental work, so they had good teeth. Guess we'll see about lower if we find the jawbone. Any idea how long it's been exposed?"

"Not long. The boy who found the skull plays around here pretty regularly. Said the tree was standing a couple weeks ago."

Hugh Barnes looked at the trees soaring around them and shrugged. "I guess he would know. If the rest of it is down there, we'll find it."

Hugh returned to his crew, staring at the skull as he did. Jack drank his coffee and watched. Being chief of police in Stillwater sure as hell wasn't going to be dull.

His mind traveled, as it had been doing since Friday night, to the image of Ellie in a well-fitting pair of jeans and a simple white T-shirt. As nice as her figure was—and he'd spent an inordinate amount of time thinking about her slightly freckled cleavage at the tip of her V-neck; he had been celibate for months, after all—it was the memory of the curve of her jaw and the way her eyes crinkled when she smiled that had been distracting him the most.

When he saw her by the concession stand, Jack had struggled to pinpoint the niggling idea in the back of his mind that he'd seen Ellie before, and not at the funeral or bank. Some other time and place. When he saw her in profile in the parking lot, his eyes lingering on the curve of her jaw, the memory of the dream hit him full force. He'd come so close to blurting it out. Luckily, he had enough hold on his foggy brain to stop himself. He didn't want to imagine the horrified expression on her face when he said a dream about her had been a happy ending to a variety of concussion-induced nightmares, one that included blowing his wife's brains out.

Jack shook his head to banish thoughts of Julie. He knew exactly how to handle his wife. Ellie Martin, on the other hand, was more complicated.

Unpacking the kitchen in the predawn hours of Saturday, Jack decided he would call Ellie that day. He had debated what to say. Surely, she knew he was interested—he all but told her standing next to her car. That had probably been a mistake. It was the concussion talking, but he didn't regret it. Though, he would if it scared her off, which he was afraid it had.

Christ, he couldn't stop thinking about her, about getting her alone and talking for hours, uninterrupted, of making her laugh. Of course, he wanted her, too, but it was nothing like the months after Julie left when he'd been driven by a physical need born of fury rather than affection. Then, he found a good-looking, willing woman—and they were all willing (and ridiculously young)—and within ten minutes, fifteen at the most, he would be fucking her. Speed was a necessity; he was on his lunch hour, after all. It was physical, raw, satiating, unemotional, and empty. That didn't stop him from doing it over and over until most of the anger at his wife had been cleansed from his system and replaced with emotional numbness and a deep mortification.

His attraction to Ellie was different—he liked her. He liked the sound of her voice, the way she smiled with one corner of her mouth, the arch of her eyebrows, the way her hair brushed against her jaw, though, man, he wished she hadn't cut it. She was intelligent, intuitive, independent, and cautious. Her attitude toward him vacillated from unguarded openness to circumspection to—he hated to admit—suspicion. She didn't trust him, but she wanted to—he could see the struggle as plainly as the chicken pox scar underneath her left eyebrow. Was she wary of him specifically or of men in general?

"Chief."

Jack turned, thankful for the interruption.

Miner walked down the trail to the crime scene it had taken all day Saturday to make. After his eyes lingered on the bruise around Jack's eye, Miner jerked his head toward the dig. "Anything?"

Jack shook his head. "Hugh said it's not too old. Won't know until he gets it back to his lab."

"How do you know this guy again?"

"He's a doctor of archaeology at UTD. He's worked with the state and Feds all over Texas."

Miner nodded. They watched the dig in silence.

"Don't suppose you can think of any missing persons reports from around here in the last fifty years off the top of your head," Jack said.

"Nope. Not adults, anyway."

Jack shrugged. "Worth a shot."

"How long'll it take?"

"No idea. Let's just hope they find the body to go with the head."

Miner grimaced.

Down the trail, a woman stood just in sight, arms crossed over her chest like it was forty degrees instead of ninety. "What do you know about Barbara Dodsworth?"

"Well, about that. I've been meanin' to tell you. I live next door."

"What?"

"Grew up on a place a bit down the road. Two hundred acres. White house a little off the road. When my dad went into the nursing home after my mom died, he gave me the place."

"Gave it to you?"

"Yeah. I would have gotten it when he dies anyway. Got some horses. You ride?"

"Horses? No."

"It's relaxin'. Anyway, I've known the Dodsworths my whole life."

"Were your families friends?"

"Not particularly. You know, neighborly, but not friendly."

Jack supposed it was a country distinction. It was lost on him.

"Graduated with Barbara back in '78."

"Tell me about her."

"Never married. George Dodsworth owned the local Ford dealership for years. Elizabeth was a homemaker. Barbara put her in the same home as my dad a few years ago. She's gone senile. The mom, not Barbara. Barbara cleans houses for a living. Has a small crew and everything."

"Record?"

"Did time over in Gatesville for check fraud back in the '90s. No trouble since. Cleans a good house. She's been cleaning our house every Wednesday for years."

"What are the chances George and Elizabeth Dodsworth killed someone and buried the body on their land?"

Miner's expression said he wasn't buying it. "Not good."

"Well, it's a theory." Jack motioned for Barbara Dodsworth to join them. "Miss Dodsworth," he said. He extended his hand. Barbara's hand was dark, bony, and calloused, the hand of a hard worker. She smelled of peppermint and smoke. "Have any idea who this might be?"

"How the hell would I know?"

"Miner tells me you've lived here all your life."

"Yeah."

"This land been in your family the whole time?"

"Yeah."

"Ever been used?"

Barbara paused. "Whaddya you mean?"

"The land. Has it always been this overgrown?"

"We used to play here when we were kids," Miner interjected.

"Don't suppose y'all saw a fresh grave when you did?" Miner's glare was answer enough. "Worth a shot," Jack said. "Did your dad have livestock?"

"No."

"Did he rent the land out to other people?"

"Not that I know of."

"For hunting or anything?"

She shook her head.

Jack turned to Miner. "Ever hunt over here?"

"Sure. A little."

"Like, starting when?"

Miner raised his eyes to the sky, thinking. "I was ten or so. Sixty-nine. Seventy? Never saw a grave."

"I'm not familiar with country ways, but why would someone own land and let it lie unused for so many years?"

"My father died back in the early '80s," Barbara said. "My mom probably didn't know what to do with it but didn't want to sell it either."

"Why haven't you sold it?"

"Because I don't own it." She paused. "It's still in my mom's name."

"She's in the nursing home, I hear."

"Yeah, and before you ask, there's no point in trying to talk to her. She hasn't spoken a coherent sentence in four years." Barbara glanced at Miner, who was fidgeting beside Jack. Jack caught his eye and Miner raised his head and looked around at the trees instead.

"I'm sorry to hear that," Jack said to Barbara. "It must be difficult to watch your parent slip away like that."

"It ain't easy. I'm just glad I can provide for her." She started to turn away. "Speaking of, I have to get to work."

"On a Sunday?"

"I take work whenever I can get it."

"Is there another way to access this land?"

"No."

"Has there ever been?"

"Not as far as I know. We're bordered on three sides by other people's land. Could have gotten in through there just as easy."

Jack nodded. "I suppose you're right." He glanced at Miner, who was studying the ground, brows furrowed. "One more question—ever come back here, Miss Dodsworth?"

"Why would I?"

Jack looked around. "It's peaceful."

Barbara sneered. "I'm too busy making a living for a peaceful walk in the woods."

"Of course. Well." Jack stuck his hand out again. "Thanks for your time. We will let you know if we need any more information. Miner," Jack said, beckoning. He walked a little away and Miner followed. Barbara stood for a moment, curiosity mixed with fear crossing her face, before walking off toward her house.

"So," Jack said. "What was with the squirming?"

"What do you mean?"

"Miner, I'm not in the mood for bullshit."

He sighed. "It's nothing to do with this."

"Why don't you let me decide that?"

"A few years ago, my dad and Barbara's mom got caught together."

"Caught together?"

"In the nursing home. In his room. You know." Miner blushed so hotly his ears turned red.

"Oh." Jack dipped his head and started laughing. He couldn't stop. He threw his head back and let loose long, lung-cleansing laughter. God, it felt good. It didn't make his head hurt either, which must mean he was getting better. He was wiping the tears from his cheeks when he realized Miner hadn't joined them.

"Come on, Miner. That's hilarious."

"It ain't when it's your dad."

"Okay. I suppose if I heard of my mom doing that I might be horrified, too. Still." He patted Miner on the shoulder. "Sorry I laughed. Back to Barbara. She's hiding something."

"She's an ex-con who has a skeleton on her land," Miner said. "I wouldn't expect her to be exactly forthcoming."

"Hmm. Maybe," Jack said. "Why would someone have land and not do anything with it?"

"Well, if you own it outright, it might be cheaper to let it lie and just pay taxes on it. Not many people make much money from running cows. If you've got another income, what's the point?"

"So it isn't unusual?"

"Not really. I just have horses on mine."

"Well, we can't do much until we know more. You good to stay here and supervise?"

"There is one thing," Miner said. Jack waited. "Back in the '80s sometime, lots of land around here got logged. They cut my dad's land and part of the agreement was I got a job lumberjacking with the company. Worst job I ever had. Almost every landowner who had a tree to sell did so. Except Elizabeth Dodsworth. It was right after her husband died and she could have used the money, all right. They tried everything they could to get the lumber from her. Never did. In the end, everyone just wrote it off as Elizabeth being eccentric. She was always a little off, even before she lost her mind."

"You know what, Miner?"

"Hmm?"

"That's the most I've ever heard you say at one time."

Miner looked caught out. "Just telling a story."

"You've got a pretty good memory, don't you?"

He paused. "Better than most."

"Thought so. Did you ever find the day laborer, Raul?"

"I did. Friday. He didn't have a lot to offer."

"Not surprising."

"Except Gilberto hadn't been around the Chevron for a few weeks. Raul suspected he got a long-term job somewhere."

"He didn't know where?"

"No. I came at it a few different ways. His story never changed."

"Believe him?"

Miner shrugged. "I believe Gilberto wasn't around, but I don't believe Raul knows nothing about Diego Vasquez."

Jack's phone buzzed in his pocket. Expecting it to be Ethan, he was surprised to see an unknown local number on the display. He answered.

"Jack McBride."

"Chief? This is Susan. Susan Grant."

"Hi, Susan. Everything okay?"

"Oh, sure. I mean, I don't know."

"What's wrong?"

"Well, I was just talking to Troy and he kinda let something slip. About Ethan."

Jack turned and walked away from Miner. "What about him?"

"He shared a picture I'm not sure he should have."

Jack had encouraged Ethan's interest in photography, hoping a hobby would distract his son from his absent mother. He even thought of counseling Ethan about what to shoot and what not to shoot but had decided his son was smart enough, and shy enough, that he would never take an inappropriate picture. Apparently, he gave Ethan too much credit. Jack closed his eyes, imagining a picture of his son's penis shooting across the Internet, artfully cropped and filtered with one of twenty options, of course.

"Of what?"

"The crime scene."

Confusion mixed with relief. "But he never went inside the Ramoses' house."

"No, not that!" Susan said, shocked. "Lord, could you imagine? No, the skull."

Jack ground his teeth. "Thanks for letting me know, Susan." He hung up before she could elaborate.

"Everything all right?" Miner drawled.

"I need to go. Hugh and his guys are going to stay here all night."

"They're gonna work through?"

"No. They'll guard the site, though. Hugh gets very protective of his bones. I'm going to have Starling check on them periodically, as well. Do you mind staying for a bit, in case Hugh needs anything?"

"Nah."

"Thanks. I'll call you later." Jack clapped Miner on the shoulder and left.

II

"Ethan!"

Jack walked in the back door and threw his keys on the kitchen table.

"In the office!"

Jack walked to the front of the house. The office was a small room to the left of the front door. When the house was built, more than one hundred years ago, it had probably been called the study or library. Dark wood paneling and bookshelves lined the walls. Jack liked the wood and the shelves but hated the dark color. It made the small room feel closed in.

"What are you doing?"

"Going through the pictures I took yesterday. What's up? I thought you were going to be gone all day."

"Let me see your phone."

Ethan handed his phone over, a wary expression on his face. Then, his expression hardened. "What did Freeman tell you?"

Jack opened the photo app on the phone and looked up. "Who?"

"GI Joe. The cop with bigger biceps than brains?"

"I haven't talked to Freeman."

"Oh." Ethan turned to the computer.

Jack forgot about the skull. "Why, what happened?"

Ethan shrugged one shoulder but didn't turn around. He was clicking through pictures of an old house, a car on blocks . . .

"He stopped me yesterday. Told me to ride my longboard on the sidewalk."

. . . a poorly paved road lined with dilapidated houses, Ellie.

Jack's heart clenched. The pictures were taken at a distance and she was completely unaware. Unguarded. Beautiful.

"Dad!"

"What?" Jack tore his eyes from the screen and back to his son. Ethan looked irritated, confused, and little afraid. Ethan glanced back at the computer screen. When he turned back to Jack, his face tightened.

"You *like* her." His voice was incredulous, angry.

The last thing Jack needed was for Ethan to suspect he was interested in another woman. Jack didn't want to deal with the drama. He tried to act as uninterested as possible and changed the subject. "You shouldn't take pictures of people without their permission."

"She didn't seem to mind."

"You met her?"

"Yeah. She told me to delete the ugly ones. Guess I'll delete them all."

God, he could be a shit. Just like his mother. Jack's mistake with Julie was rising to her bait. He refused to do it with a thirteen-year-old kid. "Do what you want."

Jack returned his attention to Ethan's phone. He opened Instagram and scrolled through the pictures his son had posted since moving to Stillwater. They were good. Just like the pictures on his computer. "Where is it? Did you delete it?"

"What are you talking about?"

"The picture of the skull you posted on Instagram. Where is it?"

"I didn't post a picture of the skull. Do you think I'm an idiot?"

"Sometimes I wonder."

Ethan leaned back in his chair and crossed his arms. "Nice, Dad."

"I just got a call from a parent saying you posted a picture of the skull on Instagram."

"Well, they're lying. I didn't."

"Why would she lie?"

"I have no idea who 'she' is so I can't tell you that."

"Don't be a smart ass."

"Why not? You're being an asshole."

Jack stepped forward. "Ethan, do not test me. Did you or did you not take a picture of the skull?"

Ethan hesitated. "I did."

"Jesus Christ!"

"But I didn't post it online! I'm not a moron, Dad."

"You took a picture of a crime scene! Do you call that intelligent?"

"Okay, no. Probably not. But it was a cool shot. When am I ever going to see another skull like that?"

"Ethan," Jack growled. "You have no idea the situation I'm in here. Everything I do and you do has to be above reproach."

"Nobody is above reproach."

"Jesus, would you stop sounding like a thirty-year-old?"

"Someone has to act like an adult around here."

"This is just like arguing with your mother."

"I guess I must be pissing you off real good."

Jack took a deep breath. He could count at least three things he regretted saying. God, he sucked as a single dad. "Why would Susan tell me you posted it on Instagram?"

Ethan paused, looked guilty. "Mrs. Grant?"

"Yes."

He looked down. "I texted the picture to Troy. He promised not to share it with anyone."

Jack felt the tension around his chest loosen. "He probably didn't."

"Then how would she know?" Ethan's face was red. Jack could tell he was getting angry with his friend.

"Maybe he tells his mother everything. Maybe she checked his text messages and found it. It doesn't matter. The lesson here is not to share stuff you don't want everyone to find out about, in text messages, emails, Twitter, Instagram, Facebook."

"Only parents use Facebook."

"You know what I mean."

"So am I grounded?"

"Yep. No phone for a week. And you have to come to the station after school until I get off work."

"That it?"

"Is that not enough?"

"It's plenty."

"Go to your room."

"I'm busy."

"Finish it later."

Ethan pushed the chair back. It rolled and hit the bookshelves. "Only five-year-olds get sent to their rooms."

"Fine. Go mow the yard."

"Seriously?"

"Yeah. Seriously."

Ethan scowled and walked off.

Ethan's phone buzzed with a text from Troy, apologizing. Jack texted back, telling Troy that Ethan was grounded and to delete the photo. The "yes, sir" return text was immediate. He opened the bottom drawer and put the phone next to another phone in a box tucked underneath a bunch of papers. He closed the drawer and went into the kitchen. Through the back screen door, Jack watched as Ethan went to the detached garage and pulled out the lawnmower. With a scowl on his face and his dark hair flopping down over his eyes, Ethan pulled the cord and the mower came to life. He didn't want to do it, but he obeyed Jack immediately. Jack sighed, slightly relieved, the hope that Ethan's attitude was due in larger part to puberty than to a true similarity to his mother.

With the sound of the mower in the background, Jack returned to the office, sat at the desk, and scrolled through Ethan's pictures of Ellie. He clicked on the thumbnails to return to the first picture, enlarged it and scrolled. Jack felt like a voyeur as he watched her enjoy her time alone. She like to read, no surprise for a bookstore owner, didn't like fantasy, drank coffee in the middle of the day, walked around barefoot, had long, narrow feet with high arches, her second toe much longer than the first. Jack lingered on the image of Ellie staring into the middle distance, concentrating. What was she thinking of? Her eyes were focused, as if calculating moves in a chess game. A few frames later, her eyes and face softened, became almost dreamy, ethereal, before morphing into the impish, lopsided grin Jack already loved. Jack hoped she was thinking of him, but he doubted it. He clicked backward and stopped. Between the daydream and the mischievousness, Ethan managed to capture an ephemeral expression that sent Jack's heart racing: desire.

It took a moment for Jack to catch his breath. When he did, he emailed the picture to his private email against the chance Ethan would follow through with his threat.

Jack scrolled forward quickly through the other pictures, making a mental note to go through their vacation pictures and pull some to hang on the walls. He leaned forward and stared at the picture of the cruiser—Freeman's by the look of it—and a red Jeep with a UT bumper sticker in front of a church. It was a sloppy picture, with no artistry or redeeming value. It looked more like one of the thousands of pictures he had taken on stakeouts. It was a picture to chronicle, not to inspire. There were only two pictures of the cars, and Freeman and the other driver were nowhere in sight. A few well-framed pictures of the church followed and the roll ended.

Why did Ethan take a picture of Freeman's car? Who owned the Jeep? What were they doing at this church? Jack checked the time stamp in the photo information. Thirty minutes had passed since the picture of a car on blocks and the picture of Freeman's car. Had Ethan been spying on Freeman? Why would he do that?

Jack printed the picture of the church, folded it, and put it in his pocket, silently thanking Ethan for giving him a good excuse to go by the bookstore and talk to Ellie.

III

Miner stopped his patrol car next to a white dually parked at the MLK Community Park on the edge of the Bottom, though calling the grassless plot of ground with dilapidated equipment a park was being generous. He got out of his car slowly and walked around to the truck's driver's side door.

"Miner."

"Buck."

Buck Pollard was a big man in his youth who had shrunk to average in his old age. A barrel chest sat atop trim hips and bowed legs. In his youth, his dark wavy hair had been his one vanity. As he aged, and the stress of his job grew, his hair turned a sleek, steel gray. A broad, trim mustache camouflaged a jagged scar on his upper lip from a bar fight in Vietnam. A full-toothed smile and crinkles around his eyes masked his humorless and calculating nature. If asked, most Stillwater residents would say Buck Pollard was a genial, friendly man. What else could they say? Buck Pollard knew the secrets of most everyone in town.

"How's Teresa?" Buck asked.

"Good, good," Miner replied.

"Still having trouble with her fibromyalgia?"

"Not too bad," Miner lied. This morning he had left his wife curled up in bed with a heating pad and a bottle of Vicodin.

"Glad to hear it."

"How's retirement?"

"Bored to death. I'm leaving tomorrow for a fishing trip in the Gulf."

"That'll be nice."

"Heard your boss got the shit kicked out of him by a Mexican."

"Yep."

"To the surprise of no one. Except maybe Jane Maxwell. What do you think of your new boss?"

"Too early to tell."

"Too early to tell?" Buck's laugh was caustic.

Miner continued, unperturbed. "Seems like a good enough FBI agent. Not sure what kind of cop he is."

"You should have gotten that job," Pollard said.

"Everything happens for a reason."

He had been relieved when Jane Maxwell broke the news to him that he'd lost the job to an outsider. He'd celebrated with a finger of Jack Daniels from a bottle hidden in his tack room for just such occasions.

"You were passed over for that job because Jane Maxwell has *plans*." He emphasized the last word with disgust. "It was a mighty artful frame-up that run me out of my job. You know it and I know it."

Miner looked off toward the river. Pollard was probably right. Miner did know that Pollard had been framed, but to prove it, Pollard would have to admit that he'd taken money in the first place, which he would never do. The framer must have known that because, besides vague statements about being railroaded out of his job, Pollard had left his thirty-four-year post as chief of police with barely a whimper. Lord knew none of the people who benefited from Buck's corruption over the years—the drug dealers who got passes, the wife beaters who were never arrested, the policemen who turned a blind eye while pocketing wads of money—would ever turn on Buck, either. As long as they laid low, kept their mouths shut, and denied, everyone would be safe.

Pollard had slowly let Miner in on it all. A hundred here and there to help with the cost of Teresa's pain meds had turned into bundles of twenty-dollar bills. Pollard always handed the money to Miner with two words: "No banks."

"You think Jane Maxwell framed you?" Miner pondered aloud.

Pollard looked unsure for a split second, as though he couldn't believe even that of his long time adversary. "Who else? She's a banker and would know all about setting up those overseas accounts."

"So what? Jane Maxwell put thousands of her own money into a foreign account with your name on it? I don't know, Buck."

Pollard shook his head. "You always were gullible, Miner. Even after being a cop all these years, you still see the good in people."

"Okay, say she did it. Why hasn't she given the information to anyone? To Newberry, huh? Or to McBride? Hell, the FBI? No way she would lose all that money just to get you to retire. And why now?"

"She's got something up her sleeve. Goddamn Nazi."

Miner didn't say anything. Calling Jane a Nazi was Buck's favorite insult, though, interestingly enough, Miner never heard him say it to anyone else.

"Tell me about the skeleton," Buck said.

"Not much to tell. It was buried in the early '60s as best we can tell. We'll comb through the missing-persons reports. Got a BOLO out on it."

"Won't get anything from that."

Miner didn't think so, either, but Pollard's confidence made him uneasy.

Pollard reached across the seat of his truck. "County records are gonna be thin for that time frame because of the fire." He handed Miner a manila envelope. "Took a look in some of my private files. This is the woman you found."

Miner didn't need to look inside the bottom heavy envelope to know what else it contained. "Private files?"

Pollard started his truck. "I'm sure I don't have to tell you to keep where you got that between us."

Cold dread settled on Miner. "Why're you giving me this?"

"I wanna help you impress your boss."

CHAPTER FIVE

Monday

I

Jack was glad he did not visit Yourkeville before taking the job in Stillwater. If he had, Stillwater's dreariness and somnolence would have been exaggerated by Yourkeville's cleanliness, organization, and energy.

Apparently, the county seat didn't get the memo that Monday morning was the usual business day off (along with the Sabbath and half of Saturday) for small-town East Texas. Downtown was bustling, due in large part to the steady stream of people coming in and out of the red stone courthouse; men in business suits, law enforcement officers, residents paying taxes, bail bondsmen talking to their clients, the stench of the county jail hovering around their crumpled clothes.

Jack found Ann Newberry's office with ease and was ushered in without hesitation by a young, fresh-faced sheriff's deputy who tried not to stare at Jack's black eye and stitched eyebrow. Ann waved for Jack to sit while she finished her phone conversation, so he sat in the leather chair, crossed his legs, and looked around.

It was an impersonal office, save the row of pictures of Ann and her daughter through the years. All the hallmarks of life were there; first day of kindergarten, Halloweens, high school graduation, college graduation, marriage and, in the place of honor on Ann's desk, a picture of three generations of Newberry women: Ann, daughter, and granddaughter in the hospital immediately after the latter's birth. Jack smiled sadly. He thought of that exact picture of him, Julie, and Ethan minutes after Ethan was born. The women in Ann's picture had the same happy pride on their faces he remembered feeling and that was caught on film for eternity, the proof now languishing in one of the many boxes of Julie's stuff he had shoved in the extra bedroom. If only that happiness could last or could be so easily remembered during difficult times.

"Well, well. Look what the cat dragged in," Ann said. She replaced the receiver.

"Not exactly the kind of first week I wanted to have."

"I guess not. How are you feeling? You look like shit."

Jack touched his bruised eye. The swelling had gone down and taken the tenderness with it. The bruise was still dark enough that people did a double take when they saw him, and stared longer than was polite. "I'm starting to remember bits and pieces of what happened."

"And?"

"I remember the storm and pulling over and Diego standing over me with my gun. Everything in between is black."

"You're lucky he didn't blow your brains out."

"I know."

"Should have called the jail for a transport."

Jack leaned forward, resting his elbows on his knees. "Don't you think I know that? I had a good reason for taking him alone—I just don't remember it."

"What is the last thing you remember?"

"Calling Ethan."

"Did you record the interrogation at the station?"

Jack smiled, bitterly. "Cameras don't work."

"Anybody watch through the glass?"

"No. Freeman says he was in his office doing paperwork the entire time."

She narrowed her eyes. "Don't you believe him?"

"Not really."

"Why would he lie?"

"That's the question, isn't it? Know him very well?"

"No. He seems to be a good enough officer, but not the type to move to the next level." She tapped her temple. "Completely lacking in intuition or imagination."

She tossed a folder onto the desk in front of Jack. "Well, here's the partial crime-scene report for the murder-suicide. Won't have the full for a couple weeks. Josh is swamped down there. Just confirms what we already figured. Rosa didn't pull the trigger. Her prints weren't even *on* the trigger."

"Sloppy."

"Yeah."

"Did Josh dust the inside of the gun? Bullets?"

"Bullets, yes. No prints. The inside of the gun, no. Want him to?"

"That'd be great."

"He did lift the serial number. Details are in the file but it was last sold to Justin Dixon, owner of Top Gun, a shooting range in the warehouse on the river in Stillwater."

"What do you know about him?"

"Blustery and opinionated. One of those 'don't tread on me' types. Runs a clean business as far as I know. My guess is he sells guns to himself, then sells them privately so people can avoid the background checks."

"Huh. Shady but not illegal." Jack opened the folder, glanced at the report, and flipped through the pictures quickly—there were the normal shots of the bodies and the scene before being dusted for prints. He closed the folder. He would look at them in more detail later.

"So," Ann said. "A skeleton in the woods?"

Jack told her about the boy at the football game, taking Ethan to see it thinking it was a cow skull, the dig to unearth the skeleton, and their meager findings.

"One shoe. A few patches of clothing. No jewelry."

"I guess a murder weapon and ID would have been too much to ask."

"At least we found the rest of the skeleton, surprisingly intact. Based on the style of shoe, and the decomposition of the clothes, Hugh estimates the body has been in the ground for nearly fifty years. He should be calling me today or tomorrow with more info."

Ann let out a low whistle. "Long time. Better you than me. Not a fan of cold cases. I'd rather work with real people than sit in a room poring over missing-persons records."

"Me, too. Which is why I'm assigning it to Miner."

She thought a moment. "Probably the best option of what you have to choose from."

"Thanks," Jack said. He knew better than anyone that he needed to upgrade his force but he didn't want to hear Ann say it. "So, we're looking for missing-persons records from the late '50s, early '60s. You have those online or boxed up?"

"Boxed up, most like. The project to put information online is always the first budget line to get cut. First of the year, we do as much as we can, as fast as we can. By June, they're pulling the money into the jail or courts. Even so, something like missing persons is pretty low priority among the records. There probably aren't many of them for the entire fifty years. I'll ask Juanita to pull them from storage."

"I'll have Miner pick them up."

"They have to stay here, Jack."

"That's hardly inter-agency cooperation."

"Maybe not, but until the records get digitized, they aren't leaving my house."

Jack picked an invisible piece of lint from the knee of his pants. "Why?"

"I don't trust Miner Jesson."

Jack raised his eyebrows in question.

"He was with Buck Pollard the longest of any deputy."

"You've said that before. Thing is, it doesn't answer the question. Unless, of course, the answer is guilt by association."

"Have you met Miner's wife?"

"No."

"You probably won't, either. Teresa's been bedridden for years. Started as fibromyalgia, which is bad enough, but recently Sam Poole suggested Chronic Fatigue Syndrome."

"That's hardly a better diagnosis."

"No. No cure, just managing the symptoms, which isn't easy, or cheap. It isn't something someone on Miner's salary can easily afford, even with the city health insurance."

Jack drummed his fingers on the arm of his chair, the wood scarred from years of use. "Is my deputy under investigation?"

"No."

"Has he ever been?"

"No."

"Cut the bullshit, Ann. Everyone tiptoes around Buck Pollard like he's a damn minefield. He serves as police chief for what? Thirty years? Retires, and then doesn't bother to even leave a note for his successor? No smooth transition, just see ya. Good luck."

"That's him giving the middle finger to Jane Maxwell. I will say this for Buck—he didn't have much crime in his town."

"Why does that sound like a backhanded compliment?"

"Because it is. Buck Pollard had a low crime rate because he didn't arrest anyone. Or, maybe I should say, he only arrested people who did something they shouldn't in public or if they couldn't do anything for him in return."

"And he got away with this for years, why?"

"Rumor has it he has dirt on everyone in the county with even a modicum of power."

"You?"

"No, not me."

"How is that possible?"

"I live a clean life."

Jack scoffed. "Jane Maxwell?"

"Wouldn't be surprised. He was never investigated. Given more Man of the Year awards than anyone in the county. He's so clean that I am 100 percent sure he's covering up something so big, it will blow this county apart if it ever comes to light."

"Why didn't you ever investigate him?"

"Never broke any law that I saw. Never directed to investigate him by the DA or anyone else."

"You didn't want the trouble."

Ann leaned forward. "I'm a damn good sheriff, Jack. When I arrest someone, I put an airtight case together and they are convicted 90 percent of the time. The DA would kiss my feet if I asked him to. I run a tight ship but I'm *elected*, not appointed. Going after a corrupt cop who is related to half the county and has the other half in his pocket would kill my career. It would be a disservice to the residents of Yourke County who rely on a competent, *clean* sheriff's department. Judge me if you want, but I don't lose one moment's sleep over it."

"If Pollard had that much power, why did he resign?"

"No one knows. One day, he gives the city manager his two-weeks' notice and was done. Spends most of his time in Galveston deep-sea fishing in his boat."

"Guess that explains why I haven't seen him since I've been here."

"Oh, I bet you have. Gone to the Chevron?"

"Sure."

"He hangs out there every morning he's in town with three other old men. Seen them?"

Jack thought back to the man who spoke to him that first day. "Yeah, okay, I've seen him."

"If Buck wants to pull strings, he'll use Miner. They're close."

Jack thought back to Miner's vote of confidence Thursday and how agreeable he had been helping Jack get acclimated, answering questions, the way he stepped up when Jack was hurt. Granted, his answers were much briefer than a man with his memory would or should provide, but Jack hadn't felt like Miner was holding anything back. Now, he wondered if Miner's affability wasn't merely a ruse to lure Jack into a false sense of security.

Jack shifted in his chair, recrossed his legs. "What do you know about Ellie Martin?"

Ann narrowed her eyes and turned her head to the side. "Why? She done something?"

"Not that I'm aware of."

Ann's face cleared and she sat back, suppressing a small smile. Jack held her gaze and tried to not to look or act embarrassed. "I'd be surprised if she did. She's been on the county Crime Stoppers board for years, since she got back from Dallas."

"She lived in Dallas?"

"For a few months. After all that happened with her husband."

Jack ran his fingers along the gashes in the arm of his chair. The question of what happened with her husband was on the tip of his tongue, but he refrained asking it. "I ask because she offered to help with questions about town history." Okay, not completely the truth. Jack hadn't talked to Ellie since Friday, but she had sort of offered to help him when they met. "I just wanted to make sure she is someone I can trust with information that the public might not be privy to."

"I would trust her completely. If you tell her something in confidence, she'll keep it."

"That was my read on her, as well. Nice to have it confirmed." Jack stood and held his hand out to Ann. "Let me know when Miner can come look through the files."

"I'll put Juanita on it ASAP."

They shook hands. Jack nodded to the picture on the desk. "That your granddaughter?"

"Yes." Ann beamed. "Madison. Best baby in the world."

"That's what all grandmothers think."

Ann walked around the desk to usher Jack out. "But she really is." She stopped him from opening the door. "About Ellie. You shouldn't have concerns about her on any level. She's good people."

Jack smiled at the colloquialism. "She seems like it."

Ann narrowed her eyes. "Should she have any concerns about you?"

"What do you mean?"

"I mean, don't fuck with her if you aren't available."

"Ann, I would never—"

She held up her hand. "Don't even. I made a few calls."

Jack went cold. "What kind of calls?"

"The kind that gave me a pretty good idea of the cloud you left under, of your behavior those last few months."

"We talking personal or professional?"

"Both."

Jack released the doorknob. "What do you want to know?"

Ann shook her head. "Nothing. I get it, Jack. I really do. If anyone can understand what it feels like to be abandoned, what it does to your psyche, it's me. Probably Ellie can, too. You got all that anger out of your system, yeah?"

Jack nodded.

"Good. I know the man you are. I like you. I'm glad you're here. You're going to be great for Yourke County."

"But?"

"This ain't Dallas. You have to be much more careful about what you do and who you do it with. Do you understand what I'm saying?"

He didn't, not really, but said, "Yes."

II

On the morning of her fortieth birthday, three years earlier, Ellie had woken up and felt her stomach laying like a blob on the bed. Horrified and disbelieving, she stripped down and stood in front of her full-length mirror. She stood there for ten minutes, wondering how, why, and when she had morphed from a star high school basketball player to a forty-year-old fat woman with dull, stringy hair, puffy cheeks, and dark circles under her eyes. Her stomach stuck out, her back was fat, and her arms were flabby. Her ass, legs, and thighs, always her best features, were spared the carnage. Mostly. Thank God.

She'd had to dig deep in her closet to find her too-tight running clothes, and never-worn shoes, all left over from an earlier weight-loss resolution. Now, the number on the scale made her cry so hard, she vomited the remainder of the candy and ice cream she had eaten the night before.

She'd walked to the end of her driveway, turned right, and started to run. Within two hundred yards, she was short of breath and wanted to stop. Instead, she kept on, turned left onto the steep, overgrown, grassy road that led to the abandoned German church. No one went up there except kids parking late at night. Ellie knew no one would be there on a random predawn Tuesday. She could have stopped at any time, but she didn't. She told herself if she made it, then she could do anything: she could lose thirty pounds, quit her boring job, and follow her dream.

She touched the wall of the church and leaned against it, arms outstretched, her breath like a jagged knife sawing through her chest. Her legs buckled and she sat heavily on the ground, the cool breeze drying the mingled perspiration and tears on her cheeks.

Through the trees Ellie could see the bend of the river hugging downtown Stillwater like a protective mother, reminding her of mornings of her childhood. Her most vivid childhood memory was of sitting on the back porch with her mother, watching the sunrise and the river transform from a black gash to a ribbon of reds, purples, pinks, and golds until it finally revealed its true state—muddy brown and shallow. Her mother, stroking Ellie's long hair, would sigh. Ellie would pat her mother's hand and say, "Maybe tomorrow it'll stay pretty, Momma." Her mother would give her a wan smile and say, "Maybe." It was years before Ellie realized her mother was not sighing about the river.

Now, three years later and fifty-five pounds lighter, she stood at the same spot and watched the river. Ellie had long since stopped being ashamed of her former fat self or impressed with her weight loss. Both selves were integral to her journey, to who she was, to her ability to accomplish those goals she set forth on her fortieth birthday. Two were crossed off the written list. One would be crossed off this week. The unwritten list, the list she carried inside, was more complicated, challenging, terrifying, and mostly unaccomplished. For now.

The sun crested, the river turned muddy, and Ellie walked down the road. When she got to River Road, she turned right and ran, quickly falling into the familiar rhythm. She slowed as she approached her old house, her body finally used to going past, around the corner to the left, across the bridge and into downtown. She opened a narrow door to the left of her storefront and jogged up the stairs. She stopped at her front door—bright red-orange for no other reason than that she liked it—caught her breath and went inside.

When she decided to move into the top floor of the building that was to house her bookstore, she had the walls torn down and had spent an entire day cleaning the eight-foot-tall windows. Light had flooded the open space and Ellie felt at home for the first time in her life. Refusing Kelly's offer to help design and decorate, Ellie went about turning the empty room into exactly what she wanted. She had a wall put up to the left of her orange door, partitioning one-quarter of the space for her bedroom. She had a small kitchen built next to the wall near the door and had a combination bathroom/laundry room installed on the outside wall. Decorating was a work in progress but leaned toward comfortable and squishy, a couch that invited curling up with a book, a campaign desk next to the windows to capture the light, flea-market tables she refinished herself. Everything about it was completely her. Six weeks after moving in, she still got a thrill walking through the door.

She went about the rest of her morning routine without thinking. Stretching, push-ups, sit-ups, and pull-ups were her least favorite part of the morning but skipping them was not an option. She was self-aware enough to know if she ever cheated on her routine or her diet even a little, she would backslide completely.

When she finished, she checked her email. Her phone rang. "Good morning," she answered.

"God, you're so peppy in the morning," Kelly said.

Ellie closed her computer and rose. "I've been up since 5:30, attacking the day." She smiled, knowing full well her enthusiasm would irritate Kelly.

"Ugh."

"You haven't had your first Diet Coke, have you?"

Kelly grunted.

"What's up?"

"I'm calling to offer my services today. I've cleared my schedule to be at your beck and call."

"Have you?" Ellie picked a protein bar from the basket on her counter, grabbed her keys, and walked out of her apartment. She jogged down the stairs. "I'm going to the store now. Let me see where I am and call you back."

"I still can't believe you aren't going to have wine and beer at your launch party."

Ellie unlocked the front door, went inside, and flipped on the lights. "I don't want to alienate half the town before I open."

"You don't want those people as customers anyway."

"Yes, I do."

"You should invite Jack McBride."

"I told Susan to mention it to him."

"Make sure he comes. We can grill him about the skeleton."

"Yeah, yeah," Ellie said, with no intention of inviting him or grilling him. She still hadn't fully recovered from their conversation Friday night. "Get your lazy butt out of bed. I'll call you later."

Ellie hung up without waiting for a response. She started a small pot of coffee and got to work.

There wasn't much left to do. The books were shelved, the display tables organized, the coffee bar stocked and clean, the buffet table for the night's reception set up, the storeroom organized. Ellie checked everything three times, sure there was no way it could all be done. There must be something she was missing. Damned if she could find it.

She dusted the shelves again. A mystery with a "cat" in the title caught her eye. She opened it to a random page and started to read. Good Lord—it was from the cat's point of view. She couldn't help but smile.

A knock on the window startled her. Jack McBride waved from the other side of the glass.

"Oh," Ellie said.

She fumbled trying to re-shelve the book and settled for laying it on top of the others. At least that would give her something to do later on. She caught sight of her reflection in the door and groaned; she still wore her running clothes, her hair was stiff with dried sweat, and she wasn't wearing an ounce of makeup. She was sure she stunk to high heaven after running six miles and working out. She didn't want to impress him, not in the least, but she was vain enough that she didn't want anyone, even Jack McBride, to see her in this state. She pointed at the sign in the window. "We're closed," she said with a smile, hoping her good nature would defer him.

Jack gave her an incredulous look, lifted the badge that hung on a chain around his neck, and said, "I'm here on official police business."

She pursed her lips. "I'm really not fit for any business, official or otherwise."

"I'm thirsty. And I can smell the coffee from here." He smiled. His teeth were so perfect and white, she expected one to sparkle. She stifled a laugh. Even with the multicolored bruise and stitched eyebrow, he was ridiculously urbane. Had he realized how out of place he was in Stillwater?

"Please?" he said.

She resolved to stay as far away from him as possible, to not even look at him, and opened the door. Who knows? Maybe if he saw her like this, he would stop flirting with her. Ellie ignored the stab of disappointment at the idea.

"Don't you want to lock the door?"

"With the chief of police here? Who would dare rob me?"

"Excellent point." He looked around her store. "Very nice. The Book Bank—is that in honor of your former employer?"

"No." She walked around the bar, a mahogany monstrosity salvaged from a historic hotel in Jacksboro. It was huge, maybe a little big for the space, but she loved it. She poured Jack a cup of coffee. "This building was a bank at one time. The competition. It's been a few things actually, so none of the bank trappings are left. Except the safe, which is the office." She placed the cup of coffee on the counter. "Cream or sugar?"

"Is your coffee that bad?"

She leaned against the back counter and crossed her arms over her chest. "See for yourself."

He sipped it. "Very good."

"How are you feeling?"

"Better and better." His smile was mischievous. He sipped again and looked up at the chalkboard menu above Ellie. "Brown Sugar Latte, Turtle Cake Latte, Raspberry Mocha, Snickerdoodle Latte? Good Lord, those sound good. What's your favorite?"

"Snickerdoodle." Ellie pushed her crunchy hair behind her ear, and looked down. Christ. She needed to shave her legs.

"Where did you learn to make a latte?"

"Hmm." Ellie paused. Part of her wanted to dodge the question, not because the answer was scandalous or even interesting. In fact, he might already know the answer, but hearing it from her would make it personal, somehow.

"Is that too personal?" he asked.

Her surprise at his use of the very word she was thinking spurred her to answer, to contradict his unsettling clairvoyance.

"I took a sabbatical a few years back. Moved to Dallas and got a job at Starbucks." His eyebrows shot up and his mouth twitched. "Don't laugh," she said, suppressing her own. "It was exactly the job I needed at the time. I had a rough year, personally and professionally. I needed a change. Like you."

"Like me." He sipped his coffee. "So, I don't know if you remember, but when we met that first day, at the bank, you offered to help me with information about the town."

"I remember."

"I suppose you've heard about the skeleton."

"I have."

He lifted one eyebrow. "That's it? Aren't you going to ask me about it?"

"No."

Jack stared at Ellie over the rim of his cup. "Hmm," he said, putting his cup down. "Why not?"

"Honestly, I doubt there's anything you can tell me I haven't already heard."

"Oh, really?"

"Really."

Jack leaned his elbows on the counter and motioned for her to continue. "Enlighten me."

"It is the skeleton of a woman, in the ground about fifty years."

"We don't know for sure if it's a woman."

"You suspect so because you found a woman's shoe. Just one, which is kind of weird."

"What else?"

"I really shouldn't."

"Please. You might know something I don't." He was enjoying himself.

She crinkled her nose. "Ethan sent a picture of it to Troy." Jack straightened up and his smile faded.

"The only reason I know that is because I was at Susan's house yesterday when she found it. I won't tell a soul. I would never."

Jack drummed his fingers on the countertop, stared into the empty pastry case. He looked at Ellie. "Why aren't there any pastries?"

"There will be tonight."

Jack pursed his lips and nodded. He studied her. "I know."

"You know about the pastries? How could you know about the pastries?"

"No," Jack said. "I know I can trust you."

She closed her eyes and shook her head. "I'm so confused." She opened her eyes. He was smiling at her, the same expression from the game. It puzzled her even more here. "Why are you looking at me like that?"

"Like what?"

"You have this, forgive the phrase, but a shit-eating grin on your face."

"Do I?" He pursed his lips, furrowed his brow, and looked serious. "Is this better?"

"No. Now you look constipated."

"What exactly is a shit-eating grin? I mean, why would anyone smile after eating shit?"

Ellie laughed. "We've moved from confusing to downright strange. What were we talking about again?"

"I don't know. I'm supposed to be solving crimes and all I want to do is drink another cup of your coffee. May I?" He pushed the cup forward.

He watched her as she poured the coffee. "Did I see you run by the house this morning before dawn?" he asked.

"You did."

"How far do you run?"

"Six miles today."

Jack whistled. "How many laps of Stillwater is that?"

"I run down almost every street in town. I end up at the church on the bluff down the street from your house."

He studied her. "Why did you want to sell your family home?"

She paused. "Bad memories."

Jack straightened. "Did something happen to you?"

She stifled a smile. Jack looked ready to go back in time and kick some ass. "No, no. Nothing like that. Maybe it's best if I just say I didn't have many happy moments there and leave it at that."

"I didn't mean to pry."

Ellie waved her hand in dismissal. "Don't worry."

He reached into his jacket and pulled out a folded piece of paper. He unfolded it and placed it on the counter. She recognized the Jeep immediately.

"Is this the German church?"

"Yes. It's abandoned."

"Why would anyone be up there?"

"That's Seth's Jeep—he's Kelly's son—and I imagine Freeman's cruiser. There's a steep trail down the backside that's good for hill work—running. Seth and Freeman have been working out together for quite a few months."

Jack nodded. "How long has it been abandoned?"

"As long as I can remember. I suppose it's Stillwater's Inspiration Point. Has been for years."

"Did you go parking behind the church, Miss Martin?"

"I refuse to answer that question."

"Why?"

"If I did, then I'm easy. If I didn't, then I'm pathetic."

"Those are two words I would never associate with you."

"Still profiling me, I see."

"Would you be offended if I said yes?"

"I guess that would depend on what the profile was." She raised her hand. "I don't want to know."

"Really? You're one of the few, then. You wouldn't believe the number of times people ask me to do it, like a party trick."

"And you lie to them."

"Every time."

"I wouldn't want you to lie to me."

He paused, held her gaze. "I wouldn't."

She swallowed, pushing down her heart, which had jumped up her throat. "That's what I'm afraid of."

She knew, as well as he did, they weren't just talking about a party trick. The same strange feeling she had during their conversations last week returned. She had struggled to find the right word for it, to explain it easily and succinctly, but for the life of her, she couldn't. Until now.

Understanding.

Was it that simple? Was it merely that they understood each other on a deep level that belied the length of their acquaintance? She barely knew this man, but it was there. Whatever *it* was. She didn't know. She didn't want to know. She was afraid to know.

"I stopped wanting to know what people thought of me years ago. Sometimes, it's unavoidable, but if it is . . ." She let the sentence trail off. *Just let it be. Turn around and walk out the door. Don't force me to make you.*

"Do you really not know what I think of you?"

"I have a pretty good idea, but I hope I'm wrong." She pulled a to-go cup from underneath the counter. "Want me to make you a latte to go?"

"Are you trying to get rid of me?"

"I am, actually. What's the official business you needed to see me about?"

He studied her for a long time. She forced herself to levelly hold his gaze, to look at him with as much neutrality as possible.

"What do you know about Barbara Dodsworth?"

She felt a small thrill of victory. "She was my babysitter."

"Really?"

"She wasn't very good. She would put me to bed almost as soon as my father left, and then sneak her boyfriends in the house. I caught her and one of them on the couch once. Miner, as a matter of fact. Very disturbing image for a seven-year-old."

Jack laughed. "That's not quite the type of information I was looking for, but interesting, nonetheless."

"Is she a suspect?"

"Not unless she was a murderous toddler. The bones haven't been specifically dated, but fifty years is the ballpark. You were right. I don't suppose I have to tell you that this is all confidential?"

"No."

Silence. Surprisingly comfortable considering all the emotions and questions hovering in the air around them. Was he waiting for her to say something? To make a move? Did he think of himself as so irresistible she would just fall at his feet as soon as he showed an interest? Ellie wasn't an idiot. She had attracted enough men in her life—not as many as she wanted, but enough—to read what he wanted easily enough.

She moved to the coffee machine and started making a Snickerdoodle latte. With a puff of steam, she cleaned out the milk wand.

"Why are you so desperate to get rid of me?"

She worked silently, hoping that if she focused enough on her task, he would magically disappear and she wouldn't have to answer. She finished the latte and looked up. He was still there. She pressed a lid on the cup, followed it with a cardboard sleeve, and placed it on the counter.

"Do you really want to know?"

"Yes."

"Because I like you much more than I should."

He couldn't suppress his grin. Her reveal had made his day. "Why is that bad?"

"Because you're married."

His smile faded. "I can explain."

Damn. Part of her had hoped he would deny it, that he would tell her she was wrong and he was divorced. She felt sick to her stomach. She could no longer fool herself into believing they were just talking, innocent conversations between two people who didn't know each other well. Of course she knew better, but it had been easy to justify her uncharacteristic behavior. Now, she couldn't decide what was more disturbing: the idea he might be a philanderer or the fact that the more she talked to him, the less she cared. She was relieved she had the courage to confront him now instead of later. She could salvage her pride and self-respect from this. Regardless of who was the most reprehensible in this situation—and it was a toss-up—Ellie wouldn't allow herself to fall in with a man who would break her heart.

Again.

"I think it's best if you just go."

He opened his mouth to say something and then stopped, picked up his coffee, and walked to the door. Ellie stared at the floor, forcing herself to not call him back, to not encourage him to explain, to not want to take what he said at face value. She brought up all the memories of the destruction of her marriage—the gossip, the humiliation, and the misery—and listened for the bell over the door to ding, signaling his departure. When it didn't, she looked up. He stood at the door, staring at her.

"It's not what you think."

The bell jingled and he was gone, leaving Ellie with the uncomfortable realization he was right.

III

Well, *that* was a disaster.

Of course there was no way Ellie would get involved with a married man. Would he want to have a relationship with someone who would?

No.

Wasn't he was drawn to Ellie because on every level she was the polar opposite of his wife?

Yes.

Oh, yes. Men would cross bars to buy Julie McBride a drink. They would cross oceans, even time and space, to be near her, with her. Lord knows enough had done so in the fifteen years they had been married. Not that Jack had ever known. He had been well and truly cuckolded.

He'd spent plenty of time the last few days thinking of this, of what drew him to Ellie. Was he attracted to Ellie for what she was or because of what she was not? He'd second-guessed himself plenty, but whenever he was with her, talking to her, he knew. When they were together, something snapped into place for him. He didn't know what it was, he couldn't explain it, define it, pinpoint it. It was like nothing he'd ever experienced. He couldn't imagine feeling it with anyone else—which was why he wanted to make sure he didn't screw it up.

When he took the job in Stillwater, he had made a conscious decision to be vague about his marriage, and why not? None of these people knew Julie and, unless something monumental happened, he would be divorced within two weeks of arrival. Then he could stop skirting questions and answer truthfully: "I'm divorced." A perfect plan, but he hadn't counted on Ellie Martin knocking him for a loop and, really, what had been the chances of that?

Now, though, his secretiveness seemed seedy, as if he were trying to hide his culpability, his guilt. He might be culpable; he resented—even hated—Julie for leaving, but he was aware enough to know his behavior played a role. Even so, he was not guilty. His faults were no larger than any other distracted suburban husband with a high-pressure career, were nothing that two people who loved each other couldn't work through if they wanted. Julie, it turned out, didn't want to. Any desire Jack had to make his marriage work a year ago was now gone.

He was tired of thinking of the past: he'd been wallowing in it for a year. He was ready to move forward. That was what taking this job, moving to this town, had been about. Ethan was settling in (at least he wasn't scowling all the time) and their relationship was still wobbly, but Jack wasn't sure how much of that was teen angst and how much was the lingering effects of his mother's absence. Jack didn't look forward to the conversation he needed to have with Ethan about his marriage—especially now that he hoped it would be followed by another conversation about a certain bookstore owner. But Jack was getting way ahead of himself. First, he needed to figure out what to say to Ellie and find a time to say it.

He took the City Hall stairs two at a time. Susan looked up when he entered.

"Hey, Chief."

"Susan."

"Where's the coffee from?"

The cup in his hand was plain brown, 80 percent post recycle, about as nondescript as you could get. "Let me guess—you don't recognize the cup. It isn't from the Chevron, Dairy Queen, diner, or one of ours."

"Yeah."

"It's from the Book Bank."

"Oh! Did Ellie tell you about tonight?"

"Tonight?"

"Her business launch? She probably figured I had already mentioned it to you. She asked me to last week and I forgot. What with your . . ." She waved her hand at her head.

"It's a party?"

"Yes. Seven o'clock. At her store. A reception. Ethan's invited, too. My kids will be there. Give you a chance to meet more people. You should come." She buzzed Jack through the door.

Jack took the invitation as a good sign. He would talk to Ellie tonight then. "I think we will."

Miner was sitting in his office at one of the two desks, looking through files. Jack took the chair in the vacant one. "Morning."

"Morning, Chief." He closed the file and put it in his desk drawer.

"What's that?"

"Just some paperwork I'm behind on."

Jack sipped his coffee and looked from the drawer to Miner. He doubted it. "You still don't think the Dodsworths dumped a body in their woods fifty years ago?"

"No."

"Okay, then. How far would you drive to dump a body?"

The officer's lips fluttered. "Five hundred miles?"

"Before interstates?"

Miner shrugged. "I'd want to get it as far away from my home as possible."

"Transporting a body out of state would make it a federal crime."

"Which means we could pass it off to the Feds," he said. Miner was one of the most taciturn people Jack had ever met, but with that suggestion, he was downright ebullient.

"Why would we want to do that? We aren't ever going to be able to establish where the woman died fifty years ago anyway. Just where she's buried."

Miner's face fell. He leaned back in his chair and sighed, resigned. "This is Texas," he said. "You can drive five hundred miles without leaving the state. Easy."

Jack stared at the map of Texas on the wall. "Using five hundred miles, staying in Texas," Jack mused, "would mean they drove from south of Houston or west of Dallas, Austin, San Antonio. If you're west of those cities, just drive into the desert. You could dump a body out near Big Bend and it would never be found."

"If you were coming from Houston, why come north five hundred miles? Go south five hundred miles and dump the body in Mexico,"

Miner said. "Hell, there're so many bodies in their desert that one more would hardly be cause for investigation."

"There's also the ocean. Go far enough out and it would never be found. If you were coming from the east, Louisiana, Mississippi, or north from Arkansas and Tennessee, why stop here? Keep going to the desert or ocean."

"Unless you knew the area."

"Which brings us back to a local," Jack said.

They stared at the map for a while in silence. Jack drank his latte and let his mind wander. It was a damn good latte.

"Problem is, Chief, there aren't any local missing-persons reports from the '60s."

Jack nodded. "That *is* a problem. I suppose to be thorough we should expand the missing-persons reports from Oklahoma, Arkansas, Louisiana, and Mississippi." He tapped a pencil on the desk. "Occam's Razor."

"What?" Miner asked.

"When you have two competing theories, the simplest solution is usually the correct one." Miner remained silent. "Especially when you consider the fact the land has been out of use for fifty years. And Elizabeth Dodsworth specifically kept it fallow."

Miner leaned forward and picked up a blue Bic pen. He held it upright, flipped it over, ran his fingers down to the bottom, and repeated the action. "Chief, I've been wondering."

"What?"

"Well, is there really much point in investigating this? A fifty-year-old murder with no identification, no evidence, and no leads? If it *was* the Dodsworths, the old man is dead and Elizabeth is senile. All finding out would do is sully their name. Got to think how it would affect Barbara, too."

"I've thought of that. But aren't you curious just a little?"

"Not particularly. Plus we've got the Ramos case."

"I'll take care of the Ramos case. You're in charge of this one."

"I'd rather pull a month of night shifts."

"I'm sure Starling would be thrilled, but no. Talked to Sheriff Newberry this morning. She's pulling missing persons files for you. Have to go through them in Yourkeville, though."

"I think it's a waste of time."

Jack watched Miner play with the pen and let the silence linger. "Is there a reason you don't want to pursue this case?"

Miner let the pen drop. "It ain't that. What if it turns out to be linked to the Dodsworths? The town won't take kindly to you coming in here and opening old wounds." Miner finally looked up and said with a sly grin. "They run you out of town, they'll put me in charge."

Jack laughed. "I appreciate your concern, but we're going to pursue this case, no matter where it takes us. Do you understand?"

Miner nodded. "Yes, sir."

"Good. Now, let's talk about the Ramos case."

"All right."

Jack smiled at the way Miner was able to draw out two syllables for so long. He drummed his fingers on the desk. "Got the partial crime-scene report when I went to Yourkeville. Rosa wasn't the shooter."

"Pretty much what we thought."

"Gun was last sold to Justin Dixon."

"He buys guns and sells them privately."

"That's what Ann said."

"Don't see him having a motive to kill them."

"We'll see."

"So, who would want to kill two hard-working Mexicans that seemed to get along with everyone?" Miner asked.

"Obviously, they didn't get along with everyone."

"How do you go from being well-liked to someone wanting to put a bullet in your head?"

"Without there being at least some small indication something was going on." Jack finished his coffee, tossed the cup into the trashcan by the door. "Have you heard anything from the Feds about Diego?"

"The Feds?"

"Yeah, didn't you run Diego through the DEA?"

"No. Did you want me to?"

Jack stared at the ground. Hadn't he asked Miner to run Diego? In this very office? Jack shook his head to clear it. It wasn't coming back. "I thought I did. I probably hallucinated it. I've been having some crazy dreams the past few nights."

The phone beeped. Susan's voice sounded through the intercom. "Chief, Juanita down at County called. Files are ready for Miner."

"Thanks, Susan." Jack stood. "That was fast. Must mean there aren't many files. Good news, huh?"

"Yeah, great. Where are you off to?"

"Back out to the Ramoses' trailer. See if we missed anything."

"All right."

"First, though, I think it's about time I met Buck Pollard."

IV

Jack got lost three times on the way to Buck Pollard's house. Miner's directions were awful, the directions of a man who knew which way to turn on every road in the county by sight but couldn't remember the road numbers. Weird for a man Jack suspected of having a perfect memory. Pollard's house was so remote, so deep in the piney woods, Jack's phone wouldn't work, making his maps app pointless. Of course his car didn't have GPS. When Jack turned around for the third time, he let the idea lingering in the back of his mind come forward: Miner purposely tried to get him lost.

He drove back to the main highway, pulled over, and called Violet, the dispatcher, on the radio for better directions. With a chuckle, Violet recited the same directions Miner had given him, this time with road numbers, before telling him that Hugh Barnes left a message. He had some preliminary information about the skeleton.

Jack called Hugh back immediately and apologized for being out of pocket.

"Why people choose to live in the middle of nowhere, I don't know," Jack complained.

"Says the man who just moved to a small town."

"But I live inside the city limits. There's a big difference."

"If you say so."

"What do you have, Hugh?"

"No date yet, but I do have a cause of death: knife between the right third and fourth ribs, next to the sternum. Serrated knife."

"So the killer was left-handed."

"Most like. She had a couple of broken ribs, long healed. Her right wrist had a partially healed spiral break. There was also a hairline fracture on her right orbital bone. Probably happened at the same time as the arm."

"Someone beat her up before she died."

"Based on the healing, a couple weeks before. A more detailed report will take a while. We're still excavating the legs."

"This is good for now. Keep me posted."

Jack put his car in drive and started. "Let's try this again."

He found it by chance when he saw POLLARD painted in faint black letters on a large, rusted mailbox with a loose red flag. Jack backed up and pulled onto the smooth oil-dirt road. Two fat sorrel horses with thick blazes stood at the barbed-wire fence, somnolent in the September heat. Their tails swished languidly at the flies on their backs. As Jack drove past, grasshoppers flew up from the wild blackberry bushes covering the barbed-wire fences on either side of the road.

The road dead-ended into the front yard of a plain, well-kept pier-and-beam house with a wide front porch. Behind the house, an old Ford tractor was parked in a wooden barn, weathered gray from years of exposure. If it weren't for the late-model dually pickup in the front yard, door open and steadily dinging in protest, Jack would have thought he had stepped back in time.

Jack unsnapped his holster and got out of his car. There was no movement anywhere. Dense woods closed in on the house from three sides.

"Hello?"

No answer. A long, large cooler and an overstuffed duffel bag were in the bed of the truck. Jack moved to the driver's side door, looked in the cab. It was clean and empty. He pulled the key out of the ignition to silence the incessant dinging. The quiet that greeted him was unsettling, unnatural. With relief, he heard one of the horses in the pasture behind him snort.

"What can I do for you, son?"

A large man wearing a low profile gray felt Stetson walked out of the front door loosely holding a shotgun in his right hand. Jack recognized him instantly.

"Buck Pollard?" he said with as much friendliness as possible.

"Yes."

"I'm Jack McBride."

"I know who you are." Pollard locked his front door. He stopped at the top of the porch steps and surveyed Jack.

"I thought I'd come introduce myself since we haven't had the opportunity to meet yet. Though—" Jack paused, as if searching his memory. "—weren't you at the Chevron the other day? No. That couldn't have been you. You would have said something, right? Introduced yourself."

"Thought you had enough on your plate."

"Thoughtful of you."

The grasshoppers and cicadas were in a contest to see who could fill the silence with the most noise. Jack made a production of putting his hands in his pockets to show Pollard he wasn't threatened by him.

"Heard you got the tarnation beat out of you," Pollard finally said.

"I did."

"Shouldn'ta taken him by yourself."

"Well, we're a little short-staffed at the moment."

"So I hear."

Jack jerked his head to the truck. "Going somewhere?"

"Fishing."

"Where?"

"The Gulf."

"What do you fish for?"

"Whatever's bitin'. You fish?"

"All the time."

"What for?"

"Information." Jack waited a beat before continuing. He hoped he was hiding his chagrin at his stupid, smart-ass answer as well as he meant to. "Thought you might be able to fill me in on the town, the officers, people."

"Miner can do that."

"Sure, but who's going to fill me in on Miner?"

"I thought you were some fancy profiler."

"Well, that's a pretty blanket term. I'm not technically a profiler. Those agents analyze crime scenes and work up a profile of who might do it. You know, serial killers are white men, twenty-five to forty. Bunch of generalities anyone who watches *Law and Order* knows."

"Bunch of bullshit."

"I wouldn't call it that exactly."

"You don't need me to explain Miner to you."

"No. I think I understand him pretty well."

Pollard stayed on his porch, gun in his hand. He turned his head and spit a long, brown stream of tobacco juice over the porch rail.

"What do you need the shotgun for?"

"Protection."

"From the fish?" Buck remained silent. Jack continued. "Did you know Gilberto and Rosa Ramos?"

"Nope."

"I thought not. You weren't much for arresting *anyone*, why mess with law-abiding illegals?"

"What do you mean by that?"

Jack shrugged. "Stillwater's crime rate is freakishly low, almost as if crimes were waved away, ignored."

"Why would I do that?"

"I know how the good ol' boy network works."

"Do you?" Disdain dripped from both words, as if there were no way a city boy like Jack understood small towns and the people in them.

"Maybe some father asks you to turn a blind eye to their kid's crimes in exchange for future favors. Maybe you catch someone dealing drugs and they offer to cut you in on the action for protection. Blind eyes being turned on wife beating, sexual assault, and child molestation. Favors could be material, could be something else. A cop who's been on the job for years could have a lot of dirt on a lot of people. Powerful stuff."

"Do I look like I'm on the take?" Pollard gestured to his house and barn.

Actually, no. Everything was well kept but average. Nothing flashy, save the truck, and Jack had seen enough duallies to know that being truck poor was almost a prerequisite for the men in Stillwater.

"No. You hide it well."

"Good luck proving anything."

"It just takes one person coming forward. Or one secret being unearthed."

Pollard stared hard at Jack before his face broke into a large grin. "You don't know shit. You just have people whispering in your ear about me, planting bugs."

"Who would do that?"

"Ann Newberry and Jane Maxwell."

"*Why* would they do that?"

"Hell if I know. Women like that hate men on principle because they think we have it easier than they do. Think on it. Has anyone else in this town had a bad word to say about me?"

Jack thought back to the residents he had met. They mostly avoided talk of Pollard but, when they did, they always shared carefully worded generalities about his dedication to his job, all of his good works, and everything he'd done for Stillwater.

"I didn't think so," Pollard said. "Newberry and I didn't get along, but she ain't got it in for me like Jane Maxwell does. That woman can hold a grudge."

"What's her grudge with you?"

"That's no business of yours."

"You brought it up. I thought you might want me to investigate something."

"I think you've got enough on your plate. Who knows, there might be a crime wave coming soon. If I were you, I'd start rounding up the Mexicans."

"Why?"

"Those two murdered wetbacks? Probably drug-related."

"Why do you say that?"

"Mexicans and drugs go hand in hand."

"We didn't find any drugs."

"Probably the person who found them took them. Sold them already, I'm sure."

"How did you know it was a double murder? I just got confirmation of that a couple of hours ago."

Pollard laughed. "People still tell me things."

"I'm sure they do. Then I suppose you heard about the skeleton we found on the Dodsworths' land."

"I heard something about it. Any idea how long it'd been there?"

"Not yet. It'll take a while to get a specific date. I'm just happy it wasn't a killing field."

Buck scoffed. "Got any leads?"

"Early days yet. Did you know the Dodsworths?"

"I know everyone in Stillwater."

"Then I came to the right place."

"I don't know what I can tell you that will help. George Dodsworth died in '84. Elizabeth is in Pembroke Arms. Can't remember her name, from what I hear."

"And Barbara?"

"Owns a cleaning business. Did time in Gatesville for check fraud. Clean since."

"Were you friends with the Dodsworths?"

"Friends?" Pollard pushed his Stetson up and scratched his head. "No."

"If you were running this case, what would be your theory?"

"Theory?" He settled his hat back in place.

"Yeah. I have one. Miner has one. I'm curious what yours is."

"Probably just someone passing through town who got caught in a bad situation."

"Accidental death?"

"Uh-huh." This stream of tobacco didn't have near the arc or distance. It landed with a splat on the porch rail. Pollard wiped spittle from his lips.

"And the killer planted her in some random, remote woods."

"Most like."

"So, you think the killer was a local."

"I didn't say that."

"Didn't you?"

"Just as like, *more* like, someone transported the body from far off. Maybe another state."

"Yeah. We're checking missing persons for the four-state area."

"Four?"

"Mississippi, too. Was there any way to access that land back in the late '50s? Besides driving right by the Dodsworths' house?"

"I don't remember. There might have been logging roads coming from the land behind."

"Logging? I thought they didn't log the area until the '80s."

"Been loggin' off and on since Stillwater was founded."

Jack looked around. "Haven't logged here, I see. Interesting Elizabeth Dodsworth didn't want them to log her land back in the '80s. Almost like she was hiding something. Wasn't much to find, anyway."

"No weapon?"

Jack shook his head. "Would've been nice, huh? She didn't have any ID on her either. Damn the luck."

"What's your theory?" Pollard said.

"Mine? Well, being an outsider, I don't have a preconceived idea of people around here. The logical explanation is George Dodsworth killed her and buried her in the woods. Maybe she was a hitchhiker, he picked her up, fucked her, then murdered her. Buried her before his wife got home."

"George wasn't the type."

"Maybe Elizabeth caught them. Killed the woman, George buried her to protect his wife."

"I can see George protecting her, but I can't see Elizabeth having the strength to stab someone."

Jack pursed his lips and nodded. "Amazing the things people do when provoked. In the heat of passion."

"True."

"Maybe George found Elizabeth and this vagrant *in flagrante*, didn't realize his wife preferred women. Went into a rage."

"Have you noticed all of your scenarios involve sex?" Pollard sneered.

"Sex is a powerful motivator. Like jealousy, anger, betrayal. All powerful motives."

"Well, you would know."

"Excuse me?"

"Jealousy, anger, betrayal as motives for murder." Pollard spit another stream of tobacco juice on the ground. "They ever find your wife, by the way?" His face was blank but his eyes were hard, calculating. "Or did they just drop the case because your momma told them to?"

There was a roaring in Jack's ears. When he spoke, it sounded like a stranger talking. "There was no investigation."

"Not what I heard."

"If you know all about it, why are you asking me?"

"Thought I'd see how honest you were."

"I've got nothing to hide."

Pollard laughed. "Everyone's hiding something. Well," the word came out like he was stretching after a long nap. "As much as I would like to sit here and help you solve your cases, I have to get on the road."

Jack grabbed Pollard's arm as he walked by. Pollard stopped, stared at Jack's hand, then moved his eyes to Jack's face. A dollop of tobacco juice hung on the bottom edge of Pollard's mustache. Pollard's arm was surprisingly hard, like the arm of a man thirty years younger.

"I don't know what you think you know, old man," Jack said between gritted teeth.

"I'll tell you what I think: I think only an idiot would grab a man who's carrying a loaded shotgun."

"I'm not afraid of you."

"You should be."

Pollard jerked his arm from Jack's grasp, walked to his truck, put the shotgun in the rack. It took all of Jack's willpower not to throw Pollard on the ground and beat the shit out of him. Pollard was in the driver's seat and was shutting the door when Jack spoke.

"Thanks for talking to me. Very informative. Learned a lot."

Jack could see Pollard's eyes calculating, wondering what Jack meant, if he was bluffing. He turned on his truck and shut the door.

Jack stood in the driveway and watched Pollard drive off.

Very informative, indeed.

V

"Does your dad ever feed you?"

Ethan, Olivia, Mitra, and Troy were sitting together near the cafeteria door. Spread before Mitra and Olivia were homemade lunches; sandwiches, vegetables, hummus, fruit, and chips. Two lunch trays of half-eaten food were in front of Troy and Ethan. Olivia watched Ethan eat with a disgusted look on her face.

Ethan wiped the dribble of gravy from his chin and swallowed. "Yes, but not homemade chicken fried steak."

"I don't know how y'all can eat that."

"Because it's good?" Troy said around a mouthful of mashed potatoes.

"Why don't you ever buy your lunch, Olivia?" Ethan asked.

"I know what they do to make the food taste so good."

"What?" Ethan asked.

"Bacon grease," she stated. She pulled the turkey off her sandwich.

"What's wrong with bacon grease?" Ethan asked.

"Besides being fattening?" Mitra asked.

"Olivia is a borderline vegetarian. She doesn't have the guts to go full bore, though. Our dad would kill her," Troy said.

"He would not."

"He wouldn't be happy."

"Why would he care?" Ethan asked.

"His dad was a cattle farmer. He doesn't trust anyone that doesn't eat meat."

"So, it's not the grease you have a problem with," Ethan said to Olivia, "it's the bacon."

"Oh, no. I love bacon."

Ethan looked between his three friends, completely puzzled. Troy shrugged his shoulders as if to say, "She's a girl, what do you expect?"

"Well, I don't care what they do to it. I didn't know cafeteria food could taste this good," Ethan said. "Every school I've been to, the food has tasted like poo."

Ethan didn't want to say it, but compared to this food, his mother's cooking was bad. Since the only meal his dad could make was breakfast, there was no comparison necessary.

"So, Mitra and I are going to study today after school. You two should probably join us," Olivia said.

"What for?" Troy asked.

"Um, for our first big test on Friday?"

Ethan paused. "Why would we start studying Monday for a test on Friday?"

"Yeah, that's overkill even for you, Olivia," Troy said.

"We thought studying a little each day would be better than cramming on Thursday night," Mitra said.

"I would, but I can't. I'm grounded, remember." Ethan cut his eyes at Troy, who looked down at his plate.

"Are you two still mad at each other?" Olivia asked.

"About what?" Mitra asked.

"Nothing," Troy and Ethan said in unison.

Mitra looked embarrassed and hurt, aware she was being left out of a secret. Ethan knew how that felt from firsthand experience. Hadn't his dad been keeping secrets from him for a year? He would rather get in trouble with his dad for telling Mitra than see her look so sad. How much more trouble could he get in, anyway?

Ethan leaned across the table. "I texted Troy a picture I shouldn't have. His mom found it and told my dad."

Mitra turned as red as the square of jello on Ethan's tray. "Oh."

"Not *that* kind of picture, Mitra," Olivia quickly said.

It took a moment or two for Ethan to realize what Olivia meant. When he did, his face turned as red as Mitra's. "God, no." He leaned forward a little more. Mitra, Troy, and Olivia all leaned toward him. "It was of the skeleton," Ethan whispered.

Mitra's eyes widened. "You didn't."

"Yeah. My dad was *not* happy."

"It was a really cool picture," Troy said.

Olivia agreed.

"Can I see it?" Mitra asked.

"Dad deleted it from my phone."

"I deleted it, too."

Mitra was dejected. Ethan said, "If I had it, I would let you see it."

She nodded and smiled. "It would probably give me nightmares anyway. Did you go around town Saturday?" Mitra asked.

"Yeah." Something kept Ethan from telling his friends about his run-in with Freeman. "Did y'all realize there are no sidewalks in Stillwater?"

"I've never thought about it," Olivia said. Her brows furrowed in concentration.

"I've noticed," Mitra said. Ethan wondered if she'd had the same problem as he had, but with residents calling the police about a strange Middle Eastern girl walking the streets.

"I guess people just don't walk many places," Troy said.

Olivia's face cleared and she took on a look of determination. "So, about studying," Olivia said. Ethan learned early on that Olivia didn't give up easily. "I'm sure your dad would make an exception for studying."

"Oh, I don't know." He didn't particularly *want* his dad to make an exception for studying.

"I'll go see my Mom at work and just happen to run into your Dad. Parents love study groups. You'll be free in no time."

"I'd hardly call study group *freedom*," Ethan murmured.

"Olivia can be convincing," Troy said.

Olivia motioned to her brother with a smile. "See? Troy agrees."

"You're going to search out my dad and ask him if I can do a study group? I don't think so."

"Why not?"

His dream of Olivia came rushing back to him in great detail. Ethan felt his face burning. "Um, because he will never let me hear the end of it."

"We're just friends."

"I know that, but he doesn't. Just don't ambush him, okay? I'll ask."

"Are y'all going to the Book Bank tonight?" Mitra asked.

Olivia's eyes lit up. "Yes! Perfect. I'll ask him then. Completely natural, because y'all will be with me when I do."

"The Book Bank?" Ethan asked.

"Ellie's launch party," Troy said.

"Oh," Ethan replied. The woman from the square, the one his dad seemed so interested in. Ethan started to think he should delete those pictures.

"Ellie's one of my mom's best friends," Troy said.

"We've known her all our lives. We used to call her Aunt Ellie until she said it made her feel old," Olivia said.

"How old is she?"

"My mom's age," Olivia said. "She is totally awesome."

"She is very nice," Mitra said.

"Are you going tonight?" Olivia asked.

"With my parents," Mitra replied.

"Dad hasn't said anything about it. We probably aren't invited."

"Oh, you're invited," Olivia said. "My mom mentioned it. You'll be there."

Ethan's embarrassment about his dream had long since vanished, replaced by the irritation he felt whenever Olivia put on her know-it-all, hyper-confident attitude. Now he didn't want to go to whatever this party was just to prove her wrong.

"I can't believe Stillwater is going to have a bookstore," Mitra said. She swirled a carrot in her hummus and took a bite.

"And a coffee shop," Olivia said.

"I won't be hanging out there. I don't like books or coffee," Ethan said, standing. "Come on, pile it on."

"Ease up, Grumpy Cat," Olivia said.

Olivia and Mitra put their trash on Ethan's tray, and he picked up Troy's to take everything to the trash.

"Isn't this sweet?"

A muscular boy with the hint of a mustache on his upper lip stood at the end of the table, blocking Ethan's way.

"I don't know, Kevin. Dumping my lunch tray has never been the highlight of my day, but I'm new to Stillwater. Maybe it is for the natives," Ethan replied.

Kevin smirked. "The natives. Funny, city boy."

"And I wasn't even trying," Ethan said, wondering what was so funny about his comment. He was trying to be insulting.

"Ready for the game this week, Kevin?" Troy asked.

Kevin Jackson stood a little straighter, as he always did when talking about football. "We're always ready to kick some ass." He slammed his fist into his palm for emphasis. Ethan tried to stifle a laugh.

"What's so funny, city boy?"

Ethan shrugged. "Can a snipe kick anyone's ass? I mean, do they even exist? What exactly is a snipe? Ever seen one? Besides on your helmet?"

Kevin stepped closer to Ethan and glared down at him. "Are you try-ing to piss me off?"

Troy stood. "No, Kevin. He's just trying to learn as much about his new school as he can."

"Ma—" Ethan started.

"Shut up, Ethan," Olivia interjected. He shot her an annoyed look.

"Yeah," Kevin said. "Shut up, *Ethan*. What kind of pussy name is that?"

Ethan put the trays down but Troy moved in front of Ethan and shook his head. Kevin smirked, before turning his attention to Olivia. "You're the one I wanted to talk to."

"Really?" she asked. Her neck turned all splotchy.

"Yeah. Want to walk to the DQ with me after school today?"

"Um," she stammered, the blush completely overtaking her face.

"She can't," Ethan interrupted. "We've got study group."

The entire table went silent. Mitra suppressed a smile. Troy was completely baffled. Olivia's splotches evened out into a bright red. Ethan could almost see the waves of anger pulsing off her.

"That's tomorrow," Olivia said, fixing her blazing eyes on Ethan, daring him to contradict her. Ethan tried to hide his mortification at saying anything and he returned her angry stare.

Olivia turned to Kevin and smiled. "I'll meet you out front after school."

"Great," Kevin said. "See ya later."

"See ya," she said.

Ethan picked up the trays. "Wow," Ethan said. "I never thought you'd go out with a bully like Kevin Jackson." He brushed past her.

She turned on him and hissed, "He's not a bully!"

Ethan dumped the trash and put the trays in the window for the dishwasher. He faced Olivia, who had followed him. "Uh, yeah. He is," Ethan said. "Or is calling people a pussy the way you bumpkins welcome people to Stillwater?" He walked back to the table, Olivia on his heels.

"You've been here a few days and you think you know everything about everyone," she said. "I'm beginning to think Kevin's right about you."

"I was obviously wrong about you. I wouldn't think you would defend a bully."

Olivia's eyes narrowed and she turned and stalked off.

Ethan, Troy, and Mitra watched Olivia go. "Well, Mitra. Hope you didn't have your heart set on studying. You just got stood up," Ethan said.

Mitra shrugged. "Tomorrow is fine."

"I can't believe Olivia would defend him like that," Ethan said to Troy, trying to ignore the stone of jealousy lodged in his stomach.

Troy shrugged. "She's had a crush on Kevin for years. You kinda ruined the moment."

"Me? He's a bully and you know it! Isn't he, Mitra?"

She shrugged and picked up her bento box. "See you in class," she said and left.

"Thing is, Kevin's not a bully, Ethan," Troy said. "He really hates you for some reason but overall he's a really good guy. Totally unlike his family."

"He just called me a pussy and he cornered me in the locker room my first day."

"You were being rude to him."

"So that justifies it?"

Troy shrugged. "No, but you being a smart-ass might explain it. I can't explain the locker room. I didn't see it."

That was the problem: no one saw it.

With no athletic clothes (of course his dad forgot) and no desire to play football, Coach Taylor had put Ethan in charge of filling water bottles for the "real" athletes. He had been alone in the locker room doing just that when he heard the clicking of cleats on the concrete floor and Kevin Jackson came around the corner, unzipping his football pants. He stopped when he saw Ethan. He walked to the urinal without a word. Ethan was fitting the tops on the water bottles when Kevin walked up behind him and stared at him in the mirror. For a moment, Ethan thought he was going to introduce himself, then Kevin straightened his shoulders and his nervousness changed to bravado.

"I wouldn't bother making too many friends. Your dad will be out of a job by the end of the month. My uncle will see to it."

"Good. The quicker I get out of this shithole of a town, the better."

Kevin grabbed Ethan's shoulder and turned him around. He was at least six inches taller and fifty pounds heavier. Ethan saw a wispy mustache on Kevin's upper lip. "Watch it, city boy."

"Great comeback, cracker."

Ethan heard the door to the locker room open. One of the coaches yelled in for Kevin. He had flipped the water bottles onto the ground and stalked out.

"You saying I made it up?" Ethan said to Troy now.

"No. But just because someone doesn't like you doesn't mean they're a bully."

Ethan wanted to argue but kept his mouth shut. He didn't want to lose his only friend after barely a week in town. They wove through the crowd of students on the way to their lockers. Olivia glared at Ethan and shouldered past them without a word. Troy watched her stomp into her class.

"It is weird, though," Troy admitted.

"What?" Ethan took his social studies book from his locker.

"Why he asked her out."

"What's weird about that?"

"He's known for years that Olivia liked him. Why did he decide to ask her out now?"

"Maybe he realized how—" Ethan stopped himself from saying something he would regret. "—much he liked her," he finished instead.

"Or maybe he's trying to make you jealous?"

"Me?" Ethan said, his voice an octave too high. "Why would that make me jealous?"

Troy rolled his eyes. "I'm not that stupid. See you in class."

Mitra walked up, holding her books close to her chest. She watched Troy walk away, disappointment written all over her face. She looked at Ethan and smiled. "Ready?" she asked.

"You think Kevin's a bully, too, don't you?"

She sighed. "I'm not the best person to ask."

"Why?"

"At one point or another, everyone has bullied me."

Ethan felt his stomach tighten. He asked the question, even though he didn't want to know the answer. "Even Troy and Olivia?"

She shrugged. "We're going to be late for class." She started walking. Ethan followed.

"How long have you lived in Stillwater?" Ethan asked.

"Ten years."

"Where are you from?"

"I was born in Houston. My parents left Iran when the Shah left. They were kids."

"Why Stillwater?"

"My dad bought an oil well servicing company here. He wanted my brother and me to grow up in a small town."

Olivia glanced up when they entered the classroom and gave Ethan a withering glare. She was making a big production of slamming books and jerking the zipper of her backpack. Damn, she had a temper. Just like Ethan's dad.

He knew Troy was right: Kevin had asked Olivia out to piss Ethan off and make him jealous. Whether Kevin was quick enough to see that Ethan liked Olivia or just assumed it because he spent so much time with her, Ethan wasn't sure. Either way, Ethan knew he needed to distance himself from her, not only because he didn't want everyone to figure out he was having wet dreams about her, but also because he didn't want Kevin Freaking Jackson to date Olivia just to spite him.

He got a funny, fluttery feeling in his stomach at that idea. It quickly changed to nausea when he thought of what the innocent-sounding walk to DQ actually meant. He'd heard through snatches of conversation that these "walks" were merely excuses to detour through an abandoned, over-grown lot and make out. The idea that this was Kevin's ultimate inten-tion—and why wouldn't it be?—made Ethan want to puke. And that Olivia, being a local and knowing much better than Ethan what a walk to DQ meant, would still choose to go with that Neanderthal made him furious.

VI

With a small pocketknife that once belonged to his dad, Jack cut the yellow crime-scene tape sealing the front door of the Ramoses' trailer. He put on gloves and went inside. He closed the door and surveyed the room.

The spicy aroma so prominent the day of the murders had dissipated, replaced with the musty smell of disuse. A thin veneer of dust covered the counters and tabletops, had settled into the fabric of the sofa and chair, and lay lightly on the carpet worn shiny and flat from years of use.

Jack dropped his duffel bag on the floor and, starting on the left, methodically began his search. Behind and underneath the sofa. Below the cushions. With a grimace, he shoved his hand between the frame of the sofa where the back met the seat and scooped out years worth of loose change, used condoms, chip bags, paper clips, pen caps, dried-out pens, plastic spoons, a butter knife, a plastic ring, a yo-yo, an empty snuff can, a tampon (unused, thank God) and a pair of panties too large to be Rosa Ramos's. He repeated the search with the chair, finding much of the same. He ran his hands under the coffee table and lifted it. Nothing but green, blue, and red gum and dried boogers.

He opened every drawer, cabinet, and appliance in the kitchen, came up with nothing interesting or out of place, and moved down the hall and into the bathroom. Despite being abandoned for a week, it smelled fresh and looked clean. A medicine cabinet full of over-the-counter drugs, condoms, tampons, a rubber bulb parents use to clear the mucus from babies' noses, a tiny set of fingernail clippers next to a larger pair for adults, a black comb with broken teeth, a can of Axe, and a small bottle of Jennifer Lopez perfume. A round hairbrush matted with black hair lay on the clean sink next to a small jelly jar holding two toothbrushes and a twisted tube of toothpaste. The toilet was clean, inside and out, but no amount of scrubbing could get rid of the years of neglect the toilet suffered before being saved by Rosa Ramos's good housekeeping. Jack lifted the lid off the back of the toilet. Nothing except a small dispenser of bleach that would release when flushed. The shower, hard-water stains notwithstanding, was spotless as well.

Jack stood in the doorway to the bedroom for a long time. It was a pocket door, necessary because having a door that would swing open would drastically reduce the floor space in the room. When he tried to close the door, it jumped off the runner and jammed into the wall. It took Jack five minutes to get the door back on track. Obviously, it wasn't closed when the killer arrived. Jack doubted Gilberto and Rosa used it at all.

The bed was next to the door of the small room. They would have seen their killer immediately, even if they had been making love, which they clearly had been. Jack turned and stood in the hallway next to the door, his back to the wall. He took his gun out and held it next to his ear. He pivoted into the doorway and pretended to shoot Gilberto, then Rosa. A few seconds was all it would have taken for a man who knew how to handle a gun. They never knew what hit them. He put his gun back in his holster.

Jack searched through the inside of every drawer, pulled them out, felt underneath, and looked inside the dresser frame. He moved it away from the wall and looked behind. He got down on his hands and knees, shined his MagLite under the dresser, then turned it under the bed. He pulled the long, thin plastic bins from beneath the bed and searched them. Nothing. Same with the closet. Nothing. He tapped his flashlight on his leg and took one last look around.

For someone who liked to hide things, according to her "brother," there was nothing interesting to be found. Were Rosa and Gilberto really this boring? Or had someone cleaned up before the police arrived? The killer? Or Diego Vasquez?

Jack moved to the nursery. Where all the other furniture in the house was obviously secondhand, the nursery furniture was new. Brand new. Underneath the crib was a plastic bag full of instructions and warranties and a Wal-Mart receipt dated August 29. Three weeks ago, Rosa and Gilberto bought $750 worth of baby furniture, toys, and clothes—in cash. Jack pulled a small baggie from his pocket, placed the receipt inside.

Besides a few unpaid bills in a kitchen drawer, Jack hadn't found evidence of a bank account or personal paperwork. He didn't expect to. Rosa and Gilberto worked in cash jobs, though what either of them could have done to earn so much cash he could only guess.

The baby's room was mostly empty since clothes, diapers, toys, and supplies had been given to the foster family. It turned out Miner had been right about the woman he gave the baby to; she was well known to the county child protective services and had taken in Mexican babies for them before.

Jack dumped the contents of the duffel bag on the kitchen table, tossed the empty bag aside, and sat down. He took all the items from the evidence bags, placed them in the middle of the table, and stared at the meager possessions the crime-scene tech had found in the bedroom the morning of the murders. The pay-as-you-go phones sat atop the print-outs of their activity over the last month. Gilberto called and texted very few people and had never set up his voice mail. Rosa made more calls, recently mostly to doctors and numbers in Mexico that Jack assumed were family members and were being traced. Her voice mail had been empty. Jack picked up Gilberto's wallet. The edges of the black leather were worn from use and the shape of the wallet indicated it was normally much fuller than Jack found it. The contents were uninteresting; driver's license, a Wal-Mart portrait of Rosa and the baby, twenty-three dollars, and a Chevron receipt for chips, Mountain Dew, and a candy bar.

Gilberto might have been the dullest murder victim Jack had ever come across. His investigation hadn't found one motive for anyone, even Rosa, to kill Gilberto. He was a good guy, hard worker, loving husband and father. He drank a lot on the weekends, but what hardworking man didn't? His drinking never led to trouble with the police; there was no record of Stillwater police ever having contact with Gilberto, or Rosa for that matter. Try as he might, Jack could not profile Gilberto. He left very little impression on the home he lived in and supported. The people who knew him spoke of him in banal generalities, as if struggling to pinpoint why they liked him and realizing maybe they didn't after all.

Jack had little doubt that Rosa had ruled the roost. The trailer spoke of a proud woman making the best of what she had. Everything was clean (the trash in the frame of the furniture notwithstanding; even the best housekeepers missed that) and obsessively organized. She was practical (using space under the bed for storage in a tiny room), conscientious (baby-proofing the house months before necessary), and frugal (food was off-brand, bought on sale and in bulk). Her one weakness, though, was family, as evidenced by using their recent cash windfall for the baby and her willingness to let her "brother" sleep on their couch and start a new life in Stillwater.

Or did she have no choice but to let Diego stay with her? Jack still remembered little from Diego's attack, but the feeling that Diego was dangerous and he was lucky to be alive was constant. Unlike questions about Gilberto and Rosa, which were answered easily, everyone was reticent about Diego. When they said they didn't know him, they were relieved.

Jack dumped Rosa's purse on the table. Her wallet was a coin purse containing her driver's license, green card (obviously fake), $3.23 in change and $289 in cash. Gum, Altoids, dental floss, two tampons, a panty liner, mascara, a half-used tube of Carmex, grocery receipts (paid in cash), the electric bill and gas bill clipped together, ponytail holders, a hair brush, a small, partially burned vanilla scented jar candle, a travel-sized package of tissues, hand lotion, and stick deodorant. Jack sighed. Nothing.

He stared at the shit spread before him. It looked more like a medicine cabinet than a purse. He picked up the scratched and scarred wintergreen Altoids tin. He opened it and wrinkled his nose as the faint scent of wintergreen wafted up to him. Inside was a necklace with a Saint Peter medal, a small key that would fit a luggage lock, and a business card with MARTES, 8:30, 24 RIVER ROAD written on the back. Jack turned the card over. SPIC AND SPAN CLEANING, BARBARA DODSWORTH, OWNER, he read. Jack flipped the card back over and stared at the address. Jack tapped the card on the table. "Huh."

He put the card down, picked up the candle, removed the lid and sniffed it. What were the chances of his murder victim being connected to his fifty-year-old murder?

He put the candle down, opened the Carmex, and smelled it. There was no such thing as coincidence, right?

He wrinkled his nose at the lotion; he hated the smell of lavender. Of course, there had to be a lot of coincidence in a town the size of Stillwater. Everyone was connected to everyone else in some way. Except him. He was well and truly an outsider.

He picked up the deodorant and pulled off the cap. He stared down into the base of it. Instead of a white slab of chalky deodorant, a piece of paper, folded tightly into a square, was wedged into the empty base. Jack removed the paper and carefully unfolded it. An old family portrait was copied crookedly on the 8x11 paper. Four unsmiling children stood around the stoic mother and father, who sat, not touching, on a settee. A plump baby in a christening gown sat on the mother's lap, her head turned toward the girl standing to her mother's left, smiling. The large, raised birthmark on the baby's cheek would have drawn the eye of the beholder, if not for the swastika armband and lightning-bolt insignia on the dour officer's uniform.

VII

Ellie had lied to Jack when she said owning a bookstore was a childhood dream. Her childhood dream had been to live inside books, to escape into worlds full of color, life, adventure and, especially, love. She woke each morning and for a few moments kept her eyes closed, hoping against hope she would open them and see the attic of the March sisters, the dormers of Green Gables, or the rough-hewn boards of Little House on the Prairie. Instead she was always greeted with a water stain shaped like the state of Maryland on her ceiling, a drunken father (when he was there at all), and an empty refrigerator.

Living inside books was a nice idea, but it didn't accomplish anything or change reality, and the reality was Ellie had a father who resented her for myriad reasons, all of which were out of Ellie's control: she wasn't a boy, and all of the property and wealth Jacob Yourke married her mother for was bequeathed to Ellie in an airtight trust. Which meant Jacob Yourke the Fourth, the direct descendant of Jacob Yourke the First, the founder of Stillwater, was dependent on his young daughter for money. Unless he wanted to get a job, which he didn't. Of course, Ellie would have given it all to her father for one kind word or even a sincere lie. However, she didn't gain control of the money until she was twenty-five. Until then, it was under the strict control of Jane Maxwell, who hated Jacob Yourke more than he hated his daughter. Which is why Gabrielle Robichaux Yourke had made Jane the executor of her will instead of her husband. She knew Jane would protect Ellie's interests. One year ago today, Big Jake Yourke had died, nursing his resentment against Ellie and Jane and plotting new ways to wrest control of his money from his daughter to his dying breath.

Ellie paused, mascara wand in her hand. It was only natural, she supposed, to be thinking of her dead father on the night she was finally putting his ghost to rest. Jacob Yourke hated books, hated anything that might make Ellie happy. Opening a bookstore on the anniversary of his death was the biggest "fuck you" she could think of. She knew its impact would have been greater if he could have seen all of the money—*his money*—she was sinking into a bookstore in a dying town full of magazine-reading rednecks during the worst economic downturn since the Depression. But, when it came to her father, her resentment and anger didn't supersede her fear of town scrutiny. There had even been a minuscule part of her that hadn't wanted him to die completely broken. As such, she played the part of dutiful daughter to the bitter end. Only two people knew the true provenance of the Book Bank; Jane Maxwell, the woman who taught her to be an implacable businesswoman, and Shirley Underwood, the woman who taught her compassion.

The alarm on her phone went off. Her twenty minutes were up. She applied a small amount of lip gloss, rubbed her lips together, and pursed them at her reflection. "That's as good as it's going to get," she said. She flipped the light off and went downstairs.

Shirley bustled around, putting the final touches on the buffet table. Her husband, Bob, organized canned drinks, water bottles, and small cups around the square bin of ice. Paige Grant stood on a step stool behind the coffee bar, writing the coffee menu on a chalkboard with much better lettering than Ellie had managed earlier in the day. A couple of Mexican women, hired for the night, walked around the store, dusting the already clean displays, killing time before their real duties began.

"Looks great, Shirley," Ellie said.

"Thanks, darlin'," she replied. She moved the plates a fraction and straightened. Then she opened her arms and walked toward Ellie. "I'm so proud of you." Ellie fell easily into the arms of the woman who had been her surrogate parent for nearly thirty years. Bob walked up and patted Ellie on the back, a significant show of affection for him.

"We both are," he said.

Ellie pushed away from Shirley but was not released from Shirley's firm grip. "I haven't done anything yet."

Shirley ran her hand fondly down Ellie's hair. "We all know that's a lie. But we also know you are self-deprecating to a fault."

"That's what Shirley's here for. To brag about you," Bob said.

Shirley looked over Ellie's shoulder, toward the door. "Speaking of . . ."

Ellie turned and saw Jack McBride walk in the door with Ethan. Ellie's stomach lurched. She'd been planning how to avoid him since Susan confirmed he was coming. How was she going to be able to avoid him if he showed up early? Of course, he walked right up to her, smiling that ridiculous, toothpaste-commercial smile.

"Glad you could make it."

"Thanks for inviting us."

"Thanks for coming. Hi, Ethan."

"Hi." His eyes barely met hers before dropping.

"Troy and Olivia are going to be here soon. Until then, help yourself to the food and drinks." She waved to the table at the back of the store. "There are some books on photography in the nonfiction section, if you're interested."

"Thanks," he mumbled.

"Ethan!" Paige Grant called to him from behind the counter. "Come over here and let me experiment on you!"

Ethan blushed and looked to his dad. "Decaf," Jack warned.

Ellie watched Ethan walk away. When she turned her attention back to Jack, he had an expectant look on his face. He opened his mouth to speak, but Ellie got there first.

Ellie stood back. "You remember Shirley Underwood," she said.

Jack arranged his face in a pleasant expression. "Of course," he said. "Good to see you again."

Before Shirley could respond, Ellie continued. "This is her husband, Bob. His law office is right across from City Hall."

Bob was a large man with a booming voice and jocular personality. He pumped Jack's hand. "Nice to meet you. I've heard a lot about you."

Jack smiled and nodded.

"You haven't called me yet," Shirley said.

"Was I supposed to?"

"As soon as you needed something," she said.

"I guess he hasn't needed anything, Shirley," Bob said.

"Don't be foolish. Of course he has. Look at that face! He's just too embarrassed to ask."

"There is one thing I need."

"Name it."

"I need to steal Ellie for just a minute." Without waiting for permission, he took Ellie by the elbow and steered her to the back of the store.

"Take her for as long as you like," Shirley cooed.

Ellie didn't like the knowing tone of voice Shirley used, nor did she like being given and taken like she was someone's possession. She pulled her elbow from Jack's grasp.

So far, the night was a disaster. Her one objective was to stay away from Jack McBride and here it was, 6:58 p.m., and he had gotten her alone. She stopped next to the buffet table, determined to not go into the back and be completely alone with him.

"So, about earlier."

Ellie closed her eyes and shook her head. "Look, let's just forget about the whole thing. Pretend it never happened."

"But . . ."

"I jumped to the wrong conclusion and now I'm mortified. Just," she sighed, met his eyes. "I really wish you hadn't come."

Jack pressed his lips together. He jingled the keys in his pockets. "What wrong conclusion?"

"That you were—" She stopped. *Interested in me. Flirting with me.* Of course she had the wrong idea, but she didn't want to degrade herself by admitting it. Why would he ask her to? Was he that cruel? "God, are you really going to make me say it?"

"I'm pretty sure you didn't get the wrong idea."

"Ellie-Bellie!"

Jack and Ellie turned in unison. Kelly Kendrick, in skin-tight jeans and four-inch stilettos, catwalked toward them, arms outstretched. She hugged Ellie, whose astonishment was due in equal parts to Jack's comment and Kelly's horrible, no good, very bad timing.

"Surely you're not already at the food, are you?" Kelly said, playfully.

Ellie tensed. "Of course not. I was showing Jack around. My guests are arriving. Why don't you finish the tour for me?" She walked off, barely registering Kelly's shocked "Yeah, sure" reply.

On her way to the door, she said hello to Seth, Kelly's son, and directed him to Ethan and Paige with instructions to make the younger boy feel welcome. The next hour flew by, with Ellie greeting people as they arrived, giving brief tours for those who couldn't figure out the layout of a one-room bookstore/coffee shop, hopping behind the counter to serve pastries and make lattes when Paige got behind, rushing around and picking up trash here and there, ringing up book sales, ordering books not in stock, taking suggestions, talking to everyone there, smiling, laughing, and still having a difficult time keeping her mind off Jack McBride. She checked on Ethan, Troy, and Olivia, who had parked themselves in the kids', section. As far as Ellie could tell, they didn't talk at all, only played on their phones. Kids. Jack moved from group to group, laughing and talking and always keeping one eye—the bruised one, of course—turned in her direction.

Kelly walked up and placed dirty cups on the coffee bar. Ellie put them in the bus tub under the back counter without a word. "What the hell was that earlier?"

"Paige, will you go check on the food table?" Ellie asked.

"Sure." Paige squeezed bleached water out of a dishtowel and left.

"So?" Kelly said.

"Can we do this later?"

"No. You should have seen his face when you stalked off. I thought the man was going to cry. Or throw up. I couldn't decide which. Maybe both."

"Whatever. You suck at reading people. Always have."

Kelly leaned over the counter and whispered. "Well, it's easy enough to tell he wants to fuck you."

Ellie put her hand over Kelly's mouth. "*Jesus*, Kelly."

Kelly pulled Ellie's hand away and held it. "Are you going to tell me what gives, or am I going to have to guess?"

Ellie sighed. "I lied when I said I didn't know if he was married. He is."

"How do you know?"

"I just do." Ellie pulled her hand free, took up a dishcloth, and started wiping down the counter.

"Well, she isn't here, is she?"

"That makes it okay?"

"It makes it not your problem. It's on him if he's cheating. Not you."

"That makes no sense whatsoever. Even if it did—" Ellie leaned forward and dropped her voice so the nearby minglers couldn't hear. "I wouldn't want to be with a man who would do that. And you fucking *know* why I wouldn't, so don't try to justify it or change my mind."

Susan walked up to the counter. "Uh-oh. Ellie's dropping f-bombs. Let me guess." She leaned forward and whispered, "Jack McBride."

"Jesus," Ellie said, lifting her eyes to the sky.

"He's not going to help you," Kelly said.

"Come on," Susan said. "Like we don't know you."

Ellie sighed. Of course they did. She and Kelly had been best friends since fourth grade. They had pulled Susan into their fold when she moved to Stillwater sophomore year in high school. Since then, the three of them had been each other's confidantes and cheerleaders. They'd had their ups and downs, their fights and outs, but they always found their way back together. Three was the perfect number for a reason, Ellie always thought. Wherever three occurred—in nature, mythology, and religions—Ellie saw the three of them, perfectly represented.

"Susan, you've been around him the most," Kelly said. "Is he anything like Jinx?"

Ellie started to interject but Susan answered. "Gosh, no. But he *is* married. Ethan wanted to call his mother after Jack's accident, but Jack told him not to. Has he made a pass at you?"

"A pass? What is this, 1957?" Kelly asked.

"Well, what's it called, then?"

"No," Ellie lied. She wasn't in the mood for bickering banter.

"Good," Susan said.

"If that's not a lie, which I'm pretty sure it is, he will soon," Kelly said. "He's been watching you like a hawk all night."

"I know. It's starting to piss me off."

"Why?" Kelly asked. "Have you forgotten that men—good looking, *eligible* men—"

"He isn't eligible," Susan said.

"—are thin on the ground in Stillwater?"

"If you don't care he's married, you make a play for him," Ellie said.

Kelly shook her head. "He'd be dead by morning."

Susan and Ellie rolled their eyes at each other. Kelly was firm in her belief that she was romantically cursed. Both of her husbands had died suddenly, and any males she got the least bit physical with suffered freak accidents soon after. She hadn't dated in fifteen years, since her last husband, Barney Kendrick, dropped dead. "And I'm not going to let you off the hook."

"What do you mean by that?"

"I mean you would love it if someone else sabotaged it so you wouldn't have to make a decision."

"I don't think that's fair," Susan said.

"Me, either," Ellie said.

"Well, it's the truth. 'With great risk comes great reward.'"

"Do you realize you just quoted Thomas Jefferson?" Ellie said.

"I got it in a fortune cookie last week." Kelly looked over her shoulder at Jack McBride. "That, sweetheart, is a risk you'd be an idiot not to take."

Susan shrugged. "You know what I think."

Paige walked behind the counter. "Hey, Mom. Ellie, I've got this now. You go out and mingle with your guests."

"Call me if you need me," Ellie said.

Determined not to seem to be avoiding Jack (though she was), Ellie made a beeline to Shirley, Bob, Jack, and Brian Grant. Jack stepped back to make room next to him. He smiled politely at her and returned his attention to Bob. Kelly and Susan joined them.

"Jack here was just asking about the Dodsworths," Bob said.

Shirley laughed. "When we got married back in '65, Elizabeth and George were already an old married couple. Of course, they were probably only ten years or so older than us. Well, Elizabeth anyway. Not all that much in the scheme of things, is it?"

"Old Man Dodsworth sold me my first car," Brian Grant said. He nudged his wife's arm. "You remember that car, don't you, Susan?"

Susan rolled her eyes. "Not as fondly as you do. Mr. Dodsworth died not long after, didn't he?"

"He was quite a bit older than Elizabeth," Bob said.

"About fifteen years," Shirley said. "Still, he couldn't have been much more than sixty when he died."

"That puts it in perspective," said Bob, who'd just celebrated his sixty-fourth birthday.

"Everyone seemed so much older then," Shirley said. "I'm sure Bob and I don't seem that old to y'all." When nobody immediately responded, she continued, "At least lie to us and tell us we don't."

"You don't seem old at all," Ellie said, dutifully and with a smile.

"He was only sixty?" Brian asked. Ellie, who was busy calculating how far from sixty she and her friends were, shared Brian's incredulity. From the expression on Kelly's face, Ellie knew her friend was thinking along the same lines.

When did we get so old?

"Well, he died soon after, so he probably wasn't in good health," Susan said.

"He was probably bored to death married to Elizabeth," Bob said.

Susan gasped. "Bob, that's awful."

"It's true," Shirley interjected. "Elizabeth, bless her heart, was sweet but dull as dishwater. I never heard her say anything original or contradictory to her husband."

"Sounds like the perfect wife to me," Brian said. Susan punched him. He pretended to be hurt and looked to Jack for support.

"I know better than to agree with that," Jack said.

"Good move," Kelly said.

"If you ask me, George tried to find the polar opposite of his first wife," Bob said. "She gave him so much trouble, he was eager to marry a doormat, even if she was a little on the crazy side."

Jack narrowed his eyes. "George Dodsworth was married before?"

"Back in the '50s. Claire was her name. Oh boy, was that woman a pistol," Bob said.

"And how would you know?" Shirley asked.

"She had this car," Bob said. His eyes took on the glazed expression so common in men who loved cars. "Canary yellow Thunderbird. She drove that car all over Stillwater, top down, her black hair tied back in a cherry red scarf, her lips painted to match." He shook his head and returned his attention to the group, who were all staring at him, some a little dumbfounded, others embarrassed. "What? I was a kid."

"Claire Dodsworth. I've never heard of her," Susan said.

"You wouldn't have. She ran off with the Fuller Brush man." Bob laughed. "I kid you not. Can't get much more postwar stereotypical than that. Unhappy housewife being swept off her feet by the traveling salesman. Doubt George Dodsworth ever said her name again in his life. He hired Elizabeth to take care of Barbara, who was a baby. Married her not long after."

"So Elizabeth isn't Barbara's mom?" Jack said.

"Not biological, but Elizabeth always treated her like she was her own," Shirley said.

"Does Barbara have any idea Elizabeth isn't her mother?" Susan asked. She looked stricken with the thought.

Bob and Shirley exchanged a horrified look. "I don't know," Shirley said. "It wouldn't surprise me if she didn't know anything about Claire."

"That's awful," Kelly said.

"Things were different back then. Scandals were talked about more in hushed tones, not flouted all over the world like today," Shirley said.

Ellie kept her eyes riveted to Shirley, fully aware that everyone, save Jack, was holding their breath for her reaction.

Shirley's eyes widened as she realized her gaffe. She hurried on. "And a better thing, too. Sweep it under the rug and don't talk about it. Barbara has had a perfectly good life without knowing about her mother."

"I don't know if you could say that," Kelly said.

"Besides drive with the top down and skip town with a traveling salesman," Jack interjected, "what else did Claire Dodsworth do to warrant that kind of silence?"

"She wasn't from around here," Bob said. "George brought her back from his time in the Army. She wasn't ever part of the town. She wasn't missed when she left."

"That's horrible," Susan said.

"But that wasn't all, was it? There was another reason why the town wanted to forget her," Ellie said. When Bob and Shirley didn't answer, Ellie answered for them. "She cheated on George, didn't she?"

They nodded.

"With a lot of men?"

Ellie felt the weight of Jack's eyes. She refused to look at him.

"Yes," Bob said. "This was all a long time ago. The early '60s sometime. Better left there, if you ask me."

Kelly gasped. "You don't think it's the first Mrs. Dodsworth you found out there, do . . ."

"No," Jack said, a little too quickly. Obviously, that's what he thought. "The remains are probably more recent than that."

Kelly's son, Seth, walked up to the group. He was tall, over six feet, his naturally lanky figure sculpted with muscles. Seth had taken to wearing clothes that showed off his chiseled physique: tight T-shirts that bunched above his biceps, athletic shirts that acted like a second skin, showing off every dip and curve of his abdomen and highlighting the way his back tapered into his narrow hips. His transformation from child to man was so unsettling, Ellie often had to avert her eyes and remind herself he was her godson. "I have to go, Ellie," Seth said. "Your store looks great."

"Thanks, Seth."

"Don't be late, honey," Kelly said. She rubbed her son's shoulder and smiled. Seth nodded at everyone and left.

"I think he's got a girlfriend," Kelly said in a stage whisper. She fished her phone out of her back pocket. "But he won't tell me who. . . . Jesus. This woman. Excuse me." She walked off, greeting her caller with much more enthusiasm and professionalism than her initial reaction foreshadowed.

"Men like their secrets," Shirley said.

"But the smart ones know better," Bob said.

Ellie couldn't help herself; she peeked at Jack. She saw tension in his jaw, his eyes narrow, but he kept them averted from her. Interesting.

"Where's the mayor? I thought for sure she would be here," Susan said.

"So did I," Shirley said. She looked around as though she might suddenly see Jane in the dwindling crowd. "I thought she would want to see the first step in her grand plan take shape."

Jack looked at Shirley. "Grand plan?"

"Ellie and Jane are working on attracting businesses back downtown and are working with a developer to rebuild the gaping holes in the square."

"I would hardly describe cold-calling developers to gauge their interest a 'grand plan.' It's all very preliminary," Ellie said.

"Sounds promising," Jack said.

"If anyone can pull it off, Ellie can," Bob said. "She's a great one for planning, our Ellie."

"I have no doubt she can," Jack said.

Brian looked at his watch. "Ellie, Susan and I need to get going. I have an early day."

"Of course," Ellie said. She moved forward and hugged Brian, then Susan. "Thanks so much for coming."

Susan held her longer than normal. "Be careful," she whispered.

Ellie squeezed her in reply. Susan and Kelly had always been the angel on one shoulder and the devil on the other. Both wanted her happiness, but disagreed on how to get there. Ellie made each of them happy about half the time. Ellie pulled out of the embrace. "Thanks for coming," she repeated.

The Grants' departure opened the floodgates for others to leave as well. Ellie was saying goodbye to people and directing Barbara Dodsworth's maids, hired for the night, in cleanup when she saw Jane's housekeeper walk in. She and Shirley both dropped what they were doing and went to the old woman.

Marta Müller stood by the front display table, holding her purse in front of her, blinking like she was seeing light for the first time in years, which was somewhat apt. Besides grocery shopping and household errands, Marta did very little outside Jane's house. She wasn't exactly reclusive, but very close to it.

"Marta," Ellie said. She put her hand on the woman's arm. "Is everything okay?"

Marta's eyes darted around the room before finally settling back on Ellie. Shirley was standing next to her now. "Marta. Is Jane all right?"

Mentioning Jane snapped Marta to attention. "Yes, Mrs. Underwood. She is well. A little under the weather. She wanted me to come and apologize for not attending your business party tonight."

"Of course," Ellie said. "Tell her I'll stop by in the morning to check on her."

The old woman nodded her head once in acknowledgment. "You have a very nice store."

"Thank you. Would you like to look around?"

"Jane is very proud of you. She is not always easy with her feelings, but I can tell. She talks very highly of you."

Ellie was taken aback. It was more than Marta had ever said to her in the thirty years she'd known her. "Thank you, Marta."

Marta nodded once, again. Ellie glanced at Shirley, who was as obviously stunned as she. Marta jerked her chin toward the coffee bar. Jack leaned against the counter, talking to Bob and Paige. "Is that the new police chief?"

"Yes. Would you like to meet him?"

"Yes."

Shirley brought Jack over.

"Jack, this is Marta Müller. She works for Jane Maxwell."

Jack's hesitation was so slight, Ellie wondered if she imagined it. His charming smile, easy demeanor, and genuine interest won Marta over immediately. Marta's whiskery face blushed, turning the raised birthmark on her right cheek a deeper shade of red.

"It is terrible, what I hear of these murders," Marta said.

"Yes. We're doing everything we can to find out what happened."

Marta jerked her head down. "It was not suicide, you are sure?"

"No. Not suicide."

"Good. They will see their baby in heaven." Some of the tension left the woman's face and she smiled, though it looked more like a grimace from lack of practice.

"Did you know Rosa?"

"No."

Jack's eyes narrowed, almost imperceptibly. When he caught Ellie studying him, he relaxed and smiled.

"Would you like something to drink or eat, Marta? Let someone wait on you for a change?" Shirley said.

"No, no. I am fine. Though a book would be nice."

"What do you like to read?" Shirley asked.

"Mystery, I think. Agatha Christie."

Shirley motioned for Marta to come with her. "Right this way."

As soon as they were out of earshot, Ellie asked, "What?"

"What, what?"

She considered calling him on it: clearly, Jack thought Marta's interest in the Ramos investigation was suspicious. She didn't say anything, though. What business was it of hers? Ellie didn't like gossip or busybodies but was acting like one herself. Instead she said, "Marta liked you."

"What can I say? The old ladies love me." He grinned.

"Then you moved to the right town."

"Can we finish our conversation?"

"Looks like Ethan wants to leave."

"He can wait."

Jack was going to pester her until he said his piece, she could tell. Better to get it over with and move on. Plus, it would be easier to ignore how good-looking he was with the huge purple bruise around his right eye.

"Sure."

At that moment, Kelly returned from the office, where she had taken the phone call from a client. "I swear that woman is going to be the end of me. I'm sorry, but I have to go."

"Party's over anyway," Ellie said.

"But I wanted to help you clean up."

"That's why I hired Esperanza and her friend. It's fine. I've got it."

"If you're sure? It's probably just as well. I'm going to be up all night pulling samples that I have already shown her and she's rejected." Kelly looked at Jack. "You leaving, too?"

"Not yet. Ellie asked me to give her security system a once over."

"I thought Michael helped you out with that."

"He did," Ellie said.

"Freeman?" Jack asked.

"I was talking to him one day about Ellie moving in upstairs and the store and everything and he offered to help her with security," Kelly said.

"Of course," Jack said. "I am familiarizing myself with as many of the business security systems as I can. I thought since I was here . . ." he let the statement trail off.

"Right," Kelly said. Ellie couldn't look at her.

"I didn't know you and Freeman were friends," Jack said to Kelly.

"Well, it's nothing romantic, I can assure you. Which, now that I think of it, I should probably be offended. He's never even made a pass at me."

Ellie laughed. "You're something else."

"Even if I dated I wouldn't take him up on it. He's a bit too," she mimed a body-building pose, "for my tastes." She addressed Jack. "Michael's been like a brother to Seth. Helping him with his fitness routine. Taught us both how to shoot, helped us buy our guns."

Ellie cringed.

"I know you don't like guns," Kelly said. "But it makes me feel safer having one around. You should have one, too. We're going to another gun show this weekend. You could get one there. Skip the background check." She put her hand up and pretended to tell Jack a secret. "She's got a record a mile long."

"No, I don't."

"Don't tell Dixon at Top Gun though. He'll be mad we aren't buying from him. I think he's a crook, but Mike likes him."

"I'm not getting a gun," Ellie said.

"Don't you think she needs a gun?" Kelly asked Jack.

"If they make her that uncomfortable then she would only ending up accidentally hurting herself or someone else."

"See?" Ellie said.

"Fine, I see I'm outnumbered." She hugged Ellie and whispered in her ear, "Take a chance. You'll enjoy it. Then call me with the details."

"Bye, Kelly."

"Bye, Chief," Kelly said in a sing-song voice. "Bye, Paige." She waved to Paige behind the bar.

Ellie sighed and with resignation, she said, "Come on." She turned and walked away without looking at him.

"Dad, come on," Ethan whined.

"This will only take a few minutes," Jack replied.

"I need to buy the book," Marta said.

"It's on the house," Ellie said.

Now that the conversation with Jack was imminent, she wanted to get rid of everyone as soon as possible. The sooner she got rid of them, the sooner she could get rid of Jack, too. "Shirley, you and Bob don't have to help clean up. These ladies and I can take care of it."

"Are you sure?"

Ellie waved her hand. "I'm sure. Go on. I'll talk to you tomorrow."

"Jack, call my office tomorrow," Bob said.

"Will do."

After hugs all around, smiles and waves, they were gone. Ethan sat on a stool at the bar. Ellie could feel his glare boring into her back and she and Jack disappeared into the office.

She leaned against the desk, crossed her arms, and waited. She met his gaze evenly and steadily and tried to remember why she had been so angry with him.

Thankfully, he didn't beat around the bush. "You've been avoiding me tonight."

"Yes, I have."

"I hope it's because you are so attracted to me, you're worried you won't be able to control yourself."

"No."

"Then it's either because you're mortified, which you said earlier, or you are so mad at me you might not be able to stop yourself from gouging my eyes out."

"That's more like it."

"You have no reason to be mortified. Which, I've got to say, I love that you used that word. Most women would say embarrassed."

"I'm glad you approve of my semantics."

He stepped close to her. His eyes lingered on her lips. She clenched her jaw and stared him in the eyes. "But you have every right to be angry with me. I am a married man and I was shamelessly flirting with you. I want to explain."

"What's there to explain? You're married. I get it."

"What do you get?"

"I'll admit I'm a bit surprised. You don't seem like the type who would do that sort of thing."

"I'm not."

"You just admitted to shamelessly flirting with me while you were married."

"Hey, you flirted with me too and you knew I was married."

"I didn't know for sure."

"Yes, you did. And you didn't care."

She waved her hand in dismissal. "Okay, fine. We're both reprehensible. This is the worst apology I've ever received, and that's saying something."

"You would like that, wouldn't you?"

"Like what?"

"You would like it if I turned out to be just like every other shitty guy you've dated, married, or fucked."

He could certainly rip her heart out like the others. "You're doing a pretty good imitation of them."

Jack took a deep breath and looked at the floor. "Okay. This is not going like I hoped at all." He raised his eyes to Ellie. "Would you just let me talk for a bit, without interrupting, please? And uncross your arms."

"Why?"

"Just humor me. Please."

She uncrossed her arms, put them down at her side, immediately felt awkward, and grasped her hands in front of her.

Jack smiled. "Thank you." He took a deep breath. "A year ago this coming Friday, I kissed my wife goodbye and went to work. When I came home, she was gone. Ethan had gone to a friend's house after school, which meant I found the note. Thank God.

"The note said she was suffocating, needed space, time to find herself." He pressed his lips together, stared hard at the floor. He jingled his keys in his pocket. "No idea of where she was going, when she would be back. Just a *if you need me, email me.* She left her phone on top of the note so I couldn't even call her. She didn't even mention Ethan." Jack paused. "It was his fucking birthday."

Ellie's head jerked back. "Oh my God."

"Yeah. When Ethan got home, I told him she had gone to her parents' house for a bit, that there was some aunt or uncle or other who was sick. He accepted it pretty easily. Eventually, he asked questions. I told him as little as possible, just that we decided to take a break for a bit, all the while emailing her and begging her to come home, if not for me at least for Ethan. Nothing."

He looked up at Ellie. "At first I was shocked, hurt. Devastated. As the weeks passed, I got angry. That's not a good emotion for me. I did some things I regret." He took another deep breath. "But it was the wake-up call I needed. Julie was gone and didn't seem to want to come back or even care what happened to her son. Once I got past the anger, I realized I didn't miss her. It had been years since we had the kind of relationship . . ." He caught himself. "Well, maybe one day I'll bore you with the details. Today, tonight, I want you to know that, yep, I'm married, but in five days I won't be."

Ellie's stomach dropped, but she remained silent.

"The state will grant a divorce if the spouse left with the intention of abandonment or has remained away for a least a year. As of Saturday, Julie's done both."

"Does Ethan know?"

Jack shook his head. "I've tried very hard not to poison him against her. Which basically means I've been lying to him for a year to protect his idea of her. I think I hate Julie for that more than anything."

Ellie stared at the floor, not trusting herself to look at Jack. She didn't know what to say or if he even wanted her to say anything. She also didn't know what to feel. Relief was the strongest emotion—relief that her initial impression of him had been correct. Relief that there was a sliver of hope of this going somewhere.

He bent down, forced her to look at him, and smiled. "I'm not some philandering husband and I'm not toying with you." He paused. "I like you very much. And I think you like me." She looked away, suddenly shy.

"We hardly know each other."

"I know enough." He said it so simply, with the confidence that there was nothing he could ever learn about her that would change his opinion. She wasn't so sure, though.

"Do you forgive me?" he asked.

She nodded. "I'm sorry I thought so little of you."

"*Señora?*"

Ellie stepped back, like she'd been punched with an electric cattle prod. One of the maids stood in the doorway, her face bland. She looked only at Ellie.

"We are almost done," she said.

Ellie cleared her throat and gave her a weak smile. "Excellent. Thank you, Esperanza. I'll be right there." The woman nodded and left.

Giddy with embarrassment, Ellie laughed and looked at Jack. Her smile faded. He was staring out the door, deep in thought.

"Jack?"

"Hmm?" He looked at her, but his mind was somewhere else.

"Ethan's waiting."

His face cleared. Jack reached out, put his hand on her hip, and pulled her to him. He smelled of long walks in the woods—pine and citrus and maybe a hint of cedar. His mouth was full, with a deep line in his lower lip that disappeared as he smiled. He pulled her closer, put his cheek against hers. His breath was warm on her ear when he said, "He can wait. You were right to think so little of me. I've been wanting to kiss you since the football game." His right hand was at the small of her back, holding her close to him. His left hand was at the base of her neck, his fingers threaded through her hair. Ellie's knees turned to water.

His lips travelled down her neck. She lifted her chin and closed her eyes, all sense of where she was forgotten. Jack interspersed kisses with whispered details of exactly what he'd been thinking the last few days. Her hands slid underneath his jacket and over his back. She trembled, imagining the vivid scene Jack described. How could anyone expect her to hold on to her objections beneath this onslaught?

"He's married, you know."

Ellie moved away so quickly she ran into the wall of the office with a resounding thud.

"Ethan!" Jack said. "You shouldn't sneak up on people like that!"

"I've been standing here a while." Ethan stared at Ellie with such hatred she felt her skin burn.

Ellie didn't know what to do with her arms. She crossed them over her stomach to try to stem her rising nausea. *Please, God. Don't let him have heard what Jack said.* She swallowed the urge to vomit, though she was fairly sure she wouldn't be able to resist later on.

After his initial outburst, Jack stared at his son in horror, completely at a loss.

"Ethan," Ellie said.

"Don't think you're special. He's screwed plenty of trashy women just like you. Why do you think my mom left?"

Jack lunged forward, sending the desk chair spinning. "That's enough. Let's go." He grabbed Ethan's arm, jerked him around, and marched him out of the office without a backward glance.

Ellie watched the chair as it spun to a stop. She buried her head in her hands and fought the urge to cry. *This is why you always go with your gut.*

She dropped her hands and sighed. She could cry later. She had to finish cleaning up, pay Esperanza and her friend, count down the register, and close up the shop.

Ethan's voice, full of excitement, rang through the store. "Uncle Eddie!"

Ellie heard Jack's voice but couldn't make out what he said. She walked out of the office and stopped at the buffet table, her eyes not believing the tableau she witnessed. Paige Grant was behind the counter, eyes round. Esperanza and the other woman stood near the door but off to the side, trying to be as inconspicuous as possible but watching everything. Next to Michael Freeman, Ethan hugged a man in handcuffs—a man who looked eerily similar to Jack.

"Eddie? What the hell are you doing here?" Jack said.

"Well, when the bat signal goes up, I am morally obligated to respond."

Jack turned to Ethan. "You called Eddie?"

"Well, yeah. When you got beat up, it was either him or Lieutenant Governor Grandma."

Jack rubbed his forehead. "Why are you in handcuffs?"

"He was speeding," Freeman said.

"Do we arrest people for speeding in Stillwater?"

"Well, he was going eighty in a thirty-five. When I stopped him, he was belligerent, uncooperative, and I suspected he was driving under the influence."

"I was not," Eddie said.

"So I searched him." Freeman didn't continue.

Jack apparently didn't need him to. He nodded his head. "Right. Thanks, Freeman. I'll take care of it."

"I should . . ."

"Nathan is probably waiting for you at the station for the shift change. Go on."

Reluctantly, Freeman left.

Jack removed keys from his pocket, stepped behind Eddie, and removed the cuffs. "Jesus, Eddie."

"Hey, that dude has a serious hard-on for authority." He looked at Ethan. "Sorry, kid."

"Like every other cop you've ever met, right, Eddie?" Jack put the cuffs in his pocket and caught Ellie's eye, who was now standing in front of the coffee bar. She couldn't read Jack's expression. Eddie rubbed his wrists and followed Jack's gaze. He smiled, a little too knowingly for Ellie's comfort.

"Come on," Jack said. "Let's go."

The tiny bell jingled over the door and they were gone. Esperanza and her friend—Ellie really needed to learn her name—were looking down at the table of books next to them.

"You can go, Paige. I'll lock up."

"Oh my God," Paige said. "They're twins."

Ellie thought of the two brothers standing next to each other, completely different and alarmingly alike.

"Apparently so," Ellie replied. "I'll get your money, Esperanza."

She got the cash from the safe and returned to the front when the door bell jingled again. Bob Underwood walked through the door.

"Will this night ever end?" Ellie said under her breath. She smiled broadly and said, "Forget something, Bob?"

"No. Is Jack gone?"

"Yes." Thank God. "Is something wrong?"

Bob glanced at the two women and away. Ellie took the hint. She paid the two ladies and they left, Paige right behind. Ellie locked the door behind them.

"What's up?" she said.

"I should probably talk to Jack about it."

Ellie lifted her hands. "Fine by me, Bob."

"Are you okay?"

She sighed. "No, I'm not. I've had a horrible night."

"I thought it all went very well."

"It did. After, not so much."

"Want to talk about it?"

Bob asked because he knew it was expected of him, not out of any real desire to know what was going on. Bless him, he was a sweet man but not one who engendered confidences. Strange, considering he was a lawyer and confidences were his business. Ellie was sure Shirley would call her first thing in the morning to grill her unless she distracted him.

"I'm fine. Did you want to talk to Ja— Chief McBride about the first Mrs. Dodsworth?"

"How did you know?"

"I could tell you were holding something back earlier."

Bob shook his head in disbelief. "I should know better than to try to fool you." He cleared his throat.

"Do you remember when she left town?"

"No. But I remember when she came back."

"She came back?"

"Yes. Nineteen sixty-one. I remember because it was my fifteenth birthday. I overheard my brother and his friend talking about her."

"Your brother? I didn't know you had a brother."

"He died in Vietnam."

"Who were his friends?"

"Walt Dixon and Buck Pollard."

CHAPTER SIX

Tuesday

I

Besides Shirley and Marta, Ellie knew Jane better than anyone else in town. What Ellie knew she had learned secondhand, pieced together from gossip, snatches of conversation when she was a child, and nuggets of information Jane let slip throughout the years.

Jane Maxwell had walked through the front door of 24 River Road in 1947 as the young German bride of Herman Maxwell, president and sole owner of Stillwater National Bank and Mayor of Stillwater for going on thirty years. Jane's arrival was a shock to the community, not only because she was at least fifty years younger than seventy-two-year-old Herman, but because Herman had long said he would never meet a woman who could hold a candle to his late wife. But Herman was a man, after all, and Jane was beautiful.

If Jane had settled in to the role of mayor's wife, the town might have embraced her, however grudgingly. Jane was not interested in bridge clubs, community service, and church, though. She wanted to work with Herman at the bank. Mellowed with age and eager to make his young wife happy, Herman agreed. He figured she would find herself out of her depth quickly and decide a life of leisure was not such a bad life after all. Much to his and every man and woman at the bank's amazement, Jane proved to have a keen financial mind, and, as time went on, her ruthless business sense became apparent. As Herman aged, Jane grew more powerful. When he died in 1965 at ninety without children, having outlived any distant family to speak of, he left everything to Jane. She had been in charge of the bank ever since.

Ellie's admiration for Jane's intelligence, independence, and determination was occasionally diminished only by an implacability that Jane masterfully hid behind common sense and practicality. Soft emotions had no place in Jane Maxwell's life, even for a ten-year-old girl with a dead mother and alcoholic gambler for a father whose fortune was entrusted to her management. Jane had delegated Ellie's emotional care to Shirley Underwood, Jane's secretary and mother of Ellie's best friend, Lisa. It was just as well; Jane terrified Ellie. As Ellie matured, the fear transformed to respect until finally settling into gratitude. Ellie cared what happened to Jane, but Jane was impossible to love.

Ellie pushed a button and a rich two-note bell rang inside the house. Marta opened the door.

"Marta," Ellie said. She forced herself not to stare at the birthmark on Marta's cheek. When she first saw the birthmark as a girl, Ellie had asked Marta about it and had received an angry retort in response. For years, Marta and her birthmark and thick German accent had always been the stand-in for the bogeyman in Ellie's nightmares. Maturity had banished the silly fear, but the birthmark still fascinated Ellie, despite herself.

"Miss Elliot." Marta was the only person in Stillwater who still called Ellie by her true name.

"How's Jane feeling?"

Marta closed the door and stood with her hands clasped in front of her. "Better this morning, though not well enough to go to work. She was sorry to miss your party last night."

"I'm just glad she's feeling better."

"I'll tell her you're here."

Marta tottered over to the staircase and climbed, clutching the banister and taking one step at a time, to Jane's bedroom on the second floor.

Ellie turned away quickly so as to not witness the maid's slow, painful progression up the stairs. She knew it was long past time for Jane to move her bedroom downstairs, for her convenience as well as Marta's. Ellie also knew it was not her place to suggest it. She held her peace and walked across the foyer to the living room, hitting every squeaky board on the way.

Maxwell Manor, as it was pretentiously named 140 years ago when Herman Maxwell's father built the house for his new bride, still retained the title of Nicest House in Stillwater despite not being updated since the 1930s, when Herman added a kitchen and turned the kitchen house into a greenhouse. Dark, ornately carved wood paneling weighted the walls and trimmed the doors. Threadbare, faded oriental rugs covered the wood floors. Heavy antique furniture sat in the same position as when it was delivered decades before. Natural light struggled to penetrate the leaded glass windows framed by heavy brocade drapes. Electric sconces, converted from gas one hundred years ago, helped as best they could, but despite their best efforts, the living room, and entire house, resembled a cave to Ellie.

She sat on the edge of a Chippendale sofa and waited. Like so many times before, she was struck by the impersonality of the room and house. There were no mementos from travels because Jane did not travel. There were no pictures of family, because she had none. The only picture in the room was one taken of Jane in 1955 when Herman made her vice president of the bank. In it, Jane's private smile could not distract from the emptiness in her eyes.

Ellie gripped her hands so tightly they throbbed. She released them and took a deep breath. She was not Jane, would not end up like Jane—alone with people only checking on her out of long-held obligations. Ellie had friends, people who loved her, cared for her, and whom she loved and cared for in return. Ellie cherished her independence, had protected it fiercely these last ten years, but not to the exclusion of human connection. A flush started on her chest and crept up her neck at the thought of Jack.

"Miss Elliot?"

Ellie jumped up at Marta's voice. "Yes?"

The old woman's face didn't show surprise or curiosity at Ellie's behavior. "Mrs. Maxwell asked if you would come to her room."

"Oh," Ellie said. "Of course."

In all her years visiting Maxwell Manor, Ellie had never been upstairs, had rarely been beyond the parlor, actually. When they reached the base of the stairs, Ellie put her hand on Marta's arm. "I can find my way. Which room is it?"

She thought the woman might protest, but after a pause, Marta replied, "First door on the left."

Ellie knocked on the door, heard Jane's muffled voice, and entered.

The room was airy and bright, at odds with the rest of the house. Plenty of muted light filtered through the sheer drapes, giving the room an ethereal feel. Midcentury European furniture with clean lines and light-colored wood floated above the dark hardwood floors, the only evidence this room was in any way attached to the rest of the house. The contrast between the floor and the furniture pleased the eye and gave a depth to the room, which was so obviously a mirror to Jane's personality: sparse, cold, unapproachable.

Jane put a frame into her bedside table and closed the drawer as Ellie entered. The room, like downstairs, held nothing personal. A vanity opposite the bed held one bottle of perfume—Chanel No. 5. A small, old-fashioned cloth-bound book was on the bedside table, the title too faded for Ellie to read.

"Good morning," Ellie said.

"That's debatable," Jane replied. Ellie chuckled, knowing this was Jane's attempt at humor.

"How are you feeling?"

"Like an old woman."

Contradicting her would only irritate and insult Jane, so Ellie replied, "What are your symptoms?"

"Are you a doctor now?"

Ellie placed a straight-backed chair near the bed and sat down. "As a matter of fact, yes. I've been taking night classes, along with working for you, managing my property, starting a business, and having a social life. I only sleep two hours a night."

"Hmph," Jane said. "I know the latter is at least true."

"Have you seen Dr. Poole?"

"No."

"Are you going to?"

"No. I know what's wrong with me."

Ellie waited for Jane to elaborate. She didn't.

"Tell me about the developers," Jane said. Enough personalizing. Straight to business.

"I'm going to Dallas on Thursday to meet with a my friend in historic preservation, as well as Liam Kelly."

"Who?"

"Harriet Kelly's son. He's made it big in video games. He bought a lot on the lake across from my place and few of his executives have, as well. I am going to talk to him about moving his business to Stillwater."

Jane nodded. "Good, good. No tax breaks, remember. We need the tax revenue to improve services and get more businesses in here."

"I know."

"I need you back at the bank, Ellie."

"Jane . . ."

"I've let you have your fun. Hire someone to run your store and get back to work where you belong."

"Jane, I've barely been gone a week."

"Precisely. Worst week the bank has had in years."

"Now you're being ridiculous."

"I am not. There is no one I trust to take care of things when I'm not there. Unfortunately, I'm getting older and days like today may become more frequent." It was the closest Jane had ever come to admitting she was mortal. Ellie knew she was being played. She wondered if all of it— missing the launch, receiving Ellie in her room—wasn't a charade.

Damn. She's good.

"It's your own fault for not grooming someone to take over."

"I groomed you."

Ellie didn't respond; there was no adequate response to what she and Jane both knew to be true. Jane moved Ellie through every position in the bank, from bookkeeper when she first arrived out of college, to the proof machine, to teller, to loan officer, to VP of loans, to VP of technology, to executive vice president. It was a rise that would have set everyone in the bank against anyone else. Ellie had a few detractors, but by and large, everyone agreed she was the only person at Stillwater National Bank who could balance Jane's dictatorial nature with compassion and kindness.

"Well," Jane said, her lips pressed into a line. "You will eventually have to choose."

"What do—"

"What is going on with Jack McBride?"

"What? Nothing." Ellie's face burned.

Jane's blue eyes narrowed. "What have you heard in town about his accident?"

Ellie swallowed. "Half the town thinks he's incompetent. The other half is skeptical, but willing to give him time."

"That's about as good as we can hope for, I suppose. If sixty percent of the town thinks he's incompetent, he'll be run out on a rail. Do what you can."

Ellie marveled at Jane's confidence in Ellie's ability to manipulate the public opinion of a few thousand people. To argue against her would be pointless. "Okay. Tell me about the Dodsworths."

"Why are you asking about the Dodsworths?"

"To help Jack McBride."

"The skeleton?"

Ellie nodded. "Did you know Claire Dodsworth?"

"Claire Dodsworth? Lord. I haven't thought of her in years. I forgot George was married before Elizabeth. It was a short marriage."

"She left him for a traveling salesman?"

"That was the rumor. She was a whore. Slept with every man in town who would have her, and plenty did."

"How old was she?"

Jane shrugged. "Probably in her late twenties. After she went through the married men in town, she started going after the boys. The original Mrs. Robinson."

"You said 'that was the rumor.' Was there a question of how she left?"

"I honestly don't remember, Ellie. She was there one day and gone the next. I'm sure someone saw her drive that car out of town, but whoever did is probably dead or senile."

"Like Elizabeth Dodsworth."

"Poor woman. At least I haven't lost my wits." Jane straightened the quilt over her legs. "Elizabeth has been peculiar for so long, it's easy to forget she was a bright young girl. Vivacious even."

"You aren't the first to say she's peculiar. Bob Underwood called her a doormat."

"Apt description. I suspect being married to George and raising Barbara took all the life out of her. Though a half-life with dull George Dodsworth was better than what she would have had."

"What do you mean?"

"Elizabeth was a Pope. Dirt poor. White trash. Lived on the edge of the Bottom, outside but just barely. Her mother had twelve kids in as many years. Elizabeth was the oldest. The mom, I can't remember her name, died with the last one and Elizabeth raised the rest. Until George Dodsworth hired her. Showed her intelligence right there."

"How do you mean?"

"How else would she have gotten out of that hovel? Best she could hope for was marrying some dirt-poor farmer and following in her mother's footsteps. Looking sixty years old at thirty. Dying in childbirth. She played George Dodsworth like a fiddle. Of course, if a man is that stupid, he deserves it. Dodsworth was never the wiser, I'm sure. He had a mother for his daughter and a wife who knew a good thing when she had it." She paused. "I'm not sure how any of this information helps Jack McBride."

"It probably won't," Ellie conceded.

"I don't know what else I can offer."

"How old was Buck Pollard during all this?"

"Buck? What does he have to do with it?"

"How old was he?" she repeated.

"Early '60s . . . I suppose he was late teens, early twenties."

"Someone Claire Dodsworth might have—"

Jane paused. Her mouth tightened before she answered. "Yes."

They stared at each other.

"Have you heard something?" Jane asked.

"Yes."

"From who?"

"Bob." When Jane looked puzzled, Ellie said, "He overheard his brother talking with Buck and Walt Dixon about Claire. That Claire had returned to town after leaving. Bob didn't remember specifics of the conversation, it was fifty years ago and he was fifteen. They teased him about Claire taking his virginity."

"Have you told Chief McBride?"

"Not yet."

Ellie was silent while Jane gazed at the window. She smiled and said, "It's interesting, if nothing else. We'll see what McBride does with the information."

Ellie shifted in her chair. Jane had a way of talking about people as though they were all acting out parts in a play she was anonymously stage-managing. Ellie didn't want to speculate on how much of her life Jane had managed and how many people Jane had manipulated through Ellie.

As if reading Ellie's mind, Jane asked in a level voice, "How is everything else going?"

Ellie took her time in meeting Jane's gaze. "Fine."

"Anything I should know?"

"No."

Of course, they both knew Ellie was lying.

II

Jack parked next to Ellie's Accord and got out of his car. His heart raced in anticipation, his stomach clenched in dread. He hadn't expected to see Ellie first thing in the morning. He needed more time to know what to say to her. Hell, he needed more time to figure out what to do.

The scene the night before with Ethan was worse than any of Jack's imaginings, and Jack had imagined plenty of different scenarios of how he would explain to Ethan that his marriage was over. Most consisted of them having a man-to-man, Ethan being upset but eventually understanding. The coldness between father and son would then thaw and return to the relationship they had when Ethan was younger. In reality, nothing like that happened. Jack felt like an idiot for thinking an immature, hormonal, angry teenager would even be capable of having such a conversation. It didn't help that the conversation started from a place Jack never envisioned or intended.

Jack should have let Ethan storm up to his room, like he started to do when they got home. Instead, Jack forced Ethan back downstairs and berated him for intruding, for saying the things he said, and for generally being an asshole to Ellie. Ethan's face took on the mottled red color of a Gala apple before he went off on Jack.

"*I'm* the asshole? What about you? You're married and all you can think about is screwing other women."

"You don't know what you're talking about."

"God, you're not even here a week and you've already all over another woman. What about Mom, huh? It'll serve you right if she doesn't take you back."

"*Her*? Take *me* back? She's the one who left, Ethan. Not me."

"The way you screw around, I don't blame her. How many women did you cheat on mom with?"

"None."

"Liar."

Jack pointed his finger in Ethan's face. "You don't know what you're talking about, kid." Spit flew out of his mouth. "I didn't cheat on your mom. Not *once* in fifteen years, though I'm pretty fucking sure she can't say the same thing."

Ethan's blush faded, but his eyes stayed burrowed into Jack's, unflinching.

Eddie had been sitting on the arm of the couch. "Jack," Eddie warned.

"No," he said. "I think it's about time Ethan heard the truth. You want to be treated like an adult? You sure like to talk like one. Okay, fine. Time to grow up, Ethan. In case it's escaped your notice, I'm the one who's stuck around, taken care of you, for the last year. Where has your mother been, huh?"

Ethan didn't answer.

"No really, Ethan. Where is she? Has she returned any of your emails?"

Ethan didn't answer.

"Has she returned your calls? Oh!" Jack went to the desk, opened the bottom drawer, and retrieved the phone. He slammed it down on the coffee table. "That's right. When she left, she left her fucking phone. I've been checking her messages for a year. The men, they've stopped calling, but you, you keep on trying. I would wait for weeks, thinking that maybe, *maybe* she would check her messages from another phone, hear your voice and call you back. She never did. Not once. I've been deleting old messages from you for months so her voice mail wouldn't fill up and you wouldn't know she didn't care enough about staying in touch."

Eddie stood and stepped in front of Jack, placing his hand on his brother's chest. "That's enough, Jack."

Jack jerked his brother's hand off. "Get your fucking hands off me."

Eddie put his hands in front of him in surrender and stepped back. Jack's heart raced. His chest heaved. Ethan stared at his mother's phone.

Jack took a deep breath. "You owe Ellie an apology. She's made it clear she wants nothing to do with a married man. It wasn't until I explained to her, told her my marriage is over, she would even consider . . ." Jack trailed off, unsure how exactly to categorize their relationship.

Ethan pulled his gaze away from the table and to his father. "What do you mean, your marriage is over?"

"Your mother abandoned us, Ethan. Under Texas state law, I can be granted a divorce after one year. I intend to do it."

Ethan struggled to keep from crying. "This Saturday?"

Jack nodded. It took everything he had to hold Ethan's gaze and watch his face crumple with the knowledge that his fourteenth birthday present would be his parents' divorce.

Ethan looked to Eddie, who was staring down at the ground, turned, and silently walked up the stairs.

Ellie opened the door to Jane's house before Jack rang the doorbell, startling both of them. He clenched his fists at his side to keep himself from embracing her, but he couldn't keep himself from smiling.

"Hi," he said. He pointed over his shoulder with his thumb. "I saw your car."

Her smile had been brief, but her blush wasn't. "What are you doing here? Did you come to talk to Jane?"

"No. Esperanza. She works here on Tuesday, right?"

"I think so," she said. She stepped out on the porch and closed the door behind her. She crossed her arms, dropped them, and clasped her hands in front of her before settling on pushing them into her pockets. Her pockets were so shallow half of her fingers were visible.

"So, about last night," he said.

"Bob came by. After you left," she said. She hurried on. "He wanted to tell you something about Claire Dodsworth."

Jack listened as she relayed what Bob told her as well as what Jane had said. "So, according to Bob, Buck Pollard had an affair with Claire Dodsworth and saw her when she returned to town."

"Maybe." Ellie shrugged. "I don't know how much you can trust fifty-year-old memories. Are you going to talk to Buck?"

An old-model Ford Taurus stopped on the road. Two women sat in the car, staring at Ellie and Jack on the porch. Jack watched them have a conversation before getting out of the car. He turned his attention to Ellie, who was studying him with a puzzled expression.

"I talked to him yesterday. He never mentioned Claire Dodsworth, and he had plenty of opportunity. Will you do me a favor?"

"Sure."

There was no hesitation in her answer. It gave him hope that maybe all wasn't lost, despite how uncomfortable she was in his presence.

"Will you tell Miner everything you just told me?"

"Sure."

"We need to talk about—other things. But I can't right now. Can I call you later?"

"Yeah. Sure." She stared at Jack, eyebrows raised.

"What?"

"Don't you need my number?"

"Oh, right." Jack fished his phone out of his jacket pocket and punched in the number she gave him. "I'm calling you now."

He heard her phone vibrate. She patted her back pocket and gave a small wave. "Bye."

She greeted the women as they passed on the driveway. Jack held his phone to his ear and listened to Ellie's voice mail. He left a message, ended the call, and put the phone in his pocket.

"Hello, Esperanza," Jack said.

"*No habla inglés,*" she replied, and walked by.

"*Hablo español,*" Jack said.

She stopped. The other woman rang the doorbell and waited without acknowledging Jack. Marta opened the door. "You're late," she said. The woman didn't reply and entered.

"Esperanza will be there shortly," Jack said.

Clearly unhappy with the change in the normal routine, Marta closed the door.

Jack didn't feel like beating around the bush. "Where's Diego?"

"*Quién?*"

"Diego wasn't in town long enough to make many friends," Jack said in Spanish. "He said he was with you the night of the murders, which makes me think you're the closest thing he has to an ally left in Stillwater."

Her expression was bland. He pulled a baggie holding a business card out of his pocket, held it up to her face to show her Barbara Dodsworth's business information. "You work for Barbara Dodsworth?" he asked.

"*Sí.*"

Jack flipped the card over. Esperanza's lips pulled down into a frown. "Rosa worked with you. Just this once, or for a while?"

She said nothing.

"I'm going to talk to Barbara, so tell me or not. I'll find out."

"Before Carmen, she worked all the time. After, she filled in for Inez a couple of weeks."

"Where all did she work?"

"Lots of places. All over town."

"Always with you?"

"*Sí.*"

"Anything happen while you worked here?"

"No."

"Find anything? Hear anything?"

"No."

Jack took Rosa's necklace and small key from his pocket, dangled it in front of Esperanza. She tried to disguise her surprise. "Recognize this?"

"No."

"Know what it opens?"

"No."

"Know whose it is?"

"No."

"Where did Rosa and Gilberto get all their money?"

"What money?"

"The cash they used to buy the baby furniture."

"I didn't know they had it."

"Was Diego with you the night of the murders?"

"Yes." She surprised herself by answering. Jack pressed on.

"Where is Diego?"

"I don't know."

"Let me see your green card."

She shifted on her feet. "It's in the car."

"Get it." Jack motioned for Esperanza to lead.

She opened the car door, sat in the bucket seat, and stared out the windshield. "Where is it, Esperanza?"

She glared at him then reached in her purse, took her wallet out, and opened it. She slid the green card out from its clear pocket and handed it to Jack. He didn't look at it. "This is a fake."

"It is not."

"I'm going to have to take you in."

"It isn't fake. I'm legal," she protested.

"Stand up."

"No. I won't."

"If you don't, I'm going to arrest you for resisting arrest."

"Diego was right about you."

"Oh really? What did Diego say?"

"He said—" She stopped, realizing she just revealed she had spoken to Diego since his escape. Her lips whitened with the pressure of keeping them closed.

Smart girl, Jack thought.

"Where is he?"

"He will kill me."

"*Who* is he?"

She shook her head, kept her lips pressed together.

"Were Rosa and Gilberto killed because of Diego?"

"I don't know. Maybe."

"Did Diego kill them?"

"No. He was with me."

"But they could have been killed because of Diego?"

"I didn't say that."

Jack put his arm on the roof of the car and loomed over Esperanza. "Here's the thing. Rosa and Gilberto were white bread."

"White bread?"

"Generic. Law abiding. Never got in trouble. Good people."

Esperanza stared at the ground and nodded her head.

"Until about a month ago. They came into a lot of money and Diego showed up. Now, I think the two are related. But, if that was the case, if they died because of Diego, I don't think he would have let me live."

She looked up slowly, stared at Jack's yellowing bruise, the stitches above his eye.

"He gave me a good beating, took my gun, torched my car. But he let me live. I don't remember much about everything that happened, but I do remember one thing. I realized that Diego, whatever his name is, whoever he is, is an evil motherfucker." Jack pointed to his eyes. "It was in his eyes. I have nightmares about his eyes. A man like Diego doesn't let a cop live. Do they, Esperanza?"

Her no was barely audible.

"Unless they want something from them." Jack stood. "What could he want from me?"

Esperanza didn't answer.

"I think Diego wants me to find out who murdered his relatives. What do you think?"

Esperanza nodded.

Jack removed the paper from his pocket, unfolded it, and held it in front of Esperanza's face. Her expression didn't change, but her shoulders drooped. Esperanza sighed. "I told her to not do it."

"Do what?"

"She wanted to get papers for her and Gilberto. Legal like. And afford nice things for the baby. I told her . . ." Esperanza's voice thickened. Tears pooled in her eyes. She wiped at her eyes angrily and swallowed. Her voice was stronger when she resumed. "Gilberto was a nice man and a hard worker, but he didn't want like Rosa, you know? He was happy with what they had. It was more than he had growing up. He didn't care they were illegal. It was enough to keep them fed, clothed, and in a nice house."

Jack nodded. "This was her ticket to a better life? Bribing an old woman?"

"She paid so fast, Rosa thought they would all be that easy. Asking for trouble. I told her. I *told* her." She pounded her fist on her leg.

"All? She was doing this with others?"

"Not yet. She hadn't worked enough to find anything. Gilberto didn't want her working. Wanted her to be with the baby."

"Where had she worked lately?"

Esperanza wasn't looking at him. Jack turned. Marta stood on the porch holding a feather duster, watching them.

Esperanza stood. "I have to go."

"What did Rosa find?"

"I told her I didn't want to be any part of it. That she might have a man to keep her fed but I didn't. I need this job. But she didn't care about anyone but herself. Oh, she said it was all for Carmen, but I knew better." Esperanza stood and closed the door of the car. "I don't know what she found. But whatever it was got her killed."

"Mrs. Maxwell is resting. She cannot have visitors."

Marta stood in the doorframe, legs apart, blocking Jack from entering.

"I didn't come to see Jane. I came to see you."

Marta blushed with pleasure briefly before suspicion took over. Her eyes darted over Jack's shoulder to where he had spoken with Esperanza and realization dawned.

"Would you like to step out on the porch?" Jack's voice was gentle. Marta closed the door and moved haltingly across the porch on arthritic knees. She sat on the edge of a wooden rocker, her feet planted firmly on the ground, her back straight and her large, calloused hands folded demurely on her lap. She looked straight ahead, as if waiting for the firing squad to get on with their business. A wave of sadness and affection washed over Jack. He handed the paper to her.

She didn't take it, only nodded.

"How much did you give Rosa?"

"One thousand dollars."

"When?"

"A month, five weeks ago?"

"Did Jane know?"

Marta shook her head. "When I came, she told me no one must know. That they would not understand. She does not know I have the picture. I hid it all these years. I wanted something of my family. There is nothing else left." The old woman's eyes were a clear blue, just like Jane's.

Jack pointed to the girl in the picture who baby Marta was gazing at adoringly. "This is Jane."

"No. That is Ingrid. *This* is Jane—Hanne." She pointed to the girl standing behind the mother. Where Ingrid had a peaceful expression, Jane's face was tight, her eyes narrowed. "This was taken in July 1936. My christening. Jane and Ingrid were twelve." She pointed at the young man standing to his father's right, proudly wearing a Hitler youth uniform. "My brother, Rolf, was sixteen. Wilfred was fourteen." She looked away. "They are all dead. Except for us."

Jack folded the paper and put it in his pocket. "Did Rosa come back to you for more money?"

"No."

"What's wrong with Jane?"

"She is old."

"Dying?"

Marta's nod was barely perceptible. "You will not tell her of this?"

"No. Thank you, Marta."

Jack walked to his car, and thought, not for the first time, how investigations were like fighting a hydra. You answer one question and two more sprout up in its place.

III

Miner visited his father at the Pembroke Arms Nursing Home three or four times a week, though he dreaded each visit. Aging smelled like piss, vomit, and shit, and no amount of Pine-Sol could mask it. Even though Policar Jesson, being healthy and of sound mind, lived in the north wing of Pembroke Arms—near the reception area and front door, so Miner never had to enter too far in the Den of Death, as he called it to himself—the smell and atmosphere of the place would follow him around, like Pigpen's cloud of dust, until Miner took a shower. Usually he timed his visits at the end of the day. This morning was different.

Paulie sat in the reception room on a dark brown leather couch, worn tan by years of use, watching Fox News and arguing with two men sitting with him. A frail old woman sat slumped sideways in her wheelchair, her chin on her chest, her rheumy eyes moving between each man as they talked. Miner couldn't tell whether she understood a word of what they said.

"Miner!" Paulie stood from the couch with more difficulty today than the last time Miner visited. Miner's heart clutched at the sight of his father, so large and robust as a young man, now stooped, gray, and thin. His smile was the same, thankfully, as was his happiness at seeing his only son. "What're you doing here so early?"

"Needed to talk to you, Pop."

An overweight man in stained khaki pants and an old mesh hat from a defunct local chicken company called out, "He's full of lies, Miner. 'Course, you know that."

Miner smiled and gave a little wave. He wasn't in the mood for banter.

Paulie sensed it, too. He masked his concern quickly. "Everyone knows you're the biggest liar of the bunch," Paulie said over his shoulder. He took Miner's arm and led him down the hall to his room.

Miner looked at the empty bed near the door of his father's room. "Don't worry, Fred's eating. Takes him forty-five minutes to eat two eggs and a piece of toast." Paulie motioned for Miner to sit. Miner shook his head. "What can I do for you, son?"

"Did you hear about what we found on Dodsworth's place?"

"Little else being talked about."

"There any way to get back there in the '50s?"

"Besides goin' by the house? Sure. They coulda gone through the Coffey place back behind, but they woulda been going through thick woods. No roads back there that I know of."

"None from logging?"

"Overgrown. Coming from our place, they woulda gone past our house through our pasture, parked at the barbed-wire fence, and walked from there. Where'dja find it?"

"Deep in their woods. Closer to Coffey's place."

"Wouldn'ta gotten past us. Same for the Jenner place on the other side." Paulie intertwined his fingers. "Dodsworth and Coffey's places were dense, overgrown woods, besides the little pastures near the houses. Woulda been hell for a car or truck to get through. A tractor maybe. But, if it's a tractor, then it's either Coffey, Jenner, or Dodsworth. At that time, Mr. and Mrs. Coffey were in their '80s, so you can pretty much rule them outta buryin' a body. Jenner's place at that time was owned by Dallas relatives. No one lived there."

Miner looked down and rubbed the back of his neck. "I just can't imagine the Dodsworths either."

"More like you don't wanna believe it."

"Do you?"

"Hell, yes. Now, if you'd said Dodsworth stole a bunch of money or diddled little boys, then I woulda been surprised. But hiding a body in the woods? Most anyone'd do that."

"I suppose so."

"You in charge of the investigation?"

"Yeah. Waste of time."

"Your chief is testin' you."

"I know."

"You like him?"

"McBride? Yeah."

"He like you?"

Miner shrugged. "Not sure."

"He honest?"

"Yeah."

"You gonna come clean with him?"

"I'm thinking about it."

"Well, today's your lucky day."

"How's that?"

"I'm gonna give you a bona fide lead."

"Oh, you are?"

"You bet. Just like on *Law and Order*. Remember back a few years ago? The incident with Elizabeth."

"I'd rather not."

"Don't be a prude, Miner. I didn't ever say much about what went on, for Elizabeth's sake, understand. What she did, that wasn't like her at all. We lived next door to the Dodsworths for forty years and she never once made a pass at me. Lord, Miner, don't make that face. Women came on to me all the time when I was younger. Elizabeth was an attractive woman, a bit timid, but pretty. When she found her way into my bed, I wasn't about to kick her out. Course, I was so shocked, it took me a while to get goin'."

Miner stared at the broken tile under Fred's bed so he wouldn't have to look at his father. A child shouldn't have to listen to such stories, even if it was in the pursuance of justice.

"You can imagine, I fell asleep right after. So did Elizabeth. Slept like a baby. That is, until she woke me up, shaking my shoulder, talking to me like I was George. She had a look in her eyes I'll never forget. She wasn't herself, and that's a fact. Well, she started screaming and yelling. That's when the nurses came in and caught us, both naked as jaybirds. You can imagine the pandemonium that caused."

"Oh, I remember."

"That day, Doc Poole came and sedated Elizabeth. Put her on sumthin'. She ain't been the same since. 'Course, Doc came and asked me a bunch of questions 'bout what happened. Accused me of enticin' her into my bed. I didn't, by the way. He all but accused me of bein' some kind of perverted old man, tryin' to have my way with a mentally deficient woman. Made me so mad, I stopped answerin'. When I did answer, I lied."

Paulie stood and stepped close to Miner. The tips of his thick, steel gray hair near his neck were still wet from his morning shower. He smelled of talcum and Stetson. A wave of nostalgia broke over Miner so hard he almost didn't hear what his father said.

"She called me George and said, 'You'd rather have her, wouldn't you?'

"'Who?' I said. I didn't bother correcting her about me being George.

"'That whore. She's coming to get Barbara,' she said.

"'Barbara's fine,' I said.

"She started to panic then. 'What if she remembers?'

"'What if who remembers what?'" I said.

"She went all vacant for a minute and I was tryin' to figger out the best way to get her outta my bed and back in her room without alerting the Nazi nurses when, clear as day, she said, 'What're you doin' here?'

"Then, she went berserk. You know the rest."

Miner nodded, still staring at the chipped tile. "So, who was she talking about?"

"Well, I don't know. But I can guess."

"Are you going to tell me or should I know?"

"Nah, you probably never heard of her. My guess is she was talkin' about George's first wife, Claire. She was a whore, by any definition of the word, and she was Barbara's mom."

"What happened to her?"

"She ran off with a travelin' salesman."

Miner sighed. "More like she was planted in the back woods." He walked to the small window and stared out at the little courtyard between the north and south wings of the home. The sky was a brilliant blue. "Why would Buck care if we found out?" he mumbled.

"What'd you say?"

Miner turned. His father stared at him with an old, familiar expression. He missed nothing.

"Pop, Elizabeth Dodsworth have many visitors over the years?"

"Just Barbara and Doc Poole. Why?"

"No one else?"

"Like who?"

"Buck Pollard."

Paulie narrowed his eyes. "No. Never seen him walk in the door. But there was some connection there. Rumor was George Dodsworth gave him a truck every five years or so until he died."

Miner heard the whine and snap of the grasshoppers outside.

Paulie's roommate shuffled around the corner. "Sorry," he said. "Didn't know you had company. Hey, Miner."

"Fred."

Fred shuffled back out.

"How's Barbara doin'?" Paulie asked.

"Fine."

"There was a time I thought you two would get married. Just think, that skeleton could've been found on your land."

"That was a long time ago, Pop."

"I'm glad you didn't. Girl was nothing but trouble. Had a lot of her mom in her."

Miner didn't want to talk about it. "Pop, why don't you come live with me and Teresa? We'll take care of you."

"You mean *you* will," Paulie said. "No, Miner. The last thing you need is one more person to worry 'bout."

"I worry about you anyway."

"Well, you shouldn't. I've got this place wrapped around my finger." Paulie slapped Miner on the back. "Now, I have to get back and win a few games of forty-two before lunch. See you in a couple days."

Miner smiled in reply. He had known that suggestion would get rid of his Pop for now. He was the most independent person Miner'd ever known. He stepped out of his father's room and wondered why he hadn't inherited his Pop's independence.

Down at the nurse's station, two black women sat behind the desk. The older woman looked up. "Hey, Miner."

"Brucilla." He walked toward them. "How you doing?"

"Fine, fine. How's Teresa?"

"About the same."

"I'll be out there Friday to check on her."

"Good. . . . I need to speak with Mrs. Dodsworth," Miner said.

Brucilla stood, walked around the desk, and started down the hall. Miner followed.

"Don't expect too much," Brucilla said. "When she does talk, it's nonsense."

"She know about the skeleton?"

Brucilla shook her head. "Barbara thought it best to keep it from her."

"Won't the other residents tell her?"

"She never leaves her room now." They stopped at a closed door about halfway down the hall. "She's on the slide. I don't expect her to live through the year."

Miner shook his head and clicked his tongue. "It's a shame. You ever heard her say anything about a woman named Claire?"

"Oh, yeah. Whenever we hear that name, we know it's 'bout to get bad."

"She say anything that makes sense?"

Brucilla shook her head. "Nah. It's all stream-of-conscious type stuff. Like reading Faulkner."

"Never read Faulkner."

"Well, it's not easy to understand. Neither is Mrs. Dodsworth when she goes into one of her fits."

Miner nodded, looked down at the floor.

"However."

Miner looked up.

"If you put it all together, there's a story there. You just have to look pretty hard."

"We still talkin' bout Faulkner?"

"No."

"You think that skeleton we found is Claire Dodsworth, don't you?"

Brucilla nodded.

"Anyone else know?"

She scoffed. "No one lasts around here long enough to put it all together."

"Were you ever going to tell?"

"I'm telling you now."

"But if I hadn't come here?"

"She's as good as dead now, Miner. What good would it do for the county to know she killed a woman?"

"Elizabeth did?"

Brucilla shrugged one shoulder. "I'm pretty sure."

They stopped talking as an old woman in a walker shuffled by. "Looking good, Mrs. Whatley," Brucilla said.

Elizabeth Dodsworth was visible to Miner through the narrow rectangular window in the door. She lay in her bed and stared vacantly out the window. She was so thin, she barely made a bump under the blanket.

"Seeing her like this breaks my heart," Brucilla said. She turned her attention back to Miner. "I knew her as children. Her family was dirt poor. Lived on the farm next to mine. We played together in the woods for a while. Until her daddy found out. Beat her something awful." Brucilla shook her head. "Elizabeth was smart. Almost as smart as me," she said, a twinkle on her eye. "When George Dodsworth hired her to take care of Barbara, I knew she'd end up marrying him."

"How'd you know that?"

"Best way to better yourself for women back then was to marry well. Then do whatever you had to do to keep your husband happy." Brucilla opened the door. "Talk to her if you want, but you won't get anything."

"Thanks, Brucilla." Miner pushed through the door. "Hey," he said. Brucilla turned. "Keep this between us."

She nodded. "See you Friday."

The door closed with a quiet click. Miner stood in the semidarkness for five minutes and silently watched Elizabeth Dodsworth stare out the window. He remembered her as a Sunday School teacher, nice but a little vacant, as if she were always somewhere else. Now, Miner knew where. He suspected they'd never know what truly happened. He didn't suppose it really mattered, after all. A woman was dead, but had anyone missed her?

A few questions lingered. How much did Barbara know, and why did Buck Pollard want him to fake the identity of the skeleton? Was he merely testing Miner to make sure he was still loyal and could be counted on to do his bidding? Or did Buck have a connection to Claire Dodsworth's death he didn't want revealed even now?

His phone buzzed in his pocket. He looked at the screen, didn't recognize the local number. He had learned it was always best to answer the local calls so he punched the ANSWER button with one hand and opened the door with the other. "Miner Jesson . . . Oh, hello, Ellie."

IV

The man behind the counter of Top Gun Shooting Range and Gun Emporium wore a camouflage T-shirt and Ducks Unlimited hat. His beady eyes were set close together in a moon-shaped face that advertised everything going through his mind like an interstate billboard.

Jack stuck his hand out and smiled broadly. "Jack McBride."

The man, wary, shook Jack's hand. "Justin Dixon."

"Nice to meet you." Jack took in the store. "Nice place you have here."

"Thanks."

Jack leaned against the glass case full of sidearms, magazines, ammunition, and knives and drummed his fingers on the top. "Don't know if you've heard; I'm in the market for a new sidearm. Mike Freeman suggested I stop by." A hairline crack formed in Justin's wall of suspicion under Jack's self-deprecating smile.

"Mike. Good customer. What are you looking for exactly?"

"Springfield Armory XDM."

"Nice gun. Don't have that in stock. Have to order it. See you've got a Beretta."

"Yeah. Sell many?"

"Eh, not a hugely popular gun. Only former military and military wannabes look for Beretta 92s."

"You own a 92?"

"No." When Justin's eyes narrowed, they disappeared into his face. It didn't engender trust. "Why?"

"Because a gun you bought was used to kill Gilberto and Rosa Ramos. Know them?"

"No. I sold that gun."

"So, you know which one I'm talking about?"

"No, I've owned a few 92s. Sold them all."

Jack pulled a piece of paper from his pocket. He slid it across the counter. Justin didn't look at it.

"This is the serial number. Would you check your records?"

"Don't recognize it."

"You didn't look at it."

He pretended to drop his eyes to the paper. "Still don't."

Jack put the paper back in his pocket. "Doesn't matter. You're the last owner of record. That makes you my prime suspect in a double murder."

"Why would I kill those Mexicans?"

"I don't know. I imagine I could manufacture a motive."

"Good luck with that. I have an alibi."

"Oh really? What's that?"

"I'm sure I can manufacture one."

Jack smiled. "Why not just tell me who you sold the gun to?"

"It was a personal sale."

"Again, you sound like you know which gun I'm talking about."

Justin paused. "I don't."

"Because if you did—"

"I don't."

"Then just give me the names of the people you've sold 92s to. Or you become my prime suspect and I turn your life upside down. Simple."

"I don't have to tell you shit."

Jack sighed and stared at the coiled snake on the flag hanging on the wall behind the counter. "We have three options here."

"No, we have one. For you to get a warrant."

"That is one option," Jack replied. "Another option is for you to cooperate fully with my investigation, creating a relationship of mutual respect with the new police chief."

"What's the third option?"

Jack took his phone out of his pocket, scrolled through the contacts, and clicked on one. He showed the screen to Justin. "See this contact? That's a buddy of mine in the ATF. One call to him and your business becomes his top priority."

"I run a legal business. Follow all of the regulations despite not agreeing with a one. Anyway, I sold those guns personally. Not through the business."

"I believe you, Justin. I really do. But my friend here isn't very trusting. Too many years of bullshit with people like you who seem more interested in making his life difficult than in helping stop crime. By the time he's finished with you, you'll regret not taking option two."

"This is harassment."

"I prefer to call it coercion."

Justin pulled a small pad of yellow-lined paper from beneath the counter. "The more things change, the more they stay the same." With a disgusted expression, he wrote down four names. "Satisfied?"

Jack looked at the list. One name jumped out.

"For now."

V

On its first full day of business, the Book Bank was hopping with a steady stream of browsers, buyers, lingerers, and coffee drinkers. A group of mothers sat on deep leather couches in the kid's corner, watching their children play. Old men sat at the front three square bistro tables playing dominoes. They were silent save the slap of the bones on the table. Ellie was refilling the coffee cups of the players and deflecting some harmless flirting when Eddie McBride walked into the store.

With everything that had happened, Ellie had given Jack's twin little thought. The whole scene the night before seemed dreamlike—honestly, more of a waking nightmare—and Eddie's part in it was muddled. He was more of an impression than a real person. When he walked through the door in the light of day, she thought it was Jack, only the bad boy version of Jack created for a cheesy television adaptation of *Dr. Jekyll and Mr. Hyde*.

"Whoa, whoa," J.B. Miller said. The coffee she was pouring spilled over the rim of the cup.

"Sorry, J.B." She placed the pot down, removed a towel from the back of her apron, and wiped the spill.

"Who the hell is that?" Walt Dixon, J.B.'s current mark, asked. Eddie sauntered to the coffee bar, his head on a swivel, smiling at people who caught his eye. J.B. turned in his seat.

"Looks like trouble to me," J.B. announced. "You gonna play that double deuce or not, Walt?"

"Damn you, J.B." Walt slapped the tile down.

"Play nice, boys," Ellie said. She picked up the coffee pot and walked to the bar.

Eddie leaned one arm on the counter and placed his order with Jennifer, a college student who would work Tuesdays, Thursdays, and Saturdays. Jennifer, fair-skinned and prone to blushing at the least provocation, was flame-red with embarrassment, and why wouldn't she be? Everything about Eddie McBride said trouble, from his tight jeans to his vintage T-shirt, from the mischievous smile to his hair brushing the collar of his shirt, from the motorcycle boots to the chain that hung in a loop down his thigh. Then there was the full arm tattoo of what looked like a phoenix. Ellie replaced the coffee pot, started making a new pot, and smiled to herself. Eddie McBride went through a lot of trouble to look the part of a bad boy.

Jennifer fumbled the paper coffee cup onto the floor. "Jennifer, why don't you go back and bring up a new sleeve of medium cups? I'll make his drink."

"Yes, Ms. Martin," Jennifer said. She focused on the ground and walked away.

Ellie tossed the fallen cup into the trash. "What are you having?"

"Brown sugar latte," Eddie replied. "You could have used the cup. I don't want to be responsible for filling landfills and killing trees."

"I absolve you of any responsibility," Ellie said.

"Whew. What a relief." He stuck out his hand. "I'm Eddie, by the way."

She wiped her hand on her apron and then shook his. "Ellie Martin."

"I thought I'd come by and properly introduce myself since we didn't get the chance last night."

"Very kind of you," Ellie said. She finished the latte, determined not to blush under Eddie McBride's examination, and placed it on the counter in front of him. "Three-oh-eight."

The thin metal chain attached to his wallet dinged on the glass case as he removed the cash. "It wasn't kindness brought me here. It was a raging curiosity to meet the woman who threw my brother and nephew into such a tizzy."

She took the money, put it in the drawer, and closed it with a little more force than necessary. "A tizzy?"

"Maybe *uproar* would be a better word." He sipped his drink.

"I don't like that one either."

"This is very good," he said.

"Thanks."

"I'm not here to judge or to berate you," Eddie said. "If you ask me, it's about time Jack felt passionate enough to fight for something."

"The last thing I would ever want is for Jack and his son to be arguing about me."

"Don't take this the wrong way, but it wasn't about you, exactly. But I'm sure Jack has filled you in."

Ellie inhaled involuntarily and straightened. Jack's voicemail had been short, to the point, and unrelated to the night before. *You're beautiful.* She'd listened to it more times than she wanted to admit.

Eddie raised his eyebrows. "He hasn't told you? Well, that's typical Jack for you."

"Is there something specific I can do for you, Eddie? Some particular curiosity you wanted solved? Or did you come here merely to size me up and to try to intimidate me? Or are you the type who is always undermining his brother out of some sort of childhood vengeance?"

Eddie leaned back. "Whoa," he said. His eyes were dancing with good humor. "You're a pistol. . . . I like you."

The phone rang. "I'm so glad. Now, if you will excuse me, I have a business to run." Ellie answered the phone and turned her back on Eddie. The call was brief, a question about the hours. When she hung up, Eddie was still there.

"Maybe we should start over," he said.

"Let's not."

"Wow, usually it takes at least ten to fifteen minutes for someone to dislike me. I guess you haven't noticed, but I am roguishly charming."

"I haven't noticed."

"You make an excellent latte."

"You've said that."

He leaned on the counter, tucking his crossed arms under his chest. "Why don't you like me?" he asked. Ellie knew by his expression it was a genuine question.

Because you are exactly like my ex-husband.

The words itched the tip of her tongue, desperate to lash out at this overconfident man. To tell him his easy charm and the sexuality that throbbed from him like ripples in water would have no effect on her. That if she gave it any thought at all—which she wouldn't—she could recite, song and verse, the ups and downs of his life. How he reveled in his role as the black sheep. How he constantly found new ways to test Jack's loyalty and the lengths he would go to to protect him, to bail him out, to give him just one more chance. How one day, Jack would finally have too much and cut him out of his life.

But she didn't. She knew her weakness would be his ammunition. She relaxed her shoulders and forced a smile, tried to make it as genuine as possible. "I'm sorry," she forced out. "It has been a busy day and I'm a bit frazzled."

He nodded. "I understand. No worries." He looked around. "I like your place."

"Thank you," Ellie replied.

"I'll be honest. When I heard Jack took this job, I didn't expect to find a place like this in it. Good coffee. Books. My kind of place. Mind if I look around?"

"Not if you buy something," she said.

"Where's your nonfiction section?"

Ellie pointed to the wall near the kids corner. "Over there."

Eddie wrinkled his nose. "I think I'll wait until the rug rats leave. I'll check out the old-timers." He leaned forward. "Don't tell them I said that."

"I wouldn't dream of it."

It wasn't long until Eddie made friends with the men. He pulled up a chair and watched J.B. and Walt play. From the expression on Walt's face, Eddie was about to take his seat. About time. She'd been waiting for a chance to talk to Walt alone all morning. She knew she should stay out of it and let the professionals do their job. But a part of her was curious.

Walt stood and gave his chair to Eddie.

"Hey, Walt," Ellie called. "Want a coffee for the road?"

Walt limped up to the counter. He was bowlegged from years of horseback riding and riding a tractor every summer since he was young enough to drive. "You keep giving away your coffee'n you'll never make any money."

"That's where you're wrong. You're my free marketing."

"Oh, am I?"

"Yes. You're going to take this cup of coffee and walk through Brookshires, telling everyone you see it's the best cup of coffee in town."

"I suppose I can do that for a pretty lady like you."

"Come back tomorrow and play dominoes."

"Does our sitting in the front window constitute free marketing?"

"Yep. You make it look busy in here."

"Well, it is."

"I want to keep it going." Ellie leaned forward on the counter. "Been meaning to ask you—what do you think of the skeleton out at the Dodsworths'?"

"Haven't given it much thought."

"Walt, you're a terrible liar. That's all anyone has been talking about for two days. Rumor is it's Old Man Dodsworth's first wife."

"Where'd you get such a crazy notion? She left town way back in the '50s."

"Did you know her? Claire was her name, right?"

"I knew of her," Walt said. He kept his eyes on his coffee cup.

Ellie leaned further forward and whispered. "Did you have a thing with her? I heard she liked younger men."

He looked up at her, his eyes narrowed. "What are you fishing for, Ellie?"

She stood and feigned shock. "Nothing, Walt. Why would you say that?"

"'Cause you aren't one to gossip and that's just what this is."

Ellie sighed. She wasn't very good at this. "You're right, Walt. Never mind." She absently wiped the counter with her towel. "The last thing the new chief needs is people spreading gossip and false stories about a fifty-year-old murder."

"Murder?"

"Well, yeah. Isn't that kind of assumed? Why else bury a body in the woods?"

Walt stared at the wall over Ellie's shoulder. She let the silence lengthen, let him think of the possibilities before saying, "There probably aren't many people around who even remember Claire Dodsworth."

"He thinks those bones are Claire's?"

"He hasn't come out and said it, but I think that's the way they're leaning."

"How do you know so much about it?"

"He was here at the reception last night, talking about it."

"Don't seem to me he should be talking about his cases like that."

"Maybe not. Or maybe he's trying to suss out information by jogging people's memories about a woman most everyone has forgotten."

Walt twisted his cup around on the counter, clearly disturbed by the information. She patted his hand. "Don't forget to go to Brookshires."

J.B. Miller let out a loud expletive. Eddie laughed. Walt picked up his cup and turned to the door. "Glad that bastard finally lost. Just wish I'd been the one to beat him."

"See you tomorrow, Walt," Ellie called.

He lifted his cup but didn't turn. "Thanks for the coffee, Ellie."

As she watched Walt leave, Ellie picked up the phone to call Jack.

VI

Ethan didn't say a word until lunch and only spoke then because Mitra asked him a direct question.

"How was the reception last night?"

Ethan's angry answer died on his tongue at Mitra's open, innocent expression. He wanted to say it sucked; that Olivia ignored him and he caught his dad groping some ugly Amazon in the office, but he didn't. "Why weren't you there?"

"Oh, my dad was sick and my mom wanted to stay home and take care of him."

"You could have come with us," Troy said.

"Thanks," Mitra said, blushing. "But I doubt my father would have allowed it. So, was it fun?"

Troy looked at Ethan warily. He had tried to draw Ethan out when they first got to school but gave up pretty quick, much to Ethan's relief. He liked Troy, but there was no way he could tell him about what happened.

"My Uncle Eddie is in town," Ethan said. It was the one bright spot to the night.

"Oh, yeah?" Troy said.

"Yeah. He's totally cool. Rides this awesome motorcycle. Brought me to school on it this morning."

"No way," Troy said. "Would he take me for a ride?"

"Sure, why not?"

"I saw him this morning," Mitra said. "I thought it was your dad for a second."

"They're twins," Ethan said, "but they're nothing alike."

"What siblings are?" Troy asked. He glanced across the cafeteria at his sister, sitting with Kevin Jackson and his group of friends. They were laughing about something. Ethan followed Troy's gaze just as Olivia looked in their direction. Ethan looked away, his face reddening. Great. Now she would think he had been staring at her. He hadn't looked at her once all day. Every time he even thought of her and Kevin Jackson, his fists balled and the corner of his right eye started twitching.

"Ethan?"

Mitra held a celery stick with a glob of hummus on the end. The concern in her eyes made him feel guilty for some reason. He always felt like Mitra knew what he was thinking, good or bad, but never judged him for it. That she somehow understood and sympathized. It kinda pissed him off.

The three talked about their classes, studiously avoiding any mention of Olivia. Ethan gathered everyone's trash, dumped it, and was placing his dirty tray in the window when he heard a low voice in his ear.

"In just a few hours, I'm going to be sticking my tongue down Olivia's throat. Again."

Ethan tensed. "Yeah, good for you." Ethan tried to walk around Kevin, but he stepped in front of him.

"If she's anything like her sister, I'll probably get my hands down her pants, too. Did you notice? She's wearing a skirt. She's practically begging for—"

Ethan wouldn't remember much about what happened next, but from all accounts, even from people he trusted like Mitra and Troy, he threw Kevin to the ground and started pounding his fist into his face.

There was screaming, yelling, and suddenly, Ethan was jerked onto his feet, his arms pinned behind him by Coach Taylor. Kevin lay on the floor, moaning, blood running from his mouth and nose. Troy was being held back by Coach Ivey. Mitra and Olivia were standing nearby in a group of eighth-grade girls, faces white with shock. A couple of Kevin's football buddies were standing by, chests heaving. One wiped a small trickle of blood from his nose and glared at Troy. The aisle of kids opened and in marched Principal Courcey, walkie-talkie in her hand, fury on her face.

"You two, come with me."

VII

After a week of relative calm, all hell broke loose in Stillwater. Calls flooded the switchboard: trespassing, slashed tires all across town, suspected drug deals, and the most disruptive of all—livestock on the road.

Jack could not believe he was staring at the asses of thirty white-faced cows as they clop-clop-clopped down Boondoggle Road. His car was parked across the road behind him, lights flashing, stopping a line of cars. Country courtesy demanded they get out and help. They formed a line on either side of Jack, flapping their arms. Occasionally, one of the farmers would release a loud two note whoop that Jack assumed was the bovine version of a duck call. He couldn't see that it did much good, other than possibly relieve the boredom of the walkers. The cows continued on their unhurried way, mooing plaintively and shitting as they walked. He'd already stepped in one cow patty, which gave everyone a good laugh. Jack figured it would be included in the *Stillwater Sentinel* crime log.

Jack and his group met up with Miner and his helpers at the pasture gate. The cows walked docilely into the pasture, Sunday strolling. Jack and Miner stood on the road. Their radios crackled to life. Violet reporting another "crime."

After Miner answered the call, Jack said, "Is this a practical joke?"

"Could be," Miner said. "It's a pretty tame one if it is. They're damn lucky no cows got killed on the road. Walt wouldn't have liked that. Wonder where he is?"

"I'm not talking about the cows, Miner."

"You're not?" He wore a studied expression of ignorance.

"We've gotten more calls today than the entire past week altogether," Jack said.

"Guess that's why it's called a crime wave." Miner mimed a wave with his hand. "It comes and goes."

Jack studied Miner. Pollard mentioned the day before to expect a crime wave. Was Miner behind it? "Where the hell is Freeman?"

"Called in sick," Miner said.

"He looked fine yesterday afternoon."

"Maybe it's food poisoning. I ate some bad shrimp once. Thought I was going to die. Haven't had shrimp since."

Jack sighed. Miner always had a story. "Which call do you want to take?"

"Slashed tires, I guess."

"Great. I get the prowler." Jack walked away, took his buzzing phone from his pocket. He ignored an unknown number and also saw he had a missed call from Ellie.

Jack turned back. "Miner." He got close enough and dropped his voice. "Did you talk to Ellie?"

"Yep. I've got some new information, too. I'll radio you when I get done. We can meet at the station."

Jack's phone rang again, with the same unknown number. Surely his number wasn't community knowledge. "Jack McBride."

"Mr. McBride. This is Dr. Courcey, principal at Eisenhower."

Through the sour taste in his throat he replied, "Miss Courcey, what can I do for you?"

She cleared her throat. "I prefer Doctor, Mr. McBride."

"And I prefer Chief McBride. What can I do for you? I'm very busy."

"I assume you aren't too busy to pick up your son."

"It's barely one o'clock."

"He's being suspended."

VIII

"Am I in the right place here?"

"Mr. Mc—Ch—" Dr. Courcey paused. "Who are you?"

"I'm Ethan's uncle, Eddie. I just got in last night."

Ethan slumped back in his chair. His dad sent Uncle Eddie instead of coming himself. So he was still mad about last night. Well, that was fine with Ethan. He was still mad at his dad. This was all his fault, anyway. If his dad hadn't been cheating on his mom, Ethan wouldn't have felt like a coiled spring all day. He hoped this caused a load of problems for his dad with the community. Maybe he would get fired and they could get out of this depressing town.

"Yes, well. Welcome to Stillwater, Mr. McBride. But I didn't call you. Nor are you on any of the forms your brother filled out. I cannot talk to you about Ethan's situation."

"Ethan's situation?" Uncle Eddie chuckled. "Sounds serious."

"It is very serious. How did you even know to come here?"

"Small town," Eddie said. "Word travels fast." He glanced at Mrs. Grant. Eddie held out his hand. "Eddie McBride."

"Susan Grant." She shook his hand briefly.

"Nice to meet you." He turned his attention to Ethan. "Hey, buddy."

"Hi, Uncle Eddie."

"See." Eddie motioned to Ethan. "He just confirmed my identity and I mean, really, Dr. Courcey." Eddie waved his hand up and down his body. "Have you met my brother? Can you doubt we are related?"

Dr. Courcey slammed a pen down on her desk. "It doesn't matter."

"Diane," Susan said. "Can we please just get on with this? He's obviously Chief McBride's brother."

"Oh, hey," Eddie said. He stuck his hand out to Troy. "Didn't mean to ignore you, dude. Eddie McBride."

Troy, puzzled, embarrassed, stuck his hand out. "Troy."

"Cool name. After Troy Aikman?"

"Yeah. How did you know that?"

"You got the look of a football star, dude."

Ethan smiled. Well, he had won Troy over. One down, two to go. If anyone could salvage this situation, it was Uncle Eddie. His dad bailing on Ethan didn't seem so bad anymore.

"So." Eddie slapped his hands together. "Did I hear something about a fight?"

"Yes, Diane," Mrs. Grant said. "What exactly happened?"

With a tight voice, Courcey shared the story.

"Ethan jumped some boy without provocation?" The disbelief was clear in Eddie's voice.

"What exactly was Troy's involvement?" Mrs. Grant said, her voice cracking on her son's name.

"He pulled Matt Huffington off of Ethan—Matt is Kevin's best friend—and punched him. Gave him a bloody nose."

Troy jumped up from his chair. His face was white, but his voice was angry. "I did not punch him." He turned to his mom. "I didn't punch him, Mom. I swear."

Mrs. Grant's entire body relaxed, but her hand still shook as she brushed hair from Troy's face. "I know, sweetie."

Ethan was sure Troy would flinch away from her hand or at least from being called *sweetie*. Instead, he stepped toward his mom, kissed her on the cheek, and whispered in her ear.

Dr. Courcey seemed relieved, as well, but it was hard for Ethan to tell. Dr. Courcey had bowed her head and was staring at the ground behind her desk. Uncle Eddie studied Mrs. Grant and Troy until Ethan caught his eye. His uncle smiled, trying to hide his concern behind his normal happy-go-lucky uncle facade. Something was going on but Ethan, for the life of him, couldn't figure out what.

"I pulled Matt off of Ethan and tossed him back," Troy said. "I think he fell over a chair. I'm sorry he hurt his nose. I was just trying to get Ethan off Kevin."

Great. Dr. Courcey was focused on Ethan again. Her eyes narrowed. "As much as you don't want to believe it, Mr. McBride, your nephew jumped Kevin Jackson. There were one hundred students who witnessed it."

"What happened, Ethan?" Eddie asked.

Ethan kept his head down and stayed silent. He couldn't tell them why he jumped Kevin. There was no way he could say what Kevin said, for one thing. He didn't think those words could come out of his mouth. For another, he was pretty sure Mrs. Grant would be mortified to hear a guy talking about her daughter like that. Dr. Courcey wouldn't believe him anyway. Most important, Ethan didn't want anyone to figure out his real motivation was jealousy.

Troy came to his rescue. "Kevin has been bullying Ethan since he got here."

Ethan flushed with pleasure. He was wrong—Troy sticking up for him (even though he'd doubted Kevin's bullying) was the best thing that could happen to him today. Well, that and Olivia not hating him for beating up her boyfriend. Since *that* wasn't going to happen, he'd take what he could get.

"Kevin Jackson?" Principal Courcey said in disbelief. "He is one of the nicest kids in school!"

"And your nephew, Diane," Mrs. Grant said, quietly.

"What are you implying, Susan?"

"Nothing. I know you're fair and would never favor your relatives. You are related to half the town, after all. But the other half of the town might talk."

"How exactly has Kevin been bullying you, Ethan?" Courcey's voice was full of mockery.

"Saying stuff about my dad."

"Is that what set you off?" Eddie asked.

Why not? It was as good a lie as any. "Yes."

"Do you really blame him?" Eddie said. "Yes, he was wrong to jump the kid, but he was provoked."

"According to Kevin, he didn't say a word to him."

"He's lying," Ethan said.

That had been the wrong thing to say, and it was made even worse when his dad took that exact moment to barge into the office.

"Well, nice of you to join us, Mr. McBride," Dr. Courcey said.

"Miss Courcey," Jack said. He turned to Ethan. Ethan scooted back in his chair and looked down. His dad crouched in front of him so that Ethan had to look at him. "You okay?"

Ethan was coming to terms with his dad's concern and the fact he wasn't spitting mad at him when his dad winked at him and stood. Ethan's mouth gaped.

"Eddie, thanks for coming down," Jack said. Eddie stepped back next to Mrs. Grant, who studiously avoided his gaze.

"So, Ethan got into a fight. Who with? Some kid named Jackson?"

"How did you know that?"

"Because my son tells me what's going on."

Huh. Ethan wasn't the only one lying.

"In fact, he told me on the first day of school that this kid and his cronies cornered him in the locker room."

"Is that true, Ethan?" Dr. Courcey asked.

"Yes."

"Why didn't you say anything?"

"I'm not a tattle-tale."

"Just a fighter," Dr. Courcey said.

"I hardly think standing up to a bully makes my son a 'fighter.'"

"Fighting is a form of bullying and we take bullying very seriously."

"Only when it's directed at a relative of yours, it would seem. Remind me again, how are you related to Buck Pollard?"

"Excuse me?"

Jack waved his hand. "It doesn't matter. You said Ethan would be suspended. For how long?"

"A week."

"Fine."

"That means he will get zeros for all of the work during that time."

"I have no doubt my son will work hard to bring his grades up as high as possible, even with that ridiculous punishment." Jack stepped close to the desk. Ethan couldn't see his face, but he heard what his dad said very clearly. "You be sure to write in your report that I told Ethan to stand up for himself and his friends, even if that means fighting."

He placed the tips of his fingers on the desk and leaned over. "I also want you to tell your uncle . . ." Dr. Courcey flinched. "Yeah, that small-town gossip works both ways. Who knew? You tell him that only a coward tries to get to someone through their kid." He turned—"Come on, Ethan"—and walked out the door.

IX

"Go inside, Ethan. I'll be right there."

Ethan hesitated, looking between Jack and Eddie, who turned off his Harley and twisted the front wheel. Jack forced a smile at his son. "Go on."

Jack sighed. The teenager he watched walk up the steps, across the porch, and through the front door looked nothing like the four-year-old Jack coached in soccer, the seven-year-old he taught to ride without training wheels, the ten-year-old who was so proud of his perfect cannonball. He rubbed his face with his hands. His bruised eye throbbed in response. It took his son getting into a fight—which Jack had encouraged him to do—for him to notice his son had a life outside of him. He turned to face his brother.

Eddie looked like a twenty-year-old slacker instead of a forty-three-year-old loser, though Jack admitted to himself it was a fine distinction.

"What were you doing at the school, Eddie? Did Ethan call you?"

Eddie sniffed, smiled, and shook his head. "God, you are so predictable, Jack."

"As predictable as you driving into my town with a pocket full of drugs."

"Your town? You've been here a week and it's *your town*?"

"Did Ethan call you?"

"No." He swung his leg over his bike and stood. "I was talking to your girlfriend when Susan called her. Rather hysterical, I think."

"My girlfriend?"

"Ellie. She's a keeper, by the way."

Jack clenched his fists and tried to keep the anger from his voice. "What were you doing at Ellie's?"

"Getting to know the locals. Playing dominoes. Drinking a really good latte. Sizing up your girlfriend."

"She isn't my girlfriend."

"Maybe not yet, but she should be. Put me in my place right off the bat. To be honest, she reminds me of Mom."

Jack turned away and ran his hands through his hair. "Jesus Christ." He turned back to his brother, put his hands together in prayer on his forehead. "Please, please stay out of it, okay, Eddie?"

"Hey, I'm not in it. I wanted to introduce myself to her and went to her bookstore. That's it. Chill out, bro."

Jack stepped forward so he was almost nose-to-nose with his brother. "*Chill out, bro?* God, you've got no fucking idea. The last thing I need is my loser brother coming here and jumping in the middle of my life. It's bad enough I bailed you out last night. I'm sure that's going to come back to haunt me. Then you show up at the school, when no one asked you, and stuck your nose in that situation."

"I'll have you know I had 'that situation' under control until you and your big ball of rage burst in. *Miss* Courcey. Could you have been any more insulting?"

"Probably, yeah."

Eddie laughed. "Your temper is going to get you in trouble, little brother. Again."

"I can handle my temper."

"Like you did last night?"

Jack shoved his hands in his pockets and looked away.

"Look," Eddie said. "I'm not about to tell you how to handle Ethan. You wouldn't listen to me if I did. But I will tell you that the only way he's going to talk to you is if you shelve the anger and talk to him like an adult."

Jack nodded. "You're right."

Eddie laughed. "What?"

Jack closed his eyes and pinched the bridge of his nose. "I keep thinking about last night. How shitty I handled it."

"Well, kids remember the apology more than the anger."

Jack dropped his hand. "Where the hell did you hear that?"

Eddie shrugged. "Some child therapist I was boning a few years ago."

"Oh, God," Jack said with a groan. "All right. What happened at school? Did Ethan explain?"

"Eh," Eddie said, shaking his hand in front of him. "He was lying about most of it. Said the kid whispered something insulting about you and he jumped him."

"Why do you think he was lying about that?"

"You two aren't exactly best buddies these days. He isn't going to care too much what people say about you." Jack's stomach clenched at the truth in Eddie's statement. "Not enough to beat the crap out of them anyway. My guess is it's about a girl."

"A girl?"

"Surely you remember being fourteen."

"Vaguely."

"Well, I remember you waking up every morning with a huge boner. Not as big as mine, of course. But it was a little impressive." He held his thumb and forefinger a couple inches apart.

Jack walked away. "Oh, hey." He walked back to his brother. "Stay away from Ellie."

"Why? Afraid she's going to like me more?"

"God, no. I'm afraid she'll be scared off by my batshit insane family."

"She doesn't look like the type to be scared too easily."

"That's what I'm counting on."

Jack knocked on Ethan's door and let himself in. Ethan was lying on his bed staring at the ceiling. Jack followed his eyes to a water stain above the bed. "What does it look like?"

"If you tilt your head just right, it looks like an F. The puffy kind girls draw," Ethan said.

Jack tilted his head. "I guess I can see that. Looks like Maryland to me." He sat on Ethan's bed. "So. Want to tell me what happened?"

"Aren't you mad?"

Jack shrugged. "I can't really be mad when I told you to stick up for yourself last week. You did have a reason for what you did."

Ethan nodded.

"Do you want to tell me what it was?"

When Ethan blushed, Jack knew Eddie was right: it *was* about a girl.

"It wasn't about me, was it?"

Ethan remained silent.

"Ethan, you know you can tell me anything. I'm not going to tell anyone. I promise."

"Even *her*?"

"Ellie? No. At the end of the day, our loyalty is to each other. To family. That's never going to change."

Ethan sighed. "He was saying things about Olivia. Dirty things."

"Troy's sister?"

"Yeah."

From the embarrassment on Ethan's face, Jack knew better than to ask specifics. He could imagine too well. "Did Troy hear?"

"If he had, Kevin Jackson would be in the hospital."

"That bad?" Jack said.

"I really don't want to . . ."

"No, no. That's fine. Well, you did the right thing."

Ethan sat up. "Really?"

"Sticking up for your friends is always the right thing. I wish it hadn't been through fighting."

"You told me!"

"I know, I know. I had no idea you would be so good at it."

Ethan leaned his back against his headboard and pulled a small down feather out of his pillow. "He picked the wrong day to piss me off."

Jack felt a wave of guilt. Kevin Jackson was the victim of Ethan's rage at his father.

"I'm sorry about last night," Jack said.

Ethan stopped picking. He looked up slowly, hopefully. "You are?"

"I shouldn't have told you about your mother that way. It was insensitive. I've tried very hard not to let my anger at your mom come across and I guess the effort of holding it in all these months burst at the wrong time."

Ethan shoulders slumped. "You're still going to divorce her?"

"I haven't heard from her in a year. She could be . . ." He stopped before he said "dead for all I know" but just barely.

"But if she came back?"

"She isn't," Jack replied.

"But if she did, you'd give her a chance, you'd let her explain?"

How could he tell Ethan of his realizations months ago? The one where he figured out he didn't miss Julie. That any feelings he had for her before she left were from obligation instead of affection. That he had known he'd made a mistake only months into his marriage. That he stayed with Julie because it was easy, it was expected of him to make it work. That Julie was a narcissist who only ever did anything with her own best interests in mind.

He couldn't tell Ethan any of that. Jack might not love Julie, but she was Ethan's mother.

"Sure. I'd let her explain."

X

Mike Freeman lived in a small midcentury Craftsman bungalow two streets from the high school. It was well kept but unremarkable, painted white with black shutters and with a concrete front porch flanked by hydrangeas. Freeman's Ford was parked in front of a detached garage behind and to the right of the house. Through the open garage door, Jack could see weight benches, dumbbells, a speed bag, a punching bag, and a treadmill.

Jack sat in his darkened car across the street one house down and stared at the red Jeep parked behind Freeman's truck, a University of Texas bumper sticker marking it as the same red Jeep Ethan had taken a picture of days before. For an hour, he heard the sound of weights clearly in this quiet neighborhood. There was no traffic. No one walking dogs. No kids playing. Just a police officer and the senior varsity quarterback working out. The light in the garage went out and Jack sat up, expecting Seth Kendrick to get in his Jeep and drive off. Ten minutes passed. The Jeep didn't move. The lights in the house didn't turn on. Jack got out of his car.

He walked down the sidewalk and past the dark house. A small dog in the house next door barked. Jack turned, walked past Freeman's house again, and went around Seth's Jeep to the cab of Freeman's truck, where he paused. The garage door was closed. Jack saw the freshly mowed back-yard, a small charcoal grill, and two canvas lawn chairs. Concrete steps with a metal pipe as a handrail led to the back door, which Jack guessed led to the kitchen. He walked around the front of the truck, past the kitchen door, and paused at the corner of the house. A line of bushes blocked Freeman's house from the yapping dog's house next door. The house was quiet. Jack let out a breath; Freeman didn't have a dog.

Jack inched forward to the side window. The room, like the rest of the house, was dark. There was a chink in the drapes but it wasn't large enough to see anything. The window, however, was open slightly, letting Jack hear everything he needed, and more than he wanted.

Thirty minutes later, Seth left and Jack went to the door. Any hope Jack had of being wrong evaporated when Mike Freeman answered the door smiling, shirtless, and holding a video game controller. His jeans were low waisted and unbuttoned. Without his too-small uniform, he looked smaller, well defined to be sure, but not the hulking muscleman he appeared in uniform. "Did you—" His smile melted into a frown. "Chief McBride."

"Mike. I wanted to see how you are feeling."

"Better."

"Can I come in?"

"Of course." Freeman stepped back, held the door open for Jack, then closed it behind him. "Let me get a shirt on," Freeman said.

"Take your time," Jack said.

The living room was sparsely furnished with a sixty-inch flat screen on a glass and metal TV stand as the focal point. The television was paused on a first-person shooter game, *Medal of Honor* or *Call of Duty*. They all looked the same to Jack. Freeman returned wearing a white T-shirt.

"*Assassin's Creed*," Freeman explained.

"I like your house," Jack said. He walked over to a bookshelf. Well-worn paperbacks, mostly military fiction Jack had never heard of, self-help books, fitness books, gun manuals, and a few romances on the bottom shelf.

"Thanks. It was my grandmother's. She left it to me."

"Did you grow up here?" Jack removed a book at random and flipped through it.

"No. I visited summers."

He put the book back. "What did the doctor say?"

"Doctor?"

"Didn't you go today?"

"Oh, no. I think it was food poisoning. I'm feeling better. Afraid to eat anything, though."

"Where did you eat? So I know to stay away from there." Jack laughed.

"It was my own cooking," Freeman said.

"Can I get a drink of water?"

"Sure."

Freeman flipped on the kitchen light, walked to the sink, and filled a glass with water. A disassembled handgun, a lint-free scrap of cloth, and gun oil sat on the Formica table.

"Wow. That's an old refrigerator."

"Yeah, it was my grandmother's. It still works, so why not use it?"

"It'll probably last forever," Jack said. He ran his hand over the curved door. "They don't make them like this anymore."

Freeman handed Jack the glass. "Thanks," Jack said. He drank the ice-less water and stared at Mike Freeman over the rim. Any uncertainty his officer had with Jack's arrival was gone. His eyes were wary.

"Want to tell me what Seth Kendrick was doing here?"

The corner of Freeman's eye twitched. "We were working out."

"I thought you were sick."

"I'm feeling better."

"After your workout?"

"He left."

"No he didn't."

"We played *Assassin's Creed* for a bit."

Jack placed the glass on the table. "Don't lie to me, Mike."

"I'm not."

Jack leaned forward and sniffed. "You smell like sex."

Jack was ready for him when he lunged. Jack stepped aside, wrenched Freeman's arm behind his back, and shoved him facedown onto the table. Big guys always overestimated themselves. Freeman yelled, his cheek splitting as it hit the gun pieces. "How long have you been fucking Seth Kendrick?"

"It's not like that."

"Really? 'Cause that's what it sounded like. You really should keep your window closed." Jack twisted Freeman's arm farther up his back.

"We aren't doing anything wrong."

"Really?"

"He's eighteen."

"He's a kid."

"His mother held him back a year. He's been eighteen for months."

"Lucky for you. Why didn't you come to work today?"

"I didn't feel good."

Jack wrenched his arm. "Bullshit."

"Okay, okay. Pollard asked me to call in."

"Why?"

"He wanted to run you around town on a bunch of fake calls."

"Why?"

"I don't know. I didn't ask."

"Why would you do what he said?"

Freeman didn't respond. Jack brought his knee up between his legs. Freeman's legs buckled and he groaned. "Let me tell you what I think," Jack said. "I think Pollard found out about you and that boy and threatened to expose you."

"He's not a boy," Freeman croaked. "*He* pursued *me*."

Jack leaned down close to Freeman's ear. "I don't fucking care. I don't care if you like men. I don't even care if you are fucking Seth, as long as it's consensual and, believe me, I'll find out. What I do care about is the fact you've been working against me for Pollard."

"I haven't. Just today."

Jack slapped cuffs on Freeman, stood him up, and pushed him down into a chair. Blood ran down his cheek. He hunched over in the chair, still in pain from being kneed in the balls. Jack pulled a chair out, slammed it down in front of Freeman, and sat down.

"Here's the deal," Jack said. "I know." He spread his hands and leaned back in the chair. "You bought a Beretta from Justin Dixon, you killed

Gilberto and Rosa." Freeman looked up. "Crime scene called today. There was a partial print on the inside of the slide assembly."

Freeman shook his head and looked down.

"Now, I can fill in the blanks through guesswork and supposition, but if I hear it from you, I'll put in a good word with the DA."

He remained silent, staring at the ground.

"Okay. Here's the story I'm going to tell: Seth Kendrick killed Gilberto and Rosa in a drug deal that went bad." Freeman's head shot up at Seth's name. "Oh, did I forget to tell you? It was Seth's print on the inside of the gun."

"That's not possible."

"Sure it is."

"He never—" Freeman caught himself. "His wouldn't be in the system."

"He would if his mother had him printed when he was a kid. My wife printed my son. In case he ever got abducted." Jack laughed. "These helicopter moms."

Freeman was breathing heavily, his face pale.

"When I leave here, I'm going to Kelly Kendrick's house to arrest Seth. My guess is he won't have an alibi for the murder. He was probably at home in bed, but kids sneak out all the time. He *might* beat the charge. It'll be tough for the DA to find a motive, but his life will be ruined. He can say bye-bye to a football scholarship. He's young, good-looking, fit. He'll be *real* popular in Huntsville."

"Okay, okay. Enough." Freeman exhaled. "I killed them."

"Why? Did Rosa clean your house?"

"What? No."

"Then, what?"

"Pollard put me up to it."

"Pollard?" Jack wasn't expecting that answer. "Why?"

"I don't know; I didn't ask."

"Someone asks you to murder two people and you don't ask why?" Freeman wouldn't look at Jack. "Why would you agree to it?"

Freeman closed his eyes. "Pollard caught us. Me and Seth. Up at the German church."

"When?"

"June."

"Were you on duty?"

"Yes."

"Go on."

"He never came out and said he would expose us, but it was there, you know? The threat. The promise to keep it secret in exchange for a future favor. I never imagined what it would be." Freeman's eyes were red.

"You did it to protect Seth. His future."

He nodded.

"What exactly did Pollard tell you to do?"

"Make it look like a double murder. Plant some drugs. I decided to make it look like a murder-suicide. Didn't figure there would be much investigation, and if there was, I could manipulate it."

"Did you plant drugs?"

"Yes. Coke, meth."

"Where?"

"In the dresser. It was gone when I took pictures."

Jack pulled a handkerchief from his pocket and gave it to Freeman. "Pollard must not have been happy when you changed the plan."

"Not really." Freeman pressed the cloth to his cheek.

"Any idea why Pollard wanted them dead?"

"No."

"Did Pollard ask you to search the house for anything?"

Freeman looked at the blood on the handkerchief, folded it in half, and pressed it to his face again. "No. Like what?"

If Pollard didn't send Freeman to find something that would tie him to the Ramoses, then why did he want them dead?

"Did someone ask Pollard to have these people killed?" Jack said.

"Buck Pollard told me to kill them and plant drugs. That's it."

Jack stood and pushed his chair under the table. "Come on. You're going to tell me this story on camera at the station." Jack grabbed Freeman's arm and jerked him out of his seat. Freeman tried to jerk away but Jack tightened his grip.

"How did you know? About me and Seth?"

"My son took a picture of your cruiser and Seth's Jeep up at the church. I didn't think much about it until I came over here tonight to check on my sick officer. The rest was just supposition and guessing. Thanks for filling in the blanks. By the way, did you harass my son?"

"Pollard told me to."

Jack slammed Freeman's face down onto the table again. He screamed. "Oh, did you trip, Mike? You need to be more careful."

"Asshole," Freeman said between gritted teeth. Jack jerked him up into a standing position again. He put his mouth next to Freeman's ear and said, with barely controlled rage, "You confess to everything and implicate Pollard, and I'll keep Seth's name out of all of this. But if you even *think* about changing your story, I will fucking destroy Seth Kendrick's life."

"You wouldn't."

"Maybe, maybe not. But do you want to take that chance?"

CHAPTER SEVEN

Wednesday

I

Ellie's apartment was dark save the bluish glow from her computer and a small desk lamp. The clock in the top right corner of her screen said 1:57 a.m. Three minutes, then to bed. She meant it this time.

She paused, listened. Was that a knock? She jumped when she heard it again, louder. She stared at the door, heard the knock again, and rose. She pulled her sweater tight across her chest and stood next to the door. "Who is it?"

"Jack."

She exhaled with relief, unbolted the lock, and opened the door. Jack leaned on the doorjamb, pale, exhausted. The bruise around his eye looked worse than when it was fresh and swollen. "What's wrong?" she asked.

His smile was wan. "Nothing, now. Can I come in?"

Ellie looked into her darkened, empty apartment. "Sure." He walked in and she closed the door. He stood a few feet from the door, looking around. She turned on a floor lamp, walked to her desk, and closed her laptop.

"I saw the light." Jack explained.

"Insomnia," she said with a shrug.

"You, too?"

"For as long as I can remember."

"Same."

"Want a drink? Beer? Wine?"

"Beer."

She pulled a beer out of the refrigerator, popped the cap, and poured herself a glass of red wine. Jack put his handheld radio on the coffee table and sat on the couch.

She walked around the island and handed him the beer. "Are you still on duty?" She settled down into the opposite corner of the couch, tucking one leg beneath her, and faced him.

He drank his beer, sighed, smiled, and looked at the label. "Yes." He turned to her. "It's been a helluva day."

She sipped her wine. "Want to talk about it?"

He rested the beer bottle on his thigh. "Maybe later. . . . I like your place."

"Thanks."

"Did Kelly help you?"

"No, Brian put the kitchen and bathroom in for me."

They drank in comfortable silence. Ellie stared at her wine and waited. She knew whatever Jack came here for would come out in time. If it didn't? She wouldn't mind. She enjoyed being near him. It was the first time they had been truly alone. She shifted on the couch at the realization.

"I heard my brother came to see you."

"He did."

"He likes you."

"Does he?"

Jack drank his beer. "Saw you called a couple times. Sorry I didn't call you back."

"That's okay," she said quickly. "I called Miner."

"Miner?"

"About Claire Dodsworth."

"Oh," he said.

"What?" She nudged his leg with her foot. "Are you disappointed?"

"Never thought I'd say it, but I'm jealous of Miner," he said with a mischievous smile.

"As well you should be," she said.

His eyes lingered on hers for a moment before his smile fell and he said, "What about Claire Dodsworth?"

She told him about trying to question Walt Dixon. "I tried to get information out of him, but he caught me out."

"Walt Dixon? That's whose cows I was herding when you called."

"I would have liked to see that."

"I stepped in a cow patty. Everyone got a big kick out of it." Jack finished his beer, put the empty bottle on the coffee table, and sat back. He settled further into the couch and leaned his head back. "How was your first day of business?"

"Good. Very good. Busy."

Jack rested his hand, palm up, on the cushion between them. Ellie shifted her wineglass to her left hand and took it. He looked at her. "Sorry I couldn't come by."

"That's okay. I know you were busy."

Jack ran his thumb along her forefinger, smiled. "You have really long fingers."

"Freakishly long."

"I wouldn't say freakish. You play piano?"

"Not very well, much to Mrs. Hennessy's dismay."

He continued to run his thumb along her hand.

"What Ethan said last night wasn't true."

"What's that?" she asked, though her stomach lurched. She had been obsessing over it all day and felt hypocritical for it. She'd been with plenty of other men. It was just . . . difficult being slut-shamed by a teenager.

"I guess Julie told him I cheated on her. Which I didn't. Not once, though God knows I had enough chances."

"You don't have to explain."

"Yeah, I do." He lifted her hand and kissed the back of it. "I have a question."

She waited.

"You don't have to answer."

"Uh-oh."

Jack smiled, shifted closer to her on the couch, and turned to face her. "Did your husband cheat on you?"

Ellie nodded.

"With a lot of women?"

She nodded again.

"That's why you were so upset with me."

"That's part of it."

"What's the other part?"

She released his hand, placed her wine glass on the table, and stood. She grabbed another beer from the refrigerator and the bottle of wine and returned to the couch. Jack opened his beer and she poured more wine. She sipped the dry red wine, letting it slide down her throat and soothe her. She met Jack's eyes levelly.

"I don't like scandal."

"Who does?"

"My life has been one scandal after another."

"Really?" Disbelief was as clear in his voice as his expression.

"Jinx was the final straw."

"Jinx?"

"My ex-husband."

Ellie knew what was coming. She'd heard it enough. Jack grinned at the absurdity of it. "His name was Jinx?"

"Yes. Should have been my first clue, huh? I was young and apparently easily swept off my feet. Dad loved him, another red flag I ignored. Married within three months of meeting."

"Julie and I were married in six."

"Then you understand."

He nodded. "Unfortunately."

"You know, I could have survived the cheating. Might have tried to make it work. But it was all a lie. Everything." She took a deep breath, tried to decide how to tell Jack what happened as briefly as possible and somehow retain a bit of his respect and her pride. She wasn't sure it was possible.

"Jinx married me for my money, my property."

"People keep saying you're the richest woman in town."

"That's an exaggeration. I have enough, but more importantly, I had what my dad wanted and thought was his. He and Jinx tried to con me out of everything.

"Jinx was very good. It took me years to realize who he really was, what his game was. And that my father was at the center of it."

"Your father?"

She sipped her wine. "His hatred for me is legendary. It's one of the reasons I'm so well liked. Say what you want about Stillwater, but there is a deep well of pity in this town that I still benefit from."

"Why does he hate you?"

"Hated. He's dead." She drank and gestured with her glass as she said, "Really, there are too many reasons, and I don't particularly want to go into it. His biggest point of contention was that my mother left me all the property and money instead of him. He spent the last thirty years of his life trying to get it away from me. Jinx was his best hope. The idea was Jinx would marry me and, when I turned twenty-five, I would turn everything over to him."

"Why would you do that?"

"My father thought I was an idiot. And desperate for a man to love me. He thought Jinx, with all of his charms and manipulation, could do the rest. He almost did." She shook her head. "Thank God I'm not a total idiot, but mostly I have Jane to thank. She never liked Jinx, though I didn't know that until the end. She knew if she railed against Jinx, it would only alienate me. Instead, she embraced Jinx. I was a little jealous, to be honest. She had never shown me an ounce of affection and there she was, practically fawning over my husband."

Jack laughed and just caught the dribble of beer falling from his chin. "Jane Maxwell, fawning?"

"I know, right? Jinx was clever and manipulative but he wasn't smart. Had absolutely no business sense. Jane made him believe he did. Kept helping him get set up in businesses that inevitably failed. But it kept him distracted from his original goal: fleecing me.

"My father wasn't nearly as good at the long game as Jinx. He drank too much and, when he did, his real feelings for me would come through."

She stared into her wine glass, wishing there were a way to drown out the memories of her father once and for all. She knew better. She'd tried, more than once, but the next morning she was always left with a raging headache, sandpaper tongue, and mortification at her weakness. The memories were more manageable and surprisingly less painful when she was in control.

She looked at Jack and smiled thinly. "My father could be cruel. Jinx was livid when Big Jake got on a roll about how worthless I was, or at least Jinx seemed to be. At the time, though, I was just happy to have someone on my side. Someone who loved me. I would have given it all over without a word of complaint."

"Why didn't you?"

"I'd like to be able to say I started suspecting something was off, but that's not it." She closed her eyes. "I was obsessed with trying to get pregnant; I had hardly any other thought in my mind. Kelly had Seth, Susan had Paige. Everyone I knew was having babies. I was desperate. And still ridiculously in love. When Susan had Troy and Olivia, one right after the other, I went off the deep end. Fertility tests showed there was nothing wrong with either of us. Of course, he was cheating on his tests, I learned later." She waved her hand in dismissal of the details. She hardly wanted to relive it. "He went along with trying for a long while, always very subtly implying the problem must be with me, that I was somehow the failure. You can imagine having sex became a chore, lost all of its appeal. Instead of having more, we had less. Well, I had less anyway. He still had plenty with women all over the county. How I didn't know is a miracle. I guess I was determined to ignore the signs.

"Jinx made the mistake a screwing a woman who hated me more than she liked Jinx. She couldn't help but tell me about their relationship, if you could even call it that. She twisted the knife a little too far, told me trying to get pregnant was futile.

"Turns out, Jinx had never wanted kids. Before we met, he had a vasectomy so he could cat around and not worry if the condom broke."

Ellie stopped. She hadn't meant to tell him all of this. She picked at the drawstring of her pajama pants, all the shame rushing back.

"Jesus. It's no wonder you think men are more trouble than they're worth."

Her head shot up. "Who said that?"

"Shirley. The first day we met."

Ellie nodded and smiled. "Sounds like Shirley. She wasn't shy in her hatred of Jinx. Strained our relationship until I came to my senses. She never judged me, never said I told you so."

Ellie took a deep breath and laughed. "Well, this is much longer than I intended, so . . . With a little help from my friends, I wised up, divorced Jinx. He ended up in the pen down in Huntsville not long after. Still there."

"And your dad?"

"Hated me until the day he died." She returned her attention to the drawstring. "The town was pretty equally divided between pity for me and scorn for my stupidity. It was all quite the topic of conversation for months. Until 9/11 came and one pathetic woman's inability to get pregnant and poor taste in men became less interesting than the threat of terrorists owning the Chevron. That's when I went to Dallas. Got a job at Starbucks."

"Which Starbucks?"

"West Village."

"I went there all the time."

"I probably made you a latte."

"I would have noticed you."

She chuckled. "I doubt it."

Jack set his empty beer bottle next to his first. "Is your bathroom over there?" He pointed to the right.

"Yes."

When the bathroom door clicked closed, Ellie collapsed back on the sofa. Why did she tell him all of that? A two- or three-sentence explanation would have sufficed. Instead she had told him most, if not all, of the sordid details. He couldn't leave fast enough. She rose, picked up of the wine and bottles in one hand, her wine glass in the other. She tossed the empty bottles, corked the wine, and finished the rest of her glass in one long gulp.

Shirley was right. She did think men were more trouble than they were worth. She hated this up and down, the uncertainty, the gut wrenching disappointment, and wasn't that always how it ended? Why would this be any different? Maybe her dad had been right; maybe there was something deep inside her that was repulsive to men.

She rinsed the wine glass and was putting it in the dishwasher when Jack came out of the bathroom. She closed the dishwasher door, wiped her hands on a towel, and turned to face him, steeling her heart for his quick exit. He looked uncomfortable, surprised. He put his hands in his pockets. "It's getting late," he said.

The microwave clock said 2:48. "Yeah. Morning comes early." Ellie walked to the door.

Jack walked to the coffee table and picked up his radio. "I have to go home and search for my video camera." He stopped in front of her. "The camera at the station is at least thirty years old. It uses VHS tapes."

"I guess Buck didn't have much use for it."

"I'm thinking of selling it online as an antique. Use the money to buy a new computer. It's an antique, too." He stepped closer. "You don't have a video camera I could borrow, do you? I really don't want to search through all those boxes."

"No, sorry."

I've never needed one. No family, remember? She restrained herself from saying it and showing him how pathetic she truly was.

"I only have the camera on my phone," she said instead. She wondered why he needed a camera. Did he arrest someone for the Ramos murders? It was on the tip of her tongue to ask, but her desire for him to leave was greater than her curiosity.

"Good idea," Jack said. "I'd be searching until next year. I forgot to label the boxes."

Ellie laughed. "You didn't."

"I did."

Their laughter died down and they stared at each other, the smiles slowly sliding from their faces.

"Thanks for coming by," she said. She put her hand on the doorknob.

"There's one thing you said that bothers me."

Just one? She lifted her eyes from the loosened knot of his tie and met his squarely. She wasn't going to become a pathetic whimpering mess just because another man was rejecting her. She could at least meet it with some dignity. It was about all she had left.

"You aren't pathetic. Someone you loved betrayed you. Lord knows I can relate. All either of us were guilty of is being too trusting."

"Has it ruined your ability to trust others?"

He shook his head. "Did it ruin yours?"

She nodded.

"Do you trust me?"

She lifted one shoulder in a half-hearted shrug. "I want to."

This was the moment to open the door without a word. He would leave, reluctant but resigned, understanding. There would be no potential for scandal or gossip, no chance of a long-lost wife returning to ruin her life. No broken heart.

No happiness. No joy. No passion.

She didn't open the door and he didn't move. He didn't want to leave, and she didn't want him to.

The kiss started slow. Tentative. Sensual. Ellie tried to focus her mind on what was happening, the feel of his lips and hands, the burning deep inside her. They would never get this moment back, the innocence of exploration and the thrill of the unknown.

His face was flushed, his breathing labored when he asked if he could stay.

She threw the deadbolt.

It happened quickly from there, the fumbling with clothes between kisses, giggling at all of the shit Jack had to take off—his gun, belt, all the goddamn buttons on his shirt, uncooperative socks. She pushed him down onto the couch and straddled him. His hands ran up and down her back as she settled on him with a sigh.

They laughed, dizzy with joy and the disbelief of where they were after so little time—and wonder at how it took so long. The mood changed suddenly and she paused, overcome by the depth of feeling she saw in his eyes. He knew exactly why and waited, patiently, while she enjoyed the feeling of him inside her. She believed they could have stayed there, filling each other, forever. Everything about the moment was perfect, too perfect to last.

II

Jack had just finished placing an online ad for a police officer when Miner walked into his office.

"What's Freeman doing in the holding cell?"

"Close the door," Jack said.

"Why? There ain't anyone left to overhear us."

"Close the door, Miner. Sit down."

Miner obeyed.

"Freeman killed Rosa and Gilberto."

"What? That's ridiculous. He don't even know them."

"Buck Pollard had him do it."

"The hell he did."

"That surprises you?"

"'Course it does." Miner's usually laconic voice was rough with anger. "Why would Buck want those two Mexicans dead? Better yet," he said, looking at Jack as he became more confident in his idea, "why would Freeman agree to do it?"

"Pollard had something on him Freeman didn't want exposed." He waited for Miner's reaction and wasn't disappointed. Miner stared at the front of Jack's desk. "*That* doesn't surprise you."

"Buck knew the secrets of everyone in town. I can't imagine Freeman's secret was so bad he'd kill for it."

"Freeman was fucking a high school senior."

Miner opened his mouth to say something.

"A male high school senior."

Miner clamped his mouth shut. Shook his head. "I don't believe it."

"Which part? That Freeman likes men? That he was fucking a kid? Or that Pollard used it against him?"

"Well, it's all pretty damn unbelievable. Who's the kid?"

Jack ground his teeth together. "It doesn't matter. Freeman changed his story and asked for a lawyer."

"Then how do you . . . ?"

"I didn't Mirandize him when I initially questioned him. None of what he told me can be used. Only his confession, which conveniently leaves out any mention of Pollard."

"But he confessed? On record?"

"Yes. I just placed a want ad for two police officers. Do you know what the most important qualification is?" Miner looked at Jack but didn't answer. "To have absolutely no ties to Buck Fucking Pollard."

Miner crossed his arms. "I sense an accusation coming."

Jack smiled. "You know what almost everyone I've met has said about you? That you were with Pollard the longest."

"Should've figgered that out for yourself by reading my file."

"You know what subtext is, Miner?"

"I ain't an idiot."

"No, but you sure don't want people to think you're as smart as you are. I wonder why that is?" Miner stayed silent. "The subtext I've gotten with just about every word said about you is I shouldn't trust you. That you're Pollard's man."

"I ain't anybody's man but my own."

Jack looked at Miner with pity. "That's not really true, is it?"

"Believe what you want. I ain't done anything against you."

"You didn't sit on running Diego through the Feds?"

"You never asked me to do that. I told you that."

"You didn't give me wrong directions to Buck's house? Hoping he would leave town before I could talk to him?"

Miner shifted in his chair. "I drove those roads for forty years without numbers on them. I don't look at the numbers, 'cause I know where I'm going. I offered to take you."

"You didn't know Pollard told people to run me around town yesterday?"

"I was running around town, too, don't forget."

Jack opened a side drawer of his desk, took out a folder, and threw it on the desk in front of Miner. "Look familiar?"

"You been going through my desk?"

"That's what you're going with? Who's Patricia Hall?"

"No idea. Louisiana woman missing since '58."

"Where did you get her information?"

"Buck gave it to me."

"When?"

"Sunday."

"Why?"

"To close the case. To keep us from finding out about Claire Dodsworth."

"Why would Buck Pollard care if we ID'd the skeleton as Claire Dodsworth?"

"Like you said earlier, I don't know but I got an idea. That's what I've been working on."

The intercom buzzed. It was Susan. "Chief? Is Miner in there?"

"Yes."

"Walt Dixon's here to see him."

"Thanks, Susan. Send him back," Miner said. When the intercom cut off Miner rose. "You can either help me or fire me. I don't give a damn which," Miner said, walking out of the office to escort his witness back.

Walt Dixon was tall, thin, stoop-shouldered, and bow-legged. A neatly trimmed gray beard and a head full of silver hair framed his leathery weather-beaten face. His hair just above his ears was permanently creased from the cowboy hat he held in his hands.

"Miner," Dixon said.

"Have a seat, Mr. Dixon." Miner motioned for a chair in front of Jack's desk. "Have you met the new chief?"

"No." Dixon stuck his hand out. "How do you do? Met your brother yesterday. He did something I've been trying to do for years. Beat J.B. Miller at forty-two."

"No kidding?" Miner said, sounding impressed.

"Nice to meet you, Mr. Dixon," Jack said. He shook the man's hand. "Please, sit down."

Dixon sat and placed his hat on the desk. Miner sat in the chair next to him. "Mr. Dixon, did you know Claire Dodsworth?"

Dixon rested his elbows on the arms of his chair and grasped his hands together. "Yeah, I knew her. Thought that might be why you called me down here, Miner."

"Why's that?"

"Ellie asked me about her yesterday. Don't know how she knew anything about it." Dixon shook his head. "I've been thinking about Claire ever since. It's been years since I thoughta her." He looked between Miner and Jack. "That's her bones you found, iddnit?"

Miner spoke up. "We think so, yes. We're trying to figger what happened to her. We probably won't know specifically. Too many people are gone from that time, but whatever you can tell us will sure help."

Dixon nodded. "Well, I'm happy to help. As long as my wife don't find out. She was none too happy to find out about my experiences with Claire Dodsworth. Don't want to open that old wound."

"Of course not," Jack said.

"Well, the first thing you need to know about Claire was she liked her men young and inexperienced. She took the virginity of just about every halfway decent looking boy in my class, and a fair few of the ugly ones. Once we got a little experience and started trying to take charge a little bit, she lost interest, moved onto the next virgin. After a while, we got smart. Just let her have her way with us. Oh we were willing, don't get me wrong."

"How old were you?"

"Fifteen. Sixteen." He shook his head. "If something like that happened now, she'd be thrown in jail and the key would be melted."

Jack thought of Ethan, a year older, being taught about sex by a twenty-something–year-old mother. His stomach churned.

"Then she lost interest. None of us heard from her for weeks. No one saw her or her car around town. Old Man Dodsworth hired Elizabeth to take care of his daughter, and said he and Claire got a divorce. I don't know where the Fuller Brush salesman rumor started. It ain't true, anyway."

"How do you know?"

"She told me, when she came back in town. It was the end of '61. Christmas Eve, as a matter of fact. I was seventeen then, my girlfriend and her family were at my parents' house, celebrating. I was just getting ready to announce our engagement when the doorbell rings. I answer it and it's Claire Dodsworth, beat all to hell. Bruised face, split lip, broken arm. Her eye looked like yours, healing, but worse looking because of it. She'd just come in on the bus and needed a ride out to Dodsworth's place. It was mighty cold that night and she didn't have a coat. Didn't have anything with her save a purse, come to think of it. Huh," Dixon stared into space. "Never thought of that before. She begged me to help her. Well, Jeanette came to the door, saw her, and had a pretty good idea why Claire came to me." The breath he blew out whistled through his front teeth. "Almost ended my engagement, let me tell you. I had to help Claire, though. She looked just awful. I got Jeanette back in the house somehow. Told Claire if she wanted my help, she would have to wait. She hid in the garage until everyone left. It was midnight before I could sneak out to help her.

"All she wanted was a ride home. She took the bus to Stillwater, see. Sold her car months before for money. The man she ran off with was the man she was with before Dodsworth. He's the one who beat her up. She got away from him somehow. She was full of remorse, wanted her life back. To see her little girl. So I took her home."

"To Dodsworth's house?" Miner asked.

Dixon nodded. "I drove off when the front porch light came on. That's the last I ever saw of her."

"You didn't wonder what happened to her?"

He shook his head. "You got to remember, I was young, in love, and afraid I was about to lose Jeanette. I was terrified we'd see Claire around town. It was weeks before I wondered what happened to her. By that time, I was just so glad she was out of town, I didn't give it much thought. No one else said a word about seeing her. It gave me a thrill to think that of all the boys she was with, I was the one she thought of for help. Boy, was I young and stupid."

"Why do you say that?" Miner asked.

"My house was one of the closest to the bus stop. I was probably the first one she found home." Dixon spread his hands, placed them on the arms of his chair, and stood. "That's it, boys. That's all I know."

"Did you go straight home?" Miner asked. "After you dropped Claire off?"

Dixon pursed his lips. "Come to think of it, no. I didn't. Me, Joe Underwood, and Buck celebrated my engagement with a bottle of moonshine Buck got from his granddaddy. Boy, was I hungover the next day. I had a hell of a time hiding that from Jeanette."

Jack didn't think Jeanette would be fun to be married to.

"Buck and Joe were leaving for the Army at the first of the year. We spent every night that holiday raising hell." Dixon shook his head. "Poor Joe. He was a POW, you know? Died in captivity. Damn shame. Great guy."

"That night, Christmas Eve, did you tell Joe and Buck about Claire?" Miner asked.

"I imagine I did. She was a favorite topic of conversation among us. We liked to compare notes. I ain't proud of it, but we were young and stupid." Dixon looked at them with a twinkle in his eye. "And Claire Dodsworth was one great lay."

"Thanks, Mr. Dixon," Miner said. He started to walk Dixon out of the office.

"One more thing," Jack said. "You and Buck still close?"

"Not so much, no. He was different when he came back from Vietnam."

"Different how?"

Dixon shrugged. "We just didn't have anything in common anymore. I had a family, a farm to run. Just drifted apart."

Jack nodded. "Ever figure out how your cows got out yesterday?"

"As far as I can tell, someone opened the gate."

"Any idea who would do that?"

"Probably some kid on a dare." Dixon put his hat on and left.

Jack walked around his desk and sat down in his chair. Miner stood near the door, feet planted apart, hands on his hips.

Jack lifted the phone from the cradle. "What?"

"We're not done."

"Miner, I've got a confessed murderer downstairs who needs to be transported to county."

"He ain't going anywhere. After all the shit you accused me of, you're out of your mind if you think I'm conducting this next interview without you. We're closing this case today. Together." He walked out of the office.

"Christ." Jack hung up the phone, took his radio from the corner of the desk, and followed.

III

Miner led Jack through the nursing home without a glance at his father or his cronies, without a comment to Brucilla at the nurses' station. He stopped at Elizabeth Dodsworth's door.

"Barbara visits her every Wednesday morning." They walked in.

Barbara sat in a chair on the far side of the bed, staring out the window. Elizabeth Dodsworth looked exactly as Miner had left her twenty-four hours before. Barbara turned, startled. "Miner?" She looked between him and the chief. "What are you doing here? I told you she can't talk to you."

"We know that, Barbara. We want to talk to you."

She looked back out the window. "I have nothing to say."

"I think you do, Barb."

Miner crouched down in front of her. If he looked hard enough, he could see the little girl he had a crush on in third grade. It was too easy to see the loose teenager she became. He thought of the time she snuck him into Jacob Yourke's house and how mortifying it had been to be caught by a seven-year-old Ellie, holding a Raggedy Ann doll. Miner gently touched Barbara's knee.

"Don't, Miner. It don't matter anymore. Hasn't mattered for a long time."

She looked over her shoulder at Jack. "What are you doing skulking around back there? Ain't you ever seen a comatose woman before? She's been like that ever since they found her in your Paulie's bed," Barbara said. "Kinda ironic, ain't it, Miner?"

"Yes, it is."

Barbara stared at her stepmother. "I wish I could say she was a good mother, but I can't. She tried, but she wasn't ever there, you know. Always lost in thought somewhere. Guess now we know where, don't we?"

"The woods behind your house," Miner said.

She shrugged.

"Do you remember anything at all?"

"About Claire?" She shook her head. "No. Not really. What is real and what is just things I've pieced together until I think they're real?"

"What do you remember?"

She smiled. "Did you know my favorite color is yellow?"

"Sure, I remember."

"You remember everything." She looked back at Jack. "He was the best boyfriend I ever had."

Jack looked away.

"You're my biggest regret, Miner."

"Don't say that, Barb."

"It's true. If I hadn't fucked everything up with you, we'd be married right now, probably have a couple of kids. Hell, we might even be grandparents." She laughed. Her smile faded as she looked out the window. "I wasn't good enough for you. For anyone. He made sure of that."

"Who, Barb? Your father?"

She jerked her head around. "My father? No. He didn't care enough about me one way or another."

"That's not true."

"I reminded him too much of my mom, I think. Probably thought I deserved everything I got. He was more concerned with saving his own hide. Or maybe hers." She spat the word toward the woman in the bed. "I guess we'll never know."

"I don't understand, Barb."

"Oh, he's done plenty to help me out of all the trouble I've gotten in over the years, that's for sure. I doubt it's out of any sort of guilt, though he's the one who's made me who I am. Who's ruined my life. That man don't feel pain, guilt, regret, remorse."

Miner looked at Jack, who had moved forward into the room. Miner kept his eyes on Jack when he asked the next question. "You're talking about Buck, aren't you? What did he do to you, Barb?" Jack's surprise was worth it. Miner felt Barbara's eyes on him.

"You caught us one time, didn't you?"

Miner nodded.

"I thought so. I never told him, you got to believe me."

"I do." It had been his own stupidity that had let Buck Pollard know Miner knew his secret.

"The first time, I was ten," she said. Her voice was clear, resigned. "Buck was new on the force, back from Vietnam a few years. War hero.

I saw him at Daddy's dealership. Daddy gave him a car every five years. Free. Didn't do that for anyone else. Only Buck.

"Hard to believe, but he was handsome. A rogue, for sure. Wore his hat at a cocky angle. Hard not to notice. He noticed me, too. He took to visiting us at night. Brought me little presents. Oh, I was in love for sure. One night, he came to the house and my parents left. Said he was going to babysit me. Well, I was thrilled. He was much better than smelly old Mrs. Robinson." She sighed. "He brought me along slow."

Out of the corner of his eye, Miner saw Jack turn away. Miner kept his eyes on Barbara, even though he wanted to cry.

Barbara sniffed, regained her composure. "It went on for years. I would do anything he asked. Pictures." She looked Miner in the eye. "He loved taking pictures of me. Then, when I got too old, I guess I was about thirteen, fourteen," and she snapped her fingers. "Just like that. I was devastated. See, I thought we were really in love. I threatened to tell on him, expose him, and he laughed in my face. Told me to go ahead, that he had something on my parents that would send them to the chair. I could tell he meant it. I'd been around him long enough to know he had a brutal streak. Buck, he wasn't one for idle threats. So I kept my mouth shut. All these years."

Miner followed Barbara's gaze to her mother. Tears were streaming down the old woman's cheeks. "Now she cries," Barbara said.

"Think she understands what you're saying?"

"Who cares? She and my father let Buck molest me for years just to save their skins."

"Then why have you been so protective of her?"

"Who knows? Misplaced loyalty? It won't change anything. Claire will still be dead, she'll still be crazy, my life will still be shit, and Buck Pollard will still walk free."

Jack stepped forward. "Did Rosa Ramos ever clean Buck Pollard's house?"

Barbara turned slowly in her chair. She glared at Jack. "What did you say?"

"Did Rosa ever clean Buck's house?"

"Once."

"When?"

"Two days before she died. He called me that afternoon. Asked me who cleaned his house. Told me she did such a good job, he wanted to give her a little something extra. He killed them, didn't he?"

Jack nodded. "He had them killed."

"Bastard." She stared out the window. "I wonder what she saw? I cleaned his house for years and never found a thing. Lord knows I looked."

"Do you know of any other girls Buck might have . . ." Miner couldn't say it.

She shrugged. "No, but I'm sure he did."

"Why?" Miner asked.

She looked at Miner with pity. "He liked it too much."

Miner stood and walked to the window. An old man was asleep on a courtyard bench, his walker in front of him. Miner's ears roared, making Jack and Barbara's conversation indistinct, white noise.

I'm sure he did.

The words bounced around his head. Was Buck molesting local girls now? The thought of that old man touching little girls made Miner's stomach lurch, his fists ball up, and his face burn with rage.

"Miner." Miner jumped when he felt the touch on his shoulder. It took a moment for Miner to focus in on Jack, to realize who he was, what they were doing there.

"Yeah. Let's go." He squeezed Barbara's shoulder. "I'll talk to you soon, okay?"

"Sure, Miner." Her voice was dead.

It broke his heart.

IV

Miner leaned across Jack and opened the glove compartment. He removed a bulging manila envelope folded in thirds and tossed it on Jack's lap. "Here."

Jack opened the envelope and went completely still. "What's this?"

"My monthly payment from Buck."

"For what?"

"Doing nothing. Turning a blind eye. Being a coward. Take your pick." Miner drummed his fingers on the steering wheel. "He's been paying me, off and on, for about ten years now. Just enough to help out with the medical bills but not enough to draw a lot of attention. No banks, he always said."

"Any idea how much he's paid you over the years?"

"Twenty thousand, give or take a few hundred."

Jack folded the envelope and put it in his coat pocket. He didn't know where to start, so he started with Barbara. Somehow he knew it was all connected. "You and Barbara were a couple?"

"Yeah, you could call it that. I'd had a crush on her for years. She was such a pretty little girl. I used to walk through the woods to her house and peek inside."

"You were a peeping tom?"

"I was ten. Eleven. I was trying to get up the courage to talk to her. To knock on the door to see if she wanted to play. I never did. 'Course, she always knew I liked her. When she got older and bolder, she pursued me. Caught me pretty quick."

"What happened?"

"She had a cruel streak in her I couldn't abide. Barbara told me later she threatened to rip off the head of Ellie's Raggedy Ann doll if she told anyone about seeing us. I mean, who says that to a child?

"It was years later, after she'd been to jail and had come back to Stillwater. Buck was helping her get her business started—he hired her to clean his house, convinced Earl to give her the City Hall job—when I made some comment about Buck always liking Barbara. I said it innocently. I remembered seeing him coming and going late at night from the Dodsworths. One night I saw her sitting on his lap. He had his back to the window so I couldn't see what was going on. But I was a kid. It never occurred to me *that* might be going on." Miner looked at Jack. "He was a *policeman.*"

The radio crackled to life. Jack turned it off. Whatever it was could wait a few minutes.

"Buck obviously thought I knew more than I did. Oh, he never came right out and said anything, never owned up to anything. But he felt threatened, for sure. Which got me thinking. When he started giving me money for Teresa, I *really* started thinking."

"Once you took the money, he had something on you."

"Yep."

"You never wondered if he was still molesting little girls? It never occurred to you to tell someone? To look into it?"

"I ain't proud of it and I ain't gonna make excuses for it except to say that for every wrong thing Buck does, he does three good things."

"Then why tell me now?"

"'Cause before I just *suspected* it. Now, I know." Miner started the car. "You'll have my resignation on your desk by the end of the day."

Jack reached out and stopped Miner from putting the car in drive. "No, I won't."

Miner's hand slipped off the drive handle. "You should arrest me for what I've told you."

"You're right. I should. And one day I might. But right now we have three officers on the force and a population that's calling in every minor inconvenience. You'll work the night shift and double shifts until I can hire a couple of people. Then, I'll figure out what to do with you. Until then, what you told me doesn't leave this car. Understand?"

"Yeah." He put the car in reverse and backed out. Jack turned on the radio.

"—oddamn it, Miner. You got your radio turned off?"

Miner picked up the handset. "Go on, Violet. What's the problem, now?"

Violet's voice trembled through the line. "Is the Chief with you?"

"Yeah, he's sitting right here."

"Get back here quick. Mike Freeman's hanged himself in the cell."

V

"State your name and address."

"Michael Wayne Freeman. 2750 Elm Street, Stillwater, Texas."

"You have the right to remain silent. Anything you say or do may be used against you in a court of law. You have the right to consult an attorney before speaking to the police and to have an attorney present during questioning now or in the future. If you cannot afford an attorney, one will be appointed for you before any questioning, if you wish. If you decide to answer any questions now, without an attorney present, you will still have the right to stop answering at any time until you talk to an attorney. Knowing and understanding your rights as I have explained them to you, are you willing to answer my questions without an attorney present?"

"Yes."

"Tell me, in your own words, what happened on Thursday morning, September 6."

"About Wednesday midnight, or is it Thursday midnight? I can never keep that straight. I went to Rosa and Gilberto's trailer house. I walked through the fields between my neighborhood and the trailer park. They're not too far from each other, did you know that?"

"I didn't."

"It's about a half-mile walk. I didn't see any cars on the roads or people.

"The trailer park was mostly dark. A couple of dogs barked, but they lost interest pretty quick. The Ramoses' trailer was dark so I went up to the back door. I was going to pick the lock, but it was open.

"I stood in the main room, letting my eyes get adjusted to the light. That's when I heard them down the hall. I started to leave, then I realized they were fucking. I pulled my gun out, walked down the hall, and shot them. Gilberto, then Rosa. It was over in two seconds. I put the gun in her hand and left."

"Why did you kill them?"

"Drugs."

"What?"

"Drugs."

"What do you mean, drugs?"

"Gilberto was my supplier."

"Supplier for what?"

"HGH. Steroids. From Mexico. But he cut me off. Started selling himself."

"*Gilberto Ramos was selling steroids?*"

"*Yes.*"

"*So you killed him.*"

"*Yeah.*"

"*Why not just find another supplier?*"

"*If you let one Mexican get away with betraying you, they'll all think you're weak.*"

"*So it was a show of force? To the other drug dealers.*"

"*Yes.*"

"*We didn't find any steroids or drugs at the scene.*"

"*I took them with me. Sold them.*"

"*This isn't the story you told me off camera.*"

"*You mean before you read me my Miranda rights?*"

"*Did someone put you up to killing the Ramoses?*"

"*No.*"

"*You did it all on your own?*"

"*Yes.*"

"*You aren't protecting anyone?*"

"*I want a lawyer now.*"

The screen turned blue. Jack stopped the video camera and turned the TV off, but the rest of his conversation with Freeman played in his mind.

"You're going to force me to bring Seth into this, aren't you?"

Freeman had leaned back in his chair. His hands were cuffed in front of him. "You don't have a print."

"You willing to take that chance?"

"You might have mine, though I doubt it. You definitely don't have Seth's. I had a lot of time to think last night, and I know without a doubt I never cleaned that gun with Seth around."

Jack had clenched his jaw. Freeman was right; there was no print.

"Where'd you go last night, anyway?" Freeman had asked. "I was sure you said not to get too comfortable. So I waited and waited. You never showed. Gave me plenty of time to think. Thanks for that."

Jack had meant to drive straight home, find the camera, and return. Then he'd seen the light on in Ellie's loft and the urge to see her had overcome his professional logic. He'd just stop for a minute; apologize for not calling or stopping by the store on her first day of business. A few minutes turned into three hours, three wonderful hours during which he was able to forget everything else going on in his life—Freeman's confession, Miner's betrayal, the divorce, his brother's inopportune arrival, his strained relationship with Ethan. Three hours that cost him his chance to nail Buck Pollard.

"I might not have Seth's print," Jack had said, "but people will believe the rumor I start about you two easy enough. Sure, some won't, but others will wonder. Everything you've done for him, every time you've been seen in public together, no matter how innocent, all of it will be remembered differently."

"Just like people will believe when I tell them about you covering for your brother," Freeman had replied. "Seems you're more like Buck Pollard than you want to admit."

Ann Newberry's voice broke through his memories. "What a load of shit."

It took a moment for Jack to realize she was talking about Freeman's confession and not his comparison to Buck Pollard. "Yep."

Jack sat on the corner of his desk and told her about his initial interview with Freeman, leaving out Seth Kendrick's name and Freeman's threat to him. Ann stood in front of the TV, her arms crossed over her chest.

"Freeman figured out I hadn't Mirandized him. Nothing he told me at his house could be used. So he changed his story."

"To protect Pollard."

"I don't think so," Jack said. "He protected his lover." Jack almost choked on the word.

Ann noticed. "I didn't know you were a homophobe, McBride."

"I'm not. I just have a hard time with the idea of an adult in a sexual relationship with a high schooler. It's wrong, even if it is consensual. Not to mention the fact he was a police officer, in a position of power. He abused a trust."

"And Ethan is just a few years younger."

"Yes, goddamn it." Jack stood and walked around the room. He felt dirty, on edge. In less than twenty-four hours, Jack had learned about three adults taking advantage of innocent children and teenagers. The situations were all unique, the participants victims of varying degrees, some not considering themselves victims at all. The idea that Ethan could be in any one of these situations made Jack feel powerless, untethered, and made him want to punch a hole in the wall or take an ax to Buck Fucking Pollard's ancient desk. He kicked his desk chair and sent it spinning into the back wall. The windows rattled with the impact.

Ann sat down. She calmly crossed her legs and clasped her hands together on her knee. If she hadn't been wearing an unflattering tan sheriff's uniform, she would have looked like a maddeningly unflappable psychologist. She didn't say a word, merely waited, an expert on the efficiency of silence.

Jack took a deep breath and returned to his perch on the corner of his desk.

"Why did he kill himself?" Ann asked.

"I don't know," Jack lied. The threat he had hurled at Freeman as he locked him in the cell that morning rang in his ears. *If you think Buck Pollard is going to protect you in Huntsville, you're a bigger idiot than I thought.*

He shook the memory from his head. "I've got ads out for officers but hiring is going to take time. I need help."

"My men will be happy with the overtime."

"I'm sure Earl will be thrilled with it, too," Jack replied, thinking of the city manager's edict just a week ago about a hiring freeze. That was before Jack got beat up and lost a squad car, and an officer strangled himself with a twisted T-shirt in the basement holding cell. Still, Jack was sure this would all be held against him, as it should have been.

"I want to get a warrant for Buck Pollard's house," Jack said.

Ann raised her eyebrows. "Based on what? A non-Mirandized interrogation of a suspect no one but you witnessed? There's not a judge in Texas who would sign that."

"That's not the basis for it. Though maybe we'll find something to tie him to the Ramos murders."

"What's the basis?" Ann asked, slowly.

He told her about Miner's investigation and Barbara's revelation. He didn't tell her about Miner's confession in the squad car. That would come out in due time, he had no doubt. But right now it was more important to keep Miner around and for Ann to trust Miner. He suspected they would all be working closely together.

"Well, I'll be damned," Ann said. She stared thoughtfully at the floor.

"You wouldn't expect that of Buck Pollard?"

"What? Oh." She blew air between her lips. "I'd expect anything of Pollard. No, I didn't know Miner was that good of an investigator."

"He doesn't look the part, does he?"

"No."

"I had my own reservations about Miner," Jack said. *Still do*, he thought. "But he's proven himself to me."

"Huh. So what's your plan? Because I know you have one. Statute of limitations is long past on Barbara's abuse. No way we can get a warrant on that."

"No. But we can get a warrant if he implicates himself."

"How will you get him to do that?"

"I won't. Miner will."

"You really do trust him."

"*Trust* is a strong word. Let's just say I'm going to give him the benefit of the doubt. For now."

"When are we doing this?"

"As soon as possible."

"Miner know?"

"Not yet."

Ann stood and smiled. "Let me make a few calls. Get some deputies over here. Then we'll see how good an actor Miner Jesson is."

Jack closed the door behind her. He walked around his desk and stood in front of the windows. The river sparkled in the midday sun. Soon, shadows from the trees on the opposite bank would creep across the water; water bugs would skim the shaded surface, tantalizing the fish. A flash of metal broke through the trees behind his house. Jack looked closely and saw Ethan and Eddie standing next to the Harley. Eddie handed Ethan a helmet and straddled the bike. Jack wasn't worried; as personally irresponsible as Eddie was, Jack trusted him with Ethan. They were probably going to get lunch. Jealousy shot through him hard and fast.

He turned from the window and stared into the middle distance. What was wrong with him? First, the burst of anger in front of Ann, now this jealousy. All day, in fact, his emotions had been bubbling near the surface—disgust and despair at Barbara's story, disappointment at Miner's confession and contempt for his cowardly actions throughout the years. Regret at the loss of Freeman and a good dose of fear at his own culpability. He should have realized Freeman was a suicide risk. Instead, he threw a veiled threat in his face and left him in the cell with a volunteer fireman to check on him occasionally. Not that he had much choice, as understaffed as they were.

He closed his eyes and pinched the bridge of his nose. Christ, what a shitty day. And it had started so well.

He sat heavily in his chair and thought of Ellie. Had it really only been seven hours since he left her bed? God, it felt like a lifetime. If he thought hard enough, he could conjure up the happiness of those hours with her. The feel of her breasts beneath his hands, the way their bodies fit together, the throaty groan she made when she came, the intensity in her eyes and the way they never left his, the way she challenged him to look away, the laughter. He'd never laughed before when making love. It had never struck him as something to laugh at, to make light of. Sex was serious business. Do this, do that, move here, hope she's in the mood to blow you, make sure she comes. It was fun in the way a good workout was fun. Sometimes you were into it and were satisfied at the end. Sometimes it was a chore, but you felt better when it was done. He couldn't imagine feeling that way about being with Ellie.

Jack sighed. He wished he'd never left her apartment. Or maybe that it hadn't happened at all.

No, not that. Never that.

But now, their first time was tied to Claire Dodsworth's affinity for teenage boys, Buck Pollard grooming little girls for molestation, Mike Freeman giving his life to protect Seth Kendrick's secret, Miner's betrayal, his own stupid mistakes. He hated them all; the town, Jane Maxwell for luring him here, his wife for leaving and setting him on this path.

"Damnit!" He kicked the middle desk drawer, the one that wouldn't open or close all the way. It popped out and he stood and kicked it again, kept kicking it until it splintered and the face fell off. Jack grabbed the broken drawer and ripped it out, spilling pens, pencils, and paperclips all over the floor. He was holding the broken drawer in his hand, chest heaving, hair flopped over his forehead, when Miner barged into the room, a panicked expression on his face.

"What the hell? Everything all right, Chief?"

Jack dropped the drawer on the floor. He smoothed his hair back from his forehead. "I'm fine, Miner. I'm glad you're here. I need you to call Buck Pollard."

"What for?"

"You're going to get him to implicate himself."

"For what?"

"Molesting girls, putting a hit on two law-abiding Mexicans, extortion, murder. Take your fucking pick."

"I don't think—"

"I don't give a goddamn what you think. You're an officer of the law and you're going to do whatever it takes to make sure Buck Pollard pays for what he's done."

VI

"Buck. It's Miner."

"Hey, Miner."

"You make it down to Galveston all right?"

"I did."

"Catch anything today?"

"Haven't gone out yet. About to. You just caught me. Did you need something or you just call to check on me?"

"You don't need checking on."

"You're right about that."

"No, I called to tell you it's all taken care of."

"What's that?"

"That skeleton. Case is closed. Just like you wanted."

There was a long pause. Miner looked across the seat at Jack, glanced in the rearview mirror at Ann Newberry. She was glaring at him. Why did she hate Miner so much?

"Buck, you there?"

"Where are you?"

"In the car. I got you on speaker phone."

"Why?"

"So I have my hands free, why else? You told us to use speaker phone as much as we can."

"So I did. So I did." There was another pause. "You alone?"

Miner laughed, tried to lace as much bitterness in it as possible. "Who the hell else would be with me? Ain't nobody left on the force hardly. Another week or two and McBride will be the only one left."

"Why, he gonna fire you?"

"No, he likes me. Thinks I like him. Pretty gullible for a fancy Fed. Chances are greater he'll get me killed somehow."

Miner felt the irritation coming off Jack in waves. Ann Newberry was smirking in the back seat.

"It's a damn shame about Freeman. He was a good officer."

"That's what I wanted to talk to you about."

"Yeah, I'll be back for the funeral."

"Not that. Freeman made some pretty serious accusations before he died."

"Is that right?"

"Said you told him to kill them Mexicans."

Buck laughed. "Did McBride believe it?"

"Yeah, he did. I think he'll believe anything bad said about you."

"Jane Maxwell's put that bug in his ear."

"Word is, she's dying, you know."

There was a pause. "Is she?"

"She's older than Methuselah. Shouldn't be much of a surprise."

Buck laughed. "Honestly, I thought she'd live forever. Outlive me for sure. Just out of spite."

"Why does she hate you?"

"Oh, we go way back, Jane and I. We've both got in our punches, though I guess she got the last one."

"You still think she framed you up?"

"Well, I sure as hell didn't open the Cayman bank account she waved in front of me." Pollard coughed and spit. "Miner, I got to go."

"McBride thinks the Mexican found something while cleaning your house. That's why you had them killed."

Buck sighed. "Like what?"

"Pictures." Miner looked at Jack. "Of little girls."

The sound of the laughter was genuine, even traveling across five hundred miles.

"He might be the worst cop I've ever heard of."

Miner laughed along with Buck. "Yeah. He ain't all he was advertised to be, that's for sure. You'd think he'd be looking a little closer at the drug angle, but it's like he don't think drugs exist in Stillwater. I guess we've done our jobs, then, huh?"

"What drug connection?"

Miner was pretty far off script but he didn't care. He had a point to make and the perfect ace to do it with.

"Diego. The brother. Or cousin or whatever. He ran him through the Feds. I took the return call yesterday. McBride was out searching for a phantom prowler. Good job, by the way, keeping us running for the last two days. You can call off your cronies, now. You've made your point."

"I'll call them off when I'm good and ready. What did the Feds say?"

"It's what they didn't say. Guy doesn't exist. I think he's a CI, working with the Feds."

They could hear the lap of water against Buck's boat, the sound of sea-gulls, a thump that was probably Buck closing the lid of a cooler. "How did you figure that out?"

"Am I right?"

"How did you figure it?"

Miner shrugged, remembered Buck couldn't see him. "I'm not an idiot, Buck. Between you putting the hit on them and the big gaping hole of information about Vasquez, I just put two and two together. Am I right?"

"Not that I know of, though if he was, it explains some stuff. Far as I know, he's just a cartel man, coming up to take over the area from our friends."

Jack clenched his fist in victory. Miner smiled at the expression of shock on Ann Newberry's face. Did he also detect a hint of grudging admiration?

"Speaking of our friends, now that I'm running the protection, I've got more money to hide. I don't know what to do with all of it."

"You're running it?"

"Come on, Buck." Miner looked at Jack. "Did you think he would stop paying because you left? He still needs assurance SPD'll turn a blind eye."

"He, who?"

Miner laughed. "I ain't saying. Knowing you, you're recording this and will use it against me. We all know how good you are at that. So, you going to tell me how to hide it? You always said no banks. I can't spend it all. I was thinking a storage facility. I don't have that much yet, but I will soon. Especially if I play the Mexicans off our friends."

"Anonymous donations are always good, but yeah. Storage is best. Just keep it out of town. I'd go at least an hour away. Maybe two. The seedier the better. Pay cash and give a false name."

Jack was motioning for him to wrap it up while texting on his phone.

"Good to know. Thanks. So, what's the weather like down there? Fishing gonna be good?"

"I hope so. You should come out with me sometime."

"I'd love to, but I don't have the time now, especially since you're running us ragged."

"I'll tell 'em to ease up a bit."

"Thanks. Oh, and Buck? I've got a little something for you when you get back. As a thank-you for all you've done over the years."

"That's mighty nice, Miner."

"It's the least I can do. When will you be back?"

"Say, Monday."

"Same time and place?"

"See you then."

Miner punched the end button and handed the phone to Jack. Jack turned the recording app off and placed the phone in the cup holder between them. He didn't say anything for a long time.

"'Pretty gullible for a fancy Fed? Chances are he'll get me killed?'" Jack said.

Miner grinned. "I haven't had that much fun on the phone since I stopped calling the 1-900 numbers."

"Jesus," Ann said, laughing.

"I'm not sure if I should be impressed with your acting abilities or worried about them," Jack said. "Any idea who Buck was working for? The drug dealers?"

"My guess?" Miner said. "Joe Doyle."

Ann whistled in the back seat.

"Who's Joe Doyle?"

"Driven past Stillwater Business Park out on Boondoggle?" Miner said. "Yeah."

"That's Doyle. Patriarch of richest family in the county," Ann offered. "Makes sense, though. He's got two or three businesses that are perfect fronts."

"Miner, how did you know?"

"I *suspected*. I know you don't believe me," Miner looked in the rearview mirror to include Ann in the comment, "but I wasn't directly involved in anything. I just looked the other way. Which is almost as bad, Sheriff, I know."

Jack stared out the car window. Miner could almost see the gears turning in his head. He turned back to Ann. "Think we have enough for a warrant for his house?"

"I'll make some calls first thing in the morning. If we get the right judge, we will be searching his house by noon."

"Not Johnston," Miner said. He cut his eyes to the rearview mirror.

"Okay," Ann said.

"Try to find one who won't advertise it all over the area," Jack said. "If that's even possible. Also, keep the Doyles out of it. The name Doyle doesn't leave this car, understood? As soon as they know we're aware of them, they'll pull back like a startled turtle. Base it on the money. He has to have some handier than a storage facility an hour away."

"Sorry I didn't pursue the molestation," Miner said. "I figgered that would throw up red flags."

"You did the right thing, Miner. Excellent work, Sergeant."

"Sergeant? I ain't no Sergeant."

"You are now."

CHAPTER EIGHT

Thursday

I

"Why do you keep staring at my breasts?"

Jack sat on the edge of Ellie's bathtub, his hands lightly resting on her bare hips while she dabbed ointment on the stitched cut above his eye. "They're right in front of me."

"Do you like them?"

"Very much."

"Are you surprised?"

"That you have breasts? Not really."

She rolled her eyes. "They were a present to myself. After I lost weight, my breasts looked like a *National Geographic* centerfold. I didn't want to look at those in the mirror for the rest of my life."

"I'm sure your boyfriends have enjoyed them."

She picked up a Band-Aid and gently placed it over the wound. "I haven't had any complaints."

"You were supposed to say I am the only one who's seen them." Jack leaned forward and kissed her nipple.

"Hmm." She smoothed the ends of the Band-Aid, and placed her hands on Jack's shoulders.

He felt her heart racing, heard her breath shorten. His fingers slid between her legs.

"Don't start something you can't finish, McBride."

He looked up at her. Her smile was slight, playful, and sensual. To his surprise, he hardened quickly. It had been years since he had been able to go twice within so many hours. He couldn't remember the last time he wanted to.

❦

"Can we just stay in here and do this forever?"

They stared at the ceiling, chests heaving, bodies covered in sweat. Jack turned to look at her. She was grinning. Who wouldn't be after that? When she turned her head and looked at him, they both started laughing.

"Why are we laughing?"

"I have no idea," she replied. "At the risk of making you even more cocky than you are . . ."

"I'm not cocky."

She rolled her eyes. "Yes, you are."

He rolled onto his side, pillowed his head on his arm, and stared at Ellie while her breathing slowed. She looked at him from the corner of her eye, crooked an eyebrow, and turned her head to his. "What?"

"Thank you."

She pursed her lips but couldn't hide the smirk. "For what, exactly?"

"Salvaging my day."

She turned on her side and propped her head on her hand. "Want to talk about it?"

"Not particularly."

She narrowed her eyes. "You aren't afraid I'll tell people, are you?"

"No. God, no. I don't want to think about it. I want to forget it."

"That's fine for now, but it won't be forever."

"What's that supposed to mean?"

"It means I'm either part of your life or I'm not. I'm too old for bullshit, Jack. For half-truths, lies, secrets. I don't want to be wondering what you're thinking, if I've somehow disappointed you, pissed you off, whatever. Not that I expect us to sit around all the time talking about our feelings. We have to be able to talk things out, to listen to each other. Full disclosure."

"Agreed." He pulled her close. He'd forgotten how sensual kissing could be, how it could be an act in and of itself, and more intimate as a result. How long into his marriage had it taken for a kiss to be either a quick, dismissive greeting or goodbye, or a gateway to sex? He couldn't remember kissing Julie this way, his body humming with contentment while in her arms.

He pulled away reluctantly. "Okay. Full disclosure."

"I didn't mean right now." She cupped his face. "Can't we have a few days of ignorance?"

"No."

"Okay, a few more minutes, then." She kissed him lightly. He pulled back when she tried to deepen the kiss.

"Ellie, I have an appointment with Bob Underwood tomorrow. Wait." Jack looked over Ellie's shoulder at the clock. 2:48 a.m. "Yep, it's Thursday. Friday morning, I'm meeting Bob."

Her expression morphed from playful to serious in a blink. "You are?"

"I have no idea how long the process will take, but it starts tomorrow." Jack smiled at her attempt to keep her expression neutral. "That is, unless you don't want me to get a divorce."

"Don't be stupid."

Jack tickled her. "Then don't look so serious."

"I feel bad rooting for the dissolution of any marriage, even yours."

"Well, don't. I'm not only rooting for it, I'm thinking of organizing a pep rally."

She ran her hand down his hip, and lifted an eyebrow suggestively. "What kind of pep rally?"

"Unfortunately, not that kind. In case you haven't noticed, I'm an old man."

"We're the same age and I'm not old."

"Well, I don't have the stamina I did when I was younger."

"And I'm in my prime."

"I've noticed."

Ellie sighed dramatically. "I guess I'll have to channel all my pent-up energy into other avenues."

"Like who?"

She punched him in the stomach. "Not funny." With a grunt, he flopped over onto his back. She nestled next to him and rested her head on his shoulder. She traced her fingers across his chest. "Did you hear about Charlie Williams?"

"The city councilman? Yeah. Is he going to make it?"

"It doesn't look good. Even if he does, he'll have to resign his position. His entire right side is paralyzed."

Jack ran his hand up and down Ellie's arm. "You've got some guns on you."

"Push-ups. They're going to have to have a special election for his seat."

"In November?"

"Yes."

Jack's hand stopped. He pulled his head back so he could see Ellie's face. "You want to run."

The corner of her mouth curled into a smile. "I was thinking about it."

"Why wouldn't you?"

"The bookstore, the downtown development plan, the bank."

"The bank?"

"Jane is sicker than she lets on and I'm pretty sure she's leaving the bank in my hands when she dies."

"Jesus. Really?"

"Yep."

"It's a private bank?"

"Yeah, hard to believe."

"I'm starting to feel inadequate."

"Why?"

"What would a woman like you want with a disgraced FBI agent turned small-town police chief? I'm beginning to think you could do much better."

"Disgraced FBI agent? What did you do?"

How much to tell her? Until Julie left, he'd led an uninteresting, average life. Career, family, friends, the occasional heart-pounding thrill of working in law enforcement. Even so, he could count on both hands the number of times he'd pulled his gun on the job, and he'd never shot it. His life had taken such a drastic nosedive there were times he thought he was living in another world, one where he had no control and no matter what he did, no matter what decision he made or path he took, it was wrong. He'd handled everything badly; he knew that as it was happening and now. Stillwater was a new start, a chance to put it all behind him and, hopefully, never talk about it again. Ellie'd been honest with him about her past; the least he could do was be honest with her. But there were some things it would be better for Ellie not to know, just as he was sure there were parts of her past she'd kept from him.

When Ellie let the silence lengthen, he said, "About this time last year, I was working a case with the ATF." He looked at her. "Ever heard of the sovereign citizen movement?"

"Vaguely."

"Some of them are paper terrorists, filing claims against the government, wasting everyone's time. Others are more traditional anti-government libertarians, with a violent bent." Jack returned his focus to the ceiling. "We had an agent under cover who finally got invited to meet with the heavy hitters. I was supposed to be her backup that night, along with an ATF agent. It was the day Julie left. I couldn't leave Ethan on his birthday. I made up some bullshit excuse, and the ATF agent said no problem, he'd handle it. It should have been a simple meet and greet. But it went south. Bad. The ATF agent was killed and my agent was wounded." Jack stared at the ceiling. "I was put on desk duty, which I've always hated. That, along with my anger at Julie, led me to do some things I'd rather forget."

Ellie stroked his shoulder and down his arm. She intertwined her fingers with his and pulled their joined hands into her chest. "Like what?"

He puffed out a laugh and rubbed his head. "A neighbor of ours, a cop who Julie had been sleeping with, got suspicious when Julie didn't return his texts and calls. I deleted all the messages from her boyfriends, probably a mistake, but I was so furious I wasn't thinking straight. The cop couldn't open an official investigation because the affair might come out and ruin his marriage. But he went to my boss, planted enough doubt to cause trouble. So, I confronted him."

Jack turned to face Ellie. Her eyes met his steadily, and she waited. "It was the first time I'd hit another man in twenty years. Not my finest hour. I felt awful about it, until rumors started swirling I'd killed Julie in a moment of passion."

"Julie's lover said that?"

"I don't know. Probably."

"How did you explain it all to Ethan?"

"I found Julie. It was ridiculously easy when I set my mind to it. I thought—still do—that she left just to get me to chase her. To feed her ego, to pull me around like some dog on a leash."

"She wouldn't come home?"

Jack pushed a piece of hair behind Ellie's ear. "I didn't talk to her. I found her with some man in California. I paid a bellboy a hundred bucks to get a picture of her so I could text it to Ethan from Julie's phone."

"Her phone?"

"She left it when she bolted."

"What a bitch."

"Exactly. Discovering she was alive was enough to appease my boss, but my career hit a wall, started going downhill. I got passed over for promotions. I couldn't travel or work late because of Ethan. I was mulling what I was going to do next, thinking about finally using my law degree, when I started working Valerie's case."

Ellie traced his lips with her finger. "Which you solved."

Jack nodded. "The official story is the suspect died in my custody. That was partially true. I was there, but I didn't kill him. My partner did. Alex is the best agent I've ever worked with, hands down. It would have been a huge loss to the Agency if the truth of what happened came out, so I took the fall."

Ellie stared at his chest, her eyes unfocused.

"Ellie?" he asked. His heart pounded in his ears. "It's too much, isn't it?"

She looked at him and smiled. "No, of course not. I'm glad you told me." She kissed the hand she held. "I hope your partner appreciated your sacrifice."

"She was the one who told me about this job. For a couple of days there, I thought maybe she had been trying to torture me. Then I met you."

"Stop being sappy."

"Sorry. So, that's it. My checkered past."

Ellie kissed him. "Thanks for telling me."

"You're welcome." He kissed her and felt much lighter than he had in months. "Enough about me. Back to the city council. Are you asking my opinion?"

She looked troubled, as if wondering herself.

"I'm sure you'd be a great councilwoman. You seem to be good at everything you do."

"I suck at relationships."

"So far I have no complaints."

"It's been twenty-four hours."

"True." She punched him again. "Seriously, that hurts. Have you seen your biceps lately? Back to you taking over the world: selfishly, I want you to run."

"Why?"

"Because then I would be assured of having one person on the city council to vote against firing me."

"Nobody's going to fire you."

"Would you blame them? I've had a pretty abysmal week."

"*Abysmal.*" She chuckled.

"You like that word?"

"Yeah, I do. You'll prove yourself to them. I believe in you."

"Oh, you do?" Jack rolled over on top of Ellie, kissed her on the nose. "I'm tired of talking."

"You said earlier you were too old to do anything more."

"That is not what I said."

"I'm pretty sure it is."

"What we have here," Jack said, moving down her body, "is a failure to communicate."

"Oh. *Oh,*" she gasped. She closed her eyes and ran her fingers through his hair. "Nonverbal communication. I like it."

II

The novelty of school suspension wore off pretty quick. Uncle Eddie had left hours before to run errands. How it took four hours to buy hamburger meat at the one grocery store in town, Ethan had no idea. Daytime television sucked and no one had updated Facebook or Instagram for hours. Ethan finally understood why his mother was always so eager to chat when he got home from school. He wished he been a little more . . .

Ethan pulled out his phone. "Google search, thesaurus, chatty . . ." Ethan recited as he tapped on his phone. "Loquacious." He blew air out between his lips. "I can't say it or spell it. Jesus. I'm talking to myself and searching for vocabulary words."

He tossed his phone aside and stared at the water stain on the ceiling. He picked up his phone and did another search. His dad was right; it was shaped like Maryland.

His dad was right. God, he hated to admit that. It was so much easier to hate his dad when he was acting like a dick and treating Ethan like a seven-year-old. When he talked to Ethan like an adult and didn't go back on his word, it was much harder for Ethan to find something to be angry about. It was a weird sensation, agreeing with his dad. Ethan was sure it would be short-lived.

He got his camera, his phone, and a Dr Pepper and went to the front porch. He sat on the swing, listened to music, and took pictures of the empty house across the street. He wondered if it was haunted; it sure looked haunted.

He was wondering if he could sneak over later and check the house out up close when he saw Olivia walking down the sidewalk. His stomach lurched. He hoped she would walk on by, though who she would be going to see on his street he didn't know. Then she stepped into his yard. *Dang it. She's coming here.* He removed his headphones and, through a dry mouth and with a tongue that had swelled like a sponge, he said, "Hey."

She stopped a few feet away. She shifted from foot to foot and shoved her hands into the pockets of her pink zip-up hoodie. Her hair was pulled back into a ponytail, except for one rebellious strand around her face that she pushed behind her ear.

"Hey."

Ethan looked around at anything but Olivia. He realized this was the first time he had been alone with her, if you could call standing in the front yard alone. "School out?"

"Yeah."

"Wow. Time flies when you're bored to death." She was looking around at anything but Ethan. He relaxed a little. "I've been texting Troy all day."

"He lost his phone for a week."

"Oh." Ethan felt guilty that he didn't lose his phone, didn't get in trouble with his dad at all. Obviously, Troy did, even though he didn't do anything more than try to help Ethan. "My dad made him go to work with him."

"Probably better than sitting around all day."

"I wouldn't count on it," she mumbled.

He would have given anything for Troy to be there, cracking a joke, keeping the conversation going. He and Olivia had nothing to say to each other, a realization that made the butterflies in his stomach shrivel up and die.

"Want a Dr Pepper?" Ethan asked.

"Sure."

He opened the front door. He thought of how proud his mom would be of him right now. First, asking if his guest wanted something to drink and then holding the door open. Olivia stopped at the top of the steps. "Is anyone home?" she asked.

"No, Dad's at work and Uncle Eddie is . . . somewhere."

She looked up and down the empty street. "I better stay out here."

"Why?"

She gave him the same look she did the first time they met. "I can't be inside alone with you."

Ethan laughed, not at her but at the idea he would have the courage to do anything inappropriate. "Whatever," he said and went inside.

He caught a glimpse of himself in the bathroom mirror as he walked by. His hair was sticking up in the back, just as it did every morning when he woke up, reminding him he didn't take a shower that morning. He wet his hand and tried to press his hair down with little success. He lifted his arm and took a whiff. Not too bad, but not great. He would be sure to stand far enough away that it wouldn't matter.

Why did she come over? Ethan wondered. It was probably to bring him homework, he supposed. He paused as he grabbed the last Dr Pepper out of the refrigerator—she didn't have a backpack. Anyway, there was no point in doing homework; Dr. Courcey had said he would get zeros on everything. He stood up abruptly, hitting his head on the refrigerator.

"Ow."

The palm of his empty hand started to sweat. He didn't want to go back outside. There were only two reasons why Olivia walked across town to see him, both of them equally terrifying. Either she liked him or she was here to grill him about his fight with Kevin. He was pretty sure she didn't like him, which left Kevin. Did she find out what the fight was about? Surely not. It would only make Kevin look bad. Chances were better Kevin spent the day trashing Ethan and making it seem Ethan jumped him for no reason at all. Considering how his last year had gone, Ethan didn't hold out much hope for Olivia's visit having a positive outcome.

When he saw her standing on the porch, arms across her chest, he knew what was coming. He shouldn't have left her alone. It had given her time to work herself up to fight with him. He held out the Dr Pepper. "Here you go."

She ignored it. "What did you fight with Kevin about?"

His shoulders slumped. He set the Dr Pepper on the porch railing, shoved his hands into his pockets, and looked down at the ground. *Maybe she'll go away if I don't answer*, he thought.

"I asked Troy and he wouldn't say."

"He doesn't know."

"Oh, he just jumped in because you're best friends?"

Ethan felt a flare of happiness. Did Troy think they were best friends? He hoped so, but he wasn't sure after the fight. Troy hadn't replied to any of his texts, though if he lost his phone and was working with his dad, Ethan understood why.

"You'll have to ask Troy why he jumped in."

"He won't tell me."

Ethan shrugged. "I don't know what to tell you."

"Why did you fight with Kevin? Was it about me?"

"Why would we fight about you?"

Olivia flinched, as if he had slapped her. Then she got mad. "God, you're such an asshole."

She walked down the porch stairs and turned. "FYI, Kevin is telling everyone you jumped him because you're jealous of him dating me. You might want to set things right with your girlfriend before you go back to school." Scorn dripped from every word.

"I don't have a girlfriend."

"Mitra will be surprised to hear that."

"She likes Troy, you idiot."

Olivia paused, surprised. "How do you know that? Did she tell you?"

"No," Ethan said, slowly. "I notice things. More than anyone else around here, that's for damn sure."

"Language, Ethan," Olivia said.

They stared at each other, both trying not to laugh. He held out the Dr Pepper. "Here," he said. She stepped up the stairs and took it.

"Thanks."

They sat on the top step as far away from each other as possible. She popped the can open with a hiss and took a drink.

"I didn't mean to be an asshole," Ethan said.

She shrugged. "I'm used to it." When she looked at him, the sliver of hair fell from behind her ear. "Where's your drink?"

Ethan picked up his empty can and shook it. "That's the last one."

"Oh, I'm sorry! Here." She held the can out. "I don't want to take your last one."

"It's okay. I've had four already today."

"Have you drunk any water at all?"

"No, Mom. I haven't."

"You are the unhealthiest guy I know." She took another drink then held out the can again. "Wanna share?"

"Sure."

He took a sip and set the can on the porch between them.

"You aren't going to tell me why you fought Kevin, are you?"

"Nope."

They stared at the street in silence. "I didn't believe Kevin, you know. When he said you were jealous."

"That's good," Ethan said, both relieved and saddened.

"I figured it was about your dad," she said. "Since Buck Pollard is Kevin's uncle."

"It was," Ethan said. He might as well grasp onto the lie since everyone assumed it anyway. Maybe it would keep Olivia from quizzing him. "About my dad."

"Oh," she said. "Why wouldn't you tell me then?"

Ethan shrugged. "Because it was a stupid thing to fight over."

"You were afraid I would think you are stupid?"

"Pretty much."

"But I already think that," she said, a wry smile tugging at her mouth.

"Ha, ha," Ethan said.

They shared their drink in silence. Ethan hoped it was the end of that conversation and wanted to talk about something else, anything to keep her here for a little longer, but he had no idea what to say.

Ethan pointed to the house across the street. "You think that house is haunted?" Ethan asked.

"There's no such thing as ghosts."

"Yes there is."

"Have you seen one?"

"No."

She spread her hands as if that explained it all.

"Have you ever seen God? Or Jesus?" Ethan asked.

"No."

Ethan spread his hands.

"That's not even close to the same thing," she said.

Ethan didn't reply. He didn't care enough about the subject to argue about it. He was completely out of conversation ideas.

"I guess Kevin said that about you being jealous to embarrass you," Olivia said.

Boy, she wasn't going to let it go.

"I guess. Who knows what goes on in that black hole he calls a brain."

"I mean, why else would he say it?"

"Can we please stop talking about it?" Ethan said.

"Fine."

"Good. What happened at school today? That didn't involve Kevin Jackson."

Olivia was deep into a rambling explanation of every word every teacher said when an old red sports car pulled up in front of the house. A petite woman with long, sandy blond hair pulled back into a ponytail and aviator sunglasses stepped out of the car and looked up and down the street. Spotting Ethan and Olivia, she closed the door and walked around her car. She wore fitted dark jeans tucked into knee-high black leather boots. Her short navy blazer covered a low-cut white T-shirt. Her high-heeled boots clicked on the sidewalk as she sauntered toward them.

"Who is that?" Olivia said, a trace of awe in her voice.

Ethan couldn't talk. He could barely breathe.

But he could smile.

III

It took all morning to get the warrant for Buck Pollard's house. When the skeleton crew of Miner, Ann, Jack, and two deputies Ann trusted to keep their mouths shut executed the warrant, it was one o'clock in the afternoon. By three o'clock, they were almost finished searching the small house with no luck. The two deputies had moved on to the barn.

Jack walked down the hall. Ann sat at a desk, rifling through files. An old desktop computer like the one at the station sat to her right, monitor on, asking for a password. *Probably bought an extra through the city and brought it home*, Jack thought.

"Find anything?"

"No, but we'll box it all up anyway."

A deputy, Ann's young assistant whose name Jack couldn't remember, poked his head in the door. "Does the warrant include a storm cellar?"

Ann's shoulders slumped. "No." Miner walked in the room. "Why didn't you tell us he had a storm cellar?" Ann accused.

Miner was taken aback. "I didn't know. It ain't like we socialized."

Ann stood and pulled her phone out of her pocket. "I'll have the warrant amended."

"The cellar. It's locked," the deputy said.

"Must mean there's something good down there."

She left the room, phone to her ear. Miner followed her toward the kitchen.

Jack sat at the desk and pulled the keyboard forward. "Bet he liberated you from the station," Jack said. He punched in the username and password Susan gave him on the first day. The screen went blue and then program icons popped up.

"Crook."

He browsed Pollard's computer. It was boring stuff. A tax software program. Microsoft Office. Email. Internet Explorer. He went into the files, noting there were only a few. Jack wondered why Pollard bothered having a computer at all. He clicked on the pictures folder, sure it would come up just as empty. There was no way Pollard was stupid enough to keep photos on a computer with such an easily guessed password.

There were fishing pictures, pictures of Buck on vacation on some island, maybe the Florida Keys. Pictures of his boat, his truck. Pictures of the previous year's Christmas were the oldest on the computer. Pictures of everyone, lots of poorly lighted pictures, pictures of the floor, the ceiling—all spoke of someone learning how to use a new, unfamiliar camera. Looking around Pollard's low-tech house, sitting at his late '90s model Dell, Jack could believe Pollard had just transitioned to digital.

He was bored. He typed M4V into the search field and hit enter. Four files showed up, all created within the last two months. Jack clicked on the most recent one and waited for the computer to open the movie program and load it. It took a while.

His phone vibrated in his pocket. He pulled it out and saw that he missed a voice mail and a call from an unknown Dallas number. The computer was still working so he swiped the message to open the voice mail. He guessed he would have to put his phone on ring, though he hated the sound no matter what the tone.

"Hey, Jack. It's me. Ellie. I'm calling from Liam's cell since I left mine at home this morning. I was distracted, spacey, though I can't imagine why."

Jack smiled. He heard the sarcasm in her voice clearly. He swiveled around in the chair and stared at Buck Pollard's queen bed. What an ugly quilt.

"I'm calling to let you know, I left my cell at home. In case you try and can't get in touch with me. I didn't want you to worry. Not that you would. Worry. Or try to get in touch with me, I mean. You know I'm out of town. But—God. I'm rambling. I tend to do that on voice mail, which is why I don't leave them. Anyway. Why I called. I'm going to text you directions to my lake house. I didn't give them to you this morning." She paused. In his mind's eye, Jack saw her chewing her lip. "That's not really why I called. I, uh. I called to tell you I miss you. Stupid, since I just saw you and will see you in a few hours. But, it's different, not being in the same town. God, I sound like an idiot. Talk about sappy. I should have stopped this message ages ago. I'll see you tonight. Ignore this message. Bye."

Jack shook his head with a smile and stared at the phone. Affection surged through him at the sound of her embarrassed, unsure voice. A small part of him had worried that she was much more lackadaisical about their relationship, that he was the one who felt more, wanted more, expected more. He wasn't sure about the last two, only time would tell with those, but he believed she felt as much as he did.

He was amazed at how much better he felt just by hearing Ellie's voice. God, she was extraordinary. Why couldn't he have met her when they were younger? They would have been that kick-ass couple everyone envied. Fulfilling careers, beautiful children, strong relationship. They would be looking forward to when the kids left and what they would do, where they would live, the exotic places they would travel. Sure, they would fight. Everyone fights. But it wouldn't be the overemotional, narcissistic bullshit he'd had with Julie. Ellie would lay it out on the table, no double meanings, manipulation, or sudden rages. They would talk, yell, be silent, reconcile, and try to remember later what the fuss had been about. At least, that was what he'd been told happened within a healthy relationship. He didn't know firsthand. But he would know and soon. He was determined to do whatever it took to make it work with Ellie. Tomorrow morning, he would meet with Bob Underwood and there would be nothing to keep them from seeing each other. Ethan would come around when he got to know her. Jack felt sure that deep down Ethan realized his mother had problems. He'd lived in the same house, after all.

Jack clapped his hands together. He was invigorated, the way he was when he drank three cups of extra-strong coffee. A bit jittery, maybe, anxious to get going and do something, anything, to make the day move faster. His watch said there were six hours until he would see her. That was a bit of a buzzkill, but he'd sat in a surveillance van in one hundred-degree heat with a gaseous agent for twelve hours before. Getting through the next six would be a piece of cake in comparison.

Jack swiveled back around to face the computer. All thoughts of Ellie vanished. Jack stopped the video.

"Miner! Ann! Come here!"

They walked down the hall, their footsteps hollow on the raised floor of the house. From the doorway, Ann called for one of her deputies to get a couple of boxes from the car. Miner walked into the room last.

"Find something?" Ann asked.

"Yeah." Jack restarted the video and stood so they could all see. The back of Jack's throat constricted and a sour, metallic taste filled his mouth. Ann's breath caught and she swore under her breath. Miner walked out of the room.

Reluctantly, Jack moved forward and turned the sound on. Miner returned.

It was a young Hispanic girl, no more than eleven, sitting on a small, thin bed built into a wall. Her eyes were resigned. She'd done this before.

"It's a boat," Ann said. "See the porthole?"

Jack nodded. "Miner, is Buck's boat that big?"

"Huh?" Miner sounded distracted. "Don't know. Maybe." He walked out of the room again.

Two people talked off camera, one voice female and heavily accented, the other Buck Pollard's.

"You want pictures, four hours, double price."

"That wasn't the deal."

"No pictures, all night. Same price."

"Why the change?"

"You take pictures and sell them. Make money. We get no cut of that."

"I don't sell the pictures."

"Then why take them?"

"I'm not paying double."

"Then no pictures."

The woman spoke in Spanish to the girl. "Show him." The girl started to remove her clothes.

When she was naked, Buck said, his voice hoarse. "No pictures. Just get out."

Ann moved forward. "Turn it off." She fumbled for the monitor power button and pushed it. With a click and a horizontal flash, the monitor died. Ann waved the deputy carrying boxes out of the room. He had to walk around Miner, who hovered in the door, staring at the floor, deep in thought.

"Miner? Care to join us?" Her voice was laced with irritation and anger. Jack knew it was more to do with what she had just seen than with Miner.

Miner walked forward, still staring at the floor.

"That sonofabitch," Ann said.

Miner's eyes were vacant, his mind somewhere else.

"What is it, Miner?" Jack said.

"I think I know where Buck hid his stuff."

"Where?" Jack and Ann asked in unison.

Miner pounded his boot on the floor, turned, and walked into the hall. He pounded his foot again.

"Sonofabitch," Ann repeated.

"Under the house," Jack said.

Miner nodded.

"Is *that* in the scope of the warrant?" Jack said.

Ann took out her cell phone. "I'll double-check." She patted Miner on the shoulder as she went past.

Jack walked up to Miner and looked his deputy in the eyes. Unlike the first day at the Ramoses', Miner's eyes met him steadily. Jack held his hand out. Miner gripped it, shook it once. "I would have figured it out eventually," Jack said, barely hiding his smile.

"Uh-huh."

"You have been wrong about one thing." Jack's phone vibrated in his pocket.

"What's that?"

He removed his phone and looked at the screen before answering. His heart stopped. Julie's smiling face looked back at him. Was Ethan calling from his mother's phone? Or was Eddie trying to freak him out?

"What's that?" Miner repeated.

"What?" Jack looked up.

"What was I wrong about?"

"Oh, you would have made a great chief." Jack walked a little away and accepted the call.

"Ethan? Why are you using your mother's phone?"

"Jack?"

The voice was high-pitched and girlish for a forty-year-old woman. It was familiar and alien at the same time. The ground started to spin. Jack put his hand on the wall to steady himself.

"It's me. I'm home."

IV

Jack burst through the front door of his house, telling himself he was wrong. He hadn't just gotten a phone call from his wife. She was gone, would stay gone until tomorrow when he filed for divorce. This wasn't happening. It was his mind playing tricks on him.

There she was. Sitting at the desk next to Ethan. Beaming. Standing up and coming toward him. Wrapping her arms around his waist, hugging him, resting her head on his chest where she had rested it thousands of times before. Her hair smelled the same, looked a bit lighter than usual. To be expected when you spend a year on the beach.

Ethan sat at the desk, beaming. Why was he smiling? Why wasn't he furious?

"Oh my God, Jack." Julie squeezed him. "I've missed you so much."

Behind Ethan, the computer screen was full of a picture of the bank. Downtown. Across from Ellie's store. The next picture in the slideshow would be Ellie, walking onto her balcony, sitting down, sipping coffee, discarding her book, the mischievous smile he loved.

But instead he saw an old house. A road filled with potholes. Two black men sitting on a porch, smoking cigarettes.

Relief rushed through Jack. Ethan had followed through on his threat. The pictures of Ellie were gone.

"Ethan was just showing me pictures of this lovely town." Julie's voice was muffled, but he heard the sarcasm.

He put his hands on Julie's shoulders and pushed her away from him. She kept her arms around his waist and looked up. Her smile now was ironic, challenging him to lash out at her in front of Ethan. Her back was to their son, so he didn't get to see the subtle change in her demeanor.

"Why do you look so surprised? Didn't you get my email?"

"No."

"I sent it. Days ago. Maybe it went into your spam folder."

"You should have called."

She laughed. "I should have written down your and Ethan's phone numbers before I left. You know I haven't memorized a number since cell phones. And, since we agreed I would leave my phone with you . . ."

She let the sentence dangle to see if he would challenge her. Ethan still smiled, though Jack thought he detected a sliver of doubt. He hoped he did.

"Your parents could have relayed the message."

"Or you could check your spam folder occasionally." Her laugh was forced and fake. How could Ethan not see through her? Julie put her hand on his cheek. "Oh, you look just terrible, honey. How do you feel?"

Jack stepped back. "Fine. Ethan, where's Eddie?"

"Ethan said Eddie is living here." Julie's lip curled. "He can leave now."

"Eddie can stay as long as he wants."

"He said he was going to get stuff for hamburgers hours ago," Ethan replied.

"Ethan, could you give us a few minutes?" Jack said.

"I wan—"

"Ethan."

Julie went over to Ethan and ran her hand through his hair. "Go on, sweetie. I'm not going anywhere."

Ethan left the office reluctantly. Jack watched him go up the stairs, heard the creak of his door. When he heard it close, he looked at Julie. She was amused.

"What the hell, Jack? A police chief?"

"What are you doing here, Julie?"

"What do you mean? I'm home."

"This isn't your home."

"Wherever you and Ethan are is my home. Though I do wonder what you did with the house in Emerson. We're both on the mortgage."

"I'm renting it out. Why are you back?"

"Ethan emailed me last week. He begged me to come home. Here I am."

"He's been begging you to come home for a year. Why now?"

"Obviously you need me."

"Actually, you are the last thing I need. What did you tell him? About where you've been?"

"I told him the truth."

"Oh really? About California?"

She didn't look embarrassed. "You know where I was? And never came for me?"

"I came. Saw you with whatever man you were fucking that month and left. What did you tell Ethan?"

"I told him I was on a sabbatical that you approved of from the beginning."

"What a load—"

"And that I did it because of a book deal I had, about a stay-at-home mom and her journey to rediscover the woman she was before her life was subsumed by her husband and his career. My agent thinks it's going to be huge."

"You're so full of shit."

"Am I?"

"So, Ethan thinks I've been lying to him all this time, that I went along with your 'sabbatical' but didn't bother to tell him? Why am I not surprised? You're here for an hour and already I'm the bad guy."

"I didn't turn you into the bad guy. What lies have you told?" She narrowed her eyes. She was checking his story against Ethan's. He wondered what Ethan told her. Had he mentioned Ellie? His fight at school and suspension? The field trip incident in Emerson?

"I told him you were taking time for yourself. That we needed a break."

"Close enough. He's so happy, he won't think too hard about the details." Her face softened. "I really did miss you, Jack." She moved to hug him again. He put his hands out to stop her.

"Don't."

She nodded. "I understand. It's going to take time. But I'm committed to putting our marriage back together. I'm at a much better place now. I understand myself, and you, better than I ever have." She ran her finger along the edge of desk and kept her eyes down. "Being away from you made me realize how much I love you, how you're the only man I have ever truly loved." When she brought her eyes back to his, they were filled with unshed tears. God, she was good. But it wouldn't work anymore. Not on him.

"We'll talk later." He turned to leave.

"When will you be home?"

"We are down to three officers and I'm working two major cases. It will be late. Well after midnight. Don't wait up."

He left, letting the screen door slap shut behind him.

V

Jack stopped short at the door of his office. For a split second, he thought someone had ransacked the place. Then he remembered his temper tantrum from the day before and the broken drawer and office supplies strewn on the floor made more sense. Susan's organization compulsion didn't extend to his office. At least, not anymore. He knew he should talk to her about Ethan and Troy's fight, but with everything else going on, he didn't have the energy for it. He had no doubt that her coolness toward him since then was rooted in something deeper, but he didn't have the space in his mind for Susan Grant and her issues at the moment.

He fell into his desk chair and stared out the window at the river. Of course Julie would come back on the 364th day, the day before he instigated the divorce. He should have done it sooner. At first he had expected her to return and they would work it out. When the rage reared its head, Jack was too busy wallowing in it to think clearly, to map out a long-term plan. Once the anger had retreated to a low simmer, he and Ethan embarked on their road trip, the job in Stillwater came up, they moved, then Ellie. If he hadn't been so distracted by life, he would have had divorce papers drawn up, signed, and ready to present to Julie the moment she returned. He didn't, and he only had himself to blame.

He rubbed his hands over his face. Ellie. What was he going to tell her? How was he going to tell her? Their relationship was too new and she was still too unsure of him, he could sense it. Despite her passion and eagerness, there was always a reticence lurking behind her eyes. Was it fear? Fear that what they had was too good to be true? He had wondered the very thing himself over the past few days. No. It was true, of that he was sure. But apparently their road to happiness was going to be full of potholes, detours, road closings, and possibly a blown bridge or two.

Or was it distrust he saw in her eyes? She said flat out she wanted to trust him, the clear implication being the jury was still out and would remain he proved himself. That he was being punished, distrusted because of the sins of past men, rankled Jack a bit. Jack didn't believe for a moment Ellie would betray him like Julie had. They were nothing alike. Why couldn't Ellie trust Jack like he trusted her?

The answer lay in the calendar on his desk blotter. One week. It was one week ago exactly that he started his job, that he met her at the bank, since Diego Vasquez escaped and sent Jack to the hospital. Seven days. Had it really only been that long? Ethan had emailed his mother that night, Jack assumed. Why did it take Julie a week to make her way to Stillwater? Where was she? Who was she with? If she'd come back earlier, Jack wouldn't have started the relationship with Ellie, which would save Ellie the emotional turmoil that was to come in—he looked at his watch—four hours.

Jack pulled the metal trashcan from beneath his desk and started cleaning up the destroyed drawer and its contents. The answer was staying busy and keeping his mind off his personal problems. It would work out. Of that he was sure. He would make damn well sure it would work out. Right now, he needed to work on a schedule incorporating the sheriff's deputies and write up the reports on the Dodsworth case and the Ramos case, though questions still lingered about both.

The exact truth of what happened between Claire, Elizabeth, and George Dodsworth would never be known. There was no one left alive to tell. Most likely it was a crime of passion. Fifty years ago, Claire had returned to Stillwater to reclaim her family, ignorant of Elizabeth Pope taking her place, and had died in the process.

Jack sat back on his heels. A wife returning after abandoning her family to find her husband happy with another woman. He couldn't ignore the parallels with his life. He only felt stupid it had taken him this long to see them. Lord knows a few months ago, Jack's rage was sufficient to harm someone, though to kill Julie? Never. A cold fear seeped into his blood at the very idea. He knew from nearly twenty years in law enforcement that anyone was capable of murder. He pushed away the knowledge of the destruction in his life that such an act would lead to.

The only person who might be able to say exactly what happened that night was Buck Pollard. He knew Claire Dodsworth had been killed by a knife at a point in the investigation when only Jack and Hugh Barnes knew it. Buck's mention of a knife was a slip, one Jack didn't think Buck realized, even now. He had been too busy showing Jack his omniscience.

Jack felt sure Pollard had gone to the Dodsworths' when he learned Claire was back in town. Did he see the murder? Or did he come upon Elizabeth and George disposing of the body? Maybe he helped. Whatever Pollard's role, George Dodsworth did whatever he could for the rest of his life, including giving his daughter to Buck as a sexual object, to keep him silent. Pollard must have realized then that harboring other people's secrets was the best way to consolidate and wield power. Again, it was all supposition, and it drove Jack crazy not knowing for sure. Pollard couldn't stay away forever. Jack would find out the truth if it was the last thing he did as police chief.

Jack threw the front of the busted drawer into the metal trashcan. The report he would write for this case would be a joke, either full of supposition and guessing or so spare with the confirmed facts as to be a report in name only. Hopefully, it would give Barbara Dodsworth some sense of closure, though he doubted it. Her parents' betrayal haunted her. Buck Pollard haunted her. After seeing the grainy video of Pollard and that little girl, Jack was determined to bring him to justice. Watching Buck Pollard be ruined, his good name dragged through the mud, would be the salve to Barbara Dodsworth's ruined life.

Though Jack knew Pollard ordered Freeman to kill the Ramoses, none of it would end up in the report, due in part to his own stupidity. It was irritating that the Ramos report, too, would be full of half-truths and lies, but the public didn't care. They wanted to know there wasn't a killer running around their sleepy little town and, if Jack was completely honest with himself, he needed to close both cases to burnish his reputation.

He also needed to set up a meeting with the newspaper, try to kiss a little Fourth Estate ass to keep the town on his side until he could steady his sinking department. Buck Pollard's complicity in the deaths of three people would be swept under the rug. For now.

Jack sat at his desk and typed up a quick press release to give to the *Stillwater Gazette*.

```
FOR IMMEDIATE RELEASE
Mike Freeman, 28, hanged himself in the Stillwater
City Hall holding cell on Wednesday, September 19,
after being charged with the murders of Gilberto
and Rosa Ramos. The couple were found shot in their
home on Thursday, September 6. In a taped and
signed confession, Freeman admitted to murdering
the Ramoses for drug-related reasons.
```

```
A 50-year-old skeleton found on Barbara Dodsworth's
land on Saturday, September 8 has been tentatively
identified as Miss Dodsworth's biological mother,
Claire Dodsworth. Because of the length of time
since the death, as well as the passing of persons
who may have knowledge of the events leading to
Mrs. Dodsworth's death, specifics of what happened
to Claire Dodsworth may never be known.
```

Jack printed the amateur press release and placed it on the corner of the desk. He supposed he needed to add "learning how to deal with local press" to his to-do list. He rubbed his forehead. It gave him a headache just thinking about it.

He knelt back under the desk to finish cleaning up the paper clips, thumbtacks, and trash he missed before when he saw it. Crammed against the back of the desk, where the drawer would have been, was what looked like a yellowed plastic wallet insert. "That's why it wouldn't close." He sat in his chair and reached under the desk.

His phone beeped. "Chief McBride. You have a visitor." The chill in Susan's voice was unmistakable.

"Who?" He stopped and listened.

"Esperanza Perez."

"Send her back."

He knelt down and looked under the desk. He grasped the plastic, worked it back and forth, and gradually pulled it free.

"*Hola?*"

Jack tried to rise and banged his head on the underside of the desk. He crawled from under the desk. "Yeah. I'm here." He stood, placed the insert on the desk without looking at it. "Come in."

Esperanza held a small wooden box in her hands. "I brought you this." She placed it on the desk.

"What is that?"

"Rosa's."

"Where did you get it?"

"It's Carmen's. I picked it up when Josephina and I got Carmen's clothes and diapers. It has her birth certificate in it. That key fits it." Esperanza turned to leave.

"Where's Diego?"

She shuddered but didn't turn around. "I hope he's dead."

Jack walked around the desk and stood in front of her. She was pale and her lips were trembling. "I got the impression he was your friend."

Her eyes were mocking. "Men like Diego don't have friends. If you don't give them what they want, they take it. You better hope he's dead, too."

"Why?"

"If he's not, your town will become a war zone."

It was a small cedar box like one Jack had when he was a kid. He knew before he opened it with Rosa's key that LANE would be stamped on the inside lid. Gloved, Jack removed the paper and unfolded it. He sat down heavily in his chair, staring a photocopied Polaroid. He pushed the box aside and lay the paper down next to the bent photo holder containing a picture of a young Buck Pollard in Vietnam, and a yellowed, heavily creased newspaper article. He sat back and stared at the evidence and wondered what other secrets were hidden beneath Stillwater's crumbling facade.

VI

Sitting in a threadbare brocade wing chair, Jane Maxwell looked diminished. Her hair was impeccable, her clothes crisp, but her pale translucent skin and the dark circles under her eyes gave her away. She was old. Dying.

She stared at the newspaper clipping and copied Nazi family photo. Though her eyes lingered over the family photo, her face was a mask of indifference. "Yes. So?"

"Care to explain?"

"Explain what? I've never seen them before."

"Really?" Jack pointed to Ingrid. "Is that you?" He looked from the picture to Jane to gauge her reaction. She was staring at him instead of the picture. He moved his finger to Jane Maxwell at twelve years old, wearing a Hitler Youth uniform. "Or is that you?"

Jane didn't reply.

"This," Jack said. He pointed to the nurse standing slightly behind a balding, bespectacled doctor in the newspaper picture. The caption placed it as Auschwitz. "Is you as well. You're older, but the resemblance is striking."

Jane's eyes were locked on Jack. "Where did you find these?"

Jack tapped the newspaper article. "This was folded inside an old photo holder, which was crammed in the back of my desk drawer. The other was in the possession of a dead woman."

Jane's eyebrows rose. "A dead woman?"

"Rosa Ramos."

"The Mexican who killed herself?" Jane asked, her voice full of incredulity.

So she *didn't* know about Rosa blackmailing Marta.

"Rosa was murdered."

"Not because of that," Jane said. She flicked her hand at the coffee table.

Of course Jack knew that. Marta had motive, but lacked the physical ability, or the mentality, to carry out a double murder. That Jane could kill in cold blood Jack had no doubt, but she had no motive. And murder would be too messy, public, and quick for the woman who was staring at Jack with shrewd, calculating eyes. Her revenge would be long, slow, painful, and private.

"How long did you bribe Buck Pollard to stay silent about your past?"

She laughed. "I didn't bribe Buck Pollard to stay silent."

"Then why did he never make it public that you worked in a concentration camp?"

"Ask him."

"You knew, though, right? That he knew you were a Nazi? That you were somehow involved in the extermination of Jews."

"Everyone was *involved*, Mr. McBride. You couldn't live in Germany during that time and not be *involved*. The people who did nothing were as guilty as the people who herded them into the gas chambers."

"How he found out isn't that hard to figure. What I wonder is why he looked in the first place."

"You will have to ask him."

"That's why you hate him so much."

"If you say so. I must say, Mr. McBride, I'm not terribly impressed with your investigative skills. You come to me with nothing but two pieces of paper I've never seen before with a lot of guessing and supposition. Are you just here to show me how smart you are? Is this what we can expect from the Chief of Police? Investigating ancient history while people die in your care? I wonder if you were the right man for this job."

"You recruited me."

"Hardly. You were recommended. Though I don't know why."

"By whom?"

"What is the point of you coming here? Are you accusing me of a crime? Of murdering those two Mexicans?"

"No, Mike Freeman confessed to that."

"Did he, indeed? Well, that's very interesting. What was his motive?"

"Do you want the official story or the truth?"

She raised one perfectly plucked eyebrow. "Both."

"The truth is Buck Pollard hired him to kill them. The official story is it was drug related."

"Are you sure the two stories are mutually exclusive?"

Jack didn't reply. How could she possibly know that?

Jane sighed. "I guess I have to do your job for you. Buck Pollard is a crime lord, for lack of a better term. A lofty name for a small-town, country crime boss, but considering all the pies he has his fingers in, it's apt. Prostitution, drugs, and protection were his biggest rackets. Extortion, of course. That's why he resigned."

"You aren't telling me anything I don't already know."

"That's a relief."

"The question is, how do you know?"

"Buck isn't the only person in town who has informants. The difference is I don't threaten the people who whisper in my ear with exposure of their weaknesses and peccadillos."

"But you threatened Pollard and he resigned."

She nodded. "He knows I don't make idle threats."

"What did you threaten him with?"

"He's been putting money in off-shore accounts for years. Much more than he made through the city or private security."

"How do you know this?"

"I looked."

"Pollard swears it isn't his account. He swears you established it to discredit him."

"I had no idea he thought so highly of me."

"Why didn't you turn that information over to the DA or the Feds so he could be investigated?"

"My primary goal was to get him out of office. I didn't see the need to rub salt in his wound. I will happily turn the information over to you so you can start an investigation."

"I'm surprised you trust me to do it."

"Why do you think you're here, Mr. McBride?" Jane leaned forward and picked up the family picture. "This was Marta's?" Jane asked.

Jack nodded.

"I did not know she had it," Jane said. "I told her when she came to me forty-five years ago to throw everything from her past away. My sister had the bad luck to be in East Berlin when the Russians came," Jane explained. "It took me years to discover she was alive. When I did, I worked to bring her here. It was my husband's last gift to me." Jane placed the paper over the newspaper clipping. "Why have you shown this to me? Surely you can't think we had anything to do with the death of those two people."

"Not directly, no," Jack replied. He pulled the Polaroid copy from his coat pocket and placed it on the table. Jane's eyes widened and her mouth turned down at the corners at the sight of the half-dressed young girl. "Do you know this girl?"

"No."

Jack narrowed his eyes. "What happened to your promise of complete honesty?"

"I don't like kids, never have. Why would I know who this girl is? Where did you get this picture?"

"Rosa Ramos had it."

"Where did she get it?"

"Buck Pollard's house."

"How do you know that?"

Jack lifted the paper. On the back was a printout of an email from Pollard to a Galveston weather watcher about fishing conditions in the Gulf. Jack lay the paper down again and sat back in his chair. "You aren't surprised."

"What does this," she said, motioning to the picture, "have to do with the other?" She waved at her family portrait.

"Rosa found your family picture in Marta's room. When Marta paid her to keep quiet so quickly and easily, Rosa decided it was an easy way to make money. When she cleaned Pollard's house, she either went snooping or maybe Pollard accidentally left this out. She made a copy on his printer, took it home, hid it, and was planning out what exactly she would ask Pollard for when she and her husband were killed. On Pollard's orders."

Jane shook her head, as if lamenting the loss of two innocent lives. But the small smile on her face spoke more of grudging admiration of Pollard's actions than disgust.

"You knew Pollard molested girls."

"I heard rumors. I told him to take it outside of town, and he did."

Jack felt his face redden in anger. "How can you possibly know that?"

"He gave me his word."

Jack's bark of laughter propelled him to stand. He walked to the fireplace and turned around. "He gave you his *word*? A child molester told you he was going to stop and you believed him? You don't strike me as an idiot, Jane. But maybe this is all just a well-rehearsed facade."

"Buck Pollard is many, many things: a crook, a child molester, a cunning manipulator. But one thing he is not is a liar. When he gives his word, he sticks by it."

"You sound like you admire him."

"I loathe him, but that doesn't mean I don't have a certain amount of respect for him."

Loathe. Jack studied the woman in front of him and tried to reconcile that strong emotion with her implacable demeanor. He knew firsthand you couldn't feel hatred without first feeling its opposite.

Jack opened his mouth to confront Jane about her past with Pollard when his phone buzzed. Ann Newberry's number popped up on the screen. He answered the phone, but his eyes didn't leave Jane.

"Ann?"

"Just got a call from the Coast Guard."

"The Coast Guard?"

"They just found Buck Pollard's boat drifting about seventy miles south-southwest of Galveston."

"Did they arrest Pollard?"

"Looks like his boat capsized in the storm last night. There's no sign of him. He's just . . . gone."

VII

Ellie pulled into the drive of her lake house at 7:30 in the evening. The sun was lowering, and a slight breeze rustled the leaves of the trees that bordered her house on three sides. The house was secluded, at the end of a long road with no other houses within sight. That would change soon. Across the lake, lots were being sold for development. Lake Yourke had suddenly become popular with Dallas businessmen looking for a tax shelter. Ellie would have to decide soon if she wanted to keep the house or not. She pulled the paper bags from Eatzi's out of her back seat and walked to the door. The sounds of cicadas, frogs, and birds serenaded her on the way.

The house was musty and hot. She kicked herself. There wouldn't be enough time for the AC to cool the house. Of course, who knew when Jack would arrive? It might be dark by the time he was able to get away. That was fine. They could sit on the back porch and drink wine. As she unpacked the bags, she made a mental note to get Barbara out here next week to give the house a good cleaning.

She put the food in the oven, opened the bottle of wine, gave the furniture in the bedroom and living room a quick dust, and went into the bathroom to freshen up. The freedom she felt without her phone earlier in the day had now, twelve hours later, turned into a distraction. What if Jack couldn't come? There was no way for him to call her. She could have swung through town and picked her phone up, but she would have been seen, would have wanted to check in at the store, and then getting away would have been impossible. Coming straight here, having Jack meet her, meant no one would be the wiser about their affair. She wasn't ready to share it with the rest of Stillwater. Although they hadn't talked about it, Ellie felt sure Jack was keeping it under wraps, as well. He had his divorce to think of. For her part, she kept it even from Kelly, which was no easy feat. There would be hell to pay in that quarter later if she found out Ellie lied to her. The one thing Kelly abhorred in friends was lying.

Ellie checked herself in the mirror for the fifth time. She felt as nervous as she had been on her very first date, when she was seventeen years old, with Joe Dan Weeks. She knew it was a pity date. She was as terrified the boy would try something as she was terrified he wouldn't. He took her up to the German church, was the first boy to feel her up, and never asked her out again. Other boys did after, but when none got farther than a handshake or peck on the cheek, everyone assumed Joe Dan had been telling lies again. Her reputation had been saved. She wished Joe Dan hadn't been so bad at feeling her up that she avoided it for so long after. It took meeting Jinx to understand what all the fuss was about. Of course, Jinx turned out to be a disaster, as well.

Things were different with Jack. For one thing, and right now the most important, the sex was amazing. There was no uncertainty or nervousness. Was it because she was mature enough and experienced enough to know what she wanted? Was it because she finally had sloughed off the guilt for wanting it or asking for it? Or was it because she had finally found the one person she fit perfectly with?

Whatever. She didn't care. She only knew she found him and was going to fight like hell to keep him, to make it work. If that meant manipulating a teenager to like her, or having to suffer through hanging around Eddie McBride, a man too similar to her ex-husband for comfort, she would do it with a big damn smile on her face.

She heard a car. She flipped off the bathroom light and went to meet Jack.

Ellie opened the door with a smile, hoping Jack couldn't hear her galloping heart. Her smile wavered when she saw him. His tread on the steps was heavy, his eyes downcast.

"Hey."

He looked up. The stress and despair on his face was shocking. He looked ten years older than he had when he left her that morning. When his eyes met hers, his face cleared and broke into a relieved smile. Without a word, she went into his arms.

He held her tightly, burying his face in her neck. "God, I missed you," he said.

She didn't want to pull away. It felt too good to be held by him. It felt right. Perfect, as if she had finally found the other half of herself that God had carved away when creating her.

"Did you have a bad day?"

"You have no idea." She pulled slightly away so she could look at him. "I just spent the last hour being interviewed by the *Sentinel*," he said.

"About Freeman?"

"And Pollard, and my brother, my personal life, and why I left the FBI." He shook his head. "As bad as it was, it wasn't even the worst part of the day."

"I'm sorry," Ellie said.

He pushed a strand of hair behind her ear and smiled. "I feel better now."

Ellie smiled and raised one eyebrow. "You do?"

Jack looked her up and down. "You clean up nice, Miss Martin. Purple is your color."

The compliment made her flush with pleasure. "You think so?"

"Hmm." His eyes lingered on her lips as he pulled her forward and kissed her deeply.

"Come on," she said, when they pulled apart. "I have a surprise for you." She led him by the hand into the house. "Okay, it's not much of a surprise," she admitted.

"It smells great in here."

"That's the surprise."

"Did you cook?"

She laughed. "Um, no. But I did make a stop at Eatzi's. I bought a bottle of wine. And dessert. I'm splurging tonight."

"What's the occasion?"

She felt her smile freeze on her face. What's the occasion? Her stomach dropped a bit. She was making too big a deal of all this. She turned away from him, smile stuck on her face so it wouldn't crumble into little pieces around her feet, and opened the cabinet to retrieve the wine glasses. She pulled the second one down and felt his arms go around her waist. He put his chin on her shoulder.

"I was joking, Ellie."

"Did you get my message?" Her voice was high. She grimaced.

"I did."

"I'm sorry about that. I ramble. I hope you got bored and cut it off before the end."

He turned her around. "And miss hearing that you missed me? Not a chance. Hearing your whiskey-soaked voice was the best part of my day."

"Whiskey-soaked voice?" She melted a little inside, though she couldn't help but think the description, in relation to her, was absurd. "Jack, you're an amazing balm for my fragile ego."

"Everything I say is true."

"It's enough right now that you think so. But I dread the day when you see me, warts and all. Do you want some wine?"

"In a minute."

His hands were on the counter on either side of her. He was searching her face, as though trying to memorize it. "What's wrong?"

"I need to tell you something."

"Uh-oh."

"Two things, actually."

Her stomach dropped again. Soon it would be on the floor. Whatever the news was, it wasn't good. She remembered their first night together, the warning that this wouldn't last fluttering through her mind as they made love, that she felt too much and it would destroy her. God, she hated it when she was right.

She held his gaze. "Just get it over with."

He took a deep breath. "First." A wavering smile broke across his face and he blushed a little. "I love you."

She stared at him, uncomprehendingly. What the hell? He couldn't be serious. He was about to say he was joking. But, if it was a joke? What an asshole. His eyes, though, gave him away.

She didn't realize she was holding her breath until his name came out as a sigh. "Jack, you can't be serious."

"I am."

"But we've known each other for a week. How can you possibly—"

"Know? I've known since I shook your hand in front of Jane Maxwell's office."

"That's crazy."

"You're right. It *is* crazy. But that doesn't make it any less true."

He put his fingers over her mouth to silence what she was about to say. "I love you. I need you to know that. To believe it. Do you believe me?"

She'd learned long ago that the eyes don't lie. The mouth can say any-thing, body language can be controlled or faked, but masking what you really felt in your eyes was almost impossible. Jack's eyes were desperate for her to believe.

She steeled herself for whatever else was coming.

"Yes," she said, more to move him on than because she truly believed him. The idea was preposterous. "What's the second thing, Jack?"

"Julie's back."

He said it quickly, like if he didn't get it out, he would never find the courage. A glimmer of relief showed in his eyes.

"Who?"

"Ethan's mother."

Ellie's spine stiffened. She stood straighter, leaned back from him slightly, but he still had her pinned against the counter. That was why he said he loved her. Not because he wanted to, or because he felt it, but because he felt he had to appease her before dropping the bomb into the middle of her heart.

"Your wife."

"Soon to be ex-wife. This doesn't change anything."

"It changes everything."

"Why?"

"Because you're married."

"I was married when I was in your bed this morning."

Her voice rose. "But your wife wasn't sleeping in my house down the road, was she?" She pushed against his chest. "Would you please let me go?"

Jack stepped away from her. She turned, poured two glasses of wine, handed one to Jack, and walked out the back door, wine bottle in hand. She was seated in an Adirondack chair when Jack came out a minute later. She sipped her wine, a 2009 Cakebread Cabernet. She had splurged. She had it once at dinner on one of her trips to Dallas and loved it. Now, here, the bitterness choked her.

Jack stood next to the empty chair. She looked up at him. "Are you superstitious, Jack?"

"No."

"You see," she pointed the finger of the hand holding the wine glass at him. "I didn't know that about you. There's a lot we don't know about each other, isn't there? Like your favorite music. I bet you like eighties hair bands. Am I right?"

He nodded.

"I'm a country music fan myself. Mostly classics. Patsy Cline, Loretta Lynn, Hank Williams. Did you guess that when you profiled me? You did profile me when we first met, didn't you?" She sipped her wine again. "I can imagine what was going through your mind. Middle-aged woman, probably a spinster or unhappily married. Easily manipulated by men. Insecure. Well-liked, but it's more pity-based than due to any redeeming quality of her own."

"You're wrong."

"Please. I know me much better than you do." She leaned her head back to take in the house behind her. "This house is cursed. My mom was driving home from this house when she drove into a tree. She did it on purpose, by the way." She took another sip. It tasted better. With the hand holding her wine glass, she pointed to the lake. "Summer, 1985, one of my best friends blew her brains out in front of me on that dock."

"Jesus."

"My dad died here, too. Last year. He didn't kill himself though. He was too big of a coward. I wish he hadn't been. Would have put us both out of our misery years ago."

"Ellie."

"And now this. I admit, it's a little melodramatic lumping the end of an affair with three deaths, but it is a death, in its own way."

Jack put his untouched wine on the railing and crouched in front of her. She couldn't see him through the tears pooling in her eyes.

"Ellie, listen to me. Look at me."

She blinked and the tears fell down her cheeks. Jack wiped them away with his thumbs. "I love you." She shook her head and looked away. *Ridiculous.*

He grabbed her shoulders and shook her. "I love you. I didn't just tell you that to soften the blow or to manipulate you. I told you that because it's true. You know what I thought when I met you? Huh? I felt sorry for all those dumb bastards who ignored you in bars, who looked past you to your friend. I saw in you what none of those idiots saw: the inner spark. You're beautiful inside and out."

"I'm really not."

"I believe you are. I will always believe that. I love you. I want to be with you. Julie coming back changes nothing. You and I will be together. I'm going to fight like hell to make it happen. I'm still meeting with Bob tomorrow and putting the divorce into motion."

She smiled. He had that look in his eyes again, like he was ready to kick some ass.

"You can't."

"Watch me."

"Jack." She took a deep breath. She was over her pity party. For now. She would have another one when he was gone, a good long one. Right now, she had to be the strong one. The logical one. "Your position here in town is too tenuous for you to be divorcing your wife within a week."

He stood. "Fuck Stillwater. People need to mind their own goddamn business." He turned his back and stared at the water.

They were silent for a few minutes. Ellie sipped her wine and considered what to do. She could let Jack do what he wanted, be the other woman, the one who destroyed a man's marriage. It would be a feeding frenzy of gossip, especially with her history. The cheated becoming a cheater, a home wrecker. Pulling apart a family and, in all likelihood, destroying Jack's relationship with his son. She would have Jack, but would they be happy?

She stood and moved next to him. "Do you want to be with me?"

He turned his head to face her. "More than anything."

"Then you cancel your appointment with Bob and try to make it work."

"But—"

"You have to at least seem to try. For Ethan's sake." Jack looked back at the lake. "He will never forgive you if you don't. And he will always resent me. He might anyway. Has he told her? About us?"

"I don't think so."

"But he might." It wasn't a question.

"I have enough on Julie to get a divorce granted and full custody."

"Good. You'll use it. Eventually."

He turned to face her fully. "What are you saying? You want me to go back and live with that woman? Sleep in the same bed as her?"

"No, the thought of it makes me want to vomit. But you have to."

Jack grimaced. "How long do I have to fake my marriage for Stillwater to accept us," he waved his hand in the air, "eventually?"

"Until the new year."

"You're out of your fucking mind."

"So, what? You're going to destroy Ethan's dream of having his family back together just in time for the holidays?"

"Why are you being so goddamn logical?" He grabbed her by the shoulders and shook her again. "Don't you care about me enough to fight for me?"

"You have no idea how much I care. I have no idea. Jack, think about it. You've come in here, and in less than a week you've turned my world completely upside down." She closed her eyes. "You tell me you love me," she said, opening her eyes, "then this. I know it isn't your fault; I'm not blaming you. God knows I could have stopped this before it ran away with us, but I didn't.

"But you can't expect me to ruin my reputation by destroying your marriage. I've worked too hard to build it back up. Even now, people don't mention me without either mentioning my father, my mother's death, Jinx, or the championship."

"Championship?"

She waved it away. There would be time enough for him to learn about *that* scandal. "This town is brutal to women who stray from the straight and narrow. Look at Claire Dodsworth. Fifty years later and what do people remember? That she was a slut."

"This isn't even close to the same thing. We care about each other." He paced up and down the deck, running his hands through his hair. He stopped. "The beginning of the year? You're asking too much."

"Do you want to be with me?"

"I do."

"That means living in Stillwater. You know that, right?"

He paused. She smiled. So, he *didn't* realize that. "I have no intention of leaving Stillwater. My life is here. My roots are here. Despite all of its problems and blemishes, I love the people, this town. Maybe if I can redeem this town, I can redeem myself."

"You don't need to be redeemed."

A boat sped across the lake, much too fast. "You don't know everything about me, Jack. You can feel for me deeply, maybe love me," she said, turning back to him, "but don't assume you know everything about me."

She continued. "If we're going to be together, and based on the expression on your face, that's a big 'if,' then we have to tread lightly with your marriage, your divorce, and our relationship."

He put his hands in his pockets. "Okay. What do we have to do?"

Ellie raised her eyebrows, surprised.

"What, were you trying to scare me off? You're going to have to do a lot more than threaten me with living in Stillwater for the rest of my life. Or imply that you have some deep dark secret. I don't care where we live, and I believe in you. I believe in what I feel for you. I'll do whatever I have to do. Say the word, and I'll do it. Even live with a woman I hate for four months."

He stood with his feet apart, his shoulders square and back, his chin lifted ever so slightly. His eyes burned with determination and resolve. Somewhere beneath the fear and grief that threatened to overtake her, Ellie felt a glimmer of something close to faith.

"You really *do* love me."

"That's what I've been trying to tell you."

She felt the smile break slowly across her face.

"Show me."

ACKNOWLEDGMENTS

The process for getting *Stillwater* into your hands has spanned ten years, numerous drafts, and lots of help from family, friends, and fellow writers.

First and foremost, thank you to my agent, Alice Speilburg, who didn't laugh when I told her I wanted to be published by the time I was 45, but went to work and made it happen.

Thanks to Nicole Frail for making the editing experience a breeze, and for knowing the perfect moment to start an email with, "Now, before you get anxious . . ." Working with you has been a blast.

Thank you to Judy and Beth for being there in the beginning, for encouraging, supporting, cheering me on, and being the best beta readers I've ever had.

Thank you to Mark for patiently mentoring me through the long, slow process of becoming a professional writer. I absolutely wouldn't be where I am today if it wasn't for you.

Thank you to Mom and Dad, for always believing in me, and to Mom specifically for the recurring dream that pulled *Stillwater* together.

Thank you to Nancy, Roy, Barbara, and Jackie for helping me find the beginning of the story.

Thank you to Corporal Tom Pressley (Retired) for answering all my police procedural questions, and to Teresa Pressley for the technical beta read. Any police procedural mistakes I made are my own.

Thanks to the members of the DFW Writers' Workshop for smacking me down and building me up when I need it. I'm a better writer for both, but especially the smack downs.

Thanks to all of my friends for the unflagging encouragement, support, and love.

Thanks to my three favorite people in the world, Jay, Ryan, and Jack. There's a little bit of the three of you in Jack and Ethan McBride. The good parts, I promise.